REVOLUTION

DEBORAH WILES

SCHOLASTIC PRESS

REVOLU

UTION

THE
SIXTIES
TRILOGY

BOOK TWO

Library of Congress Cataloging-in-Publication Data available

ISBN 978-0-545-10607-8

10 9 8 7 6 5 4 3 2 14 15 16 17 18

Printed in the U.S.A. 23
First edition, June 2014

The text type was set in Futura.
Book design by Phil Falco

for the foot soldiers

I, Too

I, too, sing America.

I am the darker brother.
They send me to eat in the kitchen
When company comes,
But I laugh,
And eat well,
And grow strong.

Tomorrow,
I'll be at the table
When company comes.
Nobody'll dare
Say to me,
"Eat in the kitchen,"
Then.

Besides,
They'll see how beautiful I am
And be ashamed —

I, too, am America.

— Langston Hughes, 1932

"A great change is at hand, and our task, our obligation, is to make that revolution, that change, peaceful and constructive for all. Those who do nothing are inviting shame, as well as violence. Those who act boldly are recognizing right, as well as reality."

— John F. Kennedy, president of the United States, announcing that a civil rights bill will be sent to Congress, June 11, 1963

We do not accept Jews, because they reject Christ, and, through the machinations of their International Banking Cartel, are at the root center of what we call "communism" today.

We do not accept Papists, because they bow to a Roman dictator, in direct violation of the First Commandment, and the True American Spirit of Responsible, Individual Liberty.

We do not accept Turks, Mongols, Tarters, Orientals, Negroes, nor any other person whose native background of culture is foreign to the Anglo-Saxon system of Government by responsible, FREE individual citizens.

— From "Why You Should Join the Ku Klux Klan," 1964

"With this faith we will be able to hew out of the mountain of despair a stone of hope. With this faith we will be able to transform the jangling discords of our nation into a beautiful symphony of brotherhood. With this faith we will be able to work together, to pray together, to struggle together, to go to jail together, to stand up for freedom together, knowing that we will be free one day."

— Reverend Dr. Martin Luther King, Jr., at the March on Washington for Jobs and Freedom, Washington D.C., August 28, 1963

"A revolution is bloody. Revolution is hostile. Revolution knows no compromise. Revolution overturns and destroys everything that gets in its way. And you, sitting around here like a knot on the wall, saying, 'I'm going to love these folks no matter how much they hate me.' No, you need a revolution. Whoever heard of a revolution where they lock arms . . . singing 'We Shall Overcome'? Just tell me. You don't do that in a revolution. You don't do any singing; you're too busy swinging."

— Malcolm X from his speech "Message to the Grassroots," November 1963

PART 1
ENCAMPMENT

I may never march in the infantry
Ride in the cavalry
Shoot the artillery
I may never fly o'er the enemy
But I'm in the Lord's army!

— Sunday school/Bible school song

AIN'T GONNA LET NOBODY TURN ME AROUND, TURN ME AROUND, TURN ME AROUND! GONNA KEEP ON WALKIN', KEEP ON TALKIN', MARCHIN' UP TO FREEDOM LAND!

From "Ain't Gonna Let Nobody Turn Me Around," traditional

The crowd assembled at the March on Washington for Jobs and Freedom, Washington, D.C., August 28, 1963.

"Wake up, America. ***Wake up!*** *For we cannot stop, and we* ***will not*** *be patient!"*

The Student Nonviolent Coordinating Committee (SNCC) Chairman John Lewis ends his speech at the March on Washington for Jobs and Freedom, August 28, 1963

All persons born or naturalized in the United States, and subject to the jurisdiction thereof, are citizens of the United States and of the State wherein they reside. No State shall make or enforce any law which shall abridge the privileges or immunities of citizens of the United States; nor shall any State deprive any person of life, liberty, or property, without due process of law; nor deny to any person within its jurisdiction the equal protection of the laws.

Section 1 — the "Citizenship Clause" — of the Fourteenth Amendment to the U.S. Constitution, July 9, 1868, which overruled *Dred Scott v. Sanford*, 1857, which held that slaves and their descendants were not protected by the Constitution and were not U.S. citizens

WELCOME TO THE 1964 WORLD'S FAIR

IN BEAUTIFUL FLUSHING MEADOWS PARK, NEW YORK!

The twelve-stories-tall Unisphere represents our growing global interdependence. The three rings around it symbolize the orbit tracks of three satellites that have circled our globe: Yuri Gagarin, the first man in space; John Glenn, the first American to orbit the Earth; and Telstar, the first active communications satellite.

SEE YOU AT THE FAIR, WHERE THE THEME IS "PEACE THROUGH UNDERSTANDING"!

Boston members of CORE — the Congress of Racial Equality — demonstrate inside the 1964 New York World's Fair, protesting racial discrimination.

AIN'T GONNA LET INJUSTICE TURN ME AROUND!

"This administration today, here and now, declares unconditional war on poverty in America. I urge this Congress and all Americans to join with me in that effort."

From U.S. President Lyndon Baines Johnson's State of the Union address, January 8, 1964

This is your FREEDOM SUMMER. It will not work without your help. COFO is asking you to provide housing for the people who are coming to work here, look for buildings which can be used for Freedom Schools and Community Centers, get names of students who want to go to Freedom Schools, let us know when you have meetings or arrange meetings so we can come answer questions about the FREEDOM SUMMER.

From the Council of Federated Organizations (COFO) brochure distributed to black citizens across Mississippi, 1964

THE MISSISSIPPI SUMMER PROJECT MAP

Many people are coming here to work during our FREEDOM SUMMER. They want to learn about Mississippi. They feel that the problems here are the problems of people all over the country. Most of them will be college students, both Negro and white.

COFO brochure, 1964

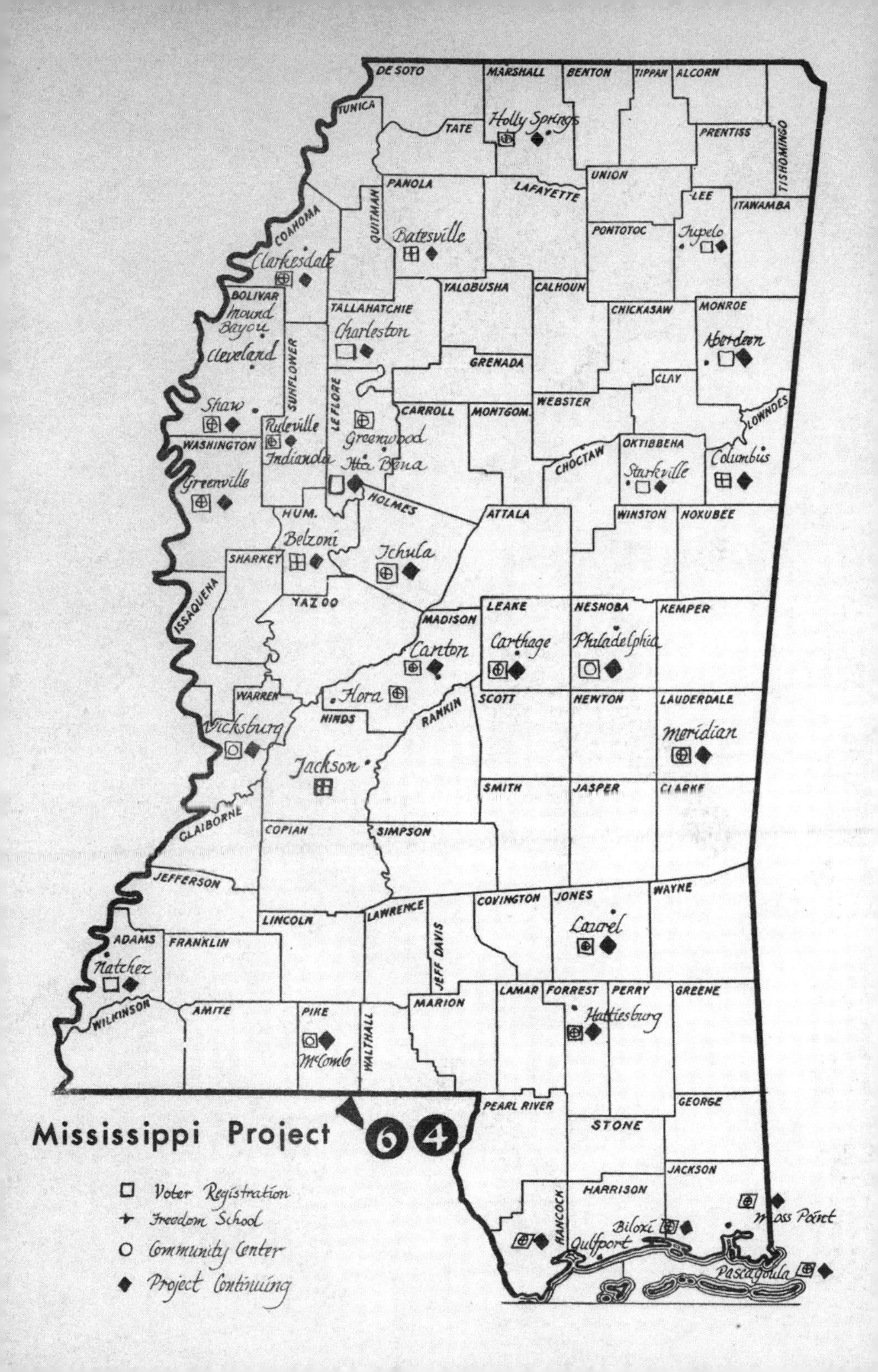

Mississippi Project 64
Voter Registration
Freedom School
Community Center
Project Continuing
DE SOTO
MARSHALL
BENTON
TIPPAH
ALCORN
TUNICA
TATE
Holly Springs
PRENTISS
TISHOMINGO
UNION
PANOLA
LAFAYETTE
LEE
ITAWAMBA
QUITMAN
COAHOMA
PONTOTOC
Tupelo
Batesville
Clarkesdale
BOLIVAR
Mound Bayou
YALOBUSHA
CALHOUN
TALLAHATCHIE
CHICKASAW
MONROE
Charleston
Aberdeen
Cleveland
SUNFLOWER
GRENADA
CLAY
LE FLORE
WEBSTER
Shaw
CARROLL
MONTGOM.
LOWNDES
Ruleville
Greenwood
WASHINGTON
OKTIBBEHA
Indianola
Itta Bena
CHOCTAW
Columbus
Starkville
Greenville
HOLMES
HUM.
ATTALA
WINSTON
NOXUBEE
Belzoni
Tchula
SHARKEY
YAZOO
ISSAQUENA
LEAKE
NESHOBA
KEMPER
MADISON
Carthage
Philadelphia
Canton
WARREN
SCOTT
NEWTON
LAUDERDALE
Flora
RANKIN
HINDS
Vicksburg
Meridian
Jackson
SMITH
JASPER
CLARKE
CLAIBORNE
COPIAH
SIMPSON
JEFFERSON
WAYNE
COVINGTON
JONES
LAWRENCE
LINCOLN
JEFF DAVIS
Laurel
ADAMS
FRANKLIN
Natchez
LAMAR
FORREST
PERRY
GREENE
WILKINSON
AMITE
PIKE
MARION
Hattiesburg
WALTHALL
McComb
PEARL RIVER
GEORGE
STONE
JACKSON
HARRISON
HANCOCK
Moss Point
Biloxi
Gulfport
Pascagoula

AIN'T GONNA LET SEGREG

ATION TURN ME AROUND!

Demonstrators try to enter a whites-only swimming pool, Cairo, Illinois, 1962.

"The white race deems itself to be the dominant race in this country. . . . But in view of the Constitution, in the eye of the law, there is in this country no superior, dominant, ruling class of citizens. . . . Our Constitution is color-blind. . . . In respect of civil rights, all citizens are equal before the law."

U.S. Supreme Court Associate Justice John Marshall Harlan, writing the single dissenting vote against *Plessy v. Ferguson*, 1896, which created a "separate but equal" society, overturned civil rights gains from Reconstruction (including the Civil Rights Act of 1866), and undermined 1868's Fourteenth Amendment to the U.S. Constitution

Brooklyn, New York, 1963. In a CORE-sponsored protest, protestors are removed from a construction site. "If we don't work, nobody works!" Hundreds were arrested, including seventeen children.

"We conclude that, in the field of public education, the doctrine of 'separate but equal' has no place. Separate educational facilities are inherently unequal."

U.S. Chief Justice Earl Warren, writing for the court, *Brown v. Board of Education*, which overturned *Plessy v. Ferguson* in 1954

"Less than seven percent of Mississippi's voting age Negroes are registered. This summer, a concentrated vote drive will be held as part of the Mississippi Summer Project."

From the *Student Voice*, the newspaper of SNCC, June 9, 1964

SNCC Field Secretary Sandy Leigh (right) and seventeen-year-old local activist Doug Smith (left) explain voter registration procedures to 103-year-old Felix Smith on his front porch in Hattiesburg, Mississippi, summer 1964.

KKK recruitment poster

"There is no state with a record that approaches that of Mississippi in inhumanity, murder, brutality, and racial hatred. It is absolutely at the bottom of the list.

Roy Wilkins, Chairman of the NAACP
(National Association for the Advancement of Colored People)

AIN'T GONNA LET MISSISSIPPI TURN ME AROUND!

"Either you believe in states' rights, home rule, or you believe in turning over this state to a black minority."

Paul Johnson, governor of Mississippi, on the campaign trail, 1963

The second trial of Byron De La Beckwith ended in a mistrial today. Beckwith, of Greenwood, Mississippi, was accused of the murder of civil rights leader Medgar Evers in Jackson, Mississippi, in June 1963. Beckwith has been released from police custody and has returned home to Greenwood. **April 17, 1964**

CROSSES WERE BURNED ON APRIL 24, 1964,

in 64 of Mississippi's 82 counties, to protest the coming summer "invasion of Mississippi." To prepare, Mayor Allen Thompson hired 100 extra police officers, purchased 250 extra shotguns, and a 13,000-pound armored personnel carrier with a submachine gun mounted on the turret. The Mississippi legislature passed a bill to "restrain movements of individuals under certain circumstances."

"Today, Americans of all races stand side by side in Berlin and in Vietnam. They died side by side in Korea. Surely they can work and eat and travel side by side in their own country."

U.S. President Lyndon Baines Johnson, State of the Union address, January 8, 1964

"I am going to Mississippi this summer to teach in the Freedom Schools . . . I want to help in whatever way I can to alleviate injustice and to help people develop self-esteem and dignity. I want to learn from people who have known more grief, humiliation, and misery than I can ever know."

Pam Parker, to members of her church, Trinity Episcopal, Solebury, Pennsylvania, June 9, 1964

Staughton Lynd, director of the Freedom Schools for the Summer Project, teaches volunteers who will become Freedom School teachers in Mississippi during their week-long training at Western College for Women in Oxford, Ohio, June 1964.

It seems almost incomprehensible at this moment that in two days the world of all of us here will change so drastically. . . . If ugly things happen to us, if death comes to us, it will be in such a way — for the same reasons that they have happened to untold numbers of Negroes for years."

From summer volunteer Zoya Zeman's diary, June 24, 1964

Summer volunteers practice peaceful nonviolent responses (such as "going limp") when "attacked" during training sessions before leaving for Mississippi, summer 1964.

AIN'T GONNA LET NO JAILHOUSE TURN ME AROUND!

SELF-DEFENSE IN MISSISSIPPI

If you are attacked:
Roll up in a knot and hit the ground.
Stay as close to your knees as possible,
legs together, because a leg sticking out
can be broken with one quick step.
Don't carry watches, pens, glasses,
and never more than five to ten dollars.
If you're caught from behind, go limp.
Watch for cars without license plates
and cops without badges.
Never be the last to leave a meeting.
Never leave alone.

The Beatles first arrive in the United States, January 1964.

Reporter to Beatles:
What do you call that hairstyle you're wearing?

George Harrison:
Arthur.

From *A Hard Day's Night*, 1964

A U.S. military advisor accompanies South Vietnamese soldiers on a river patrol near the Cambodian border in June 1964.

AIN'T GONNA LET NO HA

There are now 16,300 American military advisors in South Vietnam. South Vietnam received $500 million in U.S. aid during 1963.

"We must be strong enough to win any war, and we must be wise enough to prevent one. We shall neither act as aggressors nor tolerate acts of aggression. We intend to bury no one, and we do not intend to be buried. We can fight, if we must, as we have fought before, but we pray that we will never have to fight again."

U.S. President Lyndon Baines Johnson, State of the Union address, January 8, 1964

TRED TURN ME AROUND!

"All our dreams can come true, if we have the courage to pursue them."

Walt Disney

If we were all voting then things would be better in Mississippi. We would have enough food, more jobs, better schools, better houses, paved sidewalks.

COFO brochure, 1964

"That's all nonviolence is — organized love."

Joan Baez

"As she made the beds, shopped for groceries, matched slipcover material, ate peanut butter sandwiches with her children, chauffeured Cub Scouts and Brownies, lay beside her husband at night — she was afraid to ask even of herself the silent question — 'Is this all?'"

Betty Friedan, *The Feminine Mystique*, 1963

"The two-stage Saturn vehicle has just put into orbit the largest payload ever launched by any nation. This is a giant step forward for the United States space effort."

President Lyndon Baines Johnson, on the launching of the first satellite by Saturn I, January 29, 1964

"Sugar Frosted Flakes taste Grrrrreat!"

Tony the Tiger

"I am the astronaut of boxing."

Muhammad Ali

Willie Mays watches the ball clear the fence, May 1964.

"AND THE 'SAY HEY KID' EXPLODES!

Willie Mays owned the plate for the San Francisco Giants during the first month of play, annihilating the ball in his 43 at bats. He finished the month hitting a .488 AVG and 1.070 SLG, while bringing in 20 RBI and smacking seven bombs over the fence. Say Hey!"

AIN'T GONNA LET NO M

SERY TURN ME AROUND!

"In this summer, the stranger is the enemy in Mississippi and the short nights are longer because every man watches and every man is being watched."

Nicholas Von Hoffman, *Mississippi Notebook*, 1964

"If I have to die, I'd rather die for right. I value my life more since I became a registered voter. A man is not a first-class citizen, a number one citizen, unless he is a voter."

Reverend Joe Carter

People coming here this summer can work with you on VOTER REGISTRATION. They can knock on doors, teach the registration forms and drive people to the courthouse. They can help in any way you want them to.

COFO brochure, 1964

Reverend Joe Carter guards his house from the Ku Klux Klan after he registered to vote in West Feliciana Parish, Louisiana, 1964.

There is nothing wrong with your television set.

Do not attempt to adjust the picture . . .

You are about to experience the awe and mystery

which reaches from the inner mind to . . .

The Outer Limits.

GONNA KEEP ON WALKIN', KEEP ON TALKIN', MARCHIN' UP TO FREEDOM LAND!

WHO CAN REGISTER:

anyone, who is:

a citizen of the United States;

21 years old or over (or who will be 21 by the date of the FREEDOM VOTE)

a citizen of Mississippi.

WHERE CAN YOU REGISTER:

wherever a FREEDOM REGISTRAR is located;

at FREEDOM REGISTRATION-mobiles;

at the COUNCIL OF FEDERATED ORGANIZATIONS office nearest your home;

by sending in a blank like the one on this folder.

(look on the back for a list of COFO offices)

write: COFO STATE OFFICE
1017 Lynch Street
Jackson, Miss.
or call: 352-9605

or contact the office near you:

COFO
1323 6th Avenue N.
Columbus, Miss.
328-8916

COFO
213 4th Street
Clarksdale, Miss.
624-2913

COFO
708 Avenue N
Greenwood, Miss.
453-1282

COFO
507 Mobile Street
Hattiesburg, Miss.
584-7670

COFO
2505 1/2 5th Street
Meridian, Miss.

FREEDOM
REGISTRATIO

"The Negroes of Mississippi will not get the vote until the equivalent of an army is sent here."

SNCC Field Director Bob Moses, Greenwood, Mississippi, 1963

Mississippi Summer Project volunteers link arms to sing "We Shall Overcome" as their training in Ohio ends and they board buses to take them to Mississippi.

GONNA BUILD A BRAND-NEW WORLD!

1

Saturday, June 20, 1964

The first thing we do, me and Gillette, is make sure everybody is asleep. Daddy and Annabelle (I still can't call her Mama) go to bed after watching *The Lawrence Welk Show* on television. Parnell will be home at midnight, after he sweeps the floors and locks the doors at the Leflore Theater on the corner of Fulton and West Washington Streets. Little Audrey — champion sleeper — has been snoring for hours, so we don't worry about her.

We know what time Deputy Davis drives by our house in his black-and-white cruiser, making his rounds, and we know his route by heart, which means we know what time he passes the city pool. We've got it all figured out *yeah, yeah, yeah.*

In the bathroom, I yank on my bathing suit, which is still stretchy-cold and clammy-wet from this afternoon's swim. Gillette hisses from the hallway, "Hurry up, Sunny!"

"Hold your horses!" I hiss back. "This ain't easy!" I pull my blue sundress with the daisies on it over my bathing suit, grab my pool towel, and sneak open the bathroom door. And here is what I say then, in my most angelic whisper: "'But let patience have her perfect work, that ye may be perfect and entire, wanting nothing.' James 1:4. *Patience*, big brother."

Gillette rolls his eyes at me. "Patience, your big behind!" he says. "Let's go!"

"Shame on you!" I fling at him, and we are off. I said I wanted an adventure, and now I've got one.

Gillette is a nut. A nut like one of the Three Stooges, but not really, because Gillette is smart, real smart, even though he's my stepbrother, and I've only known him for two years — twice times 365 days of my whole life. Tonight we are celebrating two years of knowing each other and one year of being brother and sister. *Yeah, yeah, yeah.*

We tiptoe into the summer night, careful not to let the screen door slam behind us. The heat covers us like a warm velvet blanket. We are swallowed up in the muddy smell of the lazy Yazoo River just on the other side of the earthen levee. The golden glow from the streetlights lining River Road sifts through the trees and sprinkles us like glitter. Our bare feet slap the sidewalk as we race each other the six blocks to the pool.

"My behind's not big," I huff.

"I know that," says Gillette.

"Just because you're eight months older . . ."

"I know! I said I'm sorry!"

"No, you didn't," I tell him as we slow to a walk and turn onto Dewey Street. I have a sudden thought and blurt it out. "What if the invaders are already here?" I cast a quick look behind me. "What if they see us?"

Gillette looks at me like I've just started talking backward. "What invaders?"

"Didn't you see the paper?"

"Do I read the paper? No. What's happening?" Gillette doesn't seem bothered by this news, which makes me feel braver.

"I saw it when I was at Meemaw's this week. She was taking her nap and fell asleep with the newspaper over her face. I couldn't stand it, how she was snoring in all that newspaper smell, so I tried to pick it off her face, and that's when I read it, clear as day. We're being *invaded*."

"What did it say exactly?" Gillette is a facts-and-statistics man. He has everything about his favorite baseball players memorized. He can tell you how they do, from week to week during baseball season. He keeps track like that.

"I don't know!" I tell him. "It just said 'invasion of Mississippi'. . . ."

"Well, I don't see any invaders, and it looks like any other night in Greenwood. Nothing is happening. You watch too many monster movies." Gillette takes off his baseball cap — he's a Giants fan — and runs his fingers in his hair like he's combing it, but he's really getting the sweat out — I've seen him do it a hundred times.

"Do not," I say. But I do. Parnell lets me in for free at the Leflore, and I saw *The Creeping Terror* and *Beginning of the End* last Saturday at the horror-movie day double feature.

We swing left onto West Church Street. "What if Old Miss Bishop's out on her porch?" I ask.

"She won't be. Everybody's asleep."

He's right. Nary a car, bicycle, or body moves at this hour. A hound bellows with desperation from the direction of Mr. Delay Beckwith's house — one of his hunting dogs. The sound makes me shudder.

"Hurry!" I call to Gillette. We dash across the empty playground behind Jefferson Davis Elementary School, where the merry-go-round squats near the swings and watches us steal our way behind the music building to where the Greenwood City Pool lies glistening in the half-dark, its tall fence protecting it from prowlers. Then we look around to make sure we aren't spotted.

Yesterday, Gillette figured out how to jiggle the chain-link just so, so we can get in through the back gate, lock and all. Without a word, we sneak through, drop our towels, and strip to our suits. Then, smooth as seals in a calm sea, we slip into that cool, colorless water without a sound and begin to execute perfect breaststrokes, side by side, across the 200-foot length of the pool, accompanied by a chorus of crickets, the light from a cantaloupe moon, and the burble of the chlorinated water we gently shove out of our way as it ripples around our arms in the moonlight. We keep our heads above the water and take our time. That's just the way we do it.

Gillette, who delivered groceries on his bike all day, finally breaks the silence. "God, this feels great."

"Don't say *God*," I snap.

"Since when did you get religious?"

"As you can see, I'm not," I tell him, "since I'm here, breaking the law with you. Happy anniversary!"

"So what gives?"

"I dunno. Vacation Bible School. There's a prize every year for whoever memorizes the most Bible verses. I want to beat Polly."

"I'll never go to Bible School," says Gillette.

"You're lucky your mama doesn't make you."

"Did she make you?"

"No, but Daddy did." I stop talking for a moment, to catch my breath. Then I puff, "He always makes me go, every summer. He says it keeps me out of trouble."

Gillette has no answer for that. We stroke in silence. There is no relentless, steaming sun to burn us, no little kids to scream our ears off, and it amazes me how a place I know like the back of my hand in the daylight is so different in the dark. I want to ask Gillette — Mr. Personality — about Mary Margaret Fitzgerald Carr, who I think is in love with him, and I wonder if he is in love with her. But then I know Gillette saves all his love for Willie Mays, and besides, Mary Margaret is Catholic and would never be allowed to love a Methodist.

So instead of asking him about Mary Margaret, I say, "Did

you know I once rode an elephant in the parking lot at Fairchild's Grocery?"

"You never did!" says Gillette.

"Did too," I tell him. "The circus came to town, and Daddy bought tickets for the whole first grade. Me and Polly sat right up on that elephant together, just as tall as you please, like Toomai, the elephant boy."

Gillette considers this news. "What was it like?"

"High and wobbly," I say, and Gillette laughs. I love it when I can make Gillette laugh. On a night like this, it's hard to remember how much I hated him when his mama moved with him and little Audrey into our house on River Road after she married Daddy last summer. I didn't realize then how much I missed having a brother. I'd never had one.

"Backstroke," says Gillette, as we finally reach the opposite end of the pool. "Do it the way I taught you, Sunny."

The way he taught me means my arms never break the water's surface, and they move with my legs, *up-open-shut, up-open-shut*, in an underwater frog ballet.

It's a long pool, and it's hard to swim in a straight line when I'm on my back. I stare at the heavens and fixate on one "twinkle twinkle little star." Daddy told me my real mama sang that song to me when she first met me, twelve years ago. But I wouldn't know. I never knew her. Now I have Annabelle, but she's not my mama. My mama is tall and beautiful, with soft, golden hair and big, white teeth inside a lopsided smile.

When I bump into Gillette, he pushes me out of his way but he's nice about it. Gillette is nothing if not nice. "Five more minutes," he says. *Up-open-shut*.

I don't have to follow any rules in the dark, so of course I didn't walk through the showers, and I'm not wearing a bathing cap, which feels as delicious as getting out of school early on the last day. My hair floats all over the place and so does my mind.

There is nothing on this earth as good as summer. I bounce like a Ping-Pong ball with Laura Mae, between our house and Meemaw's. Daddy stocks up on Dr Pepper at the store because he knows how much I love it, especially with salted peanuts sprinkled into the bottle. Miss Cantrell makes stacks of books for me to read at the library and knows just what I like. I can spend all afternoon there reading if I want to, and the library is air-conditioned.

There's hand-cranked ice cream and all afternoon at the pool with Polly and Mary Margaret, and this year there's Gillette and baseball and always there are the scary movies that come back to the Leflore. The Man with the X-Ray Eyes *is this week's scary movie and I know Parnell will let me in free; he always does. Polly and I made him a chocolate cream pie with Laura Mae's help this morning. We're gonna have to make Parnell a hundred pies this summer because* A Hard Day's Night *is coming! Yeah, yeah, yeah!*

The paper said the "invaders" are coming, too — I don't care what Gillette says.

I lay in bed last night thinking about *The Giant Claw* and *The Mole People* and who might be clawing up out of the earth, coming for us. I never slept a wink, and then Meemaw wondered why I conked out for three hours on the floor, under the attic fan this afternoon. I told her that pie-making had worn me to a frazzle.

But I don't see a thing, right here, right now, so I start my backstroke again and I tell myself that Gillette is right, so I won't believe in invaders. *Up-open-shut. How many weeks until school starts again? How many more weeks of freedom?*

I hear the water sluice off Gillette as he climbs the ladder. I quicken my froggy pace. "You're going to hit the side," he warns.

But I don't hit the side. I don't hit the end, either. I reach behind me and touch something in the water, something soft and warm pressed into the dark corner of the pool.

Something *alive.*

And that's when I scream.

SNCC Says Headquarters Coming Here.

— Associated Press, *Greenwood Commonwealth*, June 15, 1964

"Together we will face the challenges,
and together we will plan new courses of action."

— Thatcher Walt, in an editorial for the *Greenwood Commonwealth*, June 22, 1964

Senator Stennis Calls on President,
Attorney General to Halt the Invasion of Mississippi.

— United Press International (UPI) headline, June 1964

2

I gulp a fresh lungful of air and hear a *whap!-whap!-whap!* across the wet concrete and a *crash!* into the chain-link fence. I scream my throat raw and Gillette plunges into the pool with a great splash, grabs me with both arms, and holds me tight. I choke on the water I'm trying not to swallow.

"He's gone!" Gillette shouts. "Hush your screaming! You're all right!"

But I scream some more. Gillette crushes my wrist as he hauls me to the solid steel of the ladder. In two seconds flat, I get hold of myself enough to shut up, grab the ladder, and heave myself out of the pool. Gillette is right behind me, breathing on me, hurrying. He wraps me in my towel, but we're out in the open, sitting ducks.

"What is it? Who is it? Where is it?" I hop like my feet are on fire.

Gillette pulls the towel tighter around me. "Hush, Sunny!" he says, his own voice quavering.

"It's the invaders! We've got to get out of here! Hide!"

"Sunny!" Gillette shakes me. He sounds sure of himself now. "It was just some kid! Get hold of yourself — you're going to wake the dead!" He puts his face right in front of mine and keeps talking. "I said I'd bring you if you didn't make a sound, and here you are wailing your head off!"

I am willing to be wrong. "It was a person?" My teeth are chattering. "A kid? Was he here the whole time? Did you see him?"

"I saw him."

"Who was it?"

"I don't know him," says Gillette in an even voice.

"You know everybody!"

"Well, I don't know *him*."

"Is he still here? Did he get out? Did he leave?"

"He's long gone." Gillette sounds sure.

I am out of breath. I gulp for air, which starts me on a coughing fit. Gillette pounds me on the back with one hand and grabs his towel, his T-shirt, and my sundress with the other.

"Come on, Sunny. Let's go. We're late." He hands me my dress.

"Wait a minute!" I say. "Was it that jughead Bobby Carpenter? Did you know he was going to be here? Did you set me up to be scared to death by a kid I could whup any day of the week if I saw him coming?"

Gillette shakes his head so hard he flings water from his hair in all directions. Then he dries his face with his towel and smooths his hair back along his head, flattening it like a pancake. "Why would I do that?" he asks in irritation, and I almost believe him. He pulls on his T-shirt and then his cap. "It was a kid. He had high-top sneakers."

"In the pool?"

"Not in the pool. He grabbed them by the fence and ran off. That's when I saw them. C'mon, let's get out of here."

We jiggle the fence and squeeze through the gate just as Deputy Davis swings around the circle between the pool and the playground and shines the bright, white headlights of his cruiser onto our guilty faces.

I tug my sundress over my head, blink into the lights, and swallow.

"Are we under arrest?"

Gillette stands next to me, his bathing suit dripping wet. "Don't be a nitwit," he says as Deputy Davis steps out of his car. "And don't open your big mouth, especially about why you were screaming. Let me do the talking."

"Are you out of your mind?" I sputter. Gillette may be Mr. Personality in school and on the ball field, and he may live here for the rest of his life, but he will never be from the Delta. You have to come from generations born here and buried here to be known as a true citizen of Greenwood, Mississippi.

Deputy Davis stands in front of his headlights, *lifts his gun out of its holster*, and squints through the blackness to where we stand plastered against the chain-link fence like two escapees from the state penitentiary at Parchman.

Then Gillette says, "Trust me."

And before I can think of anything to say back, he adds, "Happy anniversary."

I almost laugh, but honest, it's not funny. And then, because I won't go to my death without a fight, and because I'm not sure yet just how trustworthy Gillette is, and because I'm a big mouth, I shout, *"It's just us! Sunny and Gillette from over on River Road! Jamie Fairchild's kids! We're not invaders!"*

Deputy Davis checks his gun in its holster and starts across the grass. "Sunny?" he calls in his high nasal voice. "Is that you, Sunny Fairchild?"

"Yessir!" I call right back, my voice a croak.

Now that I know I'm not going to be shot, I need an explanation. What whopper can I make up on the spot?

"I'll tell him Bobby Carpenter made us do it," I whisper.

"It wasn't Bobby Carpenter," Gillette repeats.

Deputy Davis stops walking and rests one hand on his billy club, like he's Hoss Cartwright and we're threatening the Ponderosa, like he shouldn't have to come all the way across this wide, green, grassy lot to get us, and what are we going to do about it? So we start walking toward him.

"Then who was it, if it wasn't Bobby Carpenter?" I spit.

Gillette stares directly at Deputy Davis, but his whisper is just for me: "Sunny, it was a colored boy."

I stop in my wet tracks.

"Don't you lie to me, Gillette Robinson."

"As I live and breathe. It was a colored boy."

I am speechless.

There was a colored boy in our pool. A colored boy. And I touched him, my skin on his skin. I touched a colored boy. And then he ran away, like he was on fire.

THE MISSISSIPPI FREEDOM SUMMER PROJECT

This summer, SNCC, in cooperation with COFO, is launching a massive Peace Corps-type operation in Mississippi. Students, teachers, technicians, nurses, artists and legal advisors will be recruited to come to Mississippi to staff a wide range of programs that include voter registration, freedom schools, community centers and special projects.

The struggle for freedom in Mississippi can only be won by a combination of action within the state and a heightened awareness throughout the country of the need for massive federal intervention to ensure the voting rights of Negroes. This summer's program will work toward both objectives.

Summer volunteer Dick Landerman, a Duke University student, explains voter registration to a woman doing laundry in her backyard, summer 1964.

Voter registration workers will operate in every rural county and important urban area in the state. These workers will be involved in a summer-long drive to mobilize the Negro community of Mississippi and assist in developing local leadership and organization.

PROGRESS IN MISSISSIPPI DEPENDS ON YOU.

— SNCC recruiting brochure

3

So I run. I run like a fox run away from a hound dog. Sweet Lord, save me! Get me outta here before they catch me. Don't even stop to breathe. I was hot, so hot, and now I'll be hotter than the other side-a heaven, but I couldn't help it, just wanted to see it. They closed our pool so long ago, drained the water clean out, and now none of us have a place to swim except the muddy Yazoo or the snaky Tallahatchie, and why not that sparkling clean water for me, in that big-as-Noah's-ark pool, that pool for white folks — who says it has to be just for white folks? Don't everybody need a pool? Ma'am say that's just the way it is and I want to know why.

Twill say, "We got to go north, where the jobs are."

Jimmy say, "Ray, here, he could play ball up north."

Run, Raymond, Run! No time to think. Watch for cops. Don't let 'em see a colored boy running, ever, 'specially not at night. Don't let 'em catch you, Raymond! Run!

Run past the Cotton Boll where you can't eat the hamburgers because you colored. Trip across the railroad tracks and fall face-first into the land where your people sleep together, eat together, and sing Hallelujah in church together and keep to they own kind except when they cross the tracks to clean the white folks' houses or tend the white folks' children or pick the white folks' cotton or say yassuh and nossuh or "shine yo' shoes, sir?" or go to jail at the courthouse for no good reason.

Run past Fairchild's Grocery where Pap traded greens and

sweet taters to Mr. Jamie for bail money for Silas. Run like a fox into the deep dark night of your people.

Ma'am say, "It's just like this, Ray." Huh. Not for me. Not gon' be *just like this* for me.

Run!

4

Deputy Davis watches me and Gillette shuffle toward him. Soon we stand right in front of him, wrapped in our towels, drip-drying in the dark. A breeze tugs at the back of my neck.

Deputy Davis twitches his mouth into that *tsk* sound he always makes before he converses. "What are you two doing out here in the middle of the night?"

I want to say, *Isn't it obvious?* but I do know better than that. My lie about Bobby Carpenter feels thin, especially because Deputy Davis fishes with Mr. Carpenter and can check my story. So I don't know what to say. If I was to tell him it was an anniversary celebration, it would be too complicated and he'd still arrest us.

"It's my fault, sir," Gillette says in his most sincere voice. I blink and get ready for anything.

Deputy Davis crosses his arms. "How's that?" It's hard to see him because the headlamps are directly behind him, so he looks mostly like a life-sized silhouette of a policeman cut out of black cardboard and set in front of the bright lights of his cruiser. At least he doesn't have the red light flashing on top or the siren screaming at us. We'd scare up whole city blocks in two seconds flat.

Gillette sounds like he's Walter Cronkite delivering the television news. "Sunny lost her goggles in the deep end today, sir, and she was so upset about it tonight, I told her I'd help her rescue them. I delivered groceries all day and didn't get home before the pool closed — I even took a delivery to your house and Mrs. Davis gave me a glass of her just-made lemonade with ice and everything and let me play with the baby while she put away the groceries. Sir."

I'm impressed. I nod like my head is unhinged from my neck, while I put a look on my face that says my goggles are my most treasured possession and I will die a wretched, painful death without them. I don't own goggles.

Deputy Davis *tsks*. "Where are they?"

I swallow. And I know: He's going to tell Daddy. He's going to put us in that police car and drive us the mile to River Road and knock on our door and wake up Daddy in the middle of the night and tell him that me and Gillette are guilty of breaking the law, guilty of trespassing, and guilty of swimming for no good reason, and this is going to be far, far worse than being arrested. I'd rather starve in a cold, damp jail cell over at the courthouse than face Daddy's disappointment in me. Not to mention a whipping.

You did what, young lady? Cut me a switch off the pear tree — the longest and thinnest one you can find, 'cause that's the one that'll pop welts on your legs when I whip you with it!

I have never had a whipping from Daddy in my life — he has never even threatened me with a whipping — but this feels like a whipping offense.

"Please, sir," says Gillette. I know him well enough to know he's worried about worse than whippings, and I know that those two words — *please, sir* — really mean: *You turn us in and everybody will know it, and you'll humiliate our parents. This humiliation will be worse than the gossip that surrounded Jamie Fairchild marrying a divorced piano teacher from Neshoba County with two kids. This humiliation will mean I have to work twice as hard to be accepted in this town by everybody else's parents.*

Maybe I don't actually think these things, maybe these feelings are beyond words, but somewhere in my heart, I know this to be true. My heart pounds softly, *whoosh-whoosh-whoosh*, in my ears. Then I say quietly to the darkness and to Deputy Davis, "He's a good boy."

Our deputy seems to consider this. He tugs on the rim of his police hat, tilts his head sideways, and spits into the stubby grass. Then, mind made up, he says, "Come with me." We follow him to the back of the cruiser, where he opens the trunk and pulls out a Winchester rifle with one hand and a folded quilt with the other. He drapes the quilt over the open maw of the trunk, holds his rifle with both hands — it's almost as tall as I am — and gives us a look that says *I Am the Decider of Your Fate.*

For a crazy second I want to say, *Hunting? We're going hunting*? Why else would you carry around a rifle? But I get hold of myself, stare at the rifle, and think: *This weapon would have been no good at all against Godzilla, but it must work against invaders, and that's why Deputy Davis carries it around in the trunk.*

Tsk. "You two know that trespassing is against the law."

"Yessir." We answer in unison. We are united, guilty, and hopeful.

"You know I could arrest you."

"Yessir."

"You know I could take you to the station, make a call to your house, and wait for your parents to come pick you up."

"Yessir."

Tsk. "I'm not going to do that."

The relief that washes over me is as sweet as summer. I can practically feel Gillette go limp with deliverance. I see heat lightning off in the distance and I wonder if it will rain. We need rain.

Deputy Davis puts his rifle back in the trunk. "Here's what we're going to do," he says. *Tsk*. "I'm not going to tell your parents about this. You are."

"Sir?" says Gillette. I chance a look at Gillette and see him shaking, which is when I realize I'm cold, too. The breeze that tugged at my neck is playing in the trees now. The dry leaves rustle against one another as if they're being tickled.

"I can call this in and write you up and the whole town will know what you've been up to," says Deputy Davis. His face is not kind; it's as serious as a jail sentence.

"And I will do that, if you don't tell your folks what you've been up to."

"How will you know if we've told them?" I ask, which I know is cheeky but I can't help it.

"I'll know. And you'll know I know."

My feet begin to itch.

Daddy calls Deputy Davis a "straight arrow." He goes by the book. He doesn't make exceptions to the rules for anybody. I wonder if he's not turning us in because he has a kid of his own now. I call him Little Deputy Davis, but only when I know no one can hear me. He's a real ugly baby.

Deputy Davis picks up the quilt so he can slam shut the trunk. He opens the back door of his cruiser, spreads the quilt over the backseat, and says, "Get in. I'll take you home." And we climb right in. It's warm as toast in the backseat.

Before he shuts the door, Deputy Davis cradles his arm on the top of the car and leans toward us like he's got us where he wants us now, trapped in his sinister, gloomy cave filled with spiders, and maybe he'll let us out if he feels like it. He smells like old sweat and I realize the whole car smells clammy and hot. Thunder rumbles in the distance. I don't dare look at Gillette, but I put my hand under my towel and on top of his hand and he grabs it.

Tsk. "Think about what you've done here tonight. You've broken the law. This is how a life of crime starts. You break the law and you think you can get away with it, so you do it again.

Well, you can't get away with it. The law is the law for a reason: to protect the citizens and make this a safe place to live. Sunny, you should be ashamed of yourself — you know better. Is this the kind of reputation you want in this town?"

"Nossir," I whisper.

"You think about that tomorrow when you sit in Sunday school. This kind of behavior speaks to your character, Sunny."

I am ashamed, thoroughly and completely. *The wise shall inherit glory; but shame shall be the promotion of fools. Proverbs 3:35.*

I am a fool. This isn't an adventure. This is a catastrophe.

Deputy Davis is *tsk*ing to beat the band now, leaning in close, working up to his big finish. "Gillette, I happen to know your daddy, over in Neshoba County. He's . . . an associate of mine. You make sure you tell him, too. I'll know when you do."

At the mention of his daddy, Gillette balls his hand into a fist and swallows, a big spit-filled ball of air. "Yessir," he says.

Deputy Davis releases us from his suffocating presence, sweeps into the driver's seat like he's king of the road, and drives us home down the ghostly quiet streets of Greenwood, Mississippi.

He watches us in the rearview mirror. "Was anyone else with you tonight?" he asks. I squeeze Gillette's fist to help me keep my mouth shut.

"Nossir," says Gillette, almost too quickly.

Whoever he was, that colored boy, I decide he was the lucky one. He didn't get caught. He got away.

The cruiser stops at the curb in front of our house on River Road.

"Remember," says Deputy Davis. "I'll know."

Within two minutes we are upstairs and in our bedrooms without speaking one word to each other. I consider tapping on the wall in the Morse code Gillette's been teaching me, but somehow I know not to. Our adventure is over. "Happy anniversary, Gillette," I whisper, even though I know he can't hear me.

I crawl into bed and stare at the ceiling, wondering who that boy was in the pool, wondering if I'll be able to tell Daddy anything about tonight, and wondering what Deputy Davis will do if I don't. I wonder if all the policemen in Greenwood carry rifles in their trunks now. I wonder who the invaders are. Will I know them when I see them?

I reach into my nightstand drawer and pull out the only photograph I have of my mother. I took it from the bottom of Meemaw's underwear drawer when she was taking her bath one hot afternoon. So far, she hasn't missed it, and I really need it, so that's that.

There she stands, my mama, squinting into the sun in her shirtwaist dress and crooked smile. Around her neck, she's wearing a silver locket shaped like a heart. She's holding a suitcase. I turn over the picture and read the back again.

Miranda, age 18

What adventure was she off to? It must have swallowed her whole.

5

"Where you been?" Ma'am look me up and down quick while I drip on the floor, but get right back to the sweet taters fryin' on the stove. Smell makes my mouth water.

"River," I say, but I know she don't believe me. Nobody go to the river at night.

"Where else?" say Ma'am. "I ain't seen you since breakfast."

"Told you I was going to Browning!" I tell her. "Aunt Geneva make me stay and help Twill and Jimmy in the squash and tomatoes. Whackin' weeds all day in that field, pickin' bugs and beetles off the plants."

That true.

Ma'am say, "You get supper?" and when I shake my head, she say, "Wash up," and she turn the okra with a spatula. The grease pop.

White girl sitting at our kitchen table, smilin' at me. Never seen a white girl in this house. I stare at my shoes. I got 'em cradled in my arms like a baby.

"Why everybody up?" I ask Ma'am. "Why you cookin' so late?"

"Shhh!" Ma'am say. "Pap sleepin'." Then she tell me, "Raymond, this here Miss Jo Ellen. Jo Ellen Chapman. She gon' build us a library."

That's when I find out: White girl stayin' in our house.

I got to sleep on the floor, in Ree's room, the whole summer.

How this be?

"Hello, Raymond," white girl say. "It's nice to meet you." I don't look at her yellow hair. Ree sittin' so close she touching her, making 'mirations all over her.

She say, "We got us a Freedom Righter! Right here in our house! From the state of Maryland! Ain't that right, Jo Ellen?" She call her by her given name.

White girl nod her head. "That's right, Glory."

Ree say, "I just pick her up at the Freedom House, like a puppy dog! I seen her and a whole litter of them Freedom Righters come in on a bus — they been comin' in cars all day and now here come a bus! I spot the girl I want and grab her by the hand, and tell her, 'You comin' home with me!' And Ma'am finally say okay. Ain't that right, Ma'am?"

Ma'am give me a look says she can't tell Ree no when she like this, and then say, "Glory, I told you. You quit bothering those folks at the Freedom House." She serve up collards on a plate.

"I got me a big sis again!" say Ree. "Almost like Adele come home."

Ma'am stiffen at the stove and I run my hand over my face.

This white girl nothing like Adele. Not even close. I get me a drink of water from the bucket.

White girl say to Ma'am, "It's awfully nice of you to cook me supper this late, Mrs. Bullis."

I choke on my water. Mrs. Bullis!

Here's one way to look at it. In 1955, in Montgomery, Alabama, Rosa sat down and Martin stood up. But that's not all. That's just one piece of the big puzzle that was the civil rights movement. Here is another: One hundred days before Rosa sat down, Emmett was killed by white men, his fourteen-year-old body dumped into the Tallahatchie River near Greenwood, Mississippi, that rich, dark, flat Delta land full of swamps and rivers and cotton.

So many black men had disappeared, most of whom were never found. A black man wasn't important in the South, but a black child from Chicago whose mother made noise — now that was different. Emmett was found, and his death made the national news. His mama made sure of that. And Mississippi, the Closed Society, was on the map. Mississippi was on notice.

In 1960, Bob Moses, the soft-spoken son of a Harlem janitor, came from New York to Mississippi to see what he could see. He came because Ella sent him. Ella Baker was the mother of —

SNCC —
the Student
Nonviolent
Coordinating
Committee.

Ella respected Martin, but the civil rights group he helped start —

SCLC —
the Southern
Christian
Leadership
Conference

loved oratory and big productions and working with big government and having a shining star — the Reverend Dr. Martin Luther King, Jr. — to speak for them and lead them.

While all that was good, Ella knew it was the young people who had fire in their bellies, fire for change.

WE ARE NOT AFRAID.

Instead of one shining star, she believed in constellations, local people in Mississippi towns like Sunflower, Ruleville, Meridian, Hattiesburg . . . so many little towns where local black people were already pushing back, ready for real freedom. They just needed to uncover their shape, design, and place in the sky.

So Ella grabbed hold of Bob . . . and he grabbed right back. She sent him to Mississippi, where no one wanted to go because it was so dangerous. Blacks could not vote in Mississippi (or Alabama or Georgia or Louisiana — and elsewhere), even though more than one hundred years had passed since Abraham Lincoln had signed the Emancipation Proclamation, freeing the slaves. One hundred years since the Thirteenth Amendment had abolished slavery. Ella remembered her grandmother's slave stories, and here's what Ella said:

"Give light and people will find the way."

Bob took Ella's light to Mississippi, where there was no more slavery, because there was no more slavery in America. But in the American South, Jim Crow laws had turned the "coloreds" into sharecroppers or maids or cotton pickers. Bob was charged with making sure they had a telescope, so they could see the stars.

The people who worked with Bob before he came to Mississippi (these were Martin's people in Atlanta), wondered if he was a Communist.

(what's a communist?)

Just because:

he wasn't "one of them," from the South (he grew up in the projects in Harlem)

he observed quietly and stood in the back of the room during meetings

he read deep thinkers like Camus (his hero)

he was a deep thinker, too

he went to Harvard, he studied in Europe with Quaker peacemakers, and

he worked in Japan alongside Buddhist monks

he marched in protest with civil rights groups that weren't even Martin's — why?

He was different. Very different.
And the civil rights movement was
on notice.

In Mississippi, Bob met Amzie Moore, a World War II veteran who was now president of the local chapter of an old institution —

the NAACP —
the National
Association for the
Advancement of
Colored People.

Amzie showed Bob how to navigate Mississippi. He told him:

"What we really need is not protests,
fancy speeches in front of thousands,
not boycotts, not marches —
what we need is the right to

VOTE

THEN we can change things in Mississippi!"

So, in 1961, Bob brought black SNCC volunteers to Mississippi to work alongside the local people —

They were community organizers!

And Amzie provided a "safe house" for them. As they worked to register black voters, they were:

shot at,
beaten,
jailed, and
spat upon by whites.

Good Mississippi men like Herbert Lee and Louis Allen died because they stood for their right to vote and be treated like any white man. No one took notice of their deaths because a local black man did not make news in the South.

But everyone took notice of Bob Moses. Beaten, he quietly went right back to work with stitches in his head. Jailed, he quietly worked from jail. Shot at, he resolutely kept going, this quiet, self-possessed young man from New York. He didn't give big speeches. He didn't ask to lead. He brought the black people of Mississippi together, one small meeting at a time, one small town at a time, and asked them to lead themselves. He inspired them to discover their greatness. He told them that SNCC workers would walk beside them, go to the courthouse with them to help them register, figure out how to bail them out of jail when they were arrested, teach their children their black history, and help feed their families as they learned to be unafraid and step out of the bondage they had become used to.

In meetings, Bob stood at the back of the room and observed. When he finally spoke, he reminded people of who they already were — strong, capable, smart, worthy, and right.

He said:

> *"From the first time a Negro gets involved in white society, he goes through the business of* repressing, repressing, repressing. *My whole reaction through life to such humiliation was to avoid it, keep it down, hold it in, play it cool. This is the kind of self-repression every Negro builds into himself. But when you do something personally to fight prejudice, there is a feeling of great release."*

It's called Freedom.

And, in 1964, sitting around tables with Amzie and Ella and Allard Lowenstein, Bob organized Freedom Summer. He appealed to all those other anagrams: CORE (the Congress of Racial Equality), SCLC, the NAACP, and they gathered together with SNCC and called themselves, for this one summer:

COFO —
The Council of
Federated
Organizations

They came together like this only in Mississippi, the most racist, most dangerous state in America. Bob agreed to coordinate their efforts to open up Mississippi, to open the Closed Society.

They won't pay attention to us if we die — those were Bob's thoughts. *But bring kids here from the North, from the West — college students whose parents are doctors and lawyers and teachers — and America will pay attention. And, most important we need their help. We need to work together, black and white together.*

Now <u>this</u> was different.

One thousand souls came to Mississippi in 1964 for the Mississippi Summer Project. Most were volunteers, young college students, and white. Some were Christians, some were Jews, some were atheists. Some were doctors, some were lawyers, some were teachers. Some were ministers. Some were married and came together. For some, it was their first time away from home.

Like a small army, they marched into Mississippi's black communities to teach, to register voters, to sing at mass meetings, to live together and eat together with strangers, to risk being shot at or killed, beaten and arrested — and they were.

They were scared, and still they put one foot in front of the other. Blacks in Mississippi were scared, too. Registering to vote was an act of rebellion in Mississippi, and whites retaliated — they were scared, too. They burned crosses and bombed black citizen's homes and churches. They threw bricks and arrested the army of protestors. But still the protestors came. And black Mississippi rumbled awake. You can't wake up people after a long sleep and expect them not to be hungry.

Bob Moses was their

driving force,
quiet grace,
guiding light,
calm center,

their ever-present assurance that this nonviolent, steady stand was the way to freedom in a participatory democracy, that nobody's free until everybody's free.

"In the same way that one listens more attentively to a whisper, people were drawn to Bob . . . he was so unobtrusive that in his quiet self-possessed stillness, he fixed additional attention on himself. He seemed entirely nourished from within. If Bob walked into a room or

joined a group that I was in, I felt my chest muscles quicken and a sudden rush of exhilaration. He inspired me and touched me. I trusted Bob implicitly and felt deep affection for him."

— Freedom worker Mary King

So the army was inspired, and this was its message to the people, spread across Mississippi, one thousand strong:

Stand up and be counted!
Discover your strength! Believe in your ability to lead yourselves! And know —
Your freedom is already within you.
You must register to VOTE!
So you can change Mississippi.
Change America.
Change the world. Your fate is in your hands.

Ain't gonna let no jailhouse turn me around!

ONE MAN, ONE VOTE.

It was a revolution. It was an awakening. It was a reckoning.

Black Mississippi was on notice.

The United States government was on notice, too. In 1965, Congress passed and President Lyndon Johnson signed the Voting Rights Act, making it a federal offense to stand in the way of anyone of age who wanted to register to vote. From there began a cascade of registered black voters coming to the polls on election days.

And they did change Mississippi, the United States, and the world.

They changed themselves.

But that's not all. There is still work to be done. This is just one way to look at it, and just the beginning of the story, the barest of facts . . . just one piece of the big puzzle that was Mississippi in 1964, and Bob Moses's gentle genius, as well as the courage of an army of one thousand souls who came to stay for a summer and who left with their lives forever changed, their bellies — and their hearts — still on fire for justice, searching for the next struggle.

They put America on notice.

6

Sunday, June 21, 1964

Daddy sits at the breakfast table buttering his toast. "It's gonna be a hot one." The knife scrapes across the toast like it's buttering sandpaper. "Come tell me good morning," he says as I shuffle toward him. I yawn and try a smile. For a second, I wonder if he'll say, *Don't you have something to tell me, young lady?* and I'll dissolve into a guilty puddle of apology.

"The forecast says a high of ninety-eight today and no rain in sight," says Annabelle. "Good morning, Sunny." Annabelle is fixing her coffee while scrambling a mountain of yellow eggs in the biggest skillet and listening to the fizzle from the radio on the counter. Her hair is in a sloppy roll at the top of her head. Fat curls spiral like daddy longlegs out of control all around her face. She'll fix it, though. She never goes out in public without perfect hair.

I give Daddy the same kiss I've been giving him every morning since I can remember. "Happy Father's Day," I tell him, and he smiles at me. "Thank you, peanut."

Annabelle plops a plate in front of me — scrambled eggs, grits, a slice of bacon, and a piece of dry toast. "Thank you," I tell her. "Good morning." Daddy shoves the butter plate my way. It's already too hot to eat in this house but I don't want Annabelle to feel bad so early in the morning so I pick at my breakfast. She has put too much salt in the eggs again, but I say nothing about it. I wonder what everyone would do if I said in my most casual voice, *Ran into a colored boy in the pool last night*. . . . but I am not that crazy. I did tell Mama all about it this morning, though. Talked right to her picture and felt better about it.

Audrey marches into the room singing "I've Been Working on the Railroad" at the top of her lungs as she swings her doll, Ginny, by the hair. Gillette is right behind her. He scoops her up with a shout and deposits her in her kitchen chair after plopping Ginny in the old high chair.

"Hey!" says Audrey.

"No baby dolls at the breakfast table," says Gillette.

Annabelle smiles at her children.

Audrey pops out of her chair and smothers me with kisses. "You are *juicy* today, Sunny!" she says. She completely ignores Daddy, who smiles at me, so I hug Audrey for Daddy and send him an extra-kind smile. He sends me back a wink.

"Is it school yet?" Audrey asks as she plops back in her chair and slurps her orange juice. "I'm going to be in kindergarten!" she announces for the four-hundredth time.

"Peter Rabbit Kindergarten," I say with pride. "I went there."

"No, Audrey's enrolled at Martha Parker," says Annabelle. "I think that's a better choice for her."

I am stung, even though it shouldn't matter. Who cares what kindergarten Audrey goes to? And why isn't Peter Rabbit good enough?

"There's a kindergarten at the Presbyterian church, too," says Daddy in an offhand way.

"It's not school yet, Audrey," says Gillette. "It's still summer."

"You keep saying that." Audrey pouts while Annabelle helps her plate with steaming scrambled eggs. "Where's Laura Mae?"

"Laura Mae comes tomorrow afternoon," says Annabelle.

"These eggs are too salty!" Audrey says, but she eats them anyway.

Gillette and I still don't know how to talk about last night, so we act like we're invisible to each other.

Daddy pushes back from the table. "Time to pick up Meemaw," he says. The grandfather clock in the living room strikes six, which means it's nine.

"I have a meemaw, too," Audrey says, her mouth full of scrambled eggs. She swallows and repeats herself. "I have a meemaw, too. Back home. At our house." She sighs and her eyes fill with tears.

"This *is* home, Audrey," says Annabelle in her soft voice. I notice the dark circles under her eyes.

Audrey shakes her head. "No, it's not," she whispers. She puts down her fork and wipes at her tears with her fingertips.

"We'll go see your meemaw soon," says Annabelle. But she doesn't sound like she means it. She and Gillette exchange a look. In the year they've lived with us, they haven't been back to Neshoba County once, and it's only a hundred miles away. It's not like it's the moon. Polly's daddy goes there all the time, selling pickles and ketchup and baby food. He's a Heinz salesman and drives all over Mississippi and even to Memphis. Daddy wipes his mouth with his napkin. He smoothes Audrey's hair and she lets him. He smiles at Gillette. "How about fishing with me this afternoon?"

"Sure," says Gillette.

"It's Sunday." Annabelle points out the obvious.

"I'm sure the Lord won't mind us tickling a few fish for our supper," says Daddy. "The new minister is going to meet us, now that he and his family have settled in. He has a boy your age, Gillette. I know you'll make him welcome."

"Yessir." Gillette actually smiles and I know what he's thinking. *Now I'm not the newest kid in town.*

Annabelle doesn't protest again, so that's that. I don't want to be stuck with her and Audrey — or even worse, with

Meemaw — all afternoon, so I say, "I have a date with Polly and Mary Margaret," even though I don't.

"That'll be fine," says Daddy, "as long as it's well after Sunday dinner. You know how Meemaw is about her Sunday dinners."

"Eat your breakfast, Sunny?" Annabelle says. She never tells me what to do without making it sound like a suggestion.

"Yes, ma'am," I say. In my head, I'm already composing my note to Polly. Meanwhile, Gillette stands with his plate at the stove for seconds of grits and bacon — last night's adventure sure didn't hurt his appetite. My uncle Parnell squeezes into the kitchen behind him looking like a Yankee Doodle Dandy in the suit he wore for graduation two years ago. He heads for the coffeepot, like he always does, and announces, "I'm bringing a guest to Sunday dinner."

"Who is it?" I ask. "You're awfully dressed up."

"It's a surprise," says Parnell. "And I always dress like this for church."

He does not. "Give us a hint," I say.

"Hup-two-three-four," says Parnell.

"One, two, buckle my shoe!" spouts Audrey.

"That's right!" Parnell pours his coffee and makes no sense at all.

Daddy stands up and reaches for his suit coat on the back of the chair. "You'd better make sure Meemaw knows about it."

Daddy's out the door and Annabelle asks Parnell if he'll eat some breakfast and Parnell blows me a kiss and says he's having the chocolate pie I made him, thank you very much, and I blow him a kiss back and Annabelle says please don't eat that in front of Audrey — please — but Audrey's already begging for pie, and Parnell offers her a bite of his, and Annabelle sucks in her breath and struts to the sink and starts clanking dishes while Gillette tells Audrey there will be more pie at Sunday dinner. I announce I'm getting dressed and skedaddle up the stairs to my room, where I pull a piece of yellow construction paper out of my desk drawer and write in big letters, with a red crayon, like it's an emergency:

I am sprung
from Sunday Dinner Jail!
Meet me in our secret spot
at 4 o'clock sharp!

Then I pull up the screen on my open bedroom window and drop the folded note into the bucket hanging from the pulley rope that connects my house to Polly's like we've got a big-city clothesline high in the sky. I grab the top rope and yank it, hand over hand, until the bucket is wheeled across the space between our houses and clinks against Polly's bedroom window. I wait a minute, but she doesn't come. I keep watch while I throw on my Sunday church dress, tug on my white anklet socks, slip my feet into my church shoes, find my Bible for Sunday school, and fling a comb through the tangles in my hair. I won't let Annabelle touch my hair, and Laura Mae isn't here to braid it for me. Another glance out the window. No Polly.

"Sunny!" Gillette calls from the bottom of the stairs. "Move your big behind! Time to go!"

Interview With a White Resident of Levittown, Pennsylvania, on the Occasion of the First Black Family Moving Into Her Neighborhood in 1957

"He's got three children, and evidently he feels they will be accepted socially, and I don't feel they ever will be. The whole trouble with this integration business is, in the end, it probably will end up with mixing socially, and I think their aim is mixed marriages and becoming equal with the whites, but the only way they're going to do that is by education and bettering themselves, not by pushing in the way they have here."

Do you intend to move?

"At this time, no. It's a pretty impossible situation. We have our home here, and if the coloreds move in and run real estate values down, there are a lot of us, the G.I.s particularly, who are going to be, more or less, stuck with their homes."

What course of action are you going to follow?

"I'll do what I can to help to get them out legally and peacefully, and as far as accepting them socially, if that's what you mean, I could never do that."

7

We file into our pew — the twelfth one from the front on the right — fresh from Sunday school, and in the same order as always: Daddy on the aisle, then me, then Meemaw, and finally Parnell, who looks like a young version of Daddy, but then, he should, as they are brothers. A stranger looking at the four of us sitting there, Sunday after Sunday, as boring and unchanging as yesterday's news, would never know we've got a whole other family attached to us now and have stuffed them into our house on River Road with us.

Some Sundays I sit in our pew and pretend I've got a sudden brain tumor and forget all about Annabelle, Audrey, and Gillette, who I'm sure have picked out their own pew over at the Methodist church where we drop them off on our way to First Presbyterian. If I work hard enough at it, I can imagine the past two years were only a dream. Today I've just about decided that last night was all in my imagination. There was no colored boy in the pool, there was no swimming, and there was no running through the soft, dark night with Gillette.

Then Miss Agnes Flowers starts to pump the organ, and the choir stands up in red robes and it's time for the offering song and the offering, which means Daddy steps into the center aisle, and so does Deputy Davis. They walk together like Siamese twins to the front of the church, where our new minister, Pastor Marshall, says a prayer about how we should give all our money to the Lord, that it is fit and right to do so, and then he hands the collection plates to six ushers. Daddy and Deputy

Davis turn around and start down their aisle, handing off their plates to the first person in each row.

With Daddy ushering and collecting this month, the first person in the twelfth row is me. I don't look up as I take the plate with its envelopes and dollars and change and pass it to Meemaw, who passes it to Parnell, who passes it on down to the Smoots. Then back up the pew comes the plate and I hold it up to Daddy without looking at him. If I look at him, I'll have to see Deputy Davis. I know he's giving me the hairy eyeball.

Mrs. Marion Jackson in the choir is singing her heart out to her own special verse of "Leaning on the Everlasting Arms," and I don't even want to hear it. But it's one of my favorites and I can't help but close my eyes tight and sink right into those words:

> What have I to dread, what have I to fear,
> Leaning on the everlasting arms.
> I have blessed peace with my Lord so near,
> Leaning on the everlasting arms.

I've got plenty to dread and fear and I don't feel my Lord so near. I decide to pray right now, right through one of my favorite hymns, when Little Deputy Davis starts wailing from the tenth-row pew on the left side of the church, and Mrs. Deputy Davis scoots out the side door to hand him over to Vidella in the nursery. When I was little, I spent lots of time in the nursery with Vidella, too. Once I colored on the wall and she made me scrub it off myself. I'd much rather be sitting in church.

> Leaning (on Jesus), leaning (on Jesus)
> safe and secure from all alarms!

Leaning (on Jesus), leaning (on Jesus),
leaning on the everlasting arms!

Then, it's time for Pastor Marshall's sermon. Time for the NoDoz, as Meemaw says. But there's no dozing today.

"This morning's gospel reading is from the beatitudes, found in Matthew 5, verses one through twelve!" Pastor Marshall thunders with enthusiasm. He flops open his gigantic Bible to the Sermon on the Mount and begins.

"'And seeing the multitudes, he went up into a mountain: and when he was set, his disciples came unto him. And he opened his mouth, and taught them, saying —'"

Only Pastor Marshall is more than saying. He is holding forth. He is testifying. He delivers every one of those blessed beatitudes like he's King David and each beatitude is a rock in his mighty slingshot. *Just slay me now*, that's what I think, but of course I don't say a word.

Parnell's a mutterer, though. "Who put a tiger in *his* tank?"

"Shhhh!" Parnell is two whole years out of high school and a grown-up, but one shush from Meemaw will shut up anybody.

When Pastor Marshall gets to "'Blessed are the peacemakers . . .'" he stops. He stares at us like he's about to bore a hole in every last one of us. He repeats himself: "'Blessed are the peacemakers, for they shall be called the children of God'" and he goes on beatituding us to death. Then he closes his Bible with a thick amen, snaps off his glasses, grabs the lectern with both hands, and stands up straight. I pat myself back together.

"My message is short but heartfelt today," he says. "I know you're all hot — I see your fans waving at me across the sanctuary, and I'm not going to keep you this good morning. But I do want to talk with you about our response as Christians to the fact that Greenwood will soon fill with summer . . . volunteers . . .

from the northern and western states, who are being sent here by various civil rights organizations to register our black brethren to vote."

Well, you'd think the roof just caved in at First Presbyterian. All the air leaves the room. Every single body in front of me — and that's a lot of bodies from my twelfth-row pew — straightens like a ramrod. The bodies in my row look pretty stiff as well. I hear murmuring behind me, where the Fussells sit, but no muttering from Parnell. Meemaw doubles her fanning action, which sends whiffs of her dusting powder my way. I peek at Daddy. He's staring at Pastor Marshall as if he's got two heads.

"My Christian brothers and sisters," says Pastor Marshall. "Please."

Everyone takes a breath and I can breathe again, too.

"Mrs. Marshall and I read the papers this week, as I'm sure you have, too, and we feel moved to say something to you in the light of God's word. Senator Stennis and others — including our governor, Governor Johnson — are calling these volunteers 'invaders,' but these young people are not invaders, although they may be misguided. Most of them are college students, many of them the ages of your own children, most of them white, and most of them believing they are doing the right thing. Whether you believe they are or they aren't, the fact remains that they *will* be here. Their very presence — and their work — will shake our way of life in ways we cannot yet imagine."

People shift in their seats like they're newspapers somebody's rattling. Pastor Marshall goes on, but I don't hear a thing. All my brainpower is being used up trying to imagine what college students mistaken for invaders must look like. Or what a college student looks like, period. Parnell was a college student for one year, and he hated it. But he's Parnell, and I've known him all my life.

Meemaw stabs me with her elbow and I realize I'm bent over thinking about it, staring at my shoes.

"I want to urge the members of First Presbyterian to face these problems as Christians, to remember that we *are* Christians, and as such we are charged with keeping bitterness and hate out of our hearts and keeping alive instead a genuine concern for our brothers and sisters, be they white or colored, Jew or gentile, rich or poor, privileged or downtrodden. The good Lord expects us to be merciful to all, and to ask for mercy as well. To ask for grace. All men are equal in the sight of God and our country's Constitution. All are equal on God's earth, in God's heaven, and in this fellowship. Let us pray."

Before I can bow my head, I see Deputy Davis get up from his seat in the tenth-row pew on the left and walk out of church. Mr. Fussell does, too. So do Mr. Brand and two others.

I look up at Daddy, who is wiping his face with his handkerchief. I fan him and he smiles at me, but it's an empty smile — his mind is somewhere else. Something is wrong. I know because I get that tingle in my shoulders, that sick feeling in my gut, that horror-movie hunch, that something terrible is about to happen.

The Beatitudes, Matthew 5:1–12

And seeing the multitudes, he went up into a mountain: and when he was set, his disciples came unto him:

And he opened his mouth, and taught them, saying,

Blessed are the poor in spirit: for theirs is the kingdom of heaven.

Blessed are they that mourn: for they shall be comforted.

Blessed are the meek: for they shall inherit the earth.

Blessed are they which do hunger and thirst after righteousness: for they shall be filled.

Blessed are the merciful: for they shall obtain mercy.

Blessed are the pure in heart: for they shall see God.

Blessed are the peacemakers: for they shall be called the children of God.

Blessed are they which are persecuted for righteousness' sake: for theirs is the kingdom of heaven.

Blessed are ye, when men shall revile you, and persecute you, and shall say all manner of evil against you falsely, for my sake.

Rejoice, and be exceeding glad: for great is your reward in heaven: for so persecuted they the prophets which were before you.

8

We pick up Annabelle, Gillette, and Audrey from the Methodist church and pack ourselves like sardines, all seven of us, into our car, just like we always do after church.

We ride across the Yazoo River bridge, where Fulton Street turns into Grand Boulevard, and we're in North Greenwood, which I think of as a sort of peninsula of land surrounded by the Yazoo and Tallahatchie Rivers. Daddy says it was farmland when he was little, but now it's dotted with pretty houses and lots of trees.

Driving down Grand Boulevard means driving under a cool, wide canopy of oak trees that line either side of the road. They were planted long ago by the Greenwood Garden Club, of which Meemaw is a member. She tells us this every Sunday as we cross the bridge onto Grand Boulevard, but she's not speaking now. Her face carries a dark look, like she might explode any minute, so we all sit there and sweat in the quiet.

If you drive all the way down Grand Boulevard, you cross the Tallahatchie River bridge, and you're headed to Money, Mississippi, and all the cotton farms in that direction. That's where Gladhills, our old family plantation, sits, snugged up against the Tallahatchie. It's a wide, flat sea of cotton, baking in the sun.

But we don't have that far to go. We swing into Meemaw's perfectly swept driveway with the perfectly manicured lawn, thanks to her hired man, Wilson, and spill ourselves out of the hot-as-blue-blazes car. Parnell takes the car to go pick up his guest, Annabelle allows Audrey to ride with him, and the rest of us make our way into Meemaw's perfectly ordered house.

Meemaw marches from the car to her front door like she's an Onward Christian Soldier, which, believe me, is a sight. Meemaw is one of those people who, when she sits down, her dress floats out around her like it's a gigantic lake and she's a big buoy in the middle of the lake, bobbing along and frowning. She stomps from her front door to the kitchen and puts on her apron over her Sunday dress without even taking off her hat.

Laura Mae has left what she made for Sunday dinner covered up on the stove, and Annabelle begins taking the bowls and platters off the stove and transferring them to the dining room table.

"When you pick up Laura Mae tomorrow," Meemaw says to Annabelle, "tell her I need an extra washing day next week. Bedspreads and curtains. I'll take her Wednesday if you can spare her."

"That will be fine," Annabelle says, pleasant as you please.

"Ice in glasses," Meemaw snips at me. "Pour tea." Then she corners Daddy. "Can you believe the nerve of that man this morning? That kind of talk is not fit for church! Who does he think pays his salary? If he does not get fired for this, I don't know what this world is coming to." She wipes at her hot face with her apron.

Annabelle looks at Daddy, who shakes his head: *not now.* Gillette and I exchange a look, too. It means, *not ever, if we can help it,* and we know, neither of us is going to say a word about last night to Daddy.

The phone rings but Meemaw ignores it. Daddy turns on the attic fan and says, "Eloise, I wish you'd think about air-conditioning. It's going to be ninety-eight degrees today and it's not yet July."

"A body does not expire from a little summertime heat," replies Meemaw. "I didn't have an indoor bathroom or running water out at Gladhill Plantation growing up, much less air-conditioning, and I did just fine."

"I know," sighs Daddy, "back in the dark ages." Meemaw disappears into the dining room with fresh butter in the butter dish. The phone rings again, and again Meemaw ignores it, but she is more than annoyed. "What's the matter with decent people? Everyone knows it's dinnertime, for pity's sake."

The back screen door whips open and Uncle Vivian sweeps in with a small sack of tomatoes he puts on the counter. He spies me finishing up with my tea pouring.

"Sunshine!" he shouts. "How's my girl!" He scoops me up and spins me once around. I love this, even though I'm getting much too big for it.

"I'm fine!" I laugh. Annabelle smiles at us as she takes the biscuits out of the oven.

"How-do, Miss Annabelle?" Uncle Vivian asks her.

"I do fine, Vivian, thank you." She looks a bit puny to me, but maybe it's the heat.

"Any more of those Bee-atles?" Uncle Vivian asks me.

"Oh, yes," I tell him as I hand him the iced tea pitcher and we walk into the dining room together. "I got the new album last week. It's called *The Beatles Second Album*."

"How original," says Uncle Vivian.

"I listen to it nonstop," I say.

"Does she ever," says Gillette, who is right behind us, bringing in full glasses of the sweetest iced tea in Mississippi.

I ignore him. "I've got all the songs memorized already."

"Atta girl," says Uncle Vivian. "Sister!" He plants a kiss on Meemaw's perspiring head. Everybody's perspiring, and the house is as dark as a mausoleum, because Meemaw keeps the draperies pulled against the heat.

"Wash up, Vivian," says Meemaw, without so much as a how-dee-do. "We're starting without Parnell, since he can't have the decency to show up on time. Maybe his guest lives all the way to Memphis."

Uncle Vivian claps Gillette on the shoulder. "When you comin' out to the plantation to fish?"

"Maybe today," says Gillette as he takes his seat and looks at Daddy for confirmation.

Daddy helps Annabelle into her seat like a gentleman does and is ready with an answer. "How about after dinner and a little rest, when some of this heat has burned off?"

"That'd be fine, just fine," says Uncle Vivian. "I'll put a watermelon in the river to cool. I've got a new spot down by the Tate field, and I might even show it to you. Caught me fourteen catfish down there last week. Gave most of 'em to the coloreds."

Meemaw takes her seat without help at the head of the table. Poof goes her dress and now she's a buoy. "Fishing when you should be working," she sniffs.

"Now, Sister," says Uncle Vivian. "We're doing just fine by Mother and Daddy's money. We've got plenty of choppers this summer, plenty of pickers lined up for fall, and we're gonna have a warehouse full of cotton. We just need to get us some rain — it's been mighty dry for too long."

He seats himself at the other end of the table, and we are all gathered. Well, almost all. Uncle Vivian intones the blessing, sticks a corner of his napkin into the neck of his shirt, and says, "Pass the butter beans, please. Oh, yes." Then he changes the subject. "Gillette, you got you a girlfriend in this town yet?"

I lean my ears across the table to listen to Gillette's reply, but he just colors up as the phone rings again and Meemaw instructs Gillette to take it off the hook. He is only too happy to scoot away on the errand.

Meemaw takes a cool sip of her iced tea and says, "If you bothered to go to church on Sundays, brother, you would have heard Pastor Marshall ask the congregation today to cooperate — cooperate! — with these hooligans invading us from the North."

"Is that so?" Uncle Vivian's tone of voice changes to the one he uses when he's talking to his plantation manager. All business. He heaps butter beans on his plate and passes the bowl to me.

My every nerve is on alert. Meemaw doesn't allow anything but polite talk at the Sunday dinner table, but she's been on fire ever since those beatitudes.

Now she flings open her napkin and flaps it in her lap. "I don't know why they are here, messing in things that are none of their business. Eva Sistrunk has already seen them! She told us at bridge on Wednesday that there are just a few of them now, but more are coming — they'll just keep coming, Vivian, until we'll be overrun with them!"

"So I've heard," says Uncle Vivian with gristle in his voice. He butters a biscuit.

"She said they're all dirty, every one of them!" adds Meemaw. "They don't bathe. The boys have scruffy beards. They all wear sandals. They're *Communists*, that's what they are. Sinners, at the very least."

Meemaw takes a bite of banana pepper followed by a bite of biscuit, and swirls the iced tea in her glass, satisfied that she has conveyed the seriousness of the situation to all of us.

Daddy pours gravy on his mashed potatoes. His mouth is one thin line, his lips pressed together now, like he has swallowed a lemon.

"Sinners, Eloise?" he says. "What sins have they committed?"

I sit up straight. Uncle Vivian stops his fork halfway to his mouth.

Meemaw gives Daddy a bug-eyed look, like Cyclops but with two eyes. Even I know Meemaw wasn't issuing an invitation to a conversation.

"They live with the coloreds, Jamie! They eat with them and sleep with them! They are corrupting them right and left, filling their heads with heaven knows what dangerous notions. Stirring things up, when things are just fine the way they are. Our way of life is none of their business. Let them take the mote out of their own eye before they pretend to point fingers at us! I have absolutely forbidden Laura Mae to have anything to do with them!"

"Sister . . . ," says Uncle Vivian. He looks at Daddy. "Do we have to talk about this at Sunday dinner?"

Daddy passes the chicken platter to Annabelle and says in an even voice, "They're doing what they think is right."

Meemaw explodes. "Right! Let's talk about what's right, Jamie Fairchild. Or let's not bother. What else should I expect from the boy who stole my daughter away from me thirteen years ago and never brought her back home?"

I put my fork on my plate and my hands in my lap. Annabelle catches my eye and raises her eyebrows, flattens her lips into a sad smile. It's a kind gesture, meant for only me, but I don't want her kindness.

Daddy wipes his hand across his mouth, puts his elbows on the table, and folds his fingers like "*this is the church*" but not "*this is the steeple.*" Then he says, "I don't believe these people are sinners, any more than I was — or your daughter was! — thirteen years ago, Eloise."

I'm sitting right here! That's what I want to shout, but I don't. *Thump-thump-thump* goes my heart right behind my eyes. I open my mouth to ask to be excused but Meemaw points the butter knife at Daddy and careens in another direction.

"Don't you lecture me, Jamie Fairchild." Her voice rises, "I don't need lectures from the boy who squandered his inheritance on a life of frivolity and irresponsibility. I don't need lectures from the man who will bring home a new wife with two children and expect her to take care of that dilapidated monstrosity of a house and three children, with only part-time help."

Nobody moves. I feel light-headed and I'm afraid to look at anybody so I keep my gaze on my plate. I want so much to talk back, but I won't. Daddy wouldn't allow it. I want to hug him, though, and tell him it's all right, he's a good dad, responsibility is his middle name, and I'm a good cleaner. I will do a better job at home.

"Sister," says Uncle Vivian. "You forget yourself."

Daddy pushes back from the table and says, "I'm afraid we have to go."

Uncle Vivian puts a hand on Daddy's arm. "Just a minute, son," he says. Then he gives Meemaw a steely look. "You owe this man an apology."

Meemaw instantly becomes less poofy. She wipes at her forehead with her napkin, sighs, and says, "Of course I'm sorry, Jamie. I am. This morning has set my teeth on edge. It's this preacher that's got me overheated. And it's the heat. Maybe you're right. Maybe I do need the air-condition. But you need a full-time maid with this big brood of yours now, and I had Laura Mae first. She practically raised Miranda, and I'm not willing to give her up. I know she loves Sunny to death but you need someone for yourselves now."

Annabelle speaks up. "We do just fine, thank you, Miss Eloise." She takes one of Daddy's hands and squeezes it. "Let me help clear the table."

We have hardly started eating. This is the fastest Sunday dinner on record.

"Just a minute, now," says Uncle Vivian with his hand raised like a stop sign. He has turned into the traffic cop of the Sunday dinner table. "What did the preacher say?" His face signals stormy weather; it looked so bright and sunny when he arrived.

Meemaw, who has been clutching her napkin like she's afraid someone will try to yank it away from her, lets it go and leans back in her chair. Then she repeats Pastor Marshall's sermon, word for word ("I don't have a steel-trap memory for nothing!") while Daddy and Annabelle and Gillette and I sit in solidarity, still as stones. Meemaw waves her fork while she builds up to the "let us pray," while Uncle Vivian eats sliced tomatoes and two ears of corn and puts the empty cobs on Parnell's clean plate. Then he sits back, slowly refills his iced tea from the pitcher on the table like he's deep in thought, and says, quietly, "We'll see about that."

I look at Uncle Vivian's jaw, so thick and so determined, just like Pastor Marshall's jaw this morning. Then I think about the men who walked out of church during the "let us pray" and realize that's what Uncle Vivian would have done, too. People are picking sides, and for what, I don't know.

"It's Father's Day today," I say, just above a whisper.

"So it is," says Meemaw.

At that moment the front screen door slaps back on its hinges and here comes Audrey skipping through the living room and into the dining room singing "Tina the Ballerina" with Parnell right behind her.

"Audrey, over here," says Annabelle. "Hush, now."

"I'm hungry!" says Audrey. "Look who's come to dinner!"

Parnell has indeed brought a guest. As he enters the room we fall completely silent. A fly buzzes drunkenly near the chicken platter. The ice cracks as it settles in our glasses.

"Parnell?" asks Daddy.

"Wow," says Gillette.

"I'm sorry we're late," says Parnell. "This here is my friend Randy Smithers. He doesn't have a family to visit for Sunday dinner, and I appreciate you making room for him at your table today, Meemaw."

Randy Smithers removes his cap, clicks his heels together, and makes a little bow. "Ma'am."

Meemaw is finally speechless.

The cap. The gloves. The shiny shoes. The stripes. The medals. All those bright buttons on that handsome uniform. Hup, two, three, four. We got us a Soldier Boy for Sunday dinner.

A U.S. Special Forces advisor directs a helicopter to a landing zone in a Vietnam jungle clearing marked by a smoke grenade, August 22, 1964.

TWIST!

"If we withdrew from Vietnam, the Communists would control Vietnam. Pretty soon, Thailand, Cambodia, Laos, Malaysia, would go . . ."

U.S. President John F. Kennedy, September 2, 1963

"We'll stay for as long as it takes. We shall provide whatever help is required to win the battle against the Communist insurgents."

U.S. Defense Secretary Robert McNamara, March 6, 1964

"The Great Society rests on abundance and liberty for all. It demands an end to poverty and racial injustice, to which we are totally committed in our time. . . . Will you join in the battle to build the Great Society?"

U.S. President Lyndon Baines Johnson, May 22, 1964

A U.S. advisor/officer training Vietnamese troops in Vietnam, 1964.

ENTIRELY ASIDE FROM THE ARROGANCE

and the holier-than-thou attitude of these college students, who are going to Mississippi with no knowledge of the Negro problem, the really serious aspect of this invasion . . . is [that] it is part of an over-all scheme to destroy the United States by way of a racial revolution.

***The Clarion-Ledger*, Jackson, Mississippi, July 30, 1964**

AND SHOUT!

Chubby Checker showing a young lady how to do the Twist.

TWIST!

LBJ ALL THE WAY

U.S. presidential campaign slogan for Democratic Party nominee and U.S. President Lyndon Baines Johnson, 1964

IN YOUR HEART YOU KNOW HE'S RIGHT

Slogan for Republican Party nominee Barry Goldwater

IN YOUR GUTS, YOU KNOW HE'S NUTS!

LBJ campaign's response to Goldwater's campaign slogan

"In the name of the greatest people that have ever trod this earth, I draw the line in the dust and toss the gauntlet before the feet of tyranny, and I say segregation now, segregation tomorrow, segregation forever!"

George C. Wallace at his inauguration as governor of Alabama, 1963

Alabama Governor George C. Wallace also ran for U.S. president as a Democrat.

Ku Klux Klan rally

AND SHOUT!

This issue is clearly one of personal physical SELF-DEFENSE or DEATH for the American Anglo-Saxons. The Anglo-Saxons have no choice but to defend our Constitutional Republic by every means at their command, because it is, LITERALLY, their LIFE. They will die without it.

If you are a Christian, American Anglo-Saxon who can understand the simple Truth of this Philosophy, you belong in the White Knights of the KU KLUX KLAN of Mississippi. We need your help right away. Get your Bible out and PRAY! You will hear from us.

From a KKK leaflet circulated in Mississippi in 1964

9

Finally home, I run upstairs to my room and see that the bucket is back at my window. Inside is a note from Polly, scrawled in her writerly handwriting, on the back of my note:

Lots is popping, here at Paul!
Teletype machine ping-ping-pings!
Mama's writing a big story for the paper!
I get to help in the darkroom!
Meet me at George at six o'clock!
It won't be long, yeah, yeah!
With love from me to you! (from Paul to John!)

Just as well. I'm a wilted mess and I need time to recover. Meemaw excused herself from the table right after Parnell's entrance, took a powder, and went to bed. Daddy patted on me, which I took to be a kind of apology for everything, although I couldn't name what. There was no more talk of sinners or Communists or invaders. We entertained Sergeant Smithers ourselves and everybody got to eat after all. Sergeant Smithers talked about "our advisors in Southeast Asia" and Daddy was not impressed.

Annabelle and I did the dishes and left everything looking like it was never messed up. We left a covered plate for Meemaw's supper. Laura Mae will be happy when she sees the whole kitchen shipshape tomorrow morning. I might go over after Bible School so I can let her feed me lunch and heap praises on me for being so helpful.

The grandfather clock strikes noon, which means it's three. In the deep heat of a Sunday afternoon, our house sifts into a fitful doze. All the windows upstairs are open. The fans clack and whir. They make a rhythmic, sleepy racket. We have an air conditioner, but it's stuck in the living room window downstairs, so we bake upstairs until the sun goes down.

I never can nap on a Sunday afternoon, but Annabelle lies down with Audrey and sings her "Tammy" and rubs her back until she falls asleep. Daddy and Gillette disappear to quiet corners, and Parnell takes his soldier home, wherever that is. He'll go to work at the Leflore in a little while, but I'm not allowed to go to the movies by myself on Sunday, so instead I change into my play clothes and lie across the bed with Thor Heyerdahl and *Kon-Tiki*.

Polly loves Paul McCartney so much I think she might spontaneously combust if she ever meets him. She's convinced she's going to marry him. If I'm in love with anybody, it's Thor Heyerdahl. I've thought about this quite a bit, because I do love the Beatles — any one of them could marry me someday and that would be fine — but I'm not ready for romance yet. I am ready for adventure. So I am in love with Thor Heyerdahl and I want to set sail on *Kon-Tiki*. I want to live on a balsa-wood raft with flying fish and a talking parrot and sail across the Pacific to Polynesia.

I confessed to Polly and Mary Margaret one day that I was in love with Thor and they both said, at the same time, "That's just weird, Sunny."

"I know!" I said, and we all laughed, because it *is* weird. But I can't help it, and no one would understand it but my mama, who ran away with my daddy on an adventure and then went on another adventure herself.

I'm sure that if I could just talk with Miranda, she would say, *I miss you, Sunny, I love you! I'd come back if I could!* Only she would understand what it means to want an adventure so badly you can taste it, and how nothing will satisfy you until you get it.

Sometimes I think the closest I'll come to an adventure is lying across the bed with Thor Heyerdahl, reading *Kon-Tiki*. Nobody knows I took it from the school library on the last day of school. I just slipped it into my book bag while nobody was looking. I took it because I had read it three times already, and I needed it near me. Sometimes you just need a book near you and you can't explain why.

Here is the first sentence in *Kon-Tiki*:

> Once in a while, you find yourself in an odd situation.

No kidding, Thor. No kidding.

A knock at my door. I cram *Kon-Tiki* under my pillow. "Who is it?" I never used to close my bedroom door. Now, ever since my own invaders have moved in, I never leave it open.

"I'm getting lemonade. Want some?" Gillette. Ready to talk.

"I just thought of you as an invader," I say. We creak down the stairs and I leave thoughts of *Miranda, age 18* behind.

I love how the house feels silent and abandoned in the middle of the day. I love how peaceful and lazy the whole town of Greenwood feels on Sunday afternoons, all the stores, all the people, closed up tight like flower buds and resting until the bloom of a new week.

In the kitchen, we crack ice out of the silver ice trays in the freezer and pour some of Laura Mae's lemonade into our glasses. We're not allowed to bring anything to eat or drink into the living room — that's an Annabelle rule — so we bypass the cool front room and head for the porch. A grand porch, deep and wide, wraps itself around this old house, side to front to side. The north side is coolest in the summer.

Gillette's tackle box is open and spills out hooks, bobbers, fishing line, and lures. The transistor radio on the porch railing crackles out the ball game between the Phillies and the Mets. We sit on the low porch steps and listen to Phillies' pitcher Jim Bunning strike 'em out, one-two-three, while we stare into the tangles of honeysuckle on the far side of the dirt driveway. They are blooming for a second time this summer and the bees are busy at work, droning over all the yellow flowers.

It feels like a lifetime has passed between me and Gillette since we sat on these very steps yesterday and planned our adventure.

"Five innings and he hasn't allowed a base runner," says Gillette as the Phillies come up to bat. "So far, he's pitching a no-hitter. That's a big deal."

I ignore him. "What are we going to do?" I ask. "We haven't told them."

"It was bad timing," says Gillette.

"No kidding."

"I guess there really *are* invaders."

"No kidding," I repeat.

"I don't get it," says Gillette.

"Me, neither."

The cicadas crescendo — loud-then-soft, loud-then-soft — the song of a rich, full summer. Johnny Callison hits a home run, and the Phillies are winning 3–0.

"Yes!" says Gillette.

"How's Willie doing today?" I ask. Gillette has a Willie Mays baseball card for every year Willie has played — this is a big deal. He has memorized those statistics the way I memorize Bible verses, and there's not even a prize to win.

"The Giants are playing St. Louis, but I can't pick up that game on the radio. This one is great, though."

"Sure," I tell him. Until I met Gillette, I thought listening to baseball was like being hypnotized. It's still like that, only now I know how to listen.

"Boy-howdy, your grandmother," says Gillette, out of nowhere. "Has she always been like that?"

"Pretty much, but only when she gets riled. She's opinionated."

"No kidding," says Gillette.

"But I know she loves me," I add, and I'm surprised I feel the need to defend her.

"How do you know?" Gillette drains his lemonade.

"I don't know," I say. "I just do. Kinda like you just know your dad loves you, even when you don't see him much . . . not even on Father's Day."

Gillette dumps his ice on the ground. "I don't want to see him."

"No kidding," I say. "What does Deputy Davis mean that your dad is an associate of his?"

"My dad's a policeman. That's all." Gillette stands up and changes the subject. "Are you coming to my game on Wednesday?"

"Of course!" I say it with a little huff, as he should know by now, I always come to his ball games. He's my brother.

"Okay," he says.

"Okay," I answer.

"What about the kid in the pool?" I ask before he can walk away.

"What about him?"

"I don't know what about him," I say, "but I was wondering who he was. I was wondering if he knew any invaders."

"We'll never know," says Gillette.

"You said he's got high-tops," I point out. "White or black?" I gather our glasses and walk toward the door. I feel a plan forming.

"White," says Gillette. "They looked brand-new." And then, because he's reading my mind, he adds, "And we're not going to Colored Town to find out who he is!"

I shrug. "You've been saving for a pair of high-tops since Christmas. Half the team is saving for a pair of high-tops. Eight dollars is hard to come by. I just wanna see who's wearin' 'em over in Colored Town."

"Aren't we in enough trouble already?" says Gillette. "You think it's gonna be hard to tell your dad about last night? Wait until I have to tell mine!"

The way he sounds, almost purple, makes me turn around and face him. "Why?"

He looks at me like he's got a secret and is deciding whether or not to tell.

"Never mind," he says. "Forget it." He jumps over the porch steps and walks toward the car house where the fishing rods and the minnow buckets live.

You are a mystery to me, I think as I watch him go.

Then I hear my mysterious, adventurous *Kon-Tiki* voice whispering to me. *So is that boy with the high-top sneakers . . . Who is he?*

10

Spillin' onto the sidewalk after evenin' church, starched in they best clothes, waving fans against the hot, talkin' about registerin'. Miss Vidella Brown speakin'.

"I'm going to the courthouse to register this week. Who's with me?"

"You got that N-A-A-C-P fever, girl," say Miss Laura Mae, "'cause you sec'tree and can write down all the notes of all the meetin's. You best be careful. No register for me. They taking down names at the courthouse, put 'em in the paper, you lose your job."

"I'll get a better job, then," say Miss Vidella. "I'll vote me some people out of office!"

"Well, good for you, Vidella," say Ma'am, "but I lose my job if I do that."

"You'll lose it anyway, Libby, if certain white folks find out you've got Freedom Righters living in your house."

"Wasn't gonna do it," say Ma'am. She nod over to Ree, standing in the shade, holding that white girl's hand like it's a prize. "Just happened."

Pap shake his head — he and Ma'am been arguing about it — and say, "I can't afford to be arrested. Red Watson got his head bash in last week. He's no good to nobody now. I got a family to feed. We just gon' keep our mouths shut and our heads down until this over. I got me a good job mowing half the yards in North Greenwood, and I aim to keep it."

Freedom Man call hisself Dewey say, "Mr. Bullis, it won't be over until you have the vote. You can't get the vote unless you register."

"Easy for you," say Pap. "You leavin', end of summer. We have to live here."

"Come to the mass meeting," say Sam Block Freedom Man. He say to me and Simon and Jimmy and Twill, "We could use your help at the Freedom House. We got boxes of food and clothes and books and magazines to unpack. We got a library and a school for you to attend. Citizenship classes to take. How about it?"

Pap interrupt. "White folks drive by the Freedom House with paper bags over they license plates so you can't know 'em. They got whip antennas on they cars so they can talk to each other on the two-way."

"They bombed the last Freedom House," say Ma'am. "Threw bottle bombs through the front windows."

"I know," say SNCC Bob. "I was there."

Pap shake his head. "I'm part responsible for Simon and Jimmy and Twill — they belong to my sister, Geneva, out at Browning. Ray here, he's my boy. These white folks, they takin' down names, and I don't plan for our names to be on that list. These boys won't be coming."

Two Freedom School students.

Freedom sign made by students in a Freedom School and signed with their handprints.

11

"You're gonna croak when you hear my news!" says Polly, and before I can even adjust my eyes to the dim light in George, Polly spills. "Mr. Delay Beckwith brought a *gun* to church! A silver pistol!"

"Good golly! What happened?" I yank an old boat cushion off the shelf, inspect it for spiders, and plop myself onto it, cross-legged, on the dirt floor of the shed.

"He waved it around at the back of the church and caused a ruckus — everybody heard it, plain as day. Mr. Rivendale said, 'Now, Delay, you know you can't bring a gun to church!' and Delay — Mr. Beckwith — said, 'This is for God and Kingdom!' Mrs. Danvers was so apoplectic that Mama had to pass her some smelling salts!"

"Wow!" I am more than impressed. This is the biggest thing to happen here since Mr. Beckwith came back to town from his trial, earlier this month after being found not guilty — twice! — of the murder of that colored man in Jackson. I heard Polly's mother and Annabelle talking about it over the clothesline while Polly's mother helped Annabelle hang the sheets, talking about how proud and puffed up Mr. Beckwith looks now — "*like a peacock!*" she said — strutting downtown every day in his best suit, tipping his hat at all the ladies, and opening doors for them with a bow. "He's scary," Polly's mother said as she handed Annabelle the clothespins.

And now, a pistol! "He waved it around?"

"Yes! Everybody saw it!"

"Was it loaded?"

"Who cares, Sunny! He brought a *gun* to church!"

"Well, I, for one, would care," I say. "Then what happened?"

"Then he quit!" Polly sounds absolutely gleeful. She's wearing an enormous button that says IN CASE OF EMERGENCY, CALL PAUL.

She takes a breath and steams ahead. "Father Traynor sprinted down the aisle, ninety-to-nothin', his robes swirling like a tornado behind him. Then he stopped in front of Delay — Mr. Beckwith — and said, 'I know you want to hand me that gun peacefully, Brother Delay.' It was like being in a movie, I promise!"

I am dizzy. "Then what?"

"Then Delay — Mr. Beckwith — thought about it a minute while we all held our breaths. Then he *pocketed* his gun — he did *not* hand it over! — and started sputtering all over everybody. He said, 'There are more where this came from! My car is parked out front. I have an *arsenal* in my trunk, and we're going to need one this summer! Now, you all know me, and you know what needs to be done. Who's with me?'"

Instantly my mind goes to Deputy Davis and his rifle.

"Who went with him?" I squeak.

"Nobody!" Polly crows. "And when he saw nobody was going to come with him, he shouted, "I am a member of the Sons of the American Revolution, the Sons of Confederate Veterans, the Citizens Council, the Masons, the Knights Templar, the Shriners, the V.F.W., the American Legion, and I support various charities including the Salvation Army and this church! Also George C. Wallace, of course. But I withdraw my membership letter from the Episcopal church today! I will not be part of any establishment that will not recognize a man's God-given right to bear arms during an invasion! I quit!' And then he walked out!"

"Really!"

"I promise!" says Polly. "And I heard Mrs. Simpson say, 'Good riddance to bad news.' Then Mr. Royal said, 'He'll show up with the Baptists next week,' and Mrs. Royal said, 'They won't want him, either.' Oh, Sunny! It was *dramatic*!"

"Really!" I can only repeat myself. I don't know what else to say. No wonder Meemaw's phone rang off the hook at Sunday dinner. Won't she be surprised, when she wakes up from her Sunday afternoon coma! I itch to run inside the house and tell everybody, but Daddy might make me stay and help Annabelle for the rest of the afternoon and I don't want to get caught doing that.

Polly swipes at a fly and opens the shed door. She's delivered her big news and now she's a flattened balloon. "Let's go to Ringo," she says with a big sigh. "We'll burn up in George today. It must be over a hundred degrees. We're gonna need a new secret spot for the summer, that's for sure."

Our current secret spot — which isn't so secret — is the shed attached to our car house. It was toasty warm in frosty February when we first dubbed it George, after we saw the Beatles on *Ed Sullivan*.

Now it's summer, and George smells like old manure and garden rakes and the sweet moonflowers that climb in their vines up and over the shed. Every day at dusk, new blossoms open like big white stars and scent the air around them, and every morning they fall, dead like squashed bugs, to the ground beneath our feet. We slip-slide over them whenever we walk into George. There is no electricity, but there is enough sun coming through the two grimy windows to make George a good daytime hideout.

Polly and I have papered the walls with pages torn from *16 Magazine*. The edges curl in the humid heat, but we don't care. We think it's beautiful, and so does Mary Margaret, although she's not as big a Beatles fan as we are. Mary Margaret is in training to be a beauty queen and spends most of her time practicing her signature for when she wins the Miss Mississippi pageant in eight years and gives autographs.

She's going to be the next Mary Ann Mobley, who went on to become Miss America. Or she might settle for Lynda Lee Mead, who also was Miss Mississippi and Miss America. Mississippi has a good track record, and Mary Margaret plans to keep it that way.

"It's a long walk to Ringo," I say. "It's hot."

"Fiddlesticks," says Polly. "We haven't seen Mary Margaret since she got back from the World's Fair! You know you want to hear all about it!"

That much is true. She didn't even send me a postcard like she promised she would.

"Come on," Polly says, getting to her feet. "I'll tell you about my latest romance with Paul."

"Another one?" We take the long way, down River Road and toward the hospital, because it's the shadiest route. Old porches sigh in the heat as we walk past them on perfect sidewalks, under an oak tree canopy.

"I wrote it after church," says Polly. "Paul comes to Greenwood because he saw my letter in *16 Magazine* and it was so full of heart — and well written — he wanted to meet me. He comes to Sunday dinner and invites me to a concert in Memphis, and Mama says I can go because she's so impressed with what a gentleman he is — and cute. She knows he'll be a good chaperone but really he's in love with me, too. So we have to wait for each other for a few years, but who cares, because he's busy being a Beatle and traveling everywhere, and I have to finish school. I go to England for college, naturally."

"Naturally," I say.

"And then I go on tour with the Beatles!"

"Naturally," I repeat.

"You're just saying that," huffs Polly. "It could happen! You never know." She runs to a rock on the sidewalk and gives it a mighty kick toward the street. It sails toward a police car making its slow cruise down the street toward us.

"Sorry!" Polly yells. "I didn't see you!"

The rock lands short of the car and Officer Sundby slows down. I half expect him to get out of the car and question me about last night — I wonder if Deputy Davis blabbed about my crime to everybody at the station. But Officer Sundby just waves at us and drives on. His police radio crackles something out the open windows of his car.

"You girls be good!" he calls out to us.

"Yessir!" we call back.

"Sorry," I say to Polly. "It could happen. You're right."

"Nah, it's just a story," says Polly in a wistful voice. "But I like writing my stories."

Her shoulders are slumpy, like the *yeah, yeah, yeah* has been wrung right out of her, so I say, "You're a good writer, Polly. You said it yourself, that it runs in the family, with your mama a reporter and all. And you won that Daughters of the Confederacy writing contest last year. You even got a medal for it!"

She smiles, her voice full of hope. "And *you really never know*, Sunny."

What can I say to a girl who really believes Paul McCartney is going to show up on her doorstep? What's wrong with me that I don't believe it, too?

I stifle the urge to say "Naturally," and instead say, "That's right. You never know."

"I mean," Polly continues, "remember when we had that slumber party in the tent the last day of school and you said you hoped your mother might come home. . . ."

I feel myself flush up. I stop in my hot tracks and put my hands on my hips.

"My mother used to *live* here," I spurt. "Big difference!"

"Jeez!" says Polly. "Fine! Don't have a conniption!"

But I feel like a little conniption. "I don't know why I ever told you that, Polly! It was the middle of the night and there were stars out and I had a stomachache. I didn't mean it. I don't care."

"Yes, you do," Polly retorts. "You care as much as I care about Paul."

"It's not the same thing," I say with a sniff. But she's right. I hope all the time these days, and I don't even know why.

We walk the next block in silence while I pat myself back together.

"Do you think there's a heaven for sinners?" I finally ask.

"Why?" asks Polly. "What have you done?"

"Even if they never ask forgiveness?"

"They have to ask for forgiveness," says Polly.

"What if they don't know they're sinners? What if they don't believe it?"

"Then maybe you have to pray about it." Polly gives me a Lordy-Lord look. "Tell me what you did. I'll tell you if it's a sin."

"I haven't done anything!" I say. What a lie. "I was thinking of someone else."

"'Judge not —'" Polly begins.

"Yes," I interrupt, "I know. Matthew 7. I'm sick of talking in Bible verses."

"Let's talk in pig latin, then!" says Polly as she shakes off her hurt feelings and skips up Mary Margaret's front steps to ring the doorbell. "You can tell us both what you did!"

* * *

"Girls, girls, girls!" says Mary Margaret when she opens her front door. "I thought I might never see you again, we were gone so long!"

Then, because I am a big mouth and don't care about being polite, I ask, "Where's my postcard?"

"You can pick one out — I've got a slew of them," says Mary Margaret.

We waltz through the living room in Ringo, like we always do, past two brothers and two sisters playing rummy and Old Maid while eating Vienna sausages and sleeves of saltines, gulping Tang, and watching *Ted Mack and the Amateur Hour* on television all at the same time; past the gigantic spotlighted picture of John F. Kennedy above the television — you'd think they're trying to bring him back to life with that spotlight on him ("It's like a shrine but it isn't," Mary Margaret says, and personally I think she tacked the Fitzgerald onto her name last year after President Kennedy's assassination — she never used it before); past the kitchen where no cooking is done on Sundays because Mrs. Carr never cooks; past the screened-in back porch where Mr. and Mrs. Carr sit with their fans and newspapers, cigarettes and cocktails, and "Pearly Shells" playing on their big console stereo — "Hey, girls! What a nice surprise!"; and up the stairs to Mary Margaret's bedroom with the pink canopy bed, stuffed animals of every description, and a closet full of coordinated clothing.

"Where's Troy Allen?" asks Polly. I know she's sweet on him. I have no idea why. His head is as big as a watermelon.

"He's holed up in his bedroom, listening to the ball game and oiling his glove," says Mary Margaret. "No girls allowed." I expect Mary Margaret to ask me about Gillette next, but she doesn't.

The whole house is as cool as a Popsicle. I am jealous. We flop on Mary Margaret's rug with the roses, and listen to Mary

Margaret's long list of New York City amazements — *the Empire State Building! The Statue of Liberty! Chinatown! The World's Fair!* Oh, to have been even the littlest Carr kid, off on that adventure! Then Mary Margaret says, "Let me see that brush pile." She listens to Polly's story of Mr. Beckwith and his gun while she brushes my hair, which I am happy for her to do.

"The news is already all over town," says Mary Margaret as she works on my tangles. "I heard Mother and Daddy talking about it. St. Francis School in Colored Town is chock-full of Negro kids, of course, and the nuns say the Civil Righters are canvassing whole neighborhoods over there, trying to register the coloreds to vote in the presidential election in November. Father Nathaniel won't let the nuns have a thing to do with those Civil Righters."

"You're speaking Greek, Mary Margaret," I say as my neck snaps back under her brush. "*Ow!* Not so hard! What are 'Civil Righters'?"

"They're the invaders," says Polly in her reporter's voice. Polly owns a newspaper vocabulary that grows every day. "Mama wrote a story about them today," she says. "That's what she was writing on the Teletype for the *Commercial Appeal*. It'll be in the paper tomorrow. They're also called 'agitators,' depending on who you're interviewing."

I consider telling them what I know, what I heard at church and at Sunday dinner, but I decide against it.

Mary Margaret separates my hair into chunks for braids. "Daddy told Mother to expect long hours for him at the courthouse this summer," she sighs with importance. "But that comes with the territory when you're a lawyer." When neither Polly nor I takes the bait, she adds, ". . . The *city attorney* for the city of Greenwood."

I sigh. "Yes. Much more important than selling groceries."

"Or pickles," says Polly.

"Don't forget baby food," I say.

"Ketchup," says Polly.

"Which my dad buys from your dad and sells in our store," I say.

"Along with the pickles and the baby food that my dad sells to your dad," says Polly.

"Enough!" laughs Mary Margaret. "I'm just proud of my dad."

"We're all proud of your dad," I say dryly.

Polly fiddles with the record player, The Beatles start to sing "This Boy," and Mary Margaret changes the subject while she braids. "Troy Allen says he's pitching in this week's game. That means Gillette will play first base."

I know she's in love with him, I just know it.

But I don't discuss my friends' love lives. I just say, "Who's going to the game?" and they both say they'll go, which makes me happy. "Sno-cones!" I say. "Bring your nickels!"

Gillette and I ran into a colored boy in the pool last night — I almost say it. I *want* to say it — I want to tell them what it was like! — but I don't want to tell on myself yet, or on Gillette. It would be like breaking a promise. So I change the subject.

"I've stopped watching monster movies."

"I don't believe you," says Polly. "You couldn't stop if they paid you."

"It's true," I insist. "I've changed my ways."

Mary Margaret winds a rubber band around the end of my last braid and snaps it in place. "Good," she says. "Take a look."

I stare in the mirror she offers me and think, *Who is that girl?*

Polly and I waltz ourselves home the short way. As we come into downtown Greenwood, we pass the first clusters of people we've seen all afternoon. These are the folks who woke from their quiet Sunday stupors and decided to go to the movies. They're parking cars on side streets and stepping onto sidewalks, still dressed in their church clothes.

The Leflore has rumbled awake, too, thanks to Parnell and Mr. Martini, the manager. Mrs. Lefever will be inside, ready to shush anybody who talks during the show. On Saturdays, when there are double features and lots of cartoons, Mrs. Lefever patrols the aisles with a flashlight. She shushes the talkers and smacks kids' feet off the backs of the seats with a broom handle. She looks like George Washington on the one-dollar bill, so that's what kids call her behind her back. Mr. Guston will be upstairs in the projection room threading the movie reel through the projector and trying not to fall asleep before the reel needs changing. Sometimes Chin Lee, the Chinaman's son, shows up to help keep him awake.

There's Parnell in the ticket box, taking money and handing out tickets. I could shout hey from this distance and he would hear me, but I know he's busy, so I keep walking. The movie is *A Shot in the Dark*. Parnell says it's funny and has Inspector Clouseau in it. I'm one chocolate cream pie away from seeing it.

I'm just about to brag about that when I see a colored boy across the street all by himself. He's just standing there, near the telephone pole, hands on his hips, staring at the Leflore. A man in a car with a long whip antenna on it drives by, slows down, and shouts, "What you lookin' at, boy? You got some business to attend to over here all by yourself?" and the boy says, "No, sir!" and the man yells, "Then you best git on home!" and the boy says, "Yessir!" and does a slow trot down West Washington Street.

He's wearing brown pants that are too short for him, a T-shirt, and brand-new, white, high-top sneakers.

12

"Want a ride?" Daddy calls. His truck is right behind the car with the antenna and he sees us before we see him.

"Sure!" we chime as he pulls over at the corner. Gillette stares straight ahead, tugs on his baseball cap, and acts like he doesn't notice us. It's all I can do not to rip open the passenger side door and scream: *I have seen the colored boy in the high-top sneakers!*

But I don't have to — I can tell he saw him, too. He won't look at me, a sure sign. He just tugs his cap down farther on his head, but he knows I know. And that's enough for now. My heart pitty-pats like it did when I first saw the Beatles on *Ed Sullivan*, in that *NOTHING is as amazing as this!* way. I just want to flop down somewhere and stare at the sky and be very still and admire how life holds such surprises.

Polly and I climb into the back of the truck. We step around the cooler and tackle boxes, fishing rods, minnow buckets, and nets. "How'd you do?" I shout. My heart strums with my discovery. I smell fish — guts and scales and blood and bones — and I'm glad for my old banged-up Keds because the truck bed is awash in a scrim of old river water.

"Mostly nibbles," Daddy shouts back. "But we caught a few good ones."

So Annabelle will fry some fish tonight. "Wanna stay for supper?" I ask Polly.

"I'll ask Mama," she says.

Daddy honks at the Leflore, and Parnell waves at us through the ticket window. We bump over the curb and back onto Fulton Street. It's only a few blocks to home, but it feels good to get a ride. I can rest my body and let my mind take a breath, too, even though it's tick-tick-ticking around this latest news. *I saw you, boy in the high-top sneakers! I saw you!*

We pass the courthouse, and Polly points to the row of stately magnolia trees that spread their ancient branches down and around to the ground, like long skirts, in a line at the side of the courthouse. "How about there for George?" she asks.

What a good idea. Once we slip under that skirt of leaves, it will be easy to plant ourselves on a "swing low, sweet chariot" branch of one of those magnolias and climb higher. We'll be completely hidden from view inside a leafy canopy. No grimy windows. Lots of fresh air. Maybe even a breeze. And a great, high view of the bridge and the river — I'll bet I can see Meemaw's house across the bridge and up Grand Boulevard.

"It's perfect," I sigh. And I realize: I am beat to the bottom of my bones. My eyelids are so heavy I'm going to have to prop them open with sticks to stay awake.

"'Be ye therefore perfect,'" says Polly, "'even as your Father which is in heaven is perfect.' Matthew 5:48. I've got sixteen verses memorized. How many do you have, Sunny?"

"I've lost count," I say. "I don't care anymore." I surprise myself and realize it's true.

"You're kidding," says Polly.

"No kidding," I say. "You win."

"I don't want to win," says Polly. "I just like the game."

"I know," I say, "but I don't want to play anymore."

"Why not?"

I think about it. "I want to do something different."

"Like what?"

"I don't know. I'm itchy. I *need* something, Polly."

"What have you been up to?" she asks with suspicion in her voice.

"Nothing!" I say too brightly. And it occurs to me, I should tell Daddy about the pool. But I've got a week to think about it. A week before he takes up the collection with Deputy Davis again. Why would they need to talk to each other before next Sunday? The thought settles my mind and opens it up to new possibilities. Possibilities that include high-top sneakers.

"So what are you going to do?" Polly asks.

And suddenly I know. "I'm going to quit Vacation Bible School," I say. "For starters."

"Your daddy won't let you!"

"Yes, he will," I say. "You watch. Meet me at George — the new George — after lunch tomorrow and I'll tell you all about it. By then, I'll have it figured out."

"You're abandoning me!" Polly protests, but I can tell she's not too upset about it. Now she'll win the prize. I don't care. It's never a good prize.

Daddy takes the corner toward home and turns tight, which makes Polly and me slide from one side of the truck bed to the other. Polly laughs and flops an arm across my shoulder. I slop against the side of the truck, and, just like that, a possibility clicks into place. "Did you ever want to solve a mystery like those detectives on *Hawaiian Eye*?"

"I never saw that show. It came on past my bedtime."

"Mine, too, but I watched summer reruns at Mary Margaret's once, when I spent the night. We stayed up late and watched it with her folks. They love everything Hawaiian."

"No, they just watch everything on television."

"That, too," I say.

"I've seen *77 Sunset Strip* in summer reruns," says Polly.

"Kookie!" I say. "I'm hip!"

We chortle. "I don't understand a thing he says!" I say.

We are winding down, I can tell, just like the day. "They've always got a caper to solve on that show," says Polly. "You want to solve a mystery?"

"I want to *know* the mysteries," I say. "Don't you ever dream about running away from home on an adventure to find . . . I don't know . . . to *discover* something?"

"Love?" Polly asks with a hopeful sigh, as the truck rattles over a bump in the road and we bump with it.

Love. I unwind my friend's arm from my shoulder and take her hand in mine. Our fingers intertwine.

"I want to hold your hand," she sings softly.

I take the deepest, softest breath I can take. I think of *Miranda, age 18*, as I pull the wish from my heart and puff it, like a whisper, into the evening air, *Please. Please send me Mama to love.*

The sky is purple and orange and blue and pink, as the sun sifts through the clouds and over the earthy horizon of the Delta. The crickets begin to call from the tall grasses along the riverbank. The muddy smell of the Yazoo fills my mind with memories and dreams I have never imagined. This is the magical hour. This morning, my Sunday school teacher told us that today was the longest of the year, the summer solstice, June 21, 1964. It must be lucky to be outside, under the sky, near the end of this longest day.

I wave at a dog chasing our truck and say lazily to my love-sick friend, "Second Corinthians 13:11. 'Finally, brethren, farewell. Be perfect, be of good comfort, be of one mind, live in peace; and the God of love and peace shall be with you.'"

Amen.

PART 2
MANEUVERS

Deep and wide,
Deep and wide,
There's a fountain flowing deep and wide.

— Sunday school song

I'M GONNA LAY DOWN

MY SWORD AND SHIELD,

From "Down by the Riverside," an old spiritual recorded by Pete Seeger, Brownie McGhee, and Sonny Terry, among others

In their Sunday best, Mileston, Mississippi, summer 1964.

DOWN BY THE RIVERSIDE,

"I'm reminded . . . of an expression from the Bible: 'He loved me before he knew me.' In Georgia and Mississippi, the local people were like that. They loved us before they ever saw us. When you showed up, they didn't even ask you if you were hungry. They would just do for you like you were their own children."

Jean Wheeler, summer volunteer, SNCC

Gwen Thompson and summer volunteer Susan Schrader walk together in Meridian, Mississippi, summer 1964

DOWN BY THE RIVERSIDE

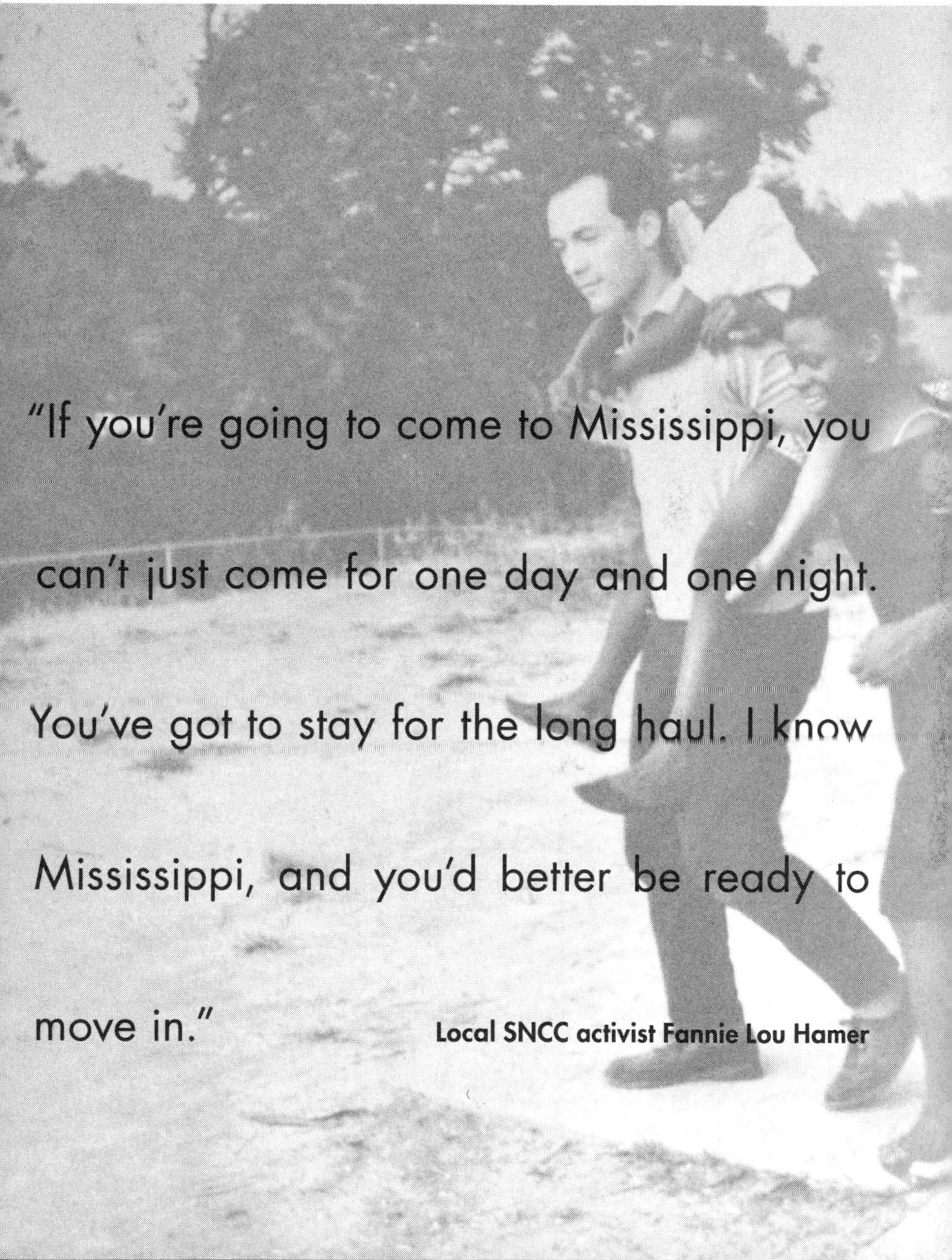

"If you're going to come to Mississippi, you can't just come for one day and one night. You've got to stay for the long haul. I know Mississippi, and you'd better be ready to move in."

Local SNCC activist Fannie Lou Hamer

Pat Thompson on summer volunteer Phil Corner's back with Dorothy Thompson at his side, 1964.

I'M GONNA LAY DOWN

DOWN BY

MY SWORD AND SHIELD,

THE RIVERSIDE,

A summer volunteer teaches a class outside at the community center in Mileston, Mississippi, summer 1964.

AIN'T GONNA STUDY WAR NO MORE

I AM SO HAPPY TO BE HERE. . . . *So far there has been no harm to any of us — (3 days here) — but we cannot allow ourselves to think that there won't be. There have been warnings. I guess that each of us made his personal decision long ago, again — several times — while in Ohio — and, every day while here — about what the Movement and what mortal potentials and limitations can be. Perhaps I* ***have*** *to believe that our project — summer '64 — will have some kind of effect — and that our ideas — about brotherhood, democracy, freedom, etc. —* ***can*** *be understood and protected more after this — at least for some people for some time. Perhaps I* ***have*** *to believe these, then, in order to face the possibility of any of us losing our lives. But I suggest that even if I didn't have to, I'd believe them anyway. We Shall Overcome.*

Freedom Summer volunteer Zoya Zeman, a student at Scripps College in Claremont, California, in a letter home to Dad, July 1, 1964

I'M GOING TO WALK WITH THE PRINCE OF PEACE

MISSING CALL FBI

THE FBI IS SEEKING INFORMATION CONCERNING THE DISAPPEARANCE AT PHILADELPHIA, MISSISSIPPI, OF THESE THREE INDIVIDUALS ON JUNE 21, 1964. EXTENSIVE INVESTIGATION IS BEING CONDUCTED TO LOCATE GOODMAN, CHANEY, AND SCHWERNER, WHO ARE DESCRIBED AS FOLLOWS:

ANDREW GOODMAN | **JAMES EARL CHANEY** | **MICHAEL HENRY SCHWERNER**

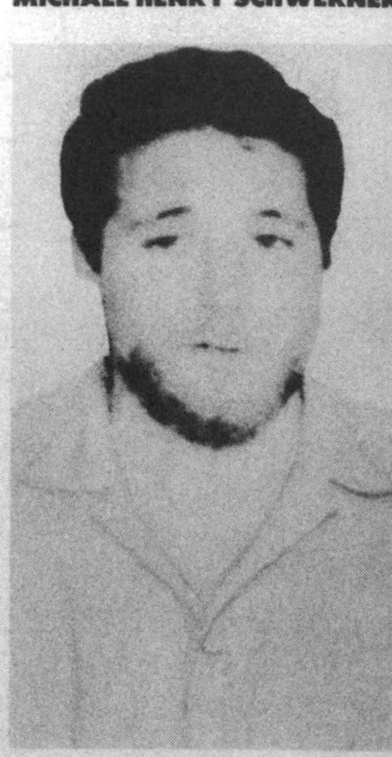

	ANDREW GOODMAN	JAMES EARL CHANEY	MICHAEL HENRY SCHWERNER
RACE:	White	Negro	White
SEX:	Male	Male	Male
DOB:	November 23, 1943	May 30, 1943	November 6, 1939
POB:	New York City	Meridian, Mississippi	New York City
AGE:	20 years	21 years	24 years
HEIGHT:	5'10"	5'7"	5'9" to 5'10"
WEIGHT:	150 pounds	135 to 140 pounds	170 to 180 pounds
HAIR:	Dark brown; wavy	Black	Brown
EYES:	Brown	Brown	Light blue
TEETH:		Good: none missing	
SCARS AND MARKS:		1 inch cut scar 2 inches above left ear.	Pock mark center of forehead, slight scar on bridge of nose, appendectomy scar, broken leg scar.

SHOULD YOU HAVE OR IN THE FUTURE RECEIVE ANY INFORMATION CONCERNING THE WHEREABOUTS OF THESE INDIVIDUALS, YOU ARE REQUESTED TO NOTIFY ME OR THE NEAREST OFFICE OF THE FBI. TELEPHONE NUMBER IS LISTED BELOW.

J. Edgar Hoover
DIRECTOR
FEDERAL BUREAU OF INVESTIGATION
UNITED STATES DEPARTMENT OF JUSTICE
WASHINGTON, D. C. 20535
TELEPHONE, NATIONAL 8-7117

June 29, 1964

"We were in this auditorium, and they tell us: 'Three people are missing.' . . . You cannot underestimate the effect that had on us. . . . And the next day we all got on the bus to Mississippi."

Hardy Frye, summer volunteer from Tuskegee, Alabama

"They're just hiding and trying to cause a lot of bad publicity for this part of the state."

Neshoba County Sheriff Lawrence Rainey on the disappearance of Michael Schwerner, Andrew Goodman, and James Chaney

"Maybe they went to Cuba."

Mississippi Governor Paul Johnson about the disappearance

I'M GONNA SHAKE HANDS WITH EVERY MAN,

"Anyone caught in the act of negro-organizing, Communist-supporting, racial-antagonizing acts should be horse-whipped, tar-and-feathered, and chased out of our beloved Southland."

Mississippi Senator Theodore G. Bilbo, from Jackson, Mississippi, *Daily News*, May 25, 1946

I'M GONNA SHAKE HANDS AROUND THE WORLD

A Vietnamese woman and children walk across a field as a hut burns at a suspected Vietcong encampment near the Cambodian border in June 1964. As part of a "scorched earth" operation, South Vietnamese troops raided the village, burning food, killing livestock, and evacuating women and children. The men of the village disappeared before the assault.

AIN'T GONNA STUDY WAR NO MORE

Sumter, South Carolina, storefront

AIN'T GONNA STUDY WAR NO MORE

13

Maybe it's that girl, Sunny. Maybe it's the boy in the pool. Maybe it's the fact that he's got to tell his father that he broke the law. Maybe it's the way Jamie Fairchild, his stepfather, hands over his pocketknife and says, "Let it go, son," when the fattest fish of the day, flopping and fighting, drags Jamie's line under a pile of old logs by the riverbank and tangles up everything.

Jamie doesn't fight it for more than half a minute. He just has Gillette cut the line and let it go. "Smart fish," Jamie says. "You got another hook and some split shot in that tackle box?"

The tackle box was first Jamie's, but now it's Gillette's. "If you don't mind that it's old and banged up, I'd like to give it to you. I caught a lot of good fish with that box at my side when I was your age." That's what Jamie had said when he handed it to Gillette last summer. Gillette didn't know what to say to that, but now he knows he didn't have to say anything. Not one thing.

They left almost everything behind. They left in the dawning light of a dewy morning two years ago, with a suitcase apiece and the clothes on their backs. His comic books were left behind. His fishing rod and gear. His BB gun. His dog, Ruth. He'd managed to cram his baseball glove into his suitcase, and then he took his Sunday school shoes out of their box and packed in his baseball cards instead. By the time his mother noticed, it was too late to go back. The next week, Jamie had bought Gillette a new pair of Sunday shoes and had left them in his new room, in his new closet, without a word spoken between them.

Jamie Fairchild came and got them that quiet, new morning. "Don't be afraid, son," was all he said. Audrey buried her face in her mother's neck and wouldn't look at anyone. She had just turned three and had celebrated at her meemaw's house the day before.

Gillette hasn't worked up to talking baseball with Jamie Fairchild yet, but he appreciates how his stepfather made sure he could play on a ball team this summer. He made sure Gillette had his own bedroom, too, in that creaky old house, and he never says a disparaging word against Gillette's father. He never says a disparaging word against anybody. Every night, when he walks through the back door, he washes his hands and sits down to the dinner Gillette's mother has made for them. He says the blessing. Then he looks up, smiles slowly, warmly, like he might melt from quiet happiness, looks at them deliberately, like he's seeing each one of them for the first time in ages, and says, "We live like kings. I love you all."

Who says that every night? Or any night?

A man like that deserves better than Gillette has given him. That's what Gillette thinks, after their fishing day. So. He is resolved. He will tell his stepfather about trespassing at the city pool. He will take the blame himself, will say it was all his idea. And maybe that will make it easier for him to tell his own father, when the time comes.

* * *

He likes his new sister but she is unpredictable, and he has learned to be predictable, at least in public. It was easier that way. It could even save your life.

This girl is loud where he is quiet. She peppers him with questions and he has no answers. She wants to do brash things and crow about them, when he knows that you don't do such things by announcing them. You do these things in secret, and you keep them to yourself.

You get along by making friends with everyone and being likeable. Not that he isn't likeable; he is. He is well-practiced at being likeable. He had to be.

He doesn't know what to make of his life right now. But he knows that his mother smiles — smiles right up to her eyes — at every moment of his stepfather's presence. Her touch is light and her movements are smooth. He knows that his little sister sings her old songs again.

And he knows that an idea has formed in his mind. That boy, that boy who wears the high-top sneakers. The fear on his face, the way he ran into that fence, came back for those shoes, and then fought that fence again to let him through. Gillette knows that fear.

And he knows there's a baseball game on Wednesday night, under the lights, at McCurdy Field. He is quite certain that he is going to hit one out of the park. Just like Willie Mays.

14

Monday, June 22, 1964

The phone rings before the sun is up, and that's saying something. When it's summer, the birds start making a racket before five o'clock in the morning, which is the time it's finally cool enough to pull up the covers and dream one last sweet dream, just before the sun beams over the horizon and starts to butter the day.

So that's what I do. My warm sheet feels just right against my chilly shoulders.

When I roll out of bed, the sun is bright through my window. As I head for the bathroom, I slide on a note slipped under my bedroom door.

GONNA TELL YOUR DAD ABOUT THE POOL.
IT WASN'T YOUR FAULT.

What? I race to Gillette's room — he isn't there. I clatter down the stairs and run past Audrey, who is tucked into a corner of the couch with her doll, Ginny, getting ready to watch *Captain Kangaroo* in the living room.

I shout for Annabelle. "Where's Daddy?"

"He had business to attend to," she calls from the kitchen.

"Where's Gillette?" I screech, as I grab on to the kitchen door frame to keep myself from hurtling into the kitchen table.

"Gillette went with him," Annabelle replies with a calm I

can tell she's practicing. Her back is facing me and her movements are slow and measured as she takes the sugar bowl down from the shelf over the sink. My mind bobs around the possibilities.

Did they leave in the dark? Why? Where did they go?

"But I need to talk to Daddy!"

"He'll be back by noon dinner." Annabelle sounds like a robot.

"That's not good enough!"

Annabelle turns to face me with a box of Morton Salt in her hand. Her eyes are shiny with tears. "Sunny," she says. "You're whining."

I let go of the door frame and drop my hands to my sides. "What's wrong?"

"Not one thing," says Annabelle. Then she fills the sugar bowl with salt.

"It was my idea!" I say. "It wasn't Gillette. I wanted to swim at night! I said no one would find out. It was *my fault*!"

Annabelle looks lost. "What are you talking about?"

I clutch at the waist of my pajama pants, yank them up, and realize Annabelle's tears are about something else entirely, and besides, I'm defending Gillette, when what I want to do is kill him.

"Nothing," I say. "I had a bad dream. But I need to talk to Daddy! It's a matter of life or death!"

Annabelle slaps the box of salt on the counter. "How did you know?" The color drains right out of her face.

"Know what? I just need to talk to Daddy!"

Annabelle's face fills in again with her usual pasty color. "I need you to get ready for Bible School."

"No!"

"What did you say?" Finally Annabelle turns her full attention to me.

"No." I fold my arms across my chest like I'm Tonto and I'm telling the bad guys they can't take over the ranch, because the Lone Ranger is on the way. I give Annabelle my stoniest stare. So what if she tells Daddy? Gillette is already getting me into more trouble than I can shake a stick at. I am going to wring his neck.

Annabelle looks from the box of salt to the sugar bowl. Her shoulders slump. She smooths her wild hair away from her face and sighs, like she's trying to make up her mind what to do now. It's early in the morning and already she is so tired she's teary, but I can't help that. I keep staring. I will bore a hole in her head with my laser vision.

Then Annabelle straightens her shoulders and says, with steel in her voice for the first time, no question, "Sunny, I know you are a good girl. It would help me so much if you went to Bible School today."

I didn't tell her to marry my father and move into this house. I'm not going to make it easy for her. Still, I shock myself when I say, "You can't make me. You are not my mother."

Annabelle unties her apron and lays it across the back of a kitchen chair.

"You're right," she says, "and I know that."

The clock strikes five, which means it's eight. The theme music for *Captain Kangaroo* dances from the living room into the kitchen.

"I don't like you," I say. My heart would tremble if I had one.

"So I see," says Annabelle.

"And you are not the boss of me," I finish.

"What a relief," says Annabelle. She takes a bowl from the cabinet and a spoon from the drawer and puts them both on the counter. Then she says, "There's a new box of Rice Krispies in the pantry and there's salt in the sugar bowl." She steps past me and walks softly out of the kitchen. *Snap, crackle, pop.*

I stand there for a full minute before I decide she's not coming back.

15

They takin' over.

We got two of 'em in our house now, sleepin' in the same bed. My bed.

They all over Baptist Town and Gritney, even in Gee Pee.

Freedom House on same street as us. People from up north keep sending boxes full of books, clothes, shoes, food. Got my good shoes from one of those boxes last year. But Pap say don't go there no more. Still, Ree there every day, can't do nuthin' with her. She singing and reading and writing at that Freedom School. Ma'am say, "Let her be," and Pap shake his head and sharpen his mower blades.

Police drive through, slow, every day, watchin', looking for invaders.

Ma'am scared about that, but still, she feed them Freedom Righters crowder peas and pinto beans and turnip greens at our table, then they wash at our pumps, sleep in our beds.

They knock on everybody's doors. "Register to vote! Be a first-class citizen!"

Some folks crazy, they say yes. Some slam doors in they faces. Miss Neddie Ruth Adams, she throw a skillet at a SNCC's head and yell, "Git!" But they don't git.

They go out to the plantations, too. "Register!"

Some SNCCs colored. Some white. They all cockeyed to a rooster.

And the white men drive by in they slow cars, so everybody afraid.

And then, mass meetin', mass meetin', mass meetin'. Ma'am drag me with her.

Old Man Jordan lead off the prayer, then talk-talk-talk and sing and testify: Miss Vidella Brown been turned away at the courthouse. Mr. Clayborn Amos arrested. Miss Julia Dupree lose her job cleanin' the white folks' house because she tried to register. Aunt Geneva put up her farm for bail money, gon' get everybody out of jail. Easter Simpson, she keepin' her mouth shut out at Gladhill Plantation, that a good job, and May Liza Jones say don't be no chicken, woman!

Freddie and Chuff, they just turn eighteen, they been run off the plantation and lose they jobs because they seen talkin' with a Freedom Worker.

"We gon' let this turn us 'round?" shouts Reverend Tucker.

Miss Flowers Watson start the singing: "Ain't gonna let nobody turn me 'round!"

Then they all singin' and shoutin'. "Will you register?"

Yes, Lord!

"Will you march downtown?"

Yes, Lord!

Marchin'. Registerin'. So what? What these SNCCs know?

Pap don't like 'em. I don't need 'em.

I can do better than they do. Reverend Tucker say they's a new law comin' next month what means I can do everything the white folks do, and I want to do that.

Gon' swim in they big pool — in the daytime. Gon' go to they movie house. Gon' play ball in that pretty white folks ball field with the white lines and the hot dogs and the bright lights.

Every day, I practice my hitting and throwing and catching so's I can get out of this town and do something big with my life.

Hank Aaron and Willie Mays did it, and they Alabama boys. I can do it, too.

Twill say, "Never seen nobody as good at all of it as you, Ray. Hittin', throwin', runnin'."

Even Freddie and Chuff make 'mirations over me. They come play sometimes, even though they growed up. They talk about Willie, tell me I can be that good, just got to practice, just got to find a way to get out there, somewhere.

"And we got to get jobs," they say. "We can't play ball like you. You just need somebody to notice you! Got to get you a talent scout, Ray."

So I make up my mind: I need somebody to take notice.

16

Believe me, there are only so many times you can sing "I've got the joy, joy, joy, joy down in my heart" before you have no more joy at all, anywhere. None. Zero. It's already as hot as blue blazes in the sixth-grade Sunday school room, and all I can feel is the hot-hot-hot-hot down to my toes. I cannot believe I'm sitting here. I didn't have any joy to begin with.

I *am* quitting Bible school — Polly gave me the "told you so" look when she saw me scoot in late — but I didn't know what else to do this morning, and I felt lowly after telling Annabelle I don't like her, so I came on to Bible School. Now that I'm here, I'm itching to leave. I notice Bobby Carpenter and his sister didn't show up at all. How did *they* get out of coming this week?

In the middle of "joy, joy, joy," I get up and move to the back of the room and sit by myself and refuse to sing the next verse. Mrs. McGinnis takes one look at me not singing "I've got that Meth-o-dist en-thu-si-as-m down in my heart!" and gives me a job to do. Great! A trip to the church secretary's office. I know the secretary is Mrs. Murchison but have no idea where her office is. This is Gillette and Annabelle's church — they've been Methodists forever, so it made sense for them to just keep going to the Methodist church when they moved in with us — and I'm sure Mrs. McGinnis just wants to get rid of me.

Fine. I will take two hours to bring back extra scissors and glue. Then Bible School will be over and I will have already slipped out to Fairchild's to see if Daddy has come back, and then I won't go home for dinner, I'll go to Meemaw's instead when the Buckeye whistle blows at noon, and I'll let Laura Mae pet on me, and I will just ignore everyone in my family and there will be swimming at the pool in the afternoon, and life will be pretty much perfect until I have to kill Gillette for squealing on me.

So I head down the stairs, around a corner, around another corner, and down a wide, quiet hallway, and this is what I hear as I get close to the exit doors:

"Why can't these children come to Bible School?"

Wouldn't it be just so fine if that jughead Bobby Carpenter was being banned from Vacation Bible School forever? There is a desk in the hallway, just outside the open door to the room where the voice comes from. I slide myself next to the desk so it's between me and the open door. My back is against the wall. Then I crane my neck over the little desk, so my right ear has the best advantage.

"They have their own church to attend," says Mrs. Murchison. I'd know that voice anywhere. Every Saturday morning I help bag groceries at Fairchild's and Mrs. Murchison gives me a nickel tip and tells me I'm a doodle. Last week, I told her I had graduated to grasshopper and she laughed.

"If they wanted to attend church here on a Sunday, could they?" asks a second unknown voice. "Is your church segregated?"

"I am not in a position to say," says Mrs. Murchison. There is starch in her voice.

The first unknown voice, which sounds like an older lady, like Mrs. Murchison, speaks again. "It says in the Bible to love the Lord your God with all your heart and all your mind and all your soul, and to love your neighbor as yourself, but here, these children of God, your neighbors, can't come to your church."

The sound of shuffling papers. Mrs. Murchison snaps, "They have their church!"

A boy's voice then, proud. "I'm a Methodist, too!"

Mrs. Murchison says, "You see? They have their own churches!"

And then a girl's voice, soft and wondery. "If it was up to you, would you let us come?" It's a colored girl. I can tell. She sounds just like Laura Mae sounds when she talks. The boy is a Negro, too. I don't even have to see them to know. My shoulders shimmer with prickly pins.

A chair scrapes. "I can't answer that question. I'd have to pray on that," snaps Mrs. Murchison. Her voice gets high and squeaky, like she's running out of air. Her solid shoes clap across the floor. "Let me see if I can find you those Sunday school giveaway pamphlets you asked me about for the colored children. That's why you're here, isn't it?"

It takes two seconds flat for Mrs. Murchison to spurt out the doorway. It takes me less time than that to splat to the floor next to the desk so I'm not seen. Mrs. Murchison zips across the hallway, enters another room, and slams the door behind her like she's got to go to the bathroom and is about to explode. I pop up and spray myself, like buckshot, around the desk and into the room with the voices.

I'm going to be stunned to see two colored children in the church office. I'm going to be surprised to get my first look at Civil Righters. But what I don't know until I round that corner, clutching the door frame so I don't fall over in my enthusiasm, is that I'm about to come face-to-face with my mother.

17

I trip to a stop. She's tall. She has long, blond hair and a crooked smile. She is wearing a plaid shirtwaist dress. I can't even stammer *Who are you?* I'm frozen in my tripped-up stance, half keeled over, arms out, head up, eyes staring at *Miranda, age 18*.

"Whoa!" She holds out a hand. "Are you okay?"

I lurch backward, straighten myself, and shake my hands like they're crawling with fire ants. *Get away! Get away!*

Not Miranda. Not my mother. It can't be my mother. She would be older now.

Eighteen plus twelve, what's that?

"She's having a conniption," says the colored girl, but I don't take my eyes off Miranda.

"Hush, Ree," says the other woman, who is much older than Miranda. "I think she's all right." Then she says to me, "*Are* you all right?"

I clasp the fingers of my left hand with my right hand. I take a slow breath, my eyes fixed on Miranda, as if she might disappear if I blink. "Yes, ma'am," I whisper.

My mind wrestles with the math. She can't be Miranda. But I want her to be. Maybe I'm wrong. I hope I'm wrong. I want to be wrong, and so I say, in my most earnest voice, which comes out in another whisper, "I'm . . . *Sunny*." I try to add *Do you know me?* But I have no breath left.

"Nice to meet you, Sunny," says not-Miranda. "My name is Jo Ellen." She gestures at her companion. "This is Vera."

"Hello, Sunny!" says cheerful Vera. "This is Glory and William."

But I don't pay the slightest attention to Glory and William, or to Vera.

Jo Ellen. Her name is Jo Ellen. She isn't my mother. *She isn't my mother.* My face fills with heat and my nose stuffs up like I'm about to cry. The air around me is suddenly alive, and I can't remember what made me so prickly-afraid just a minute ago.

"I don't think Mrs. Murchison is coming back," says Vera.

"I think we put her on the spot," says not-Miranda Jo Ellen. "It's not our job to come to the white churches and ask questions. It's not in the SNCC guidelines." She pronounces it *snick. What is snick?*

"I just wanted some more pamphlets for the children," said Vera. "I ran out of the ones I brought with me from California."

"You just wanted to stir up trouble," says Jo Ellen, but she says it kindly and she smiles that crooked smile.

"Why are you here?" I ask. My voice is a croak. I look at the colored kids and they stare at me with mute faces. I have never thought about why colored kids don't go to white churches. They just don't. I think Mrs. Murchison is right; they have their own churches. Why would they want to come to ours?

"Do you mean here, in this church, or here, in Greenwood?" asks Vera.

"Yes," I say.

Vera laughs.

"Where are you from?" I ask.

"I'm from Maryland," says Jo Ellen. "I go to college there."

The girl named Glory takes Jo Ellen's hand. Just like that. Easy. I blink.

Vera says, "I'm an old rabble-rouser from California. Near San Francisco."

My big mouth jumps into action. “Are you agitators?”

“You could say that,” says Vera. William scratches his elbow and looks uncomfortable.

“Are you invaders?”

“We’ve been called that,” says Jo Ellen, “but we don’t see it that way.”

“How do you see it?” I can’t help it; I want to know.

William pulls on Vera’s skirt and looks anxious. Vera says, “I think it’s time to go.”

Then there’s a sound from the hallway — the *whoosh!* of the big exit doors opening, and the tramping, like *hup-two-three-four!,* of the U.S. Army hustling toward us. The air closes around me, summer-thick and hot, even though there is an air conditioner in Mrs. Murchison’s office. My stomach queases into my throat.

I pitch myself to the doorway at the same time Mrs. Murchison opens the door to the room across the hall and sees me standing in her office with invaders and Negro children.

She doesn’t have to ask me what I’m doing, because Chief Lary does it for her.

“Young lady?” he says. I step into the hallway. “Did you call the police?”

Chief Lary has four policemen with him. They stand there, like soldiers waiting for orders, wondering what’s going on, hands on their weapons. One of them is Deputy Davis. I swallow hard and try not to look at him.

“Nossir,” I say. “I just came to the office for scissors and glue for Bible School. Mrs. McGinnis sent me.”

“Mildred, did you call the police?” Chief Lary asks Mrs. Murchison.

Her face blushes the color of Uncle Vivian’s tomatoes, but she says, “Certainly not!”

Mrs. Murchison's hands are full of pamphlets. The one on top reads, *LET JESUS SHOW YOU THE WAY!* "I was . . . I was . . . ," she stammers.

Vera steps into the hallway. "She was just supplying us with some reading material for the children at the Freedom School," she says, cool as you please.

The colored kids step into the hallway behind Vera, and Jo Ellen follows them.

Chief Lary clears his throat at the sight of them. It's a wide hallway, but it's getting crowded.

I've known Chief Lary all my life. He calls out the bingo numbers at the firemen's carnival every summer, and I always win at least one game. Now he takes off his glasses and begins to polish them with his handkerchief. We exchange a look, but I don't know what it means. "Have you got what you need?" he asks Vera.

Vera looks at Mrs. Murchison, who seems unsure about what to do next. Vera holds out her hands and says, "Thank you so much. The children will be so appreciative," and Mrs. Murchison hesitantly puts the pamphlets into Vera's hands, trying not to touch her. Then she holds her head up high, looks the policemen in the eye and says, "Our Christian duty. Excuse me," and walks into her office and shuts the door behind her. Glory and William each take one of Jo Ellen's hands. Deputy Davis makes that *tsk* sound. "Where's your glue and scissors, Sunny?"

"I didn't get 'em yet," I say. I cannot look him in the eye.

"Go. Now," orders Deputy Davis.

I knock on Mrs. Murchison's door and slip myself inside before she even says to come in. While I ask for supplies, I hear a muffled conversation going on in the hallway.

"Excuse me," I say, when I open the door with a bottle of Elmer's Glue and two pair of scissors in a paper sack.

"Here," says not-Miranda Jo Ellen as she steps out of my way and smiles that crooked smile. And then I see it. Jo Ellen is wearing a silver locket, shaped like a heart.

She *is* Miranda, age 18.

The conversation stops while I weave through the little crowd. My heart pitty-pats and I can barely breathe. Is anything more amazing than this? I keep my gaze on the floor and hotfoot it down the hallway, around the corners, and up the stairs, back to my Bible School classroom.

I swing into the room, toss the sack onto the table where everyone — including Polly — is throwing around construction paper and cardboard and glitter, like it's just any old ordinary day. I say in a quick, loud voice, "So sorry! Got to go! I quit!" and walk right back out, down the stairs, not around the corner, and out a different exit door.

Where I wait.

I need to be near the girl who looks like my mother.

From the Freedom School Curriculum

On Citizenship.

Question: What about Mississippi?

Answer: All over Mississippi we still see signs like "Colored Waiting Room" and "For White Only". . . . We still see Negroes going into sections where they are told to go. And, in some towns, if you protest, you are arrested or worse.

Question: Why?

Answer: Because Mississippi makes its own laws. It does not keep the law of the United States, not when it comes to race. This means if you go to a white waiting room, and some policeman tells you it is against the law — he is right. It is against the law. It is against Mississippi law.

Question: So what do you do?

Answer: You break that law. You break it because it is both evil and is against the Supreme Court of the United States — which is the Law of the whole land. You act on two higher laws — the law of human rights and the law of civil rights, because you are a human being and because you are a citizen of the United States.

Question: What will happen?

Answer: In a sense, you do not even ask what will happen. You simply do what is right because it is right. . . . It is not easy to do the right thing in Mississippi. A lot can happen to you. But a lot happened to the first Freedom Riders and the students who first went to the white lunch counters. They did it anyway. THE IMPORTANT THING IS THIS — unless we keep going and keep going to these places WHERE THE LAW HAS ALREADY BEEN PASSED IN OUR FAVOR — we will be cooperating with those people who want to keep us down. Every time you go into the "Colored" section, you are saying that Mississippi is right. When you say Mississippi is right, you are saying one thing and one thing only: I am wrong. If Mississippi is right, then Negroes are inferior.

No, Mississippi is dead wrong. BUT YOU HAVE TO SAY SO. Every time you go to the back door, you are building up segregation. Mississippi likes to say "our Negroes are happy. They do not want changes." And every time you go where they want you to go, you are saying exactly the same thing. And it is not true.

Question: Then what?

Answer: Then, if you are arrested, you get in touch with as many people as you can — COFO, the Department of Justice, the Department of Commerce, lawyers, the Civil Rights Commission. You appeal the case. You file suit against the state of Mississippi. You get the case into a federal court and out of the state courts. You fight it until some court orders [change] . . .

Before Mississippi changes there will have to be a well-planned and very strong movement among the Negro people. COFO, the people's organization, is building up that movement. It just takes more "getting ready" in Mississippi.

When Negroes have a vote, then they can help make the laws. And when Negroes make the laws . . . they will get rid of all the segregation laws. They will get rid of segregated lunch counters. They will get rid of the walls that hurt people — black and white.

18

The sky was choked with stars when they started out. The phone call had come at five in the morning, such a surprise. Jamie had to go all the way down the stairs to answer it, as the only phone in the house is in the hallway outside the kitchen.

Of course he would come. Of course. He would bring Gillette, her grandson, because Gillette knew her better than he did, and because it was Gillette's dog.

He knew about Sunny and Gillette and the pool. His bedroom windows had been open against the day's heat, and even with the fan blowing on them, he heard the cruiser stop in front of the house. He heard the car doors open and shut. He saw the police car pull away from the curb. Saw Gillette, his stepson, and Sunny, his daughter, run under the yellow moon to the side porch where they could let themselves in at the back kitchen without being heard.

He wasn't surprised when Gillette told him about it in the car on their way to Philadelphia, Mississippi, a trip of one hundred miles southeast of the Delta at five in the morning, the morning after the summer solstice. He had heard all about it already, from Deputy Davis. In addition to being a deputy sheriff, Don Davis was a braggart who would tell on his own mother if he thought it made him look good. He had told Jamie all about it the next morning before church.

* * *

"I know we did a lot worse growing up," Don Davis said in the narthex, while they waited for the choir to start singing "Leaning on the Everlasting Arms."

"I'll take care of it," said Jamie.

"I just thought you should know."

Jamie was sure the entire town knew by now, and that was one reason he would never make an issue of it.

The entire town had known all about him, Jamie Fairchild, for as long as he could remember. Growing up, he ran with the good-old bad boys and his parents didn't know what to do with him. When he was eighteen, he ran off with Miranda Rogers. He hadn't meant to do it, but Miranda wanted out of this old town, and he was bewitched. He would do whatever beautiful Miranda asked of him. He would marry her at the justice of the peace in Alabama. He would take care of everything. Then she found out there would be no money coming from his family, because he had disgraced them all. Still, he stayed. Then she had a baby she wasn't ready for — but neither was he. Then she was so unhappy. Then she left.

He returned to Greenwood, with his baby, when his parents died in a car accident — it took Parnell, who was eight at the time and with them in the car, a whole year to stop asking when they were coming home.

He gave Parnell away to Memphis relatives. He gave his baby to Miranda's mother, Eloise. He lived alone in the house on River Road, lived with his unnamed grief, and spent almost all his parents' money. The bad-boy parties in that big house were legend.

And there had been a lot of money to inherit. His father had been the president of the biggest bank in Greenwood. He had made rules. Jamie had broken them.

Before the money ran out, Jamie bought the grocery store on the corner of Main and Johnson Streets, just the other side of the railroad tracks, just on the edge of Baptist Town, which was also called Colored Town. He named the store Fairchild's. He mopped himself up. He made peace with the fact that Miranda wasn't coming home. He went to work every day. He brought his brother home. He reclaimed his daughter. He learned how to be a father. Folks in Greenwood weren't sure what to make of this new Jamie Fairchild, but they remembered his father's good name, and they patronized his store.

So for ten years Jamie has been growing up and into a man. He knows wrong, and he knows right. He has had his adventures.

This boy Gillette has already seen more adventure in one lifetime than a boy of thirteen should have to see. He knows about right and wrong. So does Sunny. But Sunny is willful, like her mother. Instead of crushing her into a circumspect box, like Miranda's parents did, squeezing, hammering, choking her with rules until she just had to pop, Jamie will allow his daughter her adventures. Then maybe she won't need to leave home with some ne'er-do-well and break his heart. And hers.

He has no idea what he is about to allow.

19

I stand between the privet hedge and the warm brick wall of the church so I can watch and listen in secret, as the little group passes me on the sidewalk. They don't look dirty, and they don't look like Communists, the way Meemaw described them. But I have never seen a Communist, so I don't know what they look like.

"We'll never find our way to the courthouse from here," says Vera. "We got so turned around trying to find the churches. . . ."

"No more side trips," says Jo Ellen.

"Did you see those policemen just standing there, trying to look menacing, rattling their weapons?" asks Vera. "I'm telling you, they don't know what to do with us."

"Don't underestimate them, Vera," says Jo Ellen. "This isn't California."

"I want to go home," says William.

"We'll take you," says Jo Ellen. She pats William on the shoulder like he's any old kid in the neighborhood. "We just want to stop at the courthouse to meet up with our group first, so they don't worry about where we are. Which way is it, Ree?"

"Don't know," says Glory. She stands a distance from Jo Ellen and Vera, like she's suddenly not sure she's supposed to be with them anymore. "I'm not allowed to come over this side of town by myself."

"Well, we'll just have to take a chance, then," says Vera.

And then, because I'm a big mouth and need to be near this not-Miranda girl, I pipe up, "I can tell you how to get there."

There is a pause as they all turn to face the privet hedge, and then Vera says, "Those bushes are talking."

I pop myself out from behind them and say, "I live practically next door to the courthouse. I can show you how to get there." Then I look around quickly to see who might see me standing on the sidewalk on West Washington Street in the middle of the morning, not in Bible School, and talking with people I don't even know, two of them colored. One long boat of a car drives by slowly and the driver, a man with white hair, eyeballs all of us. I stiffen and turn my back to the street.

Jo Ellen smiles that crooked smile. "Hey, Sunny."

I turn to look at her. I am mesmerized by her face. My shoulders soften like ice cream in the sun. "Hey."

"Could you ride with us and show us the way?" asks Vera. She opens the back door of a car parked at the curb. Glory and William pile into the backseat, lean toward us with big brown eyes, and stare at me from the open car door. For the first time I really see them. They are all arms and legs. They are wearing Sunday school clothes.

"I'm not supposed to ride with strangers," I tell them.

"But we've already met," says Jo Ellen. Her locket winks in the sun.

What to do?

"You're almost there," I say, which is true. I take a deep breath and talk fast. "You just turn right here, onto Cotton Street, go to the end, and that's River Road and the Yazoo River. Go left on River Road and you pass my house. Go right and you're at the courthouse, but that's the back, where the jail is. Actually, you want to turn right onto Market Street, before you get to River Road. That is, if you want the front of the courthouse. It takes up a whole city block. You can't miss it. There's a Confederate monument out front on the corner."

"We're so close!" says Vera, laughing. "Just a block away! We really did get turned around!" She opens the driver's side door and gets in the car.

"Want a ride home?" Jo Ellen asks me.

I look at the big, brown eyes staring at me from inside the backseat of the car. "I can run there faster than you can drive me," I say. "You can follow me if you want. I'll show you where to turn."

"Suit yourself," says Jo Ellen. She shuts the back door on the colored kids, opens the passenger side door, and swishes herself, in her shirtwaist dress, onto the front seat of the car.

I take off running, then, around the corner onto Cotton Street. Soon I hear the car creeping behind me. I cross over Market Street, turn around while running in place, jab in the right direction, and shout. "That's it! Turn right here!"

Vera toots the horn at me, waves out the window, and turns on her right turn signal. I make a plan; I'll race to the end of Cotton, turn left on River Road, and run straight for my house and my bicycle. I'll grab it quick and pedal to the courthouse so I can keep an eye on this Jo Ellen and see what she's up to, follow her if I have to. I think to myself, *I'm going to follow the invaders.*

But I can't be seen. Even though I'm not supposed to trespass, I run through the laundry hanging on Mrs. Moxie's line, around the chicken house in old Mr. Fenton's backyard, and behind the hedgerow in Polly's yard, to mine.

My bike leans against the back porch. My Beatles wig is stuffed into the handlebar basket, brown hair spilling over the sides like a hairy monster spider trying to escape.

Without stopping, I grab my bike and run it down our long dirt driveway to the sidewalk, jumping on and weaving like crazy as I do. I almost run smack into Daddy's truck, and I hardly notice at first that it is full to bursting with . . . stuff.

I just keep pedaling because I don't want them to see me and I need to gain the sidewalk, where I'll turn left — so they don't see me riding past the house — and go around the whole block in order to escape notice. It will take longer, but I won't be caught.

But a dog starts running after me. A big, red dog that has come from our porch. This dog is barking its fool head off, and coming with me down the driveway. The screen door slaps and Gillette yells, "Ruth! Get back here! Hey! Sunny! Hey!"

I can't pay attention to this dog. I hope it's not going to bite me. Is that why they went away? To get a dog?

"I'm not speakin' to you!" I scream at my brother. I kick at the dog. And I keep pedaling. The dog drops away from me, and Daddy starts yelling.

"Sunny! Get back here!"

"I'm not speakin' to you, either!" I shriek. By now I'm at the sidewalk, zooming left around the corner toward Dewey Street and out of sight.

I feel great. A thrill of freedom rushes through me, pulses in my temples, and is followed quickly by the sureness of doom. Did I really say that? Did I really just ignore my father? Did I scream at him? I am doomed. I can never go home again, never. I am going to have to run away.

20

The first thing I see after I've pedaled to the courthouse is Uncle Vivian stepping out of his big, blue pickup truck. He has parked at the opposite end of the block, on Fulton Street, near the Confederate monument. There is no sign of Jo Ellen and the rest.

I ride my bike smack under the first magnolia tree I come to. This tree could be George, or the next one, or one of the next six in a row that line this side of Cotton Street. I glide right up under those slick, shady branches. The leaves seem to part for me. I jump off my bike and leave it here, hidden. I jump up on one branch and then higher onto another. I could go much higher but I don't. I peer out from between the leaves and the few blossoms left this time of year, to see if Gillette or Daddy are coming from Cotton or Market Streets, but I don't see anyone I know. I think about what I've just done and my ears grow hot.

Uncle Vivian ambles his way along the sidewalk, past some little kids climbing on the Confederate monument, and toward the front courthouse walk on Market Street, just as the Westminster chimes in the courthouse steeple announce the three-quarter hour. Uncle Vivian tips his hat like a gentleman to a lady walking the other way down the sidewalk.

Suddenly for reasons I can't explain — maybe it's the chimes that spur me on — I scramble down my two branches, jump to the ground and out from under the tree's skirts. I race like a rabbit for Uncle Vivian.

"Whatcha doin', Uncle Vivian?" I call, just like it's the most natural thing in the world for me to be at the courthouse at this hour on a Monday.

"Sunshine!" says Uncle Vivian. He scoops me up, mid-run, and swings me around once and hugs me. "What in the world are *you* doin'?"

I laugh, even though my heart is pounding like I'm an escaped convict from the jail in back of the courthouse. "Bible School got out early," I lie.

"Well, come have dinner with me," says Uncle Vivian. "I'm just here to get my new truck tags, and then I'm going back to the plantation. Easter's cooking up fresh collards and we've got some pork — a real treat in the summertime." Uncle Vivian starts up the courthouse steps and I follow him.

"Oh, I couldn't," I say, but my mind is churning around this invitation.

"I insist!" Uncle Vivian tells me. "You can call Annabelle from the pay phone inside and let her know while I get my tags." He takes off his hat, swings open the great, wide courthouse doors, and hands me a shiny dime as we step inside.

I love the Leflore County Courthouse. It's the grandest building in Greenwood, all that white, sturdy stone, all that carving, all that heaviness, so serious, and at the same time so sheltering, with those four massive columns in front of the doors that just beckon you on in, like the columns across the front of the White House in Washington, D.C. The courthouse columns seem to say, *Come on in, we're open for business, we've been waiting for you, it's safe inside.* And it is. Cool, too. Today is another scorcher.

For as long as I can remember, I have laid on the grass near the magnolias and watched the clouds drift over the courthouse while I wait for the minute hand on the clock in the clock tower creep up to twelve. When it gets there, the whole clock tower shimmers as the chimes mark the hour.

The sound is so deep and so sonorous, it vibrates my muscles, my skin, and my bones as I lie flat on the grass, on the solid green earth while it spins around the sun. I lie there and wait for the chimes because nothing else sounds like that. Nothing else feels like that, nothing. What a wonder. And people walk by and drive by and don't even notice!

Now that we're inside the courthouse with its high stone walls, there are the familiar echoing sounds of people's shoes clacking smartly across the marble floor. I'm wearing my Keds, which make a squishy sound, and Uncle Vivian is wearing his farm boots. They make a dull *thud-thud-thud*. All the footsteps of all the busy people mingle with the echoing voices and the quiet hum of business being done. The smells of the courthouse lobby — shoe polish, floor cleaner, sweat, and cigarette smoke — are as familiar to me as the smells of the Yazoo.

Sometimes when Mary Margaret visits, she and I come here to say hey to her daddy. I really don't understand what a city attorney does. "He makes the bad people pay for their crimes," says Mary Margaret, "and he gets the good people out of jail."

Sometimes Polly and I are bored and go to the courthouse just to get some Life Savers from Mr. Benson's little candy station in the lobby. He carries Red Hots and cigarettes and Good & Plentys.

I would wave at Mr. Benson now, but he's blind — from birth, says Meemaw — sitting there behind his cart with his goodies. Still, he knows who every single person is who comes to his cart. A woman wearing a yellow hat gives Mr. Benson ten cents for some gum, and Mr. Benson's "Thank you, Mrs. Allen," echoes out into the lobby and floats up to the rounded, golden ceiling.

Uncle Vivian gives me a pat and disappears behind the door that reads TAX ASSESSOR. I stare at the bank of pay phones against the wall. I choose the one in the middle and close the folding glass door — sometimes I do this just for fun, even when I don't have to use the phone — and listen to how all the echocy sounds are muted. The light comes on in the ceiling of the phone booth, and I imagine for just a moment that I'm Clark Kent, about to change into Superman. Instead, I step on the wooden seat to reach the coin drop. I lift the receiver from its cradle.

"Number please." The Greenwood telephone operator I get is Miss May, who is about a hundred years old and knows everybody. "Would you like to make a call?"

"Hello, Miss May."

"Is that you, Sunny Fairchild?" says Miss May. "Do you want me to connect you to your meemaw? Let's see . . . she's talking to somebody else right now. Do you have a dime?"

I watched Miss May and the other operators connect all the calls in Greenwood once, on a field trip to the telephone company in second grade. There are wires and plugs everywhere, and the operators wear headphones and say, *"Number, please!"*

"Sunny?" says Miss May again. "She's off the phone. Wait to be connected, please."

"No, thank you, Miss May," I say politely. "I changed my mind." I hang up the receiver.

I wonder if I could run away to Uncle Vivian's. There are so many good hiding places on the plantation. There are barns and silos and sharecropper cabins galore, there's the gin, and there are cotton fields stretched out as far as your eye can see.

But I don't want to run away. The fizz has drained out of me. I sit on the wooden seat and think: *What do I do now?*

Once in a while you find yourself in an odd situation.

No kidding, Thor. No kidding.

21

Last night Miz Vidella Brown and her man, Sheldon Brown, sit at our kitchen table with Ma'am and Pap. Lightbulb overhead go swingin' when Pap beat the table, "No!"

Ma'am wipe sweat from her neck with a fresh-pressed handkerchief. "You got it good, Vidella. You got a good job at the white folks' church, in the nursery, in the kindergarten, you been there a long time. Sheldon, you a teacher. You teach most the kids in Baptist Town to read. What you want to mix things up for?"

Mr. Sheldon older than Pap. "I've been teaching near forty years, Libby. Never once have I had enough books or supplies or money or anything near like the white teachers have in the white schools. That means our children are at a terrible disadvantage."

"Your house full of books," say Ma'am. "You even got a television."

"You'll lose your job, you try and register," say Pap. "They takin' down names and firing people for less than that."

"They can't arrest all of us," say Mr. Sheldon.

Ree out back at the pump with Yellow-Hair, washing up for bed.

They laughing so hard it jingle the hot air.

"We've got to stick together as a community," say Vidella. "We have to stop being afraid of what will happen to us if we register! The whites want to keep us afraid. Truth is, they are afraid of *us*! There's more of us than there are of them."

"Life ain't so bad," say Pap. "We got what we need. Better than it was when I was a boy in the cotton fields, pickin' all day for not even a dollar."

Mr. Sheldon say, "If you had the vote, you would have a better job. You could own the cotton field."

Miss Vidella soft-say, "If you had the vote, Wilson, you could make sure nobody else dies like your Adele did. She needed a doctor, and nobody up at that white hospital would touch her —"

"Don't you bring Adele into it!" say Pap. He wipe at his eyes.

But Miss Vidella go on. She take Ma'am's hand but she look at Pap. "That poor child died in such horrible pain, and all for a burst appendix that any doctor could have taken care of, but the white doctors on shift refused to care for her in time. The law didn't protect her. We have to change the law, Wilson."

Pap scrape up from the table and stand by the door, open it, mad.

"Time for you to go," he say.

Nobody see me, standing inside Ma'am and Pap's bedroom, in the dark, watching. Ma'am's tears run rivers down her cheeks. Two years Adele been gone, and still nobody allowed to talk about her.

"Think about it," say Miss Vidella. "You can come with me to the courthouse tomorrow. CORE volunteers are coming with us. Do it for Adele. Do it for your children. For their children."

Mr. Sheldon and Miss Vidella go to mass meetin' and the house get real quiet. More laughing from the pump. Water sloshing out the tin tub. Slapping washcloth. Ma'am say, "That used to be Adele and Glory, out back, laughin' like fools together at the pump before bed."

Pap say, "Don't do it, Libby. It's too dangerous."

"Adele would have done it," whispers Ma'am.

"Adele ain't here," say Pap, and he sniff. "And you getting arrested ain't gon' bring her back." He walk on stiff legs out the door.

I don't make one sound.

Ma'am stare for a long time at that picture of President Kennedy in the frame on the wall by the door, like she askin' that dead president to talk to her dead daughter and tell her what to do.

22

I open the folding glass door of the phone booth and stand in the cool, clean lobby, listening to the sounds of people coming and going.

"Hey there, Miss Sunny," says Mr. Benson.

I walk to his cart. "How did you know I was here?"

"I heard you come in," he tells me. "You're with your uncle Vivian today."

"Yessir," I say. "Gee, you're good!"

"I am," says Mr. Benson. He smiles at me and his eyes crinkle at the edges even though they look right through me. "You going to the ball game tonight? My Pete's pitching."

"Nossir," I say. "I'm goin' on Wednesday night when Gillette's team plays."

Mr. Benson nods. "Is this his first season here in Greenwood?"

"Yessir," I say as polite as I can be. I know this is one way people ask about my strange family.

"Well, that's a good thing for a boy," Mr. Benson says, nodding some more. "Baseball. I'm sure he appreciates you going to watch him play."

"Yessir," I say again, although I will never watch Gillette play ball again, now that I know I can't trust him.

"I know what it's like to be the new kid," says Mr. Benson, out of nowhere.

"You do?" I finger the dime in my pocket, ponder Life Savers, and wonder if Mr. Benson is fishing for information. Some folks do.

"Well, let's just say the different kid," says Mr. Benson as he settles on getting nothing more from me.

"Yessir." I know what he means, but it isn't the same. Gillette's not blind. He's just not from around here and that's hard for folks. That, and his mama is divorced. Nobody in town is divorced. It just isn't done unless you're Elizabeth Taylor — she gets divorced all the time, but she's a movie star.

"Got some people talkin' about you in here, today," says Mr. Benson, changing the subject.

"Really?" I perk right up. "Who?"

"There was a young girl and an older lady and they was with some others, including some Negroes. Taking 'em in to register to vote."

Mr. Benson points toward the door right next to me that says, COUNTY REGISTRAR. MARTHA LAMB. I know Mrs. Lamb. She and Meemaw belong to the same ladies circle in church.

Mr. Benson continues. "Heard 'em tell one of theirs that a girl named Sunny showed 'em how to get back to the courthouse."

"That was me, all right," I say.

"I reckon so, since you're the only Sunny in town."

"I am?"

"Only Sunny I know."

"Are they still in there?" And, just like I've spoken the mysterious magic words, the registrar's door opens and out streams Jo Ellen and Vera and a colored man in a straw hat wearing a white T-shirt with black letters that spell FREEDOM NOW.

I take three steps back so they don't run over me. Three Negroes are right behind them. Policemen have the Negroes by their arms and are shoving them out the door. Vidella is one of them! Vidella, who works in the nursery at our church. She looks calmly at the floor and says nothing as she's released with a shove by the policeman. The other Negro lady looks so scared

I think she's about to cry. The Negro man with them keeps his head up straight and stares at nobody.

"That's enough for today!" the biggest policeman says. I know him. That's Officer Ramsey. His kid, Dennis, plays shortstop on Gillette's ball team.

"We're just getting started, sir," says the colored man in the straw hat. His voice is strong and sure, but peaceful.

"Don't you come back here today!" barks Officer Ramsey. "You've reached your limit of coloreds coming down here to register today! The registrar's office is closed this afternoon!"

Everyone in the lobby — and that's a lot of people — has stopped moving. The sound of Officer Ramsey's shouting bounces all over the lobby, off the stones and the marble floor and back up to the ceiling again. My knees feel wobbly.

"For what reason, sir?" asks the man in the straw hat. Officer Ramsey pulls his billy club from its holster and makes a lunge toward him.

I jump back into Uncle Vivian, who is at my side with his new truck tags. "What's going on here?" His voice booms in the big room. Everyone waits. I take his hand as if I'm suddenly six years old again and need protection from something I don't understand. His rough palm closes around mine.

Officer Ramsey gives Uncle Vivian an ugly look. "You know as well as I know what's going on here, Vivian!" He waves his stick at the Negroes and says, "We've took down your names and they'll be published in the paper!" He waves his stick at Jo Ellen and Vera and Straw Hat and says, "Y'all come back up here today with anybody else, and we'll arrest the lot of you! You've been warned!" The policeman struts back into Martha Lamb's office and slams the door so hard it shudders in its frame.

"Excuse us, sir," says Straw Hat to Uncle Vivian, so calmly. He guides Vidella and the other colored lady past us. The

Negro man follows them. The upset colored lady looks straight ahead with blank eyes and I think, *She doesn't want to see us looking at her.*

Vidella stands as straight as a light pole and looks about as proud as one. She and Uncle Vivian exchange a long look but say nothing to each other. Then Vidella sees me. She gives me the tiniest nod of her head to show she has recognized me.

Jo Ellen sees me and turns on her crooked smile, but even she looks a little quivery. "Thanks for your help today, Sunny," she says. "See you around." Then she and Vera follow Straw Hat and the three other Negroes down the stairs and outside. The buzzing sounds of people doing business start up again. They are all talking about what just happened, but their voices are so many, they bounce off the high ceiling, and I can't hear anyone clearly.

Uncle Vivian lets go of my hand and his voice is like an accusation. "Do you know these people, Sunny?"

I keep my eyes on my Keds. I tune out all the sounds of the lobby.

"Say something, young lady," he orders.

"Not exactly," I whisper.

"They seem to know you." Uncle Vivian's tone is not soft, not friendly. "What's going on?"

"Nothing!" I protest, which is true, but not good enough. I am in trouble but I don't know why.

"I'm taking you home," says Uncle Vivian, and I have no choice but to go with him and face the trouble I'm in at home, too.

"Yessir."

Uncle Vivian puts his thick farmer's hand flat on my back — it doesn't feel safe and friendly anymore — and begins to push me along as he walks *thud-thud-thud* across the wide lobby, around the little throngs of people gossiping.

I am a convicted prisoner going to her hanging. No, I am like the Incredible Shrinking Man, becoming smaller and smaller until I hate my wretched existence. I stumble beside my uncle out the courthouse doors, down the stairs, and to his truck. The noon whistle at the Buckeye blasts its earsplitting *lunchtime!* and I don't bother to cover my ears. The Westminster chimes begin to play the hour. Soon they will bong out twelve long, bottomless notes, the song of my execution.

Willie James Shaw, a SNCC worker, being arrested in Belzoni, Mississippi, for encouraging local blacks to vote in a COFO "Freedom Election." Police said Shaw was parked too close to a fire hydrant. Summer 1964.

23

Uncle Vivian pulls into our driveway, puts his truck in PARK, leans forward over the steering wheel, and peers through the windshield like he isn't sure what he's seeing.

"What in the world?"

I'm thinking the same thing. Daddy's truck is piled high with furniture and boxes. There's a dresser in the truck bed where Polly and I sat just the night before. A rocking chair is roped to the top of the cab.

Uncle Vivian turns off the engine. I'm going to have to walk up the driveway with everybody and his brother watching me trudge to my doom. And that's that.

I open the truck door, slide down to the ground, and slam shut the creaky door. A dog barks from inside our house. Great. And here comes Polly, strutting up the sidewalk from Bible School, carrying a glittery something-or-other made with Popsicle sticks.

"How was Bible School?" I ask. Dumb question. She doesn't answer me.

Uncle Vivian is beside Daddy's truck, looking at all the stuff. Polly passes me, raises an eyebrow, and says, "Ezekiel 7:25. 'Destruction cometh; and they shall seek peace, and there shall be none.'"

"Oh, go jump in the lake, Polly," I snap. "I'll bet you looked that up at Bible School, just for me." I can't think of one person I know who isn't a traitor or unhappy with me right now. Audrey? Maybe I can think of something horrible to say to her, by the time I reach the front door. Maybe I can take her doll, Ginny, and pop off her head.

Inside, it's as if everyone was talking about me and saw us coming and jumped onto the couch, where they all sit together now, looking squashed, uncomfortable, and concerned. The dog is sitting on the floor by Gillette's feet. It's a red hound dog with floppy ears, as old as Methuselah, gray around the snout. Gillette has one hand on its bony shoulder. The dog quavers at me with a bright expression but doesn't move.

There they sit, in height order: Parnell, Daddy, Annabelle, Gillette, and Audrey clutching Ginny and staring at me with big, round eyes. Audrey is practically strangling Ginny while she fidgets with impatience. Gillette puts his other hand on her knee to stop her leg jiggling. He won't look at me. *Double-crossing rat fink.* Time stretches out, even though it's only a moment that passes between all of us.

The smell of baking sweet potatoes reaches my nose. The clacking going on in the kitchen means Laura Mae must be here already, setting out the noon dinner that Annabelle probably spent all morning making. I wonder if Daddy has even been to work yet today, and who opened the store for him.

But mostly I wonder about how much trouble I'm in. Five in a row on the couch, totally silent; that's serious. Laura Mae starts humming something in the kitchen and I want to go bury my face in her apron, like I used to do when I was little, but the bodies on the couch hold me right where I am.

Uncle Vivian comes in behind me, takes off his hat, and clears his throat. Daddy stands and shakes Uncle Vivian's hand. "Thank you for bringing her home" is all he says. Annabelle is on her feet, too. Parnell moves over. "Would you like to stay for noon dinner, Vivian?" Annabelle asks. She looks at me but her face is a blank and doesn't betray her feelings.

"No, no," says Uncle Vivian. "I've got to get home." He

notices the dog but says nothing about it. He looks undecided, and starts his next sentence twice, like he's trying to get the right words out. He watches Audrey, whose left foot is waving back and forth like a flag, now that Gillette's got his hand on her right leg. A little smile plays across her face and she gives Ginny another squeeze.

Uncle Vivian coughs and tries again, in a low, confidential tone. "Jamie, there were some agitators at the courthouse just now, bringing in coloreds to register. They seem to know your girl, here . . . know her by name. It's none of my business, of course. . . ."

"Of course," says Daddy, so politely as he takes Uncle Vivian by the elbow and steers him to the door. "Thank you, Vivian."

Uncle Vivian turns, gives me a nod, and says, in such a disappointed-in-you voice, "Another day for that dinner."

"Yessir."

Uncle Vivian makes his good-byes and, from the porch, gestures toward Daddy's truck with his hat in his hand. "Interesting haul you've got there, Jamie."

"We've had a busy morning," Daddy says. He doesn't volunteer anything.

Uncle Vivian shoves his hat back onto his head, spits into the azaleas, and thuds in his boots down the porch steps. I stand just inside the screen door and watch him climb into his truck and drive away. Daddy stands on the porch until the truck is out of sight. Then he steps inside and slowly rubs his hands over his face, up and down, up and down, up and down.

Audrey sees this as an invitation. She pops off the couch and races to me, hugs me at my waist ferociously — with Ginny still cradled in the crook of an elbow — and says, "You are peachy today, Sunny!" I drop to my knees and squeeze her. My nose stuffs as my eyes well with tears. *Oh, thank you for loving me!* I want to say. *I love you, too. I even love your ratty old doll.*

Instead, I stand up, fortified by Audrey, and say, "I'm going to go upstairs to my room now." I glance at Daddy. "Please."

Audrey stares intently at my wet eyelashes and says with delight, as if she's trying to cheer me up, "Somebody's sleeping in your bed!"

"I don't feel like playing Goldilocks, Audrey."

"It's my meemaw!" Audrey is unable to contain her glee. "My Boo! She's here! She came to live with me!"

I look out the living room window at the rocking chair strapped to the top of the cab.

"We need to talk," says Daddy.

"We're going to eat first," says Annabelle, and it's not a question, it's a command. "It will be a better talk if we eat first."

I don't want to do anything Annabelle says to do, and I couldn't eat if my life depended on it. "I'm not hungry," I say.

"None for me, either," says Parnell. "I'm meeting Randy before work. We'll get lunch at Gelman's." He squeezes my shoulder as he passes me and heads out the door.

Gillette finally moves off the couch. "I'll get Boo," he says. "C'mon, Ruth." He walks past me and up the stairs. Ruth follows him, all angles and bones, silent and obedient, stuck to Gillette like glue.

Laura Mae seems to know her cue. She steps out of the kitchen with a dish towel in her hand and her apron dotted with flour and grease and says, quietly, "Dinner."

I know Laura Mae will hug me and shush me and help pat me back together. So I go to her while everyone is gathering at the table and press myself into her warm, welcoming body. I don't have to say a thing. I smell the starch in her white uniform and the sweat-smell of the day's heat coming off her that reminds me of black-eyed peas. I wrap my arms around her waist like she's my own dear mother, which I suppose she's been for twelve years, although she's really not, of course, and never could be.

Laura Mae presses her soft purple lips to the top of my head and kisses me, like a blessing. Then she says, "There now, Miss Sunny. You come eat. Make you feel better. I made you some cheese biscuits and fresh butter."

Gillette appears with Ruth and says, "Boo's snoring and I can't wake her up. She smells like Vicks VapoRub."

Annabelle says, "Poor thing. She was up all night. We'll save her a plate."

And that's how we find ourselves at our dining room dinner table at half past noon on Monday, June 22, 1964. Annabelle intones the blessing — which she never does — and then says, "This family has been through a lot today, and it's going to get harder before it gets easier. We'll need all our wits about us. We'll need each other." She takes Daddy's hand and says, "We are, each of us, important."

Daddy smiles at Annabelle. Ruth settles under the table at Gillette's feet and Daddy allows it. Laura Mae eats in the kitchen like she always does. It's the most quiet meal on record. The tea is sweet, not salty. I know because I take a sip, but I won't eat

Annabelle doesn't know the first thing about what's important. When she says, "Can I help your plate with peas, Sunny?" I can't stand any more pretend niceness.

"No, thank you," I say. I look at Daddy until he notices me looking at him. He steadily locks his eyes with mine. His face blurs in front of me as I realize my eyes are filling with tears. I blink and two fat teardrops fall onto my empty dinner plate. I stare at them and take a deep breath. I feel the sharp edge of what frightens me when I say, plainly and simply, "I don't understand what's happening."

Daddy wipes his face with his napkin, puts it in the middle of his plate full of dinner, and says to Annabelle, "Time to talk?"

"Time to talk," says Annabelle.

24

Back from moving bricks all day with Twill at a white man's house in town — got me a dollar — and they's a crowd in front of the Freedom House. Ma'am's in the thick of it.

"I can't believe it, Libby!" spout Miss Julia Dupree. "Go on with your own dear self! I'm so proud of you!"

Ma'am beam, even though she didn't pass the test, didn't get registered. Everybody make 'mirations over her. Kennedy told her to go to the courthouse. Her eyes shine like she seen the Promised Land, like she suddenly awake after a long sleep and she know what to do.

Ida Mae hold up her fist full of forms, while SNCC Dewey bring everybody inside. "You lose your job, we'll help. We've got food, we've got a little money. They can't fire all of you — they need you!"

Ma'am grab me. "This here black man CORE Sandy. All these COREs, they wear straw hats." Then, "This my boy, Raymond, Sandy. He gon' be a registered voter one day!"

Sandy say, "Good to meet you, Ray! Welcome!" He call to the crowd: "We are also registering voters for the Mississippi Freedom Democratic Party! This is a new political party that does not require you to go to the courthouse to register. You should all be registered with the MFDP! Volunteers are here to help you fill out the forms."

Ida Mae shove a form at Scarecrow Magee. "What it for?" he ask.

"For *freedom*," say Ma'am, like she in charge now. "Sign your name."

"When you start working here, Ida Mae?" I ask. Ida Mae my age.

"Just started," Ida Mae say. "You should help, too."

I wrinkle my nose at her. "You smell funny." She slap me on the arm.

"That's my Lucky Heart perfume!" Then she say, "Let me help you, Miss Libby."

Ma'am snip, "I can write it myself, Ida Mae."

"You change your mind, Ma'am," I tell her. "What about Pap?"

Ma'am wave her pen. "Pap gonna come along. All God's childrens gonna come along, and none others be forevermore left behind."

Like Adele. She don't say it, but I hear it.

"Like you and your childrens," say Ma'am. She sniff and keep writing.

Yellow-Hair come down the stairs with a stack of magazines in her hands. She nod at me, and I know it okay to nod back, 'cause we in the Freedom House, but I don't do it.

Miss Vidella Brown grab me. "Ray, the NAACP has a youth council. I want you to join it."

"What's that mean?"

"It means young Negroes will work together to make change in Mississippi — in America!"

"How we gonna change anything?" I want to know.

"We're in the middle of a revolution, Raymond, don't you know that?" She point to some womens with they sewing, talking in one corner. "They know it," she say. She point to a Ping-Pong table in the back where Simon and Jimmy and Twill slap that ball like they lives depend on it. "Your friends know it, too," she say. "They come to help."

"Here," say Miss Vidella Brown. "Read about it." She take a magazine off the top of Yellow-Hair Jo Ellen's stack and push it at me. *Jet* magazine. White man on the cover with a Negro lady, both of 'em smiling. Never seen that on a magazine. In the corner it say, WHITE UNDERGROUND MOVEMENT IN MISSISSIPPI. I thumb it open. There's the heavyweight champion of the world, Cassius Clay, in the ring in his trunks and gloves, laughin' and dancin' over four white men just lyin' there, pretending they scared. Note say, CASSIUS CLAY MAKES SHORT WORK OF THE BEATLES.

"That's the game!" shout SNCC playing with Jimmy and Simon and Twill.

He laugh like a crazy man.

The boys swarm around me and that SNCC slap me on the shoulder. "New recruit?"

"Ray," say Twill, "this here Stokely. Stokely, this Ray. He ready for the revolution!"

Lyndon Baines Johnson was born in 1908, in the Hill Country near Stonewall, Texas, in a farmhouse alongside a dirt road that hugged the Pedernales River. He was baptized in that river. He learned the alphabet from his ABC blocks, and he recited Mother Goose — also Tennyson and Longfellow! — for his doting mother. Lyndon was her firstborn and always her favorite. He liked the attention.

When his sisters were born, Lyndon took to running away from home to get even more attention, and since he always ran to the one-room Junction School, his parents enrolled him there. He became Junction School's youngest student, four years old. He wore costumes to school, often his cowboy outfit, complete with his father's Stetson hat and a toy gun. He insisted on sitting on his teacher's lap to recite his lessons.

Soon there were five children in the Johnson family,

and they moved to Johnson City, Texas, where there were tent revivals and a dance hall and swimming in the river after church. The five children ran wild because Rebekah Johnson, Lyndon's mother, tended to her health and her cultured education and left the discipline to Lyndon's father, Sam, who was often away in the legislature in Austin, where he had been elected a member of the Texas House of Representatives.

Sam knew no strangers, and everyone knew Sam, even the Mexicans he invited to Christmas dinner without telling Rebekah.

Sam wanted Lyndon to be a man's man. When Rebekah wouldn't cut five-year-old Lyndon's long blond curls, Sam waited until Rebekah was gone to church one Sunday, plopped Lyndon in a kitchen chair, and gave him his first haircut.

They were poor in Johnson City, but everybody was poor, and the Johnsons had the first bathtub in town. They loved politics and cared about the land and its people, unlike many in politics who used their position to manipulate the system for their own advantage. They agreed on so little, Sam and Rebekah, but two things they both knew and instilled in Lyndon were: Politics should help people, and any son of theirs had to grow up to teach, preach, or go into politics.

But Lyndon was wilder than wild, and no one could tame him. When his teacher kept him in for recess so he could make up his work, he stomped out of class and spit at her through a window. When he was twelve years old, he missed eighty out of one-hundred school days — even spankings couldn't get him to go to school.

Still, he loved learning. He soaked up the world like a sponge. He was smart, and a good listener. He walked and talked with the grown men who whittled on the porch at night and talked politics. He just didn't have the patience for the classroom.

Lyndon wanted people to like him and he needed to be the best at everything. He'd go hunting with the older boys, even though he hated killing small animals, so he would go behind a tree and throw up. He played baseball with those boys, even though he didn't like sports. He was loyal and he was industrious — he shined shoes, he sold litters of puppies, he chopped cotton, he herded goats. He sat in the gallery of the Texas House of Representatives and watched his father at work. Soon he was running errands there for anyone who would let him and gathering tips on the House floor. He learned how to debate.

When World War I ended, and people like Harry Truman and Arthur Chapman came home changed men, Sam Johnson moved his family back to the farm by the Pedernales River, where, suddenly, the bottom dropped out of the cotton market and — **boom** — now the Johnsons were *really* poor.

But so was everyone else.

Lyndon still hated school but managed to graduate at age fifteen. Rebekah wrote to his college teachers: "Lyndon is very young and has been considerably indulged . . . so finds the present situation very trying. To be away from home and to be compelled to study are great hardships for him. Your sympathy and encouragement will help him keep up his interest and enthusiasm."

College proved to be too much for Lyndon. He dropped out and worked on a road gang, he burned down an old barn with hooligans, he wrecked cars, he got into fights. The last terrible fight — where he was beaten and bloodied, his nose broken — led him back to college, ready to rethink. He remembered there were some people in politics — he had met them — who wanted to change the world, and who acted with the greater good of the people in mind. He was tired of being the bully.

So he went to Houston, to the 1928 Democratic National Convention, to see what he could see. What he discovered was the American political system at work, in all its grime and glory. He saw how it could be used for good or evil, and he knew that America would need men who understood this, so that good would triumph.

This is what I want, Lyndon thought. *I want to live my life in such a way that, when I've been dead a hundred years, somebody will know I have lived on this earth and done* good. *I want to be of service.*

So what did Lyndon do?

He got Cs and Ds in college. He became a teacher (and then principal! Imagine!) at the Welhausen School in the Brush Country, in Cotulla, where Mexicans made up 75 percent of the population and were separated from whites at lunch counters, parks, movie theaters, and other public places. Most of Texas was segregated, but, for the first time, Lyndon saw not poor people but people who lived in poverty, in shacks, doing backbreaking labor for so little money, their children discouraged from going to school.

The Mexicans who had stayed in Texas after the Battle of the Alamo were considered by whites as trespassers, not worthy of being called Americans, not even people. In 1921, the *New York Times* had reported, "The killings of Mexicans [in Texas] without provocation is so common as to pass unnoticed."

But Lyndon, deeply touched by what he saw, taught these children that the United States was a nation of immigrants, that they had as much right to the American Dream as anyone else.

Lyndon wanted that American Dream, too. He served in the navy, in the U.S. House and Senate, and became John Kennedy's vice president, all the while still the boy who needed to be top-dog, to be heard, to be liked, to be the best. Lyndon took his untamed feelings — all that wildness — and channeled them into the work.

Just as he had talked and walked beside the Pedernales River, and talked and walked with the Mexican children at the Welhausen School, he now talked and walked with Sam Rayburn on the floor of the U.S. Senate. He talked and walked with Claudia Alta Taylor, his wife, his Lady Bird.

And, because he was Lyndon, he needed to out-walk and out-talk everybody else. In his quest to change the world, he was loud. He complained. He cajoled. He accused. He cried. He threatened. He bullied.

The American people loved him devotedly or hated him fiercely — there was no in-between. Some say he was possessed by inner demons. Some say it was because he had grown up poor and was ashamed of that feeling, afraid of that emptiness, so he tried to fill it with things, with people, with accomplishments.

When he became the thirty-sixth president of the United States in 1964, Lyndon Johnson said, "There is a difference between being poor and being in poverty." *I should know*, he said.

Lyndon wanted to be the best president ever, better even than JFK, more beloved than FDR. He envisioned a world in which America was a shining example of generosity and compassion. He wanted to eliminate poverty and racial injustice.

So he created a plan to do that.

He called it "The Great Society."

During the Johnson administration, amazing, head-spinning legislation was passed and programs started:

The Civil Rights Act of 1964
The Voting Rights Act of 1965
The Immigration Act of 1965
The Elementary and Secondary
  Education Act of 1965
The Gun Control Act of 1968
The National Endowment for the
  Humanities
The National Endowment for the Arts
The Economic Opportunity Act
The Clean Air Act
Medicare, Medicaid, Head Start, Food
  Stamps, Urban Renewal, Rural
  Development . . .

The list goes on. And on. Head-spinning.

In 1967, Lyndon appointed Thurgood Marshall to the Supreme Court, the first African American Supreme Court justice in the land. He secured funding for space exploration, he beautified America's highways and parks, and he declared a war on poverty in this country.

But what Lyndon didn't see was that a tiny country in Southeast Asia was about to trip him up for good. Vietnam would break Lyndon's spirit and become his undoing.

He agonized over the conflict in Vietnam. Money meant for his Great Society was funneled into a war he did not want.

In his 1966 State of the Union address, he said:

"Yet, finally, war is always the same. It is young men dying in the fullness of their promise. It is trying to kill a man that you do not even know well enough to hate.

"Therefore, to know war is to know that there is still madness in this world.

"Many of you share the burden of this knowledge tonight with me. But there is a difference. For finally I must be the one to order our guns to fire, against all the most inward pulls of my desire. For we have children to teach, and we have sick to be cured, and we have men to be freed. There are poor to be lifted up, and there are cities to be built, and there is a world to be helped.

"Yet we do what we must."

HEY-HEY, LBJ!
HOW MANY KIDS DID YOU KILL TODAY?

Lyndon Johnson finally had to quit. In the middle of the 1968 presidential reelection campaign he hung his coonskin on the wall and retired to Texas, back to the banks of the Pedernales, where he built a ranch house down the same dirt road, near the farmhouse where he had lived as a boy.

He wrote his memoirs.

He walked and talked beside the river and felt empty, though not poor.

One morning, while he was still in bed listening to the mourning dove call from the dirt road outside his ranch house window, Lyndon Johnson had a heart attack and died while reaching for the phone. He was sixty-four years old.

Who did he want to call?

The Mexican children who lived in poverty?

The soldiers in the jungles of South Vietnam?

The American mothers of the dead American soldiers?

Did he want to tell Americans that he was flawed and human and had done the best that he could?

Did he want Lady Bird to come running?

She did.

Tenderly, she buried Lyndon Baines Johnson a few yards from the farmhouse in which he was born.

25

I am smothering in the turpentine smell of Vicks VapoRub. It's so hot, and the air is so thick, that everything in my room is a sponge for smells. That Vicks smell is going to soak into everything — my Beatles records, my pillow, even my stolen copy of *Kon-Tiki*. It will smell like Vicks when I take it back to school in September, yes, it will, so maybe I'll just have to keep it forever.

I turn on my box fan and put it in the window facing out to see if it can help banish the smell. I shove two pair of shorts and two tops, some underwear and socks, pajamas, toothpaste, and toothbrush into my overnight case. I take my mother's picture out of the nightstand drawer and stare at it for a good minute, ignoring the Vicks fumes all around me.

Not Jo Ellen. But almost! The same hair. The same sort of shirtwaist dress. The same sort of locket. The same crooked smile. And, I imagine, the same kind heart. It's obvious to me that Jo Ellen is kind. I don't know why Uncle Vivian can't see it.

Gently I tuck the picture of my mother into my suitcase pocket. I'm not ready to give it back yet, but I need it near me. Meemaw won't let me play my Beatles records at her house, but I put them in my suitcase, too, along with *Kon-Tiki*. I will save them from the doom of Vicks VapoRub.

Two days. I am being exiled for two days, while Daddy and Annabelle get a bedroom ready for Gillette and Audrey's grandma, so she can have a bedroom in our house, too. As if we don't have enough people living here already. *You can't just move a whole grandmother in with us and move me out like I'm a baseball card to be traded!* That's what I should have said.

And she's awful, this grandmother. They call her Boo and she looks like it, wiry hair spraying out around her head like a Brillo pad. She talks all the time. "I met my late husband, rest his soul, at the Bijou in Biloxi. He asked me to dance. Flang out his arms like he was looking at an angel — he was — and said, "Booo-tiful!" She paused for effect and a little sigh and continued, "He forever called me Boo. . . ."

"Mother . . . ," Annabelle began, but Boo smiled like a gooney bird, twirled like a crooked ballerina with Audrey, and then danced her up the stairs.

I might just hate them all.

I sit at my desk, open my Bible to the back where the concordance is that lists all the important words in the Bible and where to find them. I look up *hate* and find myself a good verse. Then I compose a note for Polly.

I know you hate me, but read this:
John 15:23. "He that hateth me hateth my Father also."
So there.
I have to live at Meemaw's for two days.
I will be at Bible School tomorrow and all week.
In the words of Paul and John:
Do you want to know a secret?
Do you promise not to tell?
I have one or two. Or ten.

I move the fan and send the note across to Polly's in our mail bucket. I don't even wait to see if she's there. I snap my suitcase shut and sit on the bed next to it and take stock. That's what Daddy said downstairs. "Take stock, Sunny. Think about what's important."

"Like what?" I asked him.

"Like your freedom, for one thing," he answered. I thought to tell Daddy of the Freedom Worker in the T-shirt that said FREEDOM NOW — that seemed pretty important — but I didn't.

"Your freedom comes so easily to you," Daddy continued. "You have the freedom to wander all over Greenwood. You come and go as you please. You have all summer to do the things you want to do, sunup to sundown. Until you break the law. Then you no longer have your freedom."

Then he gave me my punishments — *consequences*, he called them. I can't go to the pool or the movies for two weeks. And I have to finish this week's Bible School. I have to apologize to Mrs. McGinnis for leaving her class. Gillette and I have to spend one whole day picking up trash in and around the school playground. That will pay back the city for our trespassing offense. Deputy Davis expects us to show up at eight tomorrow morning.

Then I have to spend the next two weeks helping at the grocery store instead of getting in Annabelle's way all day.

Well, lah-dee-dah! I'll be glad to be out from under Annabelle's thumb! That's what I should have said.

I'm not allowed in the courthouse, either, although Daddy didn't ask me what Uncle Vivian was talking about, he just said it's not a place for me to go alone right now.

It's so unfair. I should have said that, too. I clutch my pillow, flop on my back, sling my legs across my suitcase, and think of everything I should have said downstairs.

The whole time Daddy was talking, he was sitting forward in his chair in the living room, with his elbows on his knees, talking with his hands, and sweating until Annabelle thought to turn on the air conditioner.

"You're not to torture your brother over this," he said.

I don't have a brother, that's what I should have said.

"He's just as guilty as you are and he was brave to tell me. That was the right thing to do."

I shot a sideways look at Gillette, who sat glumly at the opposite end of the couch. He kept that red dog right next to him the whole time. Gillette's got his own share of troubles for the next two weeks, but he can still play baseball, and I can still go to his games. I won't.

Then, just when I thought we'd get the punishments out of the way and talk about what's happening all over Greenwood, Daddy said, "And now, let's talk about Boo." He cleared his throat. "Boo is here because . . ." But he couldn't finish his sentence, he just fidgeted until Annabelle went and stood next to him, put her hand on his shoulder, and smiled at him, one of her sickly-sweet smiles.

Then Daddy tried again. "Boo is here because we're going to have a baby."

"*Boo is going to have a baby?*" I actually said that, even though I know better. Then I said, "She's a *grandmother*!" and I waved my arms in a little twirl for effect.

"No!" said Daddy. "Not Boo! Me!"

"*You're* having a baby?" I would not make it easy for him. He has not made it easy for me.

Daddy's face turned the color of a fire engine. A happy fire engine. "No!" he said, and then, "Well, yes!" He cleared his throat yet again and repeated himself. "We're all going to have a baby."

Daddy grabbed Annabelle to him and kissed her. She laughed like a happy kumquat.

Gillette started rubbing his forehead with his fingers, back and forth. He already knew. I'll bet they all knew except me.

"Is this for real?" I asked. "Aren't you too old for babies now?"

What I should have said — shouted — was, *There are too many people in this house already! I don't want a baby making it worse! How could you be so selfish?*

"I know it's a surprise," explained Daddy. "It surprised us, too!" He sounded like he'd just won the big prize of the night at bingo.

I should have said, *Where are you going to put a baby? It's not going in my room! No sirree!*

I squash my pillow to my face and scream into it. I can't even think about babies! I need answers for what's happening *right now.*

"Are we going to have a baby *today*?" I asked.

"Of course not," said Annabelle. "He — or she — will arrive around Thanksgiving."

I ignored Annabelle and looked straight at Daddy. "Then why did you leave at five o'clock this morning?"

Daddy's face darkened. "We were going to bring Boo here this fall, but there were extenuating circumstances."

"What's that?"

"It's hard to explain, Sunny. It was a grown-up decision to bring Boo here now."

Gillette finally spoke. "My dad tried to shoot my dog," he said flatly. "At five o'clock this morning. And that's why we went to Philadelphia."

My breath hitched in my throat. The clock struck ten, which meant it was one, and we all waited in silence for it to finish.

Then Annabelle asked, "How did you know that, Gillette?"

"Boo told me," Gillette said. "I asked her. She said Dad would have hit Ruth, too, if he hadn't been so angry and weaving all over the place, and if she hadn't brought Ruth into her house and locked all the doors."

Annabelle licked her lips like she was trying to find something to say to this. Now it was my turn to rub my forehead.

Gillette's voice was shaking. "Boo said he was up all night and out with the boys. She watched him come home from her house across the street, and then Ruth was there, on the porch and barking like she always does at Dad, and he was mad, and —"

"She didn't need to tell you all that," Annabelle interrupted. No longer a happy kumquat.

I finally looked Gillette full in the face. He returned my gaze. He was tortured by this, I could see, and in that moment, I wanted to help him.

I spring off my bed with that thought and fling my pillow at the headboard. This will never do, feeling sorry for Gillette.

What I should have said was . . . what should I have said?

The rest was a blur, downstairs. I still don't understand why the Negroes need the vote and can't have it, why the white people are so upset, why the police are so strange, what the unrest is about, and why the agitators are here. Three of them have gone missing. They went missing last night, on the summer solstice, in Philadelphia, where Gillette and Daddy went this morning.

I asked Daddy the question I most wanted to know the answer to: "What's going to happen?"

"We're going to watch, Sunny," he answered me, "and stick together. Everything will be all right."

"Whose side are we on?" That was the other question I needed to ask.

"It's more complicated than that," Daddy said. "We'll keep talking. Right now, I need to get you to Meemaw's and I need to get to work. I've got a refrigerator on the blink."

"I don't want to go to Meemaw's," I told him.

"It will be like old times," Daddy said.

"I didn't like the old times," I answered.

We were done. Daddy smiled me away. "Go get packed, honey."

A clink brings me back to my bed, by my suitcase. I have mail. I grab it from the bucket and read it, hungry for any good word from my friend. Even a bad word will do.

> *I never said I hated you. Mary Margaret says you need help. She is making pimento cheese sandwiches. We are bringing them to your meemaw's when Mama goes to the courthouse to take some pictures of some doings for her latest news article. She's writing a big story and she's just as happy to see me rescuing you.*
>
> *She'll drop us off.*
>
> *Here's some help from the Beatles (and me):*
>
> *"I told you before, you can't do that!"*

She doesn't hate me. I pick up my suitcase and trudge down the stairs, but not before I stand in the hallway in the wide space by the front windows, the alcove where I used to play dolls and dress-up and school. Now Audrey plays in the dress-up box and chalks on the chalkboard and colors on my old dolls. Soon there will be a baby who will do the same thing. It used to be just Daddy and Parnell and me. It used to be there was no unrest. Everybody was happy. Nobody was mistreated. And there was enough love to go around without heaping a whole lot of extra people into everything.

26

His mother calls it "borrowing trouble," the kind of thinking that gives you dark thoughts about things that *could* happen but probably won't. The kind of thinking that gives you a stomachache and makes it hard to eat your dinner. "We really don't know what the future will bring," his mother always says. "It's best to let the day take care of itself. There's enough to do each day."

He didn't tell Jamie that Deputy Davis said they had to tell on themselves. He didn't tell Jamie that he was supposed to tell his father about his trespassing. And he doesn't want to tell his father. He's afraid to do it. Not that his father would care about the trespassing — he wouldn't.

He would, though, very much want another opportunity to set Gillette on the straight and narrow, as he calls it. To punish him for wrongdoing, and to be able to tell his friends he did it. "Got to keep a young boy in line, yes sirree." Gillette has heard this before. He knows he is difficult for his father. His father calls him a mama's boy, and perhaps he is. That's all right. Boo always told him that the world needed tenderizing, and the stronger the man, the more tender he could be.

He was glad he didn't have to see his father. The whole time they were loading furniture, he was afraid his father would show up with his anger and his bad aim, but Boo said he'd already left again.

At least he got his dog back before anything worse could happen to her. Ruth and Gillette were born in the same month of the same year, a lucky sign. They had never been separated until Jamie came to pick up Annabelle and Audrey and Gillette that summer morning and take them to Annabelle's sister's in Winona. He had missed the dog more than he'd missed his father; and his father, he was sure, hadn't missed Gillette at all. He could be sad about that, or it could be just part of letting the day take care of itself. It was something to live with, that's all.

And now this girl, his sister. She doesn't understand — how could she, with a father like Jamie?

Not going to the pool for two weeks? Piece of cake. Gillette could do that with his eyes closed. New baby coming? Piece of cake. He's already been through that, with Audrey. And with this baby, he won't have to be vigilant. He won't have to protect her. He can just love her. Or him. A brother would be nice.

She pouts, this girl. She wants her way. She won't speak except to wisecrack. And now she won't come to his baseball games. No matter. He doesn't need her to come. He did the right thing. When you come clean, when you tell the truth, you lift a great weight off your shoulders. It's not that you don't ever do anything you shouldn't do ever again, of course not. You're human, and sometimes the vagaries of life are just too delicious to ignore. Sometimes you are impetuous. Sometimes you are impulsive. And sometimes that's okay. Sometimes it's not. It's just that, when you know you're caught and you've done something you shouldn't have done, you own up to it.

And you think about it. Is this who I want to be? Does this hurt others? Does it scare them? Is it right? What *is* right? What is wrong?

Gillette knows about these questions because he has watched his father for a long, long time — a boy in his situation gets used to watching. And here's what Gillette thinks: His father hasn't asked those questions. His father just knows, just believes that he is right. But how do you know such things? That is the question. That's what Gillette wants to know now.

This selfish, stubborn girl, Sunny, would rather spend all her energy believing she is right and not asking questions, guaranteeing that no one finds out who she really is, not even herself.

And here's one more thing, something this girl would dearly love to know. At his last three ball games, he has spotted a boy standing by the box elders near the third-base line, in Gillette's line of sight from center field. He has been watching, quietly watching each ball game, almost blending in to the tree bark. A boy in Converse All Stars. A boy in high-top sneakers.

27

Wednesday, June 24, 1964

I am living in exile, I am reading *The Good Earth,* and I am suffocating.

I'm suffocating because O-lan smothers her baby right after she is born, because the whole family is starving and they can't afford to feed the second baby girl, as there is a famine throughout China, and everyone in the provinces is dirt-poor and starving. It breaks my heart. So I am suffocating, right along with second baby girl, and I am realizing my own great fortune to have been born, only baby girl, into a family of plenty. Relatively speaking.

If we *really* had plenty, Meemaw would have her whole house air-conditioned, so I am also suffocating because it's so dang hot in here I might just expire. If I expired, I wonder who would really miss me. Soon there will be a third baby girl in our family, and that means there will be less love and less plenty to go around and no one will even notice me anymore. Or maybe there will be a boy. Which would be even worse.

But right now, there's enough plenty. I lie on the cool wood floor of Meemaw's wide hallway as I read, and I drink an Orange Crush. Meemaw lines her whole refrigerator door with Orange Crushes each summer, and she allows me one whenever I visit. I have to remember kindnesses like this when Meemaw is snipping at me to be a better person, which is all the time.

I'm reading *The Good Earth* because it was on Meemaw's bookshelf in the boxy hallway that's big enough to be its own room, the hallway with the attic fan in the ceiling, the hallway where I try to stay cool enough not to expire, while Laura Mae shells lima beans on the back porch, and Meemaw naps away the hottest part of the day with the *Greenwood Commonwealth* over her face.

"Try this one," Meemaw had ordered as soon as I showed up at her house the day before yesterday. She thrust the book into my hands. "I know Pearl Buck."

Meemaw knows everybody. And that's part of the problem. She knows Miss Hazel Smith at the *Lexington Advertiser*. She calls her every Wednesday when the paper appears, to let her know that she got something wrong — usually it's her editorial "taking up for the coloreds" — or that something is misspelled. She's a stickler for correct reporting and good punctuation. "I wasn't a schoolteacher for forty-two years for nothing!" That's what she says, every Wednesday when she calls Miss Hazel.

Yesterday, on the first full day of my exile, Meemaw put on her Sunday dress and gloves and took me to the Greenwood Public Library because she had a luncheon to attend at the Confederate Memorial Building as a member of the Daughters of the Confederacy, and Laura Mae was at my house helping Annabelle fix up a bedroom for Boo. "I don't want you out of my sight," said Meemaw, which told me she knew about my trespassing at the pool, although we didn't discuss it.

That suited me fine, as the library, which is so close to the Confederate Memorial Building it's almost attached, is one of my favorite places in Greenwood. It's air-conditioned, too. I wandered the stacks. I learned that word — *stacks* — from Miss Cantrell, the librarian, who had a pile of books for me to decide about. I read an entire *Boys' Life* in my favorite comfortable chair, in the frosty quiet. When my mind got tired of words, I lay on the carpet in the picture book section and studied the mural on the walls, something I almost never take the time to look at anymore.

It's a painting that goes all the way across the children's section of the library, way up high, on three walls, even into the rounded corners, and it tells the story of cotton in Greenwood. When we went on a field trip to the library in third grade, we learned about how cotton is king in the Delta, and how this mural showed the whole process, from planting to chopping to picking, to taking the cotton in wagons from the gin to the giant compress in town where it gets baled, and then shipping it on boats and in boxcars, all over the world. It's our biggest business in Greenwood — Cotton Capitol of the World.

I stared at the Negroes under the vast blue sky of the mural, standing in the cotton fields, their long, white sacks bulging with the cotton bolls they're bending to pick. The white overseers are on horses, watching them, and I thought, *That's what it looks like at Uncle Vivian's plantation every September — an ocean of cotton, a wave of pickers, a great white-capped sea on the flat Delta land, as far as the eye can see.* Sometimes Uncle Vivian rides a horse, too, but mostly he drives his big, blue truck into the fields to check on things. The artist — I still remember her name: Miss Lalla Walker Lewis — got it just right.

Instead of going home after the luncheon, Meemaw took me to Goldberg's for a new pair of school shoes. When I protested, "But it's only June!" Meemaw came back with, "You can't expect that wife of your father's to have time for shoe shopping now," which at first I thought was a complaint, but then I decided was a little excuse for Meemaw to spend time doing things with me that Annabelle had taken over when she married Daddy and moved in with us.

Meemaw showed me off at Goldberg's, and then at the post office, where she stopped in to buy stamps and to tell Mrs.

Baylor she would be hosting bridge with her granddaughter's help on Wednesday, and I smiled like Pollyanna at Mrs. Baylor as she looked me over. I wondered if Meemaw was trying to say she was proud of me, or if she was trying to recover my reputation.

We walked down the steamy sidewalks of Greenwood together, me and Meemaw, perspiring in the afternoon sun, her with her big, brown purse in the crook of her elbow — and missing her nap for me — and me carrying my new shoes in their box, when a man approached us from the opposite direction and made Meemaw stiffen.

It was Mr. Byron De La Beckwith himself, dressed like a dandy and walking like a banty rooster, smiling and nodding to anyone whose eye he could reach. When he saw us take note of him he stopped walking, took off his hat, and bowed from the waist, a deep, exaggerated bow.

"How-do, Mrs. Rogers?" he said to my grandmother.

Meemaw reached down and took my hand in hers. "How are you, Delay," she said in a voice that meant she didn't want an answer.

Mr. Delay blocked the sidewalk with his bow, with his arm extended to the curb, his hat in his hand going out even farther, and Meemaw was both annoyed and anxious. I pictured Polly's story of Mr. Delay and his gun in church and wondered if he had it in his suit pocket right now. He didn't look even mildly hot as he said, "Your beautiful granddaughter, I presume?"

Meemaw held my hand tighter and said, in a not-unpleasant voice, "Yes, this is Jamie's daughter, I'm sure you know." She didn't mention my name, and she gave me the tiniest shove with her clasped hand that led me to try to take a step around Mr. Delay.

"And Miranda's daughter, too, of course," said Mr. Delay. "How *is* Miranda? Where does she make her home now?"

You'd have thought Meemaw had been slapped. She swayed a bit — I could tell because I was holding her hand — and acted like she was going to have to take a step back, but she didn't. "Of course," she said in a sure, clipped voice. "Miranda's daughter, too. Excuse us, Delay."

But Mr. Delay ignored us wanting to get around him. "My, my how you've grown, young lady!" he said to me, tipping his hat back onto his head. "How old are you, now, sugar? And how is your *daddy*, may I ask? And his lovely bride? How is his *business* faring?" His tone of voice was syrupy sweet, but it was laced with something terrible.

I didn't want to say one word, and Meemaw didn't give me time. She pushed harder with her hand and I took a step that landed me off the curb and into the street near a parked car.

"We're all just fine, Delay." Meemaw even forced a smile as she began to steer me around him. "I'm afraid we're late for an appointment. It's good to see you looking well. Good afternoon to you."

And with that, Meemaw followed me around Mr. Delay and we were soon past him and at Meemaw's car, where we scrambled into it like we were being chased by Martians in *The Angry Red Planet*. Meemaw started the engine and we gunned it out of the parking place and all the way home.

She didn't say a word about it, so neither did I, but when nighttime rolled around and I was in my pajamas and fresh from my bath, wet hair and all, Meemaw came into my bedroom to tell me good night. I was in bed, with *The Good Earth* on my nightstand next to the three postcards I took from Mary Margaret's. I was supposed to take one. The picture of my mother was under my mattress. I had two fans blowing on me, but they just shoved the hot air around. The fact that I was wet helped.

Meemaw sat on the edge of my bed. With her thumb and index finger she delicately lifted stray hairs from my forehead, one after the other, and rolled them behind my left ear.

"How's your book?" She picked it up and opened it to a random page.

"Sad," I said. "Just plain sad."

"It gets better," she said. She smelled like butterscotch candies. She always has one in her mouth if she's not sleeping or eating. "Keeps the moisture in," she always says.

I nodded. "Thank you for the shoes, and for our afternoon." I wanted her to know I noticed her attentions.

"You're welcome, sweet girl."

My heart melted. It was an invitation. "What was she like?" I asked.

Here is the story Meemaw told me:

It rained for seventeen days straight in Lavatek, Alabama, before the day I was born. The dirt roads were slop and the cotton crop was threatened. On the eighteenth day of rain, as the clouds parted and the September sun lathered itself like soap over that steamy coal-mining town, here I came.

"Was Daddy a coal miner?"

"For a little while, but coal was playing out in Alabama. They lived in a company town, and lived a . . . common . . . life. He thought . . . I don't know what he thought. It didn't work out. Your father ran off with my daughter — your mother — against my wishes."

I licked my lips. "It broke your heart," I said.

"Yes."

"Were they in love?" I whisper it.

Meemaw takes a deep breath and sighs in such a way that her lips pop and her cheeks puff out. "I think they were, yes."

It was hard for her to say this to me, and maybe it was hard to say to herself, too.

My father tiptoed into the coal company hospital room where my mother, propped against pillows, beautiful after birth, held me in her arms. She wore a lacy, blue bed jacket tied in the front with a white silk ribbon. Her face was streaked with happy tears. Mama and Daddy took turns cradling me and gazing into my big, brown eyes — they didn't know what to make of this miracle they had so unexpectedly been blessed with.

I interrupted again. "And Mama sang to me. 'Twinkle, Twinkle, Little Star.'"

"Yes," said Meemaw. Her eyes had delicate tears in them now. "Then she said, 'What shall we name her, Jamie?' while at the same time your daddy pointed out the window and said, 'Look, Miranda, it's sunny!' And so, just like that, you became . . . Sunny."

I want to believe this story. It's the story Meemaw told me even though she wasn't there. It's the story Daddy won't talk about.

I was itching to pull the photograph out from under my mattress. I wanted to tell Meemaw about the girl who looks so much like her Miranda. But I sensed the invitation time was closing. And I needed to know something else.

"What does Mr. Delay want?" I asked.

"Pay him no never-mind," said Meemaw. "That's just who Delay is and always has been."

"He doesn't like Daddy," I said.

"Shhhhh," said Meemaw. "Your daddy can take care of himself."

"He upset you," I said, meaning Mr. Delay, but maybe Meemaw thought I meant Daddy.

"I've been upset before," said Meemaw.

"You were upset when Mama left," I offered, even though what I wanted to ask was *Why didn't she come back with Daddy? What happened?* But I was afraid to go that far.

"Yes," said Meemaw. "I was upset. But look what gift she brought me. You."

Which goes to show you. You never know about a person. You just never know.

28

I know all they strange names now. Willie Peacock, Sam Block, Bob Moses, Bob Zellner, Dewey Greene, Stokely Carmichael, Casey Hayden, Annelle Ponder, Linda Wetmore, Sally Belfrage, Eli Zaretsky, Monroe Sharp. I lie on my pallet on the floor at midnight, stare at the moon out the window, and spell out all the names I can remember, even Yellow-Hair Jo Ellen, and they put me right to sleep. They from Mississippi, they from everywhere else. They walkin' the streets of Colored Town, registerin' voters for the MFDP. They SNCCs, COREs, NAACPers. And they all COFOs this summer, but that don't matter to me. What matter is they love meetin's and I hate meetin's. I want to DO something. Where this revolution? That's what I ask Twill and Jimmy and Simon.

Stories from the pulpit, every Sunday, from mass meetings every week.

Reverend Johnson shout, "For one hundred years, slavery has been illegal, and yet we are still slaves!"

Reverend Ebbie say, "They ain't no jobs up north! That's just something they say to get rid of you, now that they don't need so many of you to pick their cotton, now that they've got tractors to do it for them. Don't go! Stay here and fight for your rights!"

Reverend Tucker say, "President Johnson WILL sign into law the Civil Rights Act of 1964, and we NEED to be ready! We NEED to continue to go to the courthouse and register to vote! Sign a pledge to go to the courthouse, and take home a bag of groceries! Let's help one another, brothers and sisters. Let us pray."

They's dozens of Freedom Righters now, living with folks dotted all over Baptist Town and Gritney. Even in Gee Pee. They come to church with us, sing with us. Can't get shed of 'em anywhere. I think they plan it that way.

Pap and Ma'am not speakin'. Ma'am lose her job ironing for Deputy Davis family, but she still holding her head up high. Last night she make hot water corn bread and cabbage and fried a fat rabbit Scarecrow Magee brought her. "I registered, Miss Libby!" he say.

"Come on in and eat with us!" Ma'am beam. She make 'mirations all over Scarecrow Magee, a man who gots only three teeth in his head and less brains.

Yellow-Hair Miss Jo Ellen and Blue-Hair Miss Vera stay out of Pap's way. But SNCC Bob visit Pap every day and say the same thing: "Mr. Bullis, it's your right as an American citizen to vote. If you vote, you can change things. If enough of you vote, you can elect a new sheriff, you can elect yourselves, you can change this town."

Pap coming to the door with his rifle in his hands now.

"This is a nonviolent movement, sir," say SNCC Eli. His hands shake around his clipboard full of register papers.

"Then you move your New York nonviolent white feets off my front porch!" say Pap. "Both of yous!"

SNCC Bob look at me. "We've got the new issue of *Jet* at the Freedom House," he say. "Willie Mays is on the cover. You can listen to the baseball games on the radio, too, anytime. Come help us — we've got plenty for you to DO."

Ain't doin' nothin', watching Ma'am and Pap spit at each other, working on the farm at Browning for Aunt Geneva, pickin' up odd jobs some days. Pap won't let me chop cotton. Nothin' but the heat to keep me company, and not even Twill and Simon to play ball with, now that they at the Freedom House most every day. So I swallow and march off the porch with SNCC Bob and SNCC Eli, Pap yellin', "You come back here, Raymond!" and Ma'am saying, "You let him go!" At the Freedom House, SNCC Bob say to SNCC Stokely and CORE Sandy, "We can't keep them from guns. It's legal, and they've always carried them."

That the truth. Pap always say, "The whites know we got our rifles, and we'll use 'em. They shoot into my house, I'm gonna shoot right back. It keeps 'em scared of us." Scarecrow say, "How else I gon' shoot rabbits?"

29

Saturday, July 4, 1964

So my exile wasn't as bad as I thought it would be. Still, for two weeks I have felt like Frankenstein's monster, lying under that heavy gray sheet on a cold steel table, waiting for the great ray that first brought life into the world. But in two more days — the day after tomorrow — there will be lightning and thunder above me, the sheet will be rolled off, the bandages taken away, the dials turned, and — *it's alive!* — I will go to the movies! And the pool! All in the same day. I have it all planned out.

We are having a cookout today with Polly's family, in honor of Independence Day, but I consider it a party to welcome me back to my regular summer routines, including the pool and the Leflore Theater. Parnell said he'd kept my favorite seat warm for me, and he would buy me popcorn, licorice, and a Dr Pepper. *He loves me, yeah, yeah, yeah.* I wave at him whenever I walk by the Leflore, which is every day, and sometimes I take him a tuna fish sandwich I made myself, just because he is so good to me. Sometimes I see Randy Smithers standing at the ticket booth in his uniform, talking to Parnell. I wave at him, too. He's coming to the cookout today. I'm glad Parnell has found a new friend, and I wonder if he has any regular clothes.

We invited Meemaw to the cookout, too, but she won't come. I asked her why and she told me a long-winded story about her great-great-uncles who were killed at the Battle of Vicksburg during the Civil War. So that's that.

I've been smothering under a heavy, gray sheet because that's what it feels like to be grounded for two weeks. Not that there weren't good things. Like reading in the Greenwood Library all morning — I read every book about adventure I could find. Like lunch at Polly's most days because I didn't want to be near Annabelle or Boo or Gillette, who, it turns out, couldn't go to the pool or movies, either, but that didn't seem to faze him.

Gillette's not planning a big comeback like I am. I've decided that Gillette is an inward boy. He seemed satisfied to spend his grounded time listening to ball games on the radio and oiling his glove, going to practice, and playing ball games I didn't go to.

Gillette and I don't speak, not even about the high-top boy — High-top. Once, when I was feeling my most snippy about Gillette's betrayal, and because it's hard work not speaking to people you used to like, Gillette came out on the side porch, where I was reading *Robinson Crusoe* while lying in the porch swing, and I said, "Well, well, if it isn't Tom Terrific and Mighty Manfred the Wonder Dog!"

"Shut up." That's what Gillette said, without even looking at me. He said, "C'mon, Ruth." And the old dog scribbled down the porch steps and off to practice with Gillette. That dog sleeps with Gillette and spends every waking moment by his side. She has started to fill out and isn't quite so bony anymore, but she still moves like she has the arthritis, except when she's barking at bicycles.

Annabelle has filled out, too. Suddenly her cheeks have color again and she doesn't boo-hoo at the drop of a hat, and she spends long days with her mother, the always-talking Boo — washing curtains and cooking dinner and planning a nursery — that's what I heard her call it. A nursery for the baby. We have seven bedrooms in this big, old house, three on a third floor nobody ever went to but Parnell, because his room has always been up there. Most of the bedrooms were all closed up, the whole time I was a little girl. Now, one by one, they've been opened again, cobwebs dusted, broken-down old furniture removed, floors and walls scrubbed clean and painted, windows washed, curtains sewn and hung, and Audrey underfoot, into every bit of it with Annabelle, as excited as she is. I escape at every opportunity.

Boo is my cross to bear. She makes escape difficult. I can't get away from her, or her Vicks-y smell, no matter where I turn. "Won't you eat something, Sunny, dear? I brought my jars of peach pickle with me from Philadelphia. They won a prize in last year's Neshoba County Fair!"

"No, thank you," I tell her. "I'm on a hunger strike." I'm not, of course. It just makes me feel good to say that to Boo, who, it turns out, won't tell on me. She is like Annabelle in that way, or Annabelle is like her, I guess. I only talk to Annabelle when I have to and she knows it.

Daddy knows it, too, which is why, during my Frankenstein days, he took me to the store with him after lunch except Wednesdays, since all the stores in Greenwood close after lunch on Wednesdays. "Everyone has a siesta!" says Boo. Then she sips something purple in a tiny glass and siestas herself to a nap.

Some afternoons, I stayed at Fairchild's until closing, at six o'clock. I sat in the back and read all the comic books I wanted from the magazine rack while Daddy closed out the registers and put the money in the safe for the night. Isaiah Nixon mopped the floors after closing and he'd just mop right around me, with his giant bucket and mop, as I read my magazines and waited for Daddy to be done. "No need to move, Miss Sunny," he'd say, so I wouldn't.

Sometimes Annabelle and Audrey met Daddy at the store before closing. Daddy tripped the switch on the pony out front so Audrey could ride it all she wanted without putting in any coins, and sometimes Audrey would let Daddy ride her home in his truck after Daddy showed Annabelle more about the bookkeeping. Sometimes Ruth wandered off from the ball field or the house and showed up at the store, all shaggy and hot and begging for water and a treat, her tongue hanging out like she was about to expire. We put her in the truck with Daddy and we all went home for the supper that Laura Mae kept warm for us.

Gillette banged in late from practice or a baseball game — now that it's high baseball season and there are so many boys on so many teams, there's a game to play in or a game to watch almost every night. I don't go to any of them.

I learned how to make the signs Daddy painted each week that advertised the specials: BANANAS 10 CENTS A POUND! IMPORTED FROM HAWAII, OUR NEWEST STATE! I sat next to the adding machine at Daddy's desk in his office, with tempera paints and poster board, and painted pineapples and green beans and bunches of broccoli and then set out the signs where Daddy told me to. I got good at it.

Mr. Arnold, who is in charge of the bakery, gave me a fresh jelly doughnut whenever I made new signs for the bakery department. My fingers would be sticky all afternoon, even after I'd washed them.

Mrs. Murchison even complimented my work one Saturday and I smiled at her, as if nothing unusual had passed between us, as if we'd never met in her office with Negroes and Freedom Workers, too, as if she'd never said, *They have their own churches!* and then walked across the hall and called the police.

* * *

One day, Pastor Marshall's wife came to shop in the store with two of her children. She wore her gloves and a hat and held her head up high, like she was practicing perfect posture. The air in Fairchild's, which always smells like bacon and lettuces and yeasty bread and sawdust and air-conditioning in the summer, was laced with the smell of uncertainty then, and there was a hush from some of the white customers — you could feel it. It was a bristly feeling.

We have been to church every Sunday since Pastor Marshall's beatituding sermon, and we will be there tomorrow. Something has changed in church, too. Greetings are formal and polite. People sit down too quickly and they don't linger after. There aren't as many glad handshakes. The air feels unsettled. Even the hymns are less enthusiastic. I wonder if we are all confused.

So I watched people come in and out of Fairchild's these past two weeks, because that's what Daddy said we were going to do, watch. Here is what I observed:

There are just as many Negro customers as there are white, maybe more, as our store is located on the edge of Colored Town. Also because it's a good store. Negro employees, who have worked for my daddy forever, cut open the boxes and stamp the cans with prices in purple ink and keep the shelves stocked. They make boxes for the cakes in the bakery. They keep the meat department clean, and they put produce back into the walk-in coolers at closing every day.

Only white employees work the registers and I know them all: Mrs. Maple, Mr. Crenshaw, Mr. Lewis. The butcher, Mr. Nethery, is white. So is Mr. Arnold, the baker. So is our produce manager, Mr. Waycross. Negroes bag groceries right next to me and Gillette when we help bag, and we know them all by name. I've known them all my remembered life: Isaiah and Joe and Porter and Thaddeus. They laugh and joke with Daddy and call him Mr. Jamie. "Yessir, Mr. Jamie." We have one bathroom and we all use it. We have one drinking fountain, and we all drink out of it. These are the things I noticed while I was grounded.

These are things I didn't talk about with Polly and Mary Margaret during my Frankenstein days, but we had plenty of other things to discuss. The three of us found the just-right branches under the magnolias at the courthouse — where I retrieved my bike — and climbed higher and became more sure of ourselves as we established our new secret clubhouse, the new George. We climbed wearing our Beatles wigs and clutching a *16 Magazine* each, which we tore to shreds in our climbing efforts.

"Another new album! This month! And the movie in August!" shouted Polly from her branch.

"Oh, we'll have to go to Joe's Records to get it!" shouted Mary Margaret from her branch, breathless. Then, "I have to tell you girls, this is a lot of work." She brushed bits of bark off her pants.

"I know!" Polly shouted. "On both counts!"

"I know!" I agreed, situating myself with my back against the tree's mighty trunk. "I'll find out from Parnell when the movie comes to the Leflore so we can go see it together!" I didn't tell them I've bicycled past the Leflore almost every day and have seen High-top there three times, standing across the street at the light pole at the Texaco service station, near the gas pumps, hands on his hips, staring at the ticket booth.

We sang "A Hard Day's Night" at the top of our lungs, or at least what we could remember — we're still learning it, as the record album just came out.

So there were good things about the Frankenstein days. And there were not-so-good things.

Meemaw canceled Sunday dinners when Boo moved in with us. I didn't see Uncle Vivian for two whole weeks. I missed him. I overheard snippets of conversations between Daddy and Annabelle, and I tried to listen in when I heard Annabelle say, "I know it's a risk, but I think it's important," but Daddy knew I was there and gave me a job to do.

I climbed up to George by myself some mornings. I watched for Jo Ellen but never saw her at the courthouse. I did see Negroes picketing the courthouse one day, with some ministers — they wore their minister collars — walking back and forth quietly with signs that said FREEDOM NOW and ONE MAN, ONE VOTE. I itched to get closer, but Daddy had told me I couldn't go to the courthouse, and I obeyed him.

Chief Lary shouted through a megaphone at the pickets and told them they couldn't be more than ten people — I counted seventeen — and they had to be over eighteen, and from Leflore County. Then a bunch of other policemen came out and arrested some of them.

This was shocking to me, and I didn't tell anyone, even though one of the protestors was Pastor Marshall and I saw another white minister, too. Neither of them were arrested.

After that, I couldn't move for a long time. I considered how there were now a lot of things I wasn't telling anyone, and I didn't know how long I could keep this up, or why I was holding on to all of it. Then the courthouse clock struck twelve and the mysterious Westminster chimes began to ring through me, and I felt how small I was in the big, confusing world, and yet how connected I was to everything vibrating around me, and somehow — I don't know how — that made me feel better.

Eight SNCC field workers including Bob Moses, director of the Mississippi Voter Registration Project of COFO, and James Forman, Executive Director of the Student Nonviolent Coordinating Committee, were released from Leflore County jail, where they were being held on charges of disturbing the peace and disorderly conduct. The eight men were arrested . . . while walking with a group of Negroes who sought to register.

Upon their release, this morning the eight issued the following statement:

WE MAINTAIN THAT UNDER THE LAWS AND CONSTITUTION OF THE UNITED STATES THAT WE HAVE A RIGHT TO ENCOURAGE PEOPLE TO VOTE. WE FURTHER HOLD THAT PEOPLE HAVE A RIGHT TO PEACEFULLY WALK TO THEIR COUNTY COURTHOUSE, ESCORTED BY WHOMEVER THEY CHOOSE. WE MAINTAIN THAT ANY LAW ENFORCEMENT OFFICER HAS THE OBLIGATION TO PROTECT ALL CITIZENS FROM HARM AND ESPECIALLY PEOPLE WHO WANT TO REGISTER TO VOTE

THEREFORE WE WILL CONTINUE TO WALK WITH PEOPLE TO THE COURTHOUSE FOR THE PURPOSE OF VOTER REGISTRATION, AND WE CALL UPON THE CITY POLICE OF GREENWOOD NOT TO INTERFERE WITH THIS DUTY WE ARE PERFORMING FOR OUR COUNTRY.

IF THERE SHOULD BE A POTENTIAL DANGER TO OUR SAFETY WE ASK THE POLICE TO ARREST THOSE WHO WOULD HARM US AND NOT TO ARREST US. SHOULD THEY TRY TO STOP OUR ORDERLY, PEACEFUL AND QUIET WALK TO THE COUNTY COURTHOUSE, THEN WE HAVE NO OTHER ALTERNATIVE THAN TO GO TO JAIL, ONCE, TWICE, OR AS MANY TIMES

AS NECESSARY TO OBTAIN THE RIGHT OF OUR PEOPLE TO VOTE.

— From the UPI clippings and journals of Sara Criss, Greenwood Bureau Chief for the Memphis *Commercial Appeal*, summer 1964

30

Me and Twill and Jimmy and Simon. What we do with these SNCCs?

Only so many boxes we can unpack. Only so many magazines to read.

Blacks in some these magazines nuthin' like the black folks I know.

None of 'em lives in Mississippi.

All of 'em rides Greyhound, wears fancy clothes and shoes and watches, buys fancy refrigerators, plays golf. Golf!

Then I see it. They's a story in *Ebony* about a minister in Cleveland, Ohio, got crushed to death under a bulldozer 'cause he was standin' there, with a bunch of other folks, tryin' to stop that bulldozer from building a segregated school . . . a school just for white kids.

And he a white man. In Ohio. Reverend Bruce Klunder.

All the other protestors black.

I stare and stare at that page, those terrible pictures.

Pictures of black folks in a ditch, daring that bulldozer to dump dirt on them, cover them up.

Picture of Reverend Bruce Klunder in front of that bulldozer, dead. Dead.

His wife say, don't be afraid of no conflict, don't run away from violence. She say, waitin' around for evolution too slow! We need a revolution. Now.

I throw that magazine on the floor. There ain't no revolution in this Freedom House.

Ain't no bulldozers here. Just floors for me to sweep while I listen to the ball game on the radio. Just papers, forms, clipboards, telephones, two-way radios in SNCC cars so's Greenwood operators can't listen in on phone calls, just sweaty volunteers with typewriters, books upstairs in the library and Freedom School, where Yellow-Hair Jo Ellen teachin' African history, black history to Ree and bunches of kids who show up every day.

What good all that?

CORE Sandy pick up my magazine and look at Reverend Bruce Klunder.

"He was one of us," he say. "A CORE volunteer, through and through. Only twenty-seven years old. He had two children." He take off his straw hat and shake his head.

"I want to DO something," that's what I say.

"We do something every time we register another voter in the state of Mississippi," say CORE Sandy. "Don't you realize that? Registering to vote is direct action! Come out with me today and see how it's done."

"I seen it!" I spit. "I seen you come to my door, and my pap ready to shoot you!"

"Lots of people are afraid," say CORE Sandy. "But they sign up anyway. It's the only way we'll change the law in Mississippi."

"Look like the law ain't so good in Ohio, neither," I say.

"It takes all of us working together," say CORE Sandy. "We're doing spade work, Ray, that's what it is, digging, digging, digging, a little at a time."

"You won't let us go to the courthouse," I say. "You won't let us protest. What else can we do?"

"You're not old enough for that yet," say Sandy. "But you will be, soon. There's no need for you to get arrested yet."

"Maybe they is," I say. "I quit. Simon! Jimmy! Twill! Let's go!"

We talk it over. We gon' make our own council. We gon' call ourselves

The FreedomMakers.

31

Monday, July 6, 1964

It's before six o'clock when I wake up on my freedom day, but the sunlight is streaming into my room in that early-morning-sunbeam way it has of being brilliantly, brightly sunny but not yet hot. Bits of dust dance in the light, particles I can't see without the sunbeams showing them off. I used to think they were fairy dust.

Sunbeams always make me think of that Sunday school song I sang when I was a little girl. I lie there with my eyes closed and hum the tune, sing the words in my head, and pretend I'm six again, when just me, Daddy, and Parnell lived in this house and everything was simple, and I always knew just what to do.

Jesus wants me for a sunbeam
to shine for him each day
In every way try to please him
At home, at school, at play.

A sunbeam! A sunbeam!
Jesus wants me for a sunbeam!
A sunbeam! A sunbeam!
I'll be a sunbeam for him.

Jesus wants me to be loving
And kind to all I see

Showing how pleasant and happy
His little one can be

A sunbeam! A sunbeam!
Jesus wants me for a sunbeam!
A sunbeam! A sunbeam!
I'll be a sunbeam for him.

Then I listen to the sun. You can hear sunbeams if you get very still and listen carefully enough. They make a quiet, insistent sound, like they are trying very hard to do their very important job, and would, if you would just let them do it. I lie in my bed and let the sunbeams bathe my closed eyes, cover my soft cheeks, and warm my crooked little heart.

I will never be a sunbeam. It's not in me. I think I knew this, even when I was six.

I don't even know what *good* means. Loving and kind in all I see? Pleasant and happy? Even the sun can't be pleasant and loving all the time. It hasn't rained here in weeks, and people's gardens are shriveling. The cotton is baking. The fields are cracking like the Sahara Desert. Uncle Vivian and all the other farmers in the Delta must be worried. There's a fine coating of dust on everything in this heat with no rain. My lips are even coated with it when I come in from outside.

My doorknob rattles. I have taken to locking my door ever since Gillette betrayed me. I can tell by the kind of rattle it is that it's Audrey.

"Just a minute!" Audrey is the best thing that's happened to our house. She is the most honest person I know. She slips her sweet arms around my waist for a sleepy hug and murmurs, "You are swimmy today, Sunny!" and I laugh.

"Are you going, too?" I ask.

"I have school?" she says it like a question, just like Annabelle used to do.

"Not yet," I say. "Two more months." I hold out the fingers on one hand. "Not long."

Audrey sighs. "Can I get in your bed?" I let her. I tuck my sheet around her as she sighs a little-girl sigh, shoves her long hair out of her face, looks at me with sleepy eyes, and whispers, "I miss my daddy," like she's telling me a big secret.

I am surprised at that, but I suppose she would miss her daddy, even if he's not a good person. "You can share mine, if you want to," I whisper, but she doesn't answer me.

Audrey curls into a ball under the sheet, letting the sunbeams play over her little self, while I go down the hall to the bathroom to brush my teeth and put on my bathing suit. The pool doesn't open until one o'clock, after lunch, after swim practice and swim lessons, but I want to announce to everybody that things are back to normal and I am back in business. I need to send Polly a note, but it can wait until Audrey leaves.

When I come back to my room, Ruth is curled against Audrey — they are spread out together, soft and snugged up to each other, like butter on toast, and the two of them are sleeping in my bed. Audrey has her head buried in the back of Ruth's neck, and her arm draped around Ruth's skinny middle. Ruth's graying snout is on my pillow. She opens one lazy eye, sees that it's me, and closes it again. Her tail thumps once to let me know she's seen me.

I take my blue sundress with the daisies off the peg behind my bedroom door, pull it over my suit, and tiptoe out of my room. I close the door ever so quietly behind me.

The sunbeams are doing their job.

32

I slip on my Keds, grab my bike where I left it against the porch, and start pedaling. I careen right, onto the sidewalk, and head to town. I'm going to say hello to my pool, even though it's not yet open.

I feel *that good.*

The city drains the water out of the pool every Sunday and refills it before opening again on Monday. I'll say hello now, and then I'll be back, waiting at one o'clock, and I'll be one of the first people to jump into that clean, sparkling, cold water I've missed so much. I'm going to do a cannonball off the diving board.

Hello, you! That's what I'll say when I get to the fence. *Have you missed me? Last time I was here, it didn't go so well, did it? I'm sorry I screamed. Bet I scared you to death. Scared me, too. Did you know there was a colored boy in your water? Don't worry — I haven't told anybody.*

I ride past the back of the courthouse, where the county jail stands three stories high. Did the pickets go to jail? They must have. Are they still there? How long does someone have to stay in jail for picketing?

This is enough to destroy my good mood. Immediately, I decide to sing for the prisoners, just in case they're in there. I want them to know, I understand what it's like to lose your freedom and be in exile. I'll sing because it's over and I don't want it to happen again. I can't be a sunbeam, but I can obey the law, and I will.

This is a good place to sing because the Yazoo is on my left, and so is the bridge into North Greenwood, and the jail is on my right, but there aren't any houses for me to wake up, so I serenade the prisoners and the policemen — I wonder if Deputy Davis is working. Who cares! — with "Oh, What a Beautiful Mornin'," the song we sang in chorus for this year's sixth grade graduation. It's one of my favorites.

I glide past the jail and courthouse parking lot singing. Two Negro workers are painting a school bus black in the parking lot. One is lettering the side of the bus with *Greenwood Police.* He waves his brush at me in a friendly way, and I wave back and launch right into the third verse, which is my favorite: *All the sounds of the earth are like music!* Because they are. The birds are singing with me.

Then my big finish: *I've got a beautiful feeling, everything's going my way!*

Yes sirree it is. I've done my time, and now I'm free. I sing for those who are still prisoners, and for the lazy old Yazoo, and for the beautiful bridge over the Yazoo, and maybe even to show off to Deputy Davis that he doesn't have any power over me anymore. I spent a whole morning picking up after Greenwood's litterbugs two weeks ago, and that's that. I have paid my debt to society.

I turn right onto Fulton and pass a row of magnolias, but not the ones where George is. George is in the magnolia row on the opposite side of the block. I reach the corner where the Confederate monument stands tall and I blow it a kiss. I stay on Fulton Street and realize I've decided to visit the Leflore as well.

I haven't been able to look at the Leflore Theater without an ache since I've been grounded. Two blocks up and I am filled with glee when I see it, its marquee dark but readable.

The Moon-Spinners
starring
Hayley Mills

I love Hayley Mills. She's only a few years older than I am. She was so good in *The Parent Trap* and *Pollyanna*, and now here's another Hayley Mills movie. How lucky that I didn't have to miss it.

The sun warms my shoulders and soon I smell the streets of town — gasoline and oil and rubber from tires, and a tar smell, a newspaper smell, and some sort of suds from somewhere. I fancy I can even smell the buttery popcorn leftover from yesterday's movies at the Leflore. *Soon*, I tell it, as I zoom past. *Soon. I'll see you later tonight.* There are service stations on the three corners opposite the Leflore, and they are all closed. Soon enough, cars will pull in for gas and an attendant in a snappy uniform will fill up the tank, check the oil, and wash the windshield. Parnell had that job when he was in high school.

Everything is closed up at this hour, but there are signs of life everywhere.

A police car cruises by me and I wave. I get a curious wave back. Nothing to fear here! No unrest as far as the eye can see. We're all safe and sound. And I'm an A-number-one citizen again. A Negro taxi goes by with a Negro maid in it, wearing her uniform, on the way to work. Laura Mae might pass me any minute — she comes to work in a taxi each morning, and Daddy drives her home at night, even if she has been over at Meemaw's. A big stake-bed truck rumbles by, Negroes spilling out of it, on their way to work at a plantation for the day.

Cars trickle into town, some heading west, toward the Buckeye, where the cotton seed is turned into oil, and the Coca-Cola plant, where you can stand outside any day but

Sunday and stare in the big window and watch Coca-Cola bottles ride by on the big conveyor belts. Some cars head south toward the cotton compress.

A train whistles as it draws close to the crossing. I've watched in September, when the trains pick up thousands of bales of cotton from the compress — some of it Uncle Vivian's — and the whole town of Greenwood is filled with tiny cotton wisps that drift on the tiniest breeze and catch on telephone poles and car wipers and window ledges, as the compress works through the fall, until frost, baling the cotton that the pickers have picked and the cotton farmers have brought in on their giant wagons. A truck won't be big enough for the workers that will be needed in the fall to bring in the harvest — they'll send buses, then.

I turn onto Wright Place and see the front entrance of the pool straight ahead of me as Wright Place hits Cotton Street. "There it is! Oh, I have missed you," I whisper. But I'm brought up short by the cars that pull up in front of the pool just as the gate comes into view. One of them is the police car I saw earlier.

Three men get out of their cars with signs and hammers. I edge myself next to a shade tree across from the electric company and watch the men hammer the signs into fence posts beside the front gates and at the corners of the chain-link. One of the men says, "Community center, too," and another says something I can't hear, and then they are gone.

As soon as the cars are out of sight, I sprint to the gate to read the signs.

POOL CLOSED

UNTIL FURTHER NOTICE

BY ORDER OF GREENWOOD POLICE DEPT

AND MAYOR'S OFFICE

I peer through the chain-link and see that the pool hasn't been refilled after its Sunday emptying. I grab my bike and start pedaling furiously down Cotton Street, across the railroad tracks, and left onto Johnson Street. I am out of breath, and everything I see is a blur. My mind is racing, racing.

A clutch of men are gathered outside Angelo's, talking with their hands on their hips and their voices full of feeling. Some are drinking coffee in white mugs, the steam spiraling out into the sour morning. Daddy comes here for coffee with his friends before Fairchild's opens for business, so I glide my bike to a stop and lean it against the corner of the store.

"Excuse me," I interrupt, breathless. "Is my daddy inside?"

"Here he comes right now, little lady," says Dr. Norwood, nodding toward the Howard Street corner.

"Thank you!" I rush to meet Daddy, to tell him all about it. But he already knows.

"Sunny, go home. I'll be there for noon dinner, and we'll talk about it."

"But —"

"Home. Now."

I watch the men greet Daddy and him greet them back. There's a gruffness in everyone's voice, and Daddy disappears into Angelo's. The men watch me as I get my bike and walk it away from the store and up the sidewalk. I hear Dr. Norwood say, "Disgrace . . ." And another man say, ". . . over my dead body." It's all so terribly unfriendly. I run alongside my bike until I can jump on and pedal furiously for home.

So much for my beautiful morning.

We urge business owners affected by the Civil Rights Bill to resist its enforcement by all lawful means. We will support anyone involved in litigation for refusal to serve Negroes. You will have the backing of this community including financial assistance from the White Citizens Legal Fund. . . . We call upon every citizen in this community white and colored to join with us in giving no aid or comfort by word or deed to the advocation of forced integration.

— Statement from the Executive Committee of the Greenwood Citizens' Council, July 1964

"Our police force always maintained law and order and will continue to do so, but we cannot be expected to help the federal government integrate public places."

— Mayor Charles Sampson, Greenwood, Mississippi, 1964

33

When I get home, I jump off my bike, race up the back porch steps, and jerk the kitchen screen door so hard it slaps back against the house. Laura Mae is alone in the kitchen, taking bacon out of the cast-iron skillet with a long fork. Suddenly I'm starving. I hug Laura Mae and she hugs me back absentmindedly.

"There, there, Miss Sunny," she says.

"They've closed the pool, Laura Mae! Why?"

Laura Mae uses her body to push me away from her enough to make sure the bacon grease won't pop on me. "Now, Miss Sunny," she says, "you know that pool don't open until after noon dinner."

"No, it's closed! For good! I saw the signs. Until further notice!"

Laura Mae says, "I don't know about decisions like that. You get your breakfast?"

I shake my head.

"Put some bread in the toaster. I'll make you some eggs, just the way you like 'em. This will be the last breakfast I make for you in this house."

I open the bag of Sunbeam Bread. "Why?"

"You got a new maid comin'." Laura Mae says it quietly, like she doesn't want to upset me, but needs to tell me something. "I'm going back to Miss Eloise, all the time. She needs me."

"She doesn't need you at all!" I say. "Not like I do!"

Laura Mae breaks eggs into a bowl and begins to whisk them together. "Well, it's decided," she says. "I hates to leave you, but you'll be over to visit me at your meemaw's, I 'spect, just like old times. You growing up. You got you a mama now."

"I have no such thing!" I protest. "Annabelle's making you go! I hate her!"

Annabelle walks into the kitchen. I know she heard me. "Where's the hot-water bottle, Laura Mae?" she asks.

"It be under the 'lectric blanket in the hall closet, Miss Annabelle," says Laura Mae. My toast pops up and I put it on a plate without looking at Annabelle. I start buttering it as I go silent.

Boo walks into the kitchen with a thermometer. "A hundred and two. We should call the doctor. Will he make a house call?"

"I think so," says Annabelle. "I've never asked before."

"Dr. Norwood will come," I say, "if you call him early and ask Miss Slater to put you on the list. Who's sick?" I think of Dr. Norwood at Angelo's just minutes ago. *Disgrace.*

"Thank goodness," says Annabelle. "Thank you, Sunny, I'll call him right away. Audrey has a stomachache and a fever." She leaves to call the doctor's office.

The skillet sizzles as Laura Mae pours in my eggs and starts stirring. Boo says, "What a good help you are, Sunny!" Then she looks at my outfit. "Going swimming? Can I come? I've got a suit!"

"No, ma'am," I say. "Nobody's going swimming. The pool is closed today."

"Suit yourself!" Boo laughs at her own joke as she leaves the kitchen.

I would never take her to the pool with me. We took her to Sunday dinner at the Crystal Grill and Boo talked through the entire meal like she'd recently been let out of prison and had had no one to talk to for years. I had to show her where the bathroom was, and on the way she talked to the colored help in the kitchen, washing the dishes. She told Mr. Liollio her entire life story while Daddy was paying the bill, and Mr. Liollio is from Greece and hardly speaks English. She ordered two pieces of mile-high pie — the coconut and the lemon ice box. We all just sat there, smiling and nodding, and sometimes we could work in, "Pass the butter, please."

"It's Mr. Jamie's decision," says Laura Mae, getting back to our conversation. She dishes my eggs onto my toast plate and puts two pieces of bacon next to them. "That Miss Annabelle, she not so bad."

"She's terrible," I say. "And she's not my mother."

Laura Mae has nothing to say about that. "You need all-day help now, with all these people in this house, and I can't give you that. I already raised up two generations of babies — I got the gray hairs and bad back to prove it — and I'm too old to raise another. Be easier for me out at Miss Eloise, and easier for her, too. She wants me."

"I want you, too," I tell her.

"I know, honey girl. And I want you. You come see me all the time, hear? Ain't nothin' changed between us." She puts my plate on the table and says, "Eat. That brother of yours already done had his breakfast and gone out to somewheres. You be the last one left."

"Eat with me, then," I say.

"Oh, no," says Laura Mae. "That's not right. You a big girl now. You *Miss* Sunny."

"I liked it better when I was just Sunny."

"Well, you growing up. Ain't nothin' a body can do about that." Laura Mae fills the kettle with water and puts it on the stove to heat. "Let me see if I can fill up that hot-water bottle for Little Miss Tummy." She turns to me as she dries her hands with her apron. "That new brother," she says. "You miss him."

"Do not," I sniff.

"I know what I know," says Laura Mae. She passes Parnell coming into the kitchen as she's leaving.

"Good morning, Mr. Parnell."

"Good morning, Laura Mae."

Parnell, who never eats breakfast unless it's pie, heads straight for the coffeepot.

"Hey, squirt."

I jump up and stand by the coffeepot. "Parnell, they've closed the pool! Until further notice! I saw them put up signs!"

"Yep," says Parnell. "They're closing the library, too. And just you wait, most of the restaurants in town will close. I'll bet the Crystal Grill isn't serving today."

"Why? What's happening?"

"Civil Rights Act. Don't you watch the news?"

"No, I never watch the news. What is it?"

"It's a new law. President Johnson signed it the other day."

"Why do we have to close the pool and the library and restaurants?"

"We don't have to close them. But if we keep them open, they have to be open to everybody."

"But they *are* open for everybody! *Everybody* I know goes to the pool. *Everybody* goes to the library."

"Not if they're colored," says Parnell. He puts cream in his coffee and three teaspoons of sugar.

"What does that have to do with anything?"

"It has everything to do with it."

"But they have a pool," I say. I remember Mrs. Murchison. *They have their own churches.*

"I guess that's not enough," says Parnell. He bends over and takes a slurp of his coffee to drink down the excess.

"Is the Leflore closed?"

"Nope," says Parnell. "The owners told Mr. Martini to keep

the theater open and obey the law. I've got to sell a ticket to whoever wants to buy one."

"Why can't we do that at the pool?" I ask.

Parnell puts his cup on the counter and looks at me, like he's trying to decide what to say. "Sunny, have you ever seen a Negro in the Greenwood City Pool?"

My face turns the color of a ripe summer cherry. "No."

"Have you ever seen a Negro in the library?"

"No."

"Have you ever seen a colored kid play on a baseball team or sit at a desk in your classroom at school?"

"No."

"When we ate Sunday dinner at the Crystal Grill, did you see any Negro families eating there?"

"No," I say. "They never do."

"Well, now they can do these things, that's what the new law says."

"Why do they want to?"

Parnell sighs. "I don't know, Sunny. Why do *you* want to?"

"I've just always done them," I say. "But they've always done them, too, haven't they? I mean, they've got restaurants in Colored Town and stores and schools, too."

"That's what folks here think," says Parnell. "'We've always done it this way — separate but equal, and everybody's happy — so why change it?'"

"So why do we have to change it?"

"Because it's a federal law now. That means all over the United States colored people can swim in the same pools and eat at the same restaurants and go to the same schools as whites."

"I don't understand," I say.

Parnell takes a long, appreciative sip of his coffee and says, "People in Washington, D.C., don't understand, either. We don't like the U.S. government telling us what to do here in Mississippi. So folks are closing up, until they can figure it out."

"The Leflore isn't closing," I point out.

"No," says Parnell. "And it will be fine. The coloreds don't go to the movies anyway. They can't afford it." He says it like he's trying to convince himself.

I think of Vidella at the courthouse two weeks ago, being threatened with arrest by the police, the pickets outside the courthouse. "Does this have something to do with the invaders?"

"I don't know about the invaders." Parnell looks at his watch. "I've told you everything I know. Is it enough?"

"Enough for now," I say.

"Does it earn me a chocolate cream pie?" Parnell smiles at me.

"Yes. Two pies."

"Atta girl," says Parnell, just like Uncle Vivian. "I've got your seat saved for the show."

"I'll be there. Is Randy Smithers coming?"

"Why would you ask that?" I've surprised Parnell.

"Oh, I don't know. I just see him sometimes at the box office, talking to you."

"We've got a lot to talk about. In fact, I'm on my way to talk with Randy right now."

"You like him," I say.

"Let's just say I like the possibilities," Parnell replies.

"What does that mean?"

"It means I'm late." Parnell gives my chin a tug and walks out the kitchen door with his coffee.

Laura Mae comes back to the kitchen with the hot-water bottle and begins filling it with the water from the kettle. She hums an old hymn I know and can't remember the name of.

"Laura Mae, would you help me make another pie for Parnell?"

Laura Mae screws the top onto the hot-water bottle. "I 'spect I can, if this girl ain't too sick today, Miss Sunny. I'll let you know."

I sit down in my chair and finally start eating my breakfast. And it comes to me to ask, "Laura Mae, do you want to swim in the city pool?"

"Heavens, no, child. Can't swim anyways. Never learned."

"Do you want to go to the library sometime?"

"Don't read books."

I stab another bite of eggs with my fork. "Laura Mae, do you want to register to vote?"

Laura Mae puts the hot-water bottle in the sink and turns to me. "What's this about, now?"

"Nothin'," I say. "I was just wondering. Are you happy, Laura Mae?"

Laura Mae shakes her head and says, "People need to mind they own business here. That's all I'm saying."

She takes the hot-water bottle upstairs, and I wonder just what my business is.

The City Council urgently appeals to the parents of all children to keep them away from dangerous situations created by the Civil Rights Act. As much as the City Council dislikes the thought, it is forced to face the fact that the federal government by court decree and the enactment of the Civil Rights Act has taken away from the State of Mississippi and local authorities the power to decide how racial relations shall be conducted, and has taken unto itself the authority formerly vested in the states and municipalities. As long as racial relations were in the hands of the State of Mississippi and its local authorities, they were handled in such a manner as to avoid the racial violence, discord and strife prevalent in the North, but the Federal Government has now decided unwisely on a different and disastrous method of handling the matter. It is apparent that the method of handling racial matters decided upon by the Federal Government will promote racial strife, discord and violence. The City Council regards this with abhorrence but cannot shut its eyes to fact. We hope that good judgment on the part of the citizens of our City, both white and colored, will keep these troubles to a minimum, and we shall of course do our best to see that this is done. As one step toward attaining this end, we ask the parents of children to carefully control their actions during the trying years ahead.

— Statement from the City Council of Greenwood, Mississippi, published in the *Greenwood Commonwealth*, June 1964

34

"They've canceled the talent show at the community center, and I'm not going to climb an old tree to tell you about it!"

Mary Margaret hangs up. I stare at the phone. I call Polly. Then Mrs. Carr calls Annabelle to tell her she's bringing Mary Margaret to me and Polly because Mary Margaret is so overwrought Mrs. Carr can't do another thing with her, and Annabelle tells me — like she's issuing a command — that I'm in charge of this because Audrey is sick.

"How sick is she?" I ask.

"She'll be fine," says Annabelle in a clipped voice. People are either clipped or overwrought these days.

"Is she still in my bed?"

"She's in mine," says Annabelle. She walks past me with a glass of ginger ale and some saltine crackers on a plate. I wonder if I should go upstairs and say hey to Audrey, check on her myself, but I don't feel invited. In the end, I decide she might be contagious.

And that's how Polly and I end up sitting with Mary Margaret on the wide, earthen levee across from my house, staring at the river and trying to keep Mary Margaret from flinging herself into the Yazoo. Not that she'd actually do that, but really, we're worried about her. She hasn't combed her hair and she's not wearing lip gloss, her signature cosmetic. And she's crying. Buckets. It's all tumbling out.

"I was going to win!" she sobs. "There was going to be a talent scout down from Memphis! It was my chance to be famous!"

Polly gives me a look and I return it.

"There'll be another show, Mary Margaret," I say.

Which makes her cry harder. "Mary Ann Mobley's starring in television shows now! She's making a movie! And she didn't become Miss America overnight!"

"She had to become Miss Mississippi first," says Polly, trying to be helpful.

"I know that!" sobs Mary Margaret. "That's not what I meant. She started off in talent shows, right in her hometown. I'm sure of it. How else does a talented singer get noticed? And she has a record now, too!" Fresh tears.

"But it's a terrible record," Polly points out.

"You're not helping," I say. I hand Mary Margaret another tissue. "Look, I have an idea. Let's get you cleaned up, Mary Margaret, and let's go downtown. We can find out when the new Beatles album is on sale at Joe's, and I'll bet Mrs. Neely will have lipstick or perfume samples at the cosmetics counter at Barrett's — and you're her favorite, because you appreciate all the new colors. Remember last time, she penciled your eyebrows and put your hair in a French twist? We can get a Coke."

Mary Margaret blows her nose and gulps some jagged breaths. "I know you don't think this is important," she says.

"Yes, we do," I tell her.

"It's important to you," says Polly. "That's good enough for us."

Mary Margaret's eyes brim with fat tears as she gives us a weak smile. "Thanks. You're true friends. *I'm just so disappointed!*" She says it in the same tone someone would say *I've just been murdered!* Then she blows her nose and says, "And to think all this has happened because of those Civil Righters and their holier-than-thou ways! They're stirring up everybody. Making the Negroes feel like they're missing out on something." She hiccups.

"It's not the Civil Righters, Mary Margaret. It's the new law," I say.

"Same thing." She sniffs and dries her eyes. "It's all about the Negroes. They want to be in the talent show, they want to vote. Same thing. They never wanted to do these things before. My dad spends half his life at the courthouse now, because so many of them are being arrested. Mother says she might as well move a cot into his office for him."

"I saw some of them get arrested." I just say it, just like that, and surprise myself.

"You didn't," says Mary Margaret in a shocked tone.

"When?" asks Polly. "Where?"

"At the courthouse, a few days ago. It was awful." I can tell I'm talking fast, but I can't help it. I'm so glad to be telling someone. "There were Negroes, and I think they live here, but there were some Freedom Workers with them — Civil Righters. Some of them were Negroes, too — they wore straw hats — and some were white. Some of them were handcuffed and taken away and all they did was picket the courthouse with signs. Maybe that's against the law, I don't know."

"How did you see all this?" asks Polly. "Were you in George?"

I nod. "You were in Bible School. I was just sitting in George, minding my own business and, wham, it all happened. Also, one of them was our minister, but he wasn't arrested."

"Oh, wow," says Mary Margaret. "This is bad, a minister."

"He wasn't arrested."

"But he could have been!"

"That much was in the paper," Polly says. "The Teletype in our kitchen clicks all the time now, with Civil Righter stories, and notes from Mama's editor in Memphis, telling her to go interview somebody or take a picture or get a story. Mama says, 'I used to report on cotillions and teas, and now look at me!'"

"Does she still get her name in the paper?" asks Mary Margaret.

"Oh, no," says Polly, suddenly on fire to explain it to us. "Her byline for the civil rights stories is always 'UPI' and the dateline is 'Greenwood, Mississippi.' So when we get the *Commercial Appeal*, I look for her stories." Polly sounds anxious, her voice too high and tight.

"She's real careful how she writes them up," Polly continues. "I mean, folks in town know it's her, writing the UPI stories, of course, and she doesn't want any trouble because of what she writes — some people would be real unhappy to have their personal unpleasant news reported all over the country, she says — but she still has to be fair and say the truth, because that's what a reporter does."

Polly takes a breath and keeps going. "I saw that write-up, Sunny. It said 'five white ministers.'"

"I only saw two," I tell her.

"Five ministers!" says Mary Margaret. She crosses herself.

"Maybe it's happened more than once," says Polly. "I don't see everything she writes. I did hear her tell Dad that she thinks it's mostly the Civil Righters making the trouble."

"What are the ministers trying to do, marching with the Civil Righters and the coloreds?" Mary Margaret tears up again. "They're only making it worse! And now we can't do anything in this town!"

"We can go to the movies," I point out. "The Leflore is still open, and I'm going tonight for the first time in two weeks. Want to come with me? It's *The Moon-Spinners* with Hayley Mills!"

"I can't. I'm going with my family this weekend," says Mary Margaret.

"Sorry, I saw it yesterday," says Polly, "with Jodie Lynn Bayard."

"Why in the world would you go to the movies with Jodie

Lynn Bayard?" shrieks Mary Margaret. "She's the most untalented girl in Greenwood!"

"No, she isn't," I tell her. "That's me."

"At least you're interesting," says Mary Margaret.

"Thanks a lot."

"You'll like it, Sunny," says Polly. "It's about a girl trying to solve a mystery."

I sigh and look for a four-leaf clover in the grass. I'm going to have to celebrate my freedom all by myself, because nobody at my house wants to go, and I'm not about to ask Gillette.

As if she's reading my mind, Mary Margaret asks, "Is Gillette home?"

"I don't know where he is," I say. "I hardly see him anymore. We're not speaking."

"Why not?" asks Mary Margaret.

"Because he's a rat fink. I don't want to talk about it."

"You're missing all of his games," says Polly.

"I don't care," I say, but I *am* missing them, in more ways than one.

"I saw Gillette last night," says Mary Margaret, "when we were taking Mae Alice home. He was on his bike in Baptist Town, about eight o'clock."

"What?"

"I *know*," says Mary Margaret solemnly. "Daddy didn't see him, but I did. He was on a side street, coming toward us. He had his Giants cap on and his baseball glove dangling from the handlebars. He wouldn't recognize our car, and he looked like he was in a hurry. I didn't mention it to Daddy."

Now it's my turn to be surprised. "Wow," I say. "That explains a lot."

"Like what?" asks Polly.

"Like why Gillette is gone early in the morning and why he gets home so late from ball practice."

"I wonder what he's doing over there," says Mary Margaret.

"Are you sure it was Gillette?"

"I'm sure." Mary Margaret sighs. "I'd know that face — and that cap — anywhere."

Besotted. That's what she is. I knew it.

And we're not going to Colored Town to find out who he is!

Huh. So you said, my brother. So you said.

35

We been skipping Freedom House to play ball at the colored field until dark. Show up and other kids show up, and you got a pickup game. We don't got teams like the white kids do, but we make 'em up every time, plenty of kids, and I shine. I know I'm good. I know I am. So's Twill, who can hit harder than anybody. He give me lots of practice catching in the outfield.

It's so hot I see stars when I run too fast. "Water," I say. Simon, Jimmy, Twill, and me, we walk to Beulah's Café, 'cause Miss Beulah give us water free from the hose if we ask permission.

Mr. Amzie Moore there, talking at tables, eatin' chicken and mashed taters, fried okra, sweet tea. Look mighty good. Smell even better. And Beulah's got the air-condition.

"Make these boys a plate," say Mr. Amzie. Then he ask us, "Where have you been?"

Mr. Amzie a NAACP man. He work with Miss Vidella Brown, and they all show up at the Freedom House, like good COFOs.

"We quit," say Twill. "Nothing to do but unpack boxes and sort papers."

"Those papers are important. They're going to help us elect the first Negro president of the United States."

Twill hoot. "How?"

"Son, you get enough black voters on the voting rolls in this country, you can do anything, don't you know that? The vote! That's power!"

Twill shake his head. I don't see how signing no paper gon' make no difference."

"My friend Aaron Henry is running for president of the United States, on the Mississippi Freedom Democratic Party platform," say Mr. Amzie. "We are going to Atlantic City, to the Democratic National Convention in August, and we need registered voters, so we can be seated in place of the all-white Democratic Party, and so the world can see that Negroes want a say in their government and are willing to stand against the status quo!"

We all stare at him like he suddenly got religion and be talking in tongues.

"Those pieces of paper are important," he say, "and we have much work to do."

"We got our own work to do," say Jimmy. "We the FreedomMakers."

"That so?" say Mr. Amzie. "Let me see you make some freedom, then."

"Give us a job," that's what I say.

Mr. Amzie wipe his mouth with his napkin. "The new law has been passed — the Civil Rights Act. It says, in part, that any man, no matter the color of his skin, can use any public facility now — parks, restaurants, drinking fountains, restrooms. . . ."

"Pool?" I say it.

"Pool," say Mr. Amzie. "But they closed the city pool this morning."

Ain't never gonna get to feel that water in the daylight. Ain't never gon' have to meet that girl who ran into me, neither, so silly talkin' about ridin' elephants in Fairchild's parking lot.

"Ball fields?" say Jimmy.

"They got lights at the white ball fields," say Twill. "New law gonna give us lights over here?"

"Shoot. We don't even got lights at my house!" say Jimmy. "'lectric been cut off 'cause we cain't pay the bill."

Mr. Amzie say, "The NAACP Youth Council is considering a task force to test the accommodations clause of the Civil Rights Act — the clause that says you have the right to enjoy the library, the soda fountain, the theater —"

"The movies?" I interrupt.

"We got the Walthall," say Simon.

"But it ain't like the Leflore," I tell him.

How long I been starin' at that place, wondering what it like inside?

Mr. Amzie drink his sweet tea. "The Youth Council is full of young men and women your age and we need you. Come to our next meeting. Is dinner enough to bribe you?" Everybody smile.

Beulah bring us plates of the best food in Baptist Town. We eat like we been starving in the desert with Moses.

36

At the end of the day, I'm back downtown for my movie. I run up the stairs on the side of the building, to the very top of the Leflore, where there is a landing and a door that opens into the projection room. I pound on the door with my fist, hoping Mr. Guston will hear me and let me in. Sure enough, he does.

"Hello, little miss!" he says. "Excuse me." He leans over the landing and spits a stream of snuff into the alleyway below. "I thought you must be the Chinaman's son, only it ain't Saturday and he cain't pound on a door that good."

"No, it's me!" I grin like my face might split at my lips. I don't know what I want Mr. Guston to say, or why I'm here. I'm just so happy to be here, period.

"Well, come on in," Mr. Guston says. "You gonna watch from up here with me tonight?"

I shake my head. "Nossir. I just wanted to say hey and tell you not to fall asleep!"

Mr. Guston laughs and spits again. "I ain't," he says. "Even without Chin Lee, my little alarm clock."

Chin Lee's family owns Lee's Grocery in Baptist Town. It's a lot smaller than Fairchild's, and they have mostly a colored clientele, according to Daddy. The Lees live in the back of the store, and one of Chin Lee's older sisters was in my class this year. Her name is Joy. I don't really know her — nobody does — but I remember when we wrote autobiographies, she stood up and read hers, which started, "Some of my people came to this country almost a hundred years ago, to build the railroads, and some were recruited to come south and work on plantations after the Civil War, to take the place of the freed Negro slaves. But they weren't suited to farmwork so they started grocery stores in the old plantation commissaries, and the Negroes stayed on and worked the plantations as sharecroppers. The Chinese came to this country to earn money to send back home to their families. The Negroes were brought here from Africa, against their will."

Well. Nobody knew what to say to her after that. I heard she is going to St. Francis School in Baptist Town next year.

I never see Joy in town. Maybe she's always helping at their store. But Chin Lee is only five years old, like Audrey, and he comes to town on Saturdays by himself, when everybody and his brother comes to shop, and he wanders all over the place — everybody knows him — and then climbs these stairs and watches the cartoons and old movies in the afternoon, and pokes Mr. Guston when it's time to change the reels. I can't imagine Audrey wandering anywhere by herself.

Mr. Guston scratches his head and stares at me, and I realize I can't think of another thing to talk about with him.

"Well, I'd better get my ticket," I say.

"Enjoy the show," says Mr. Guston.

I can't describe how delicious it feels to be back at the Leflore after a two-week exile. I clatter down the outside stairs and decide to just notice, or watch, as Daddy says we should do now. I don't notice any coloreds trying to buy a ticket from Parnell. I don't see one Negro, not even High-top.

As I get in line to get my ticket, I hear a man in a blue shirt talk about the Negro theater on Walthall Street. I didn't know about that. Another man says there's a colored balcony at the Paramount and that should be good enough for any Negro. I know about the Paramount. I don't like to go there. It smells and they don't show good movies.

I'm the only kid in line, but there will be others already

inside. Maybe not many, though, because it's a Monday night, and there's a ball game at McCurdy Field, and reruns of *The Outer Limits* on television, which I like, but I like the movies better.

I can smell the starched cotton shirts and pressed pants and new sweat from the other bodies waiting in line, as I watch the traffic signal change from red to green. The metal light pole makes tiny clicking sounds inside as it begins to cool down after being baked all day by the steely summer sun. It's the same sound our cookie pans make when Laura Mae pulls them out of the oven and transfers the cookies to paper grocery sacks she cuts open and lays on the counter for the cookies to cool on. Then she puts more cookie dough on the hot pan and runs it back in the oven.

"I'll wrap you up some biscuit," said Laura Mae when I told her I was going to the movies and wouldn't be home for supper. I couldn't even say thank you. I just hugged her like there might be no tomorrow, and she said, "Ain't nobody know you like I do, Sunny . . . how you likes your hair braided — tight but not too tight — how you likes your chocolate milk, how you loves you brother even when you say you ain't . . . you come to your meemaw's and see me." Her hug was fierce and she had tears in her eyes, and that made me feel better. And she called me Sunny. Just Sunny. It was then that I realized she did know me better than even Daddy did. I made a note to ask if I could eat supper at Meemaw's tomorrow night.

For a movie that's been here two whole weeks, there are more people buying tickets than I would guess for a Monday night — which Parnell declares the slowest night of the week. They are mostly men, hardly any women. *Where are the wives?* I notice things like that.

"Is it 'bachelor night' at the movies?" I ask Parnell when it's my turn. I want him to appreciate my joke but he just shoves my ticket under the glass and says, "Enjoy the show," like he says to everybody else. He always does that. Mr. Official, at his Official Job. "Next!"

It's so cool inside it's like walking into the huge refrigerator at the back of Fairchild's, and I forgot to bring my sweater. At the candy counter, Mrs. Ferguson hands me what Parnell promised: popcorn, a package of red licorice, and a Dr Pepper.

"Parnell paid for it," she says, just like always, when I ask.

"Thank you." I put my face right next to the Dr Pepper fizz in my cup and let it spritz my cheeks.

"Hey, Mr. Martini," I say as I juggle my snacks and try to hand him my ticket. I think Mr. Martini must wear Dippity-Do in his thick, black hair, the way he always slicks it back and has a loopy curl just-so in the front. He's a fussy and fidgety sort, and he acts like he's not going to answer me. So I try again, with more enthusiasm.

"Hey there, Mr. Martini!" I nod to my ticket sticking out of my pocket.

"Sunny!" he says as if he just noticed I was standing there. He takes my ticket out of my pocket and tears it in half. "Our best customer. Good to have you back."

I *am* his best and most loyal customer, even though I never pay him.

"Is the movie good?" I ask.

"Have you ever seen a bad movie here?" he asks me. He seems friendly but distracted as he takes tickets and smiles and says welcome.

"Never," I say solemnly.

Mr. Martini is standing under the buffalo carving, which is my favorite of all the carvings on the lobby wall that depict the history of Greenwood, although Daddy says there would not have been buffalo east of the Mississippi River, which is where the Delta is. There would have been Indians, though — the

Choctaw and Chickasaw, including Choctaw Chief Greenwood Leflore, who was here first and signed the Treaty of Dancing Rabbit Creek way before the Civil War. That's when most of the Indians moved to Oklahoma. Miss Coffee, my fourth-grade teacher, would be proud of me for remembering.

Mr. Martini looks past me to the front doors, and then to Mrs. Ferguson, who shakes her head. Then Mr. Martini says, "Excuse me, Sunny, I've got work to do here. Enjoy the show." He slips the tip of my ticket stub back in my pants pocket for me because I have no hands left to take it with. I am dismissed. Nothing to do now but go through the swinging doors into the theater.

Parnell has tied a ribbon across my favorite seat. He wasn't kidding when he said he had saved it for me.

I sit down and arrange my Dr Pepper, my popcorn, and my package of licorice on the floor in front of me. The lights are lowered. The curtains are pulled back. I hear the whir of the projector. The newsreel and the previews of coming attractions are about to start. I have the whole front row to myself.

I'm back at the Leflore. All's right with the world.

37

Everybody got religion at the Freedom House. New law say anybody can go to the movies and sit in the cushy seats with the white folks. New law say anybody can eat a hamburger at the Cotton Boll. New law say anybody can swim at the white folks pool, if they open it up again. New law makin' people happy, but I say, let's prove it.

Here I am, sittin' in the Youth Council meetin' at the Freedom House, mad.

"You're not eighteen, Ray," say Mr. Amzie. "You've got to be eighteen before you can risk arrest like this, and even then, you need your parents' permission. You haven't been through the training, either. Younger youth council members are going to man the phones and provide support — we're going to need lots of support."

"I'm almost fifteen," I say. "Old enough."

Miss Vidella Brown shake her head at me. Simon, Jimmy, and Twill, they stare at they shoes. Support. It mean more papers. More phone calls. More cleaning up. More errands. More nuthin'. Miss Vidella hand me two dollars. "This is to pay Mr. Lee at his store, for sending over the ice and the lemonade tonight. Will you make sure he gets it tomorrow?"

I stuff the money in my pocket but I don't want to do it. I want to quit. "Yes'm."

"Testing the new law is outside the purview of COFO," say SNCC Bob. "Our job is to register voters, and to run a Freedom School and a community center, not to test the Civil Rights Act."

I don't care what they do. I'm startin' to make my own plans.

"There's a mass meeting tonight, and I want us all to attend," say Mr. Amzie. SNCC Bob and SNCC Dewey sittin' with us, nod they heads. "Maybe you can ask your pap to come, Ray," say SNCC Bob.

"So's he won't shoot you? Pap do what he want," I say, "and I do, too. I don't want no more mass meetin', pray to Jesus, all sing together now."

"You're just hot," say Miss Vidella. "It's so hot in here." She fan herself with a stack of register forms.

"I'm mad, Miss Vidella," I say. "I'm mad. When we get to DO something?"

Before she can answer me, I tell 'em all. "I'm gon' home."

But halfway across the street, I change my mind, don't go home.

I'm a FreedomMaker. I go to the movies.

"It's already started," say the man in the ticket booth.

"I got money," I say. I shove a dollar of Mr. Lee's money under the glass.

Man shake his head, but he give me back a ticket and seven cents.

He don't say one word.

I don't say one, neither.

Just push open that door and walk inside, like I belong there, because the law say I do.

38

The opening to *The Moon-Spinners* lets me know we're in an exotic place. On a beach! Surrounded by mountains! And there's the beautiful sea, and Walt Disney presents in Technicolor!

And then there's a bus — chugging along country roads in a place that looks nothing like Greenwood, Mississippi. *The Island of Crete*, it says on the screen, and there's Hayley Mills, in the crowded bus — people stand in the aisles carrying braids of onions and garlic and one dead fish that swings absentmindedly in front of Hayley's face. Even reciting "Jabberwocky" doesn't help her fend off the smell.

Nikky — that's Hayley's name in the movie — and her aunt Fran finally get off the bus at their stop and walk with their suitcases up the the rocky path to an adventure.

I open my licorice for part one, start on my popcorn for part two, and by the time we're into the third act, I'm halfway through my Dr Pepper. I'm on the edge of my seat as Stratos tries to run over Mark with a motorboat in the cove. Then, without warning, something flies by my head and explodes into a million pieces on the floor in front of me. *Crash!*

At first, I think it's part of the noise from the motorboat, but it's too close to me, and it's out of place, and I realize — it's real. Instinctively I duck to the floor and upset my Dr Pepper — ice scatters everywhere — and I cut my knee on a piece of glass. On the screen, Mark and Stratos are fighting in the boat while I'm on my hands and knees in front of my seat, kneeling in the sticky goo of my drink and the pieces of glass from whatever crashed in front of me — a bottle? I'm afraid to lift my head, afraid to move.

Another missile flies by me and smashes closer to the screen. I hear someone shout, "You git outta here, boy! Git!" Then there are lots of voices yelling and calling names, and the sound of people shoving, fighting. More bottles, more trash, and I don't know what to do.

Where is Mr. Martini? Where is Parnell? I want to yell, *Stop the movie! Turn on the lights!* But I don't know who these people are, and I don't want them to hurt me.

I consider crawling over to the aisle, but I'm afraid I'll cut myself again, so I stay in a squat in front of my seat while the movie plays and the theater comes alive behind me. People bump into seats and tumble over them and scream and shout and run up the aisles. So many bottle bombs shatter around me, I feel like I'm inside a war, until finally the movie stops in mid-frame and the lights come on and Parnell is calling for me.

"Sunny! Sunny!" His feet tramp the aisle, running toward me, and I'm in his arms and he carries me to Mr. Martini's office, where he puts me in a chair and says, "Stay here!" in a command that would glue anybody to the spot. Then he's gone, slamming the door behind him.

There's angry shouting in the lobby and shoving — something comes crashing down — and I'm scared. A body booms against the closed door of the office with an *oomph!* and I shrink back in fear and look for a place to hide.

"Let him go!" Mr. Martini shouts from the lobby. "All of you! Out! Everybody out!" And, like a monster dying at the end of a bad movie, there is less and less noise, and I begin to breathe again.

My knee stings. It's bleeding a tiny river down into my white sock, but I ignore it and crack open the door instead, so I can see what's happening. The lobby is emptying out, but there's a great crowd growing outside, pressing close to the doors. Mr. Martini locks the doors and says, "That's enough. I'll call the owners tonight. We can't do business like this."

And then I see him with Parnell and Mr. Martini, standing there in his white, high-top sneakers, in those same brown pants and white T-shirt. Shaking but standing up straight, with a defiant look on his face.

"What are you doing, boy?" Mr. Martini asks him.

"I came to the movies," High-top says.

"You picked the wrong theater."

"You sold me a ticket," says High-top. "Law says you have to do that."

"The law might say so, but this crowd thinks otherwise," says Mr. Martini. "How are you going to get out of here?"

"I called the police," says Parnell.

"The police aren't going to be helpful here," Mr. Martini observes.

"I'll call a cab," says Parnell, "One of the colored cab companies will come get him."

Mr. Martini shakes his head. "Who's going to pay for that?" To High-top he says, "When you walk out of here, I can't be responsible for you, boy. Those men out there, they're likely to beat you up from the door to the car. Can't you see you're just making trouble for yourself?"

"Call SNCC," says High-top. "They'll come. I got the number. Show me the phone."

"You bring those agitators down here, they're going to get beat up, too," says Mr. Martini. "I don't care if they're white or colored."

Agitators means Jo Ellen. *Don't call Jo Ellen,* I pray. *Not Jo Ellen.*

Police car sirens wail and Mr. Martini lets a clique of officers come in. Deputy Davis is one of them. Quicker than you can say jackrabbit, they arrest High-top.

"I got a right to be here," he protests, his chin sticking out. "Law says I can come in here."

Deputy Davis says, "The law don't say you can disturb the peace, boy, and that's what you're doing." *Tsk.* "You're under arrest for disturbing the peace."

"I didn't do anything," says High-top. He's trying to sound brave, trying to hold his head up. "I just come to the movies. I bought my ticket like anybody else and sit down to watch the movie like anybody else."

Now Deputy Davis is in High-top's face, angry. "What's your name, boy?" He pulls his handcuffs off his belt.

"Raymond Bullis," says High-top.

Raymond Bullis. His name is Raymond Bullis.

"You're going to jail, boy," says Deputy Davis, his voice more high and nasal and angrier than ever. "You're going to jail for disturbing the peace . . . and because I don't like your face or your attitude."

Tsk. Then he says, "Do you want to file charges, Martini?" and Mr. Martini says no, no, nothing like that, not tonight, please, just go.

Deputy Davis shoves High-top — *Raymond* — out the door and into the crowd. The shouting and shoving starts again. The other policemen part the crowd enough for Deputy Davis to cram Raymond into his police car.

I was in that car just two weeks ago. And now it's Raymond's turn. Arrested for coming to the movies. For having a face Deputy Davis doesn't like. For disturbing the peace. He's on his way to jail at the courthouse.

I open the office door until it creaks. I look at Parnell and Mr. Martini and they startle, as if they'd forgotten I was there. The crowd outside has magically thinned and disappeared.

"Where are Mrs. Lefever and Mrs. Ferguson?" I ask.

"They're long gone home," says Mr. Martini. "I shooed 'em right out when the trouble started."

"Let's get you home," says Parnell. "I'll be back, Mr. Martini. I'll help you clean up."

"Thank you, son," says Mr. Martini. "Let me call Guston and tell him he can come down." He hands me his handkerchief. "You're bleeding on my rug," he says.

"I'm sorry," I tell him. The top of my sock is soaked red. "There's a piece of glass in my knee."

Parnell puts me back in my chair and carefully pulls out the glass with the handkerchief. I try not to cry. "You're fine," he says, pressing the handkerchief on my cut, but his voice shakes. I'm shaking, too.

Mr. Martini holds the back of his neck with his hand and rubs it. "Good night, Sunny," he says.

"Good night," I tell him. Mr. Guston knocks on the front door, and Parnell lets him in. He looks surprised to see me. I try a wan little smile, and Mr. Guston pats me on the shoulder. I feel suddenly exhausted, like I might have to sleep for a hundred years.

And all I can think on the short drive home is this: *That crazy, crazy boy.*

Because he *is* crazy. And he has a name. Raymond. His name is Raymond. He can't be any older than I am.

Suddenly I know just what I need to do. I need to tell Gillette.

Dear Folks

. . . COFO is discouraging any public accommodations demonstrations — Moses feels such demonstrations would bring down all the weight of Mississippi oppression and squelch us. The summer project is having a revolutionary effect in many communities — police are actually upholding law and protecting us and Negroes. . . .

— Summer volunteer Matthew Zwerling in a letter to his parents, Israel and Florence Zwerling, July 3, 1964

On July 10 the Executive Committee of the Greenwood Citizens' Council urged owners of businesses affected by the Civil Rights Bill to "resist its enforcement by all lawful means." In a five-point statement they promised support to anyone involved in litigation for refusal to serve Negroes. "You will have the backing of this community including financial assistance from the White Citizens' Legal Fund," the statement said. It stated further: "We call upon every citizen in this community white and colored to join with us in giving no aid or comfort by word or deed to the advocation of forced integration."

— From the journals of UPI reporter and Greenwood, Mississippi, resident Sara Criss

39

I wake up screaming in the middle of the night and Boo is there. She's sitting on the side of my bed, right next to me, her knobby fingers combing through the tangled hair on my pillow, her voice calm and soothing.

"Shhhhh . . . shhhhhh . . ."

At first I cling to her like she's Laura Mae, or my own mother, even Jo Ellen, and then I wake up to where I am and I realize who she is and push her away.

"What are you doing here?"

Boo stands up, takes a step, and sits in her rocker, which is in my room. Her shawl falls off the back of the rocker and she picks it up, lays it across one arm of the chair. She's wearing a long, white nightgown, and the moonlight that comes through my windows makes her look like an angel, which I know she's not.

She motions to her rocking chair. "I brought it in here myself, after the second time you woke up screaming. I told Jamie to go back to bed, I'd sit with you. Annabelle wanted to do it, but she was afraid you wouldn't let her, and she's got to get her rest, so I shooed her back to bed, too. I'm a night owl anyway, up at all the wee hours — I don't need nearly as much sleep as I used to. You wait until you're older like me, you'll see, that's the way it is."

What a mouthful. I consider it, as a tiny breeze plays through the window screen. I'm sweating — my hair clings to my face and I'm suddenly cold. I pull up my sheet. "How is Audrey?" I whisper. I hardly remember Parnell bringing me home, the sting of Mercurochrome on my knee, the worry on Annabelle's face, the tucking into bed by Daddy.

"She's fine," says Boo. "Everyone is fine. You've had a bad scare. I'm just here to sit with you through the night. Try to get some sleep. I'll be right here."

I don't know what to say to that. "Where's Gillette?" I whisper. There was something I wanted to tell him, but I can't remember what it was.

"He's fast asleep," says Boo. "The whole house is asleep, darlin'. Do you want a drink of water?"

"Yes, please." And just like that, Gillette's grandmother brings me a drink of water.

"There," she says after I've drained the jelly glass from the bathroom. "That's better."

"Yes," I say. "Thank you."

"You're so welcome."

Boo's rocking chair creaks in the dark while the crickets sing an opera outside my window, and the watery smells of the Yazoo mix with the medicine smells of Boo's VapoRub. I lie in bed and drift in and out of sleep on a raft bobbing over the ocean with talking parrots and flying fish. Every time I open my eyes, Boo is there.

"We're going to have company for tea on Wednesday," she says.

"Tea?" I don't know what that is. Maybe I'm dreaming this conversation.

"Tea," says Boo. "Annabelle has been planning it for some time."

"Annabelle," I say, and I drift. I see Meemaw, bobbing like a buoy on the sea of her sadness. Then there's Jo Ellen and her locket, her crooked smile. I think she loves me. "Mama," I say.

"Yes!" says Boo, surprise in her voice.

"No," I say, and I try to rise to the surface of consciousness. "Not Annabelle," I murmur, and I hear Boo's soft sigh.

"Annabelle doesn't think you should come to tea, but I do," says Boo. "I think it's important you be there."

"Important," I say, and fall into a doze.

When I rouse myself again, Boo is still there. I am feeling more myself. Boo smiles at me in the moonlight and I don't mind.

"I don't understand what happened tonight," I finally say.

"Would you like to tell me about it?" Boo asks.

"No."

"Fair enough," says Boo.

I sleep then and have no more dreams. When I'm finally awake for good, Boo is sewing a button on one of Audrey's dresses. It's gray-light, and the first songbirds are making a racket. Boo and I watch each other as the moon goes to sleep and the sun begins to creep into the sky. And here's what Boo says to me:

"There are all kinds of ways to be in the world. And no matter what has happened to us, or what we have been told, or what we have believed, we get to choose our way."

I blink but say nothing. Boo pulls my summer blanket up to my neck, and tucks it in. She pulls her shawl around her shoulders. Crows call from somewhere near the levee. They must see something shiny in the almost-light.

"Those men last night," I say.

"Hmmm . . ." Boo keeps her eyes on her sewing but nods, encouraging me.

"I think they would shoot a dog."

"They might," says Boo. And then she says, "What would you do about that?"

I have no answer. I don't understand the question.

Boo says, "I'm going to let you sleep a little longer, and I'm going to go back to bed now. Do you think you'll be all right?"

I give my head a short, tiny nod, but I'm not sure I want her to leave.

"That's a good girl," says Boo. "I'll get my chair later." She plants a Vicks-y kiss on my forehead and I let her. She opens my bedroom door and there's Ruth, lying on the hall floor, across my doorway.

"Ruth!" whispers Boo. "What a good girl. Come on in. We need you here."

Ruth taps softly across the floor and helps herself onto the foot of my bed like she's been invited, which, I suppose, she has. After Boo leaves, Ruth inches her way to my side in an insistent way, like she knows it's where she belongs. I make room for her to lie beside me in all her warm, red softness. I slip my arm around her and she sighs.

Her breath moves in and out, in time with mine, stretching a little bit longer each minute, encouraging me to do the same, until my breathing matches hers, slowly in-and-out, in-and-out, in-and-out. With her steady breathing, one calm breath after another, she seems to say, *Safe . . . here, safe . . . here, safe . . . here.*

And that's when I cry.

40

First time at the jailhouse. Breathe in and out. That's all.

Deputy Davis poke me. Shove. "You're a troublemaker, aren't you, boy?"

My mama ironed for Miz Davis for ten years until she lost her job tryin' to register, and he don't know me, don't know my name, don't care.

"You Libby Bullis's boy?"

So he do know. "Yessir." I keep my eyes on the floor. Try not to shake. Emmett Till got killed for less than this, not long ago. Ma'am and Pap know his people.

Deputy Davis make suckin' sounds when he talk, like a boot pullin' out the mud.

"Now listen to me, boy." That's what he say. "Those idiot white kids are gonna go home when this summer is over, and your mama still won't have a job, and you'll never find one, either, because no one in this town is gonna hire you after this stunt you just pulled."

"Yessir." I hold my breath and wait for what come next.

White man in blue suit come in the room. "Don," he say. "A moment."

Deputy Davis leave and come back a long while later. Then he say, "I'm going to do you a favor, boy. I'm not going to put you in jail, on account of my past . . . relationship . . . with your family. Professional relationship. I'm going to let you make a phone call, and have your mama come pick you up."

I almost tell him, *We don't got no phone*, 'cause we don't.

But then I remember, SNCC gots a phone.

"Then I don't want to see you here again, you hear me?"

"Yessir." I call the number — I got it memorized — and a car full of SNCCs comes to get me.

SNCC Stokely don't have to tell me, "This is why it's important to have someone in the office, on the phone, all the time. This is support, Raymond."

Pap and Ma'am come to the Freedom House to get me. They been worried sick since they heard. Somebody already gone to our house to let them know where I am and that I all right. Support.

Everybody on our street turn out at the Freedom House. Folks come from the mass meetin', on they way home. News travel fast. "Your boy all right?"

Food to eat, out of nowhere, and I think: I spent Mr. Lee's dollar. So thirsty. Somebody hand me water. Everybody touch me, touch my head, my shoulders, my arms, my face, touch my hands with they hands, asking me if I all right, everybody ask me to tell the story.

Pap start to cry. I ain't seen him cry since Adele died. It makes up my mind for me.

Miss Jo Ellen put her arm around Pap's shoulder. "He's all right," she say.

I breathe deep. My neck hot. "I'm going back," I tell 'em. "I'm not gon' stop. Me, Simon, Jimmy, Twill, we the FreedomMakers. We got us a cause."

Everybody quiet.

Somebody start the song. "I got the light of freedom . . ." and they all sing.

Pap look as old as Methuselah when he say, "I can't stop you."

Then, real slow, he walk to the desk full of papers and pick up a form, look at it long. Then he write his name on the line. Wilson Bullis.

Spade work.

Another voter register for the Mississippi Freedom Democratic Party.

41

Tuesday, July 7, 1964

Just when I think things can't get any stranger, here comes Vidella to our back door. Vidella, who I've known all my Sunday school life. Vidella, who looked at me like she did at the courthouse. Vidella, who, it turns out, I don't know at all.

I am sitting on the couch with Audrey and Ruth, trying to pat myself back together this morning while watching the most boring television program on the face of the earth — *Romper Room* — when I hear Annabelle welcome Vidella, call her Mrs. Brown, and tell her she's glad to see her.

I don't even get off the couch. I'm protesting the fact that Laura Mae is gone for good. Instead of bacon and eggs this morning, which Laura Mae made every day she worked for us, there were cereal bowls laid out and a box of Rice Krispies. I just said no, thank you to that and Annabelle said, "Suit yourself," and headed to the dining room.

That's not entirely true. She asked me how I was. "Did you finally get some sleep, Sunny?"

She tried to touch my shoulder but I pulled away. "You don't have to be nice to me," I said.

"I know that," said Annabelle.

She used that clipped tone of voice again, which made me feel bold enough to say, "My mother knew my daddy all her life. They went to school together. He was very in love with her."

"I'm sure he was," said Annabelle.

I know it's not nice. But I've held in my true feelings long enough. I don't like her.

Audrey, who is feeling better, is glad for my company. She whispers, "I'm a Do Bee, Sunny," and snuggles against me, with her old baby blanket in her lap and Ginny in the crook of her arm while Miss Nancy on *Romper Room* gazes into her Magic Mirror and recites the names of all the kids she can see at home.

Audrey says, "She never sees me."

I sigh and wrap my arm around Audrey. "I see you," I tell her, "and that's even better. Miss Nancy is a nearsighted knucklehead."

Annabelle walks into the living room with Vidella. Vidella is not wearing a uniform, but Annabelle is wearing an apron and has a wooden box in her arms.

"My mother's silver," she says to Vidella, and smiles. "It will need a good polishing. I'll help you."

"Let me have it," says Vidella. "You don't need to be toting something that heavy."

Annabelle smiles a thank-you. "Girls, this is Mrs. Brown. She's going to be working with us here at the house for a while."

"For the summer?" I ask.

"We'll see how long," says Annabelle. "As long as she wants to."

"But she works in the kindergarten at our church!" I say.

"Not anymore," says Annabelle. She points out Audrey and introduces her to Vidella.

"I'm sick," says Audrey in a small voice.

"We can do something about that," says Vidella.

Then Annabelle gestures to Vidella and me and says, "I see you two know each other already from church."

"Yes, ma'am," I say in an obedient voice, but what I really want to say is, *Did they fire Vidella at church? Was her name in the paper like the policeman at the courthouse said it would be? Did Uncle Vivian tell on her? What happened?*

Vidella says, "Hello, Sunny."

Instead of asking my questions, I just say, "Hello, Vidella."

"Mrs. Brown," corrects Annabelle, cool as an air-conditioned room.

I lick my lips. "Mrs. Brown," I say. It feels strange coming off my tongue. *Mrs. Brown.*

Vidella — Mrs. Brown — who stands straighter than anybody I've ever seen, even Mary Margaret, nods at me the way she did in the courthouse. A look passes between us, but neither of us says anything about that day to the other.

"I found this paper in your front yard," says Vidella to Annabelle, and she begins to work it out of her dress pocket with her fingertips, even with the silver chest in her arms.

"It's probably a sale circular," says Annabelle in an uninterested voice, not even looking at it as she walks back to the dining room. "Just leave it on the table with the newspaper, if you don't mind. I want to get a start on polishing this silver for tomorrow's tea."

"Yes, ma'am," says Vidella.

"Just 'yes' is fine," calls Annabelle.

Vidella gives me a knowing glance as she leaves the rolled-up blue paper on top of the coffee table. It's just like Annabelle to be too distracted to see it, but I know what it is without even unrolling it, even though I haven't seen one for months. Daddy won't allow me to read them if I find them first, but he's not here, so I pick it up and unroll it as soon as I hear the clatter of forks and spoons. It begins, like they all do, with the heading, A DELTA DISCUSSION.

A Delta Discussion

Citizens of Greenwood and surrounding areas, we feel that we should discuss with you some of the events and circumstances surrounding those events which have recently occurred in our area during "the long hot summer of agitation" inflicted upon us by the imported Communists and their fellow travelers in our midst. As you know, the Leflore Theater is likely to be one of our most persistent trouble spots. The reason for this is plain. The theater is owned by a group of out of state people whose only interest in Mississippi and her citizens is money. The manager is a Massachusetts born man who has apparently never cared to adapt himself to our local customs. Within ten minutes after the so-called Civil Rights Bill was signed, this man gave orders to his ticket agents to sell tickets to all applicants. His employees, all native born Mississippians, meekly agreed to go along with him, and the trouble makers appeared. They knew in advance that they would receive support from the theater manager, owners, and its jellyfish sorry employees. It should be kept in mind that if this theater sells no tickets, it cannot continue to operate. It is our intention to see that continued patronage of this theater by anyone receives full publicity. We fully support the right of any man to operate his business as he sees fit but we also intend to focus the glaring light of publicity on any business owner or manager, local or imported, who deliberately disregards our local customs in his business operation. We recognize the Civil Rights bill as a mislabeled, unconstitutional, freedom-destroying, vicious, and un-American piece of legislation and we do not intend to obey it under any circumstances.

I finish reading it for the second time just as Gillette walks through the living room toward the kitchen. Ruth gets up from her place at Audrey's feet and follows Gillette through the room.

"I want to talk to you," I call to my brother.

"Not interested," Gillette replies.

"Really?" I follow him into the kitchen. "You will be, when you hear what I have to say."

Gillette fills a bowl with Rice Krispies. "No, I won't," he says. "And you forget: I can't be trusted." Gillette sloshes milk into his bowl.

I blink and change tactics. "I know where you go at the end of the day." I say it like a threat.

Gillette spoons cereal into his mouth. "I don't care if you do."

"I almost got killed last night!" I hiss, low enough that Annabelle and Vidella won't hear me. I hope I don't sound as desperate as I feel.

"Don't tell me about it," Gillette says. "You look like you're all in one piece. And you've still got a big mouth."

"You are hateful!" I say, too loudly. "You should be apologizing to me!"

We stand in the kitchen facing each other, Gillette crunching cereal at the sink, staring at his bowl, and me staring at Gillette as he eats, my arms folded across my chest, the hate sheet rolled in one hand.

"You're the one who told on me! Why are you so mad at me now?"

Gillette drinks the milk left in his bowl and then says, "C'mon, Ruth, I'll let you out." He opens the back kitchen door and follows Ruth onto the back stoop and down the steps barefoot, still in his pajamas, wearing his Giants cap. I follow him.

He turns to me when he gets near George and says, fire in his voice, "So now you want to talk? You never gave *me* a chance to talk, did you? You never asked me why I did it. You don't care that I must have had a reason. Did you ever stop to think about how I might feel? You don't want to know anything about me, not really. You only care about yourself!" His face is still puffed from sleep, and his eyes are rimmed red.

"What was I supposed to do?" I shout. "I had no choice! You left me a note saying you were betraying me!" I wave my arms for effect.

"It was five o'clock in the morning!"

"So?"

"I had a few other things on my mind," says Gillette, "not that you would care about that. And I left you a note. I cared enough about you to do that."

"If you cared about me, you would never have betrayed me."

"I betrayed myself, too, then. We were in it together, in case you've forgotten. And here's the good news, Sunny: You don't have to sneak around hoping Deputy Davis doesn't tell your dad about this one day. It's done. It's over. You paid your dues. You did your time. You didn't have to tell. And now, your life is back to normal."

"My life is anything *but* normal, buddy boy!"

"And you think mine is? Grow up!"

"What's going on out there?" Annabelle calls from the open dining room window.

"Nothing!" we shout, in unison.

I turn my back to the window and face my brother. "I *hate* you."

"That goes double for me," he says.

"Fine."

"Fine!"

I shove the hate sheet into his hands. "Read this," I command. I stalk back to the house and stomp upstairs to my room. I don't care if I wake up Boo, I don't care if I wake up the neighborhood.

I slam my bedroom door and throw myself across my bed. Even though I hate Gillette with the white-hot heat of a thousand Mississippi suns, I need him to read that hate sheet. Something in me tells me he will know what to do, that he has been scared like this before, and that he can help me. Because I'm scared, and I have no one else I can talk to about it. I am holding on to so many secrets that need telling, I'm likely to pop. There is no one who will understand them like Gillette will. If anyone has held on to secrets in his lifetime, it's Gillette.

WE ARE TRAVELING IN THE FOOTSTEPS OF THOSE WHO HAVE GONE BEFORE AND WE'LL ALL BE REUNITED ON THAT NEW AND SUNLIT SHORE

From "When the Saints Go Marching In," an old spiritual

THE Civil Rights Act of 1964

What's in it . . .

How you can use it to obtain the Rights it guarantees . . .

All persons shall be entitled to the full and equal enjoyment of the goods, services, facilities, privileges, advantages, and accommodations of any place of public accommodation . . . without discrimination on the ground of race, color, religion, or national origin. . . . Any inn, hotel, motel, or other establishment which provides lodging to transient guests. . . . any restaurant, cafeteria, lunch-room, lunch counter, soda fountain . . . any motion picture house, theater, concert hall, sports arena, stadium or other place of exhibition or entertainment . . .

From Title II, the public accommodations clause of the Civil Rights Act of 1964

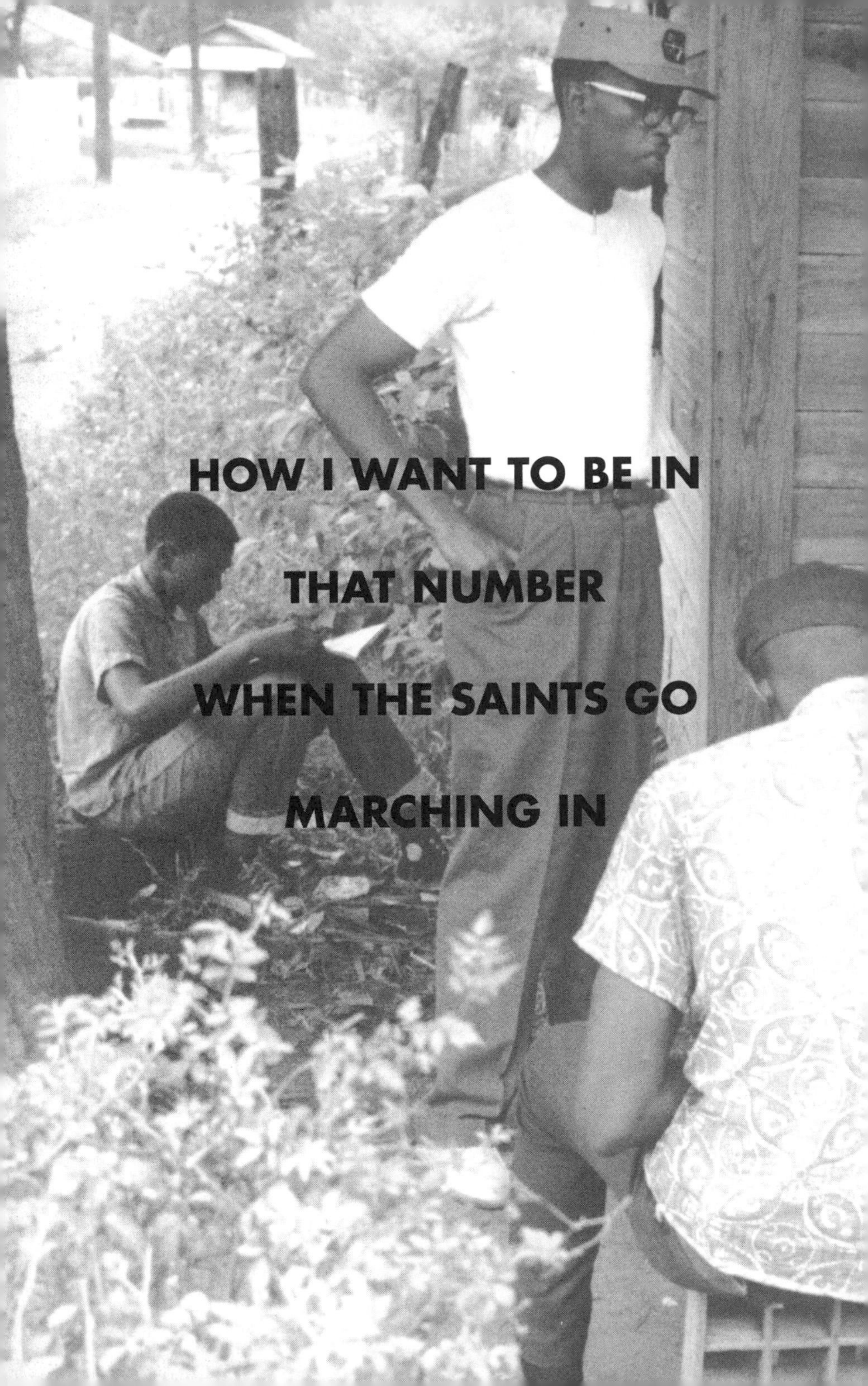
HOW I WANT TO BE IN
THAT NUMBER
WHEN THE SAINTS GO
MARCHING IN

Young men get their first look at magazines such as *Ebony* and *Jet* at the COFO house in Hattiesburg, Mississippi.

FBI photograph of the burned station wagon driven by James Chaney, Andrew Goodman, and Mickey Schwerner, which was found shortly after their disappearance.

WHEN THE MOON TURNS

RED WITH BLOOD

O WHEN THE MOON

TURNS RED WITH BLOOD

I WANT TO BE IN

THAT NUMBER

"I feel that God had a purpose in creating the races separate. I am so proud of negroes who are so proud of being negroes. They are what God made them. And I'm proud of being white because I am what my white race has made me. I am white today because my parents practiced segregation."

Mary Cain, editor, *The Summit Sun*, Pike County, Mississippi

SOME SAY THIS WORLD OF TROUBLE
IS THE ONLY ONE WE NEED
BUT I'M WAITING FOR THAT MORNING
WHEN THE NEW WORLD IS REVEALED

Two African American boys work in the "Freedom Press Office" at their Freedom School in Hattiesburg, Mississippi, summer 1964.

WHEN THE REVOLUTION COMES

WHEN THE REVOLUTION COMES

The news just suddenly broke out as a shock. The people were scared and angry, saying "Why would any person want to take the lives of three boys?"

The people in the country were scared and some were even scared to come to town. I feel sorry for those boys and I think they should be found. The missing boys were a shock to some. The white wasn't so sad.

They found their station wagon. It was burned. Some people think they are dead. Some say the police are not looking as hard as they should be and most people think they cut them up in little pieces and threw them in the river.

Frances Lee Jeffries, child reporter, *Freedom News*, volume 1, issue 1, July 8, 1964

HOW I WANT TO BE IN THAT NUMBER WHEN THE REVOLUTION COMES!

42

By noon dinner everyone knows about the hate sheet thrown in every front yard in white Greenwood. Meemaw has come over for noon dinner to talk about it, because she heard I was at the Leflore last night. I don't know why I ever in my right mind thought I could do anything in this town without everyone finding out.

I wander into the kitchen, at loose ends. "Where's Daddy?"

"He's got a meeting — he'll eat in town," says Annabelle. Daddy never misses noon dinner.

"What about Parnell?"

"Parnell didn't sleep here last night," says Annabelle.

"What?"

"Parnell is a grown man," says Annabelle. "He doesn't have to account for his whereabouts."

"That grown man needs a home of his own," huffs Meemaw.

"He's just now nineteen," says Annabelle. Sticking up for Parnell! Well!

"He's twenty, if he's a day," says Meemaw.

"Is he all right?" I ask.

"He's fine," says Annabelle. "He called."

Vidella puts an enormous platter of sandwiches on the kitchen table and Meemaw eyes it with the same expression she'd use to eyeball a platter of fish guts. Annabelle hands me two paper plates from the cupboard and says, "Help yourself to a sandwich," which means I'm not to sit down with the grown-ups and neither is Polly, who is on her way over.

Annabelle is changing right before my eyes. No more questions. Only orders. I stand there trying to figure out how to disobey this one.

Polly comes through the back door with her mother, who has a gigantic bowl of potato salad in her arms and says, "There's enough here for today and tomorrow, too — you know I can't come, but I'm with you in spirit. And, of course, I can't write it up for the paper."

"I know that," says Annabelle, "and I don't want you to. Thank you, Carol Ann."

I'm about to ask what's going on, when Polly's mother says, "How are you, Sunny?"

"I'm fine, thanks," I tell her. I don't want to talk about it. My knee hardly hurts anymore. I sent a note to Polly this morning and got one back from her, saying her mother reported the "disturbance at the Leflore" as a UPI story about testing the Civil Rights Act. I'm itching to read how she wrote it up. I decide I want to read the newspaper every day from now on.

"I've got five minutes," says Polly's mother. "Bill Storey at the *Appeal* wants me to interview some of the summer volunteers at the COFO Freedom House in Baptist Town, and Jack Bayard from the *Commonwealth* is going to go with me. It's just routine, but they are planning a Freedom Day, and Bill wants to know what they want."

"Can we come?" I ask for both me and Polly.

"Absolutely not!" snorts Meemaw, and that decides the matter.

Boo, Meemaw, Annabelle, and Polly's mother settle themselves quickly at the kitchen table, like they are attending a meeting. Maybe they are. Vidella takes the potato salad from Polly's mother. Polly stands next to me and pinches my arm in a friendly way. "I should have known better with a girl like you," she croons in a whisper. I pinch her back and sing, "That I would love everything that you do, and I do, hey hey hey, and I do!" *Yeah, yeah, yeah.*

Polly switches songs. "I'll give you all I've got to give, if you say you'll love me, too," she sings, louder. Not to be outdone, I come right back with, "I may not have a lot to give, but what I've got I'll give to you," and we both laugh at how well we're memorizing the songs from *A Hard Day's Night*.

Polly's mother sighs. "I think I may go crazy before these Beatles are over."

"They'll never be over!" says Polly. I hand her one of my paper plates and we reach for sandwiches. Vidella pours us each a glass of milk.

"This is not to be borne!" says Meemaw about the hate sheets, or Polly's and my singing, or the Civil Rights Act, or the sandwiches. I don't know. Vidella puts a plate of sliced tomatoes on the table and a bowl of steaming creamed corn, too. Boo fills her plate enthusiastically. Her Vicks-y smell is better today. It doesn't knock me over.

When no one answers Meemaw right away, she asks Annabelle, "How's your new maid working out?" with Vidella standing right there, dividing up the potato salad, some for our lunch table and some for tomorrow.

Annabelle doesn't miss a beat. "How are you working out, Mrs. Brown?"

Meemaw's face colors up. "Really, Annabelle."

"I made some fresh iced tea," says Vidella without a smile. "Would you like some, Miss Eloise?"

"Of course I would," says Meemaw. As Vidella pours her tea, Meemaw adds, "I hope you appreciate this new job, Vidella."

"Of course I do," says Vidella. There is grit in her voice. I reach between Boo and Meemaw for half a peanut butter and jelly sandwich.

Meemaw says, "It must be hard on a family when someone is fired, but then, some people forget the way of things. . . ."

I straighten up like I've been stuck with a stick.

"Eloise!" says Annabelle.

And then, because I can't help it, I open my big mouth and ask.

"Why were you fired, Vidella? You've had that job forever!"

Vidella removes her apron and hangs it on the peg by the stove. The air in the room is suddenly way too hot and thick, and I wish I could take back what I just said.

"I tried to register to vote," she says to the wall in a matter-of-fact voice. Then she turns to face us. She looks at me first, as if she's trying to decide whether to tell everyone she saw me there.

Then she looks at Meemaw, "That job meant a lot to me, Miss Eloise. I taught kindergarten and tended nursery for a good portion of the white children in Greenwood for almost sixteen years. I loved that job and I loved those children."

"Now, Vidella, you were an *assistant*," Meemaw intones, but Vidella comes right back at her with more.

"When I tried to register, the church council wanted me fired. But the membership vote came back in my favor. There's good Christian folks in that church, and I don't want to be the cause of any trouble or distress. I *will* be back at the courthouse to register. So I quit. I wasn't fired. I just want to be clear about the truth of it."

Vidella wipes her hands on a dish towel. "Excuse me," she says. "I've got a sick girl to tend to today. I promised her we could fix that." She leaves the room without another word.

Meemaw looks like she's just taken a bite of those fish guts. She says to Annabelle, "Are you going to let your help talk to me like that, in your house?"

Annabelle says, "Sunny, you and Polly go have a picnic in

the backyard." All the women around the table look at us and wait for our "yes, ma'am," which we give them.

Polly — who looks like she's been hit by lightning — puts a tuna fish sandwich on her plate and follows me to the swing on the side porch, where we can eat and listen and peek in, if we're quiet. She's not about to tell me we're not doing as we're told. She wants to hear this as much as I do. *Atta girl*, I feel like telling her. The songbirds are going crazy. I want them all to stop singing, so we don't miss a word.

"Of course, times are changing, and we must change with them," says Boo. She's still back on what's not to be borne with Meemaw. She doesn't know what Meemaw means, either, but she's taking a stab at it while eating an egg salad sandwich.

"July, our good relations with our Negroes is fast disappearing," says Meemaw. "Nobody trusts anybody anymore."

July! Boo's real name is July!

"How do you mean?" asks Boo, as if she has no idea what Meemaw is talking about.

"Our Negroes are frightened and confused," says Meemaw. "They no more want to mix with the whites than we want to mix with them. They have no ambitions to be bank presidents or lawyers and such, and they couldn't do those jobs if they wanted to — they're not suited to them. They can't learn like we can. Vidella and the others have been influenced by these invaders from the North who have no understanding of our way of life."

"I believe the *whites* are frightened and confused," says Annabelle. "Aren't you, Eloise?"

Meemaw harrumphs. "Laura Mae is my bellwether. She is so afraid those white students are going to come to her door and harass her, she just lies out there in her bed with the lights out and the door locked, hoping they leave her alone. If it wasn't for those agitators, we wouldn't be in this predicament!"

Polly and I move as one person, like a giant amoeba, off the swing and to the window, where we have a better view.

"If whites weren't frightened, they wouldn't be arresting teenaged Negro boys and taking them to jail when they've not broken the law," says Annabelle.

"Wow," Polly whispers to me, and all I can think is, *Who is this Annabelle?*

"Whether or not he's broken the law is debatable," says Meemaw. "Our laws are not the same as their laws." She takes a sandwich and looks at it like it might give her leprosy. "Standards have really come down in this household, and quickly," she says.

"We've got a lot to prepare for," says Annabelle. "A sandwich is what we've got to offer today, Eloise. We didn't know you were coming."

Now it's my turn. "Wow."

Meemaw sits up straight in her chair and murmurs, "I don't know what this world is coming to."

Boo says, "There will be more arrests."

Polly's mother says, "I'm worried about their 'Freedom Day.' They're bringing all the coloreds to the courthouse to register, hundreds of them."

"You see?" says Meemaw. "They've got them all worked up and thinking they need something they don't even understand."

"The roughneck whites in this town are just as bad," says Polly's mother, "stirring up the white community. You can't say a word against them, with their Citizens' Council — they'll run you out of business or scare you out of town."

"We're members of the Citizens' Council," says Annabelle. "We're afraid not to pay the membership. Jamie has to keep the store open."

"We are, too," says Polly's mother. "We all walk a fine line. We've got friends in the Citizens' Council, good people. . . ."

Meemaw interrupts. "Now, we've got just a sliver of white hooligans in this town — in any town! — who behave badly." Immediately I think of our encounter with Mr. Delay and I realize Annabelle is right. Meemaw is frightened, too. She wouldn't have dared to say a disparaging word to Mr. Delay and she couldn't wait to get away from him.

"That sliver is mighty vocal," says Polly's mother.

"Everyone is afraid," says Boo, "all over Mississippi. There's a terrible feeling of defeat and despair. We're all worried about what tomorrow may bring."

"They found the car in the Bogue Chitto Swamp," says Polly's mother. "It didn't make the local papers, of course, but it came over the Teletype. That car was burned to a crisp and buried tail up."

"It was on the nightly news," says Annabelle.

Boo adds, "It's only a matter of time before they find those boys." She and Annabelle exchange a dark look, like they know some secret they can never tell.

Meemaw stands up and brushes crumbs from her dress. That's our signal to go back to the swing and we make a dash for it.

"The whole country must think we're heathens down here," says Meemaw. "I watch Walter Cronkite give the news every night. You'd think we're all KKK members, to hear him tell about what's happening in Mississippi. I know you all think I'm strident, but I want the same thing you do. I want everything to be peaceful again. How are we going to repair the damage done to our relations with the Negroes when these agitators leave?" I hear her shove her chair under the table. "Time for *Guiding Light*."

"I'll join you," says Boo. Imagine that. She says to Annabelle, "We can finish planning after I see what's happening with my story."

"I'll need a nap before I go home, Annabelle," says Meemaw.

"You can use Sunny's room," says Annabelle.

I could make money renting out my room.

"I've got to go," says Polly's mother. "Fill me in with the details later, will you?"

As the back screen door bangs shut, me and Polly scramble to her mother's car. We are sitting in the backseat like little innocents when she slips into the front and starts the engine.

"I don't want to stay home alone," says Polly. "I don't feel safe today."

"And Annabelle wants us out of the house," I add. "She didn't say I couldn't come."

Polly's mother puts the car in REVERSE, twists herself around to look behind us, lays her arm across the neck of the front seat to steady herself, and backs out of our driveway.

"You can wait in the car," she says with a sigh. "I won't be long."

And that's how me and Polly end up riding with her mother and Mr. Bayard to the Freedom House in Colored Town.

43

Miss Jo Ellen, she ask Ma'am at breakfast, "Could you spare Raymond today, Mrs. Bullis?" Then she say to me, "Ray, I wonder if you could help me at the Freedom School for a little while today."

Ma'am say, "He'll be happy to help if he don't have paying work lined up yet — do you, Raymond?"

I shake my head no. "But —"

"No but," say Ma'am. "This here girl your comp'ny! If she need you to go to the moon for her, you say yes."

"I appreciate it," say Miss Jo Ellen.

"Yes, ma'am," I say, not happy.

"Just yes is fine," say Miss Jo Ellen. "Can you call me Jo Ellen?"

"No, ma'am," I say.

Glory skip ahead, on the way to the Freedom House. Miss Jo Ellen say, "I want you to help me understand some of my students, and to interpret what I say for them."

"You speak Russian to 'em?"

"No, of course not," say Miss Jo Ellen, "but they keep telling me they can't understand me, and you've heard me talk and talk, and you don't seem to have trouble with it."

"You talk funny," I tell her.

Jo Ellen smiles. "I think *you* talk funny."

"You just got to speak slower and pronounce your words," I tell her.

Upstairs at the Freedom House, kids show up, Ree's age and on up to twins Freddie and Chuff, who come for magazines and Ping-Pong.

"We don't want no more coloring or painting!" say Chuff. "We don't got no more room left on these walls!" Chuff pull a book from a box. Here — teach us something from this schoolbook. Is this a schoolbook from a white school?"

"Yes, it is," say Miss Jo Ellen. She open it up. "1930!" she say. But she start to read.

"Go slow," I say.

"The history of America begins in England. All Americans come from Europe."

Miss Jo Ellen take a deep breath, close the book, and look at all the faces sitting there in the hot, sweaty and waiting. Nobody say one word.

"What's wrong with this passage?" Miss Jo Ellen ask.

"What that mean?" say Freddie.

Miss Jo Ellen look at me. "Slow," I say.

"Did all Americans come from England?" she ask.

Ree shoot up her hand. "Yes! The book say so!"

Miss Jo Ellen say, "The book is wrong."

"Can a book be wrong?" ask Mercy Mayfield.

"Yes," say Miss Jo Ellen. Everybody likes that. "People came to America from many different countries, all around the world, for many different reasons. Where else do Americans come from?"

Hands go up. Miss Jo Ellen put a globe on the desk and spin it. "Help me pick people, Ray."

I pick on kids and I tell her what they say if she can't hear 'em right.

Sidney Phillips say, "France?"

"Yes!"

Ralph Muster say, "Italy?"

"That's right," say Miss Jo Ellen. "Let's make a list." She get out a fat black marker and big paper, tack it to the wall.

Chuff say, "I bets they came from Germany — I heard about Germany, my pap tells stories about the war, sad stories, and scary, too."

Miss Jo Ellen look at me. "Germany," I say.

"Yes!" say Miss Jo Ellen. She write it down.

"I think Mexico," say Caroline Mayfield, Mercy's sister.

"Absolutely," say Miss Jo Ellen.

"What about China?" say Laurette Magee, "I think the Lees come from China."

"Yes, they do," say Miss Jo Ellen. She add China to the list.

No more guesses. "Nowhere else?" Miss Jo Ellen ask.

Silence.

Miss Jo Ellen look at us like she want to scoop us up and slather us with everything she know.

"What about Africa?" That's what she ask us.

Nobody say one word. Then Ree raise her hand, unsure.

"Does that count?"

Miss Jo Ellen wipe her hand across her mouth, lick her lips, and say, "Yes, Ree. That counts."

Just Jo Ellen.

44

I have gone in the car with Daddy when he's taken Laura Mae home, but I've never been this deep into Colored Town. We ride slowly down McLaurin Street, through Laura Mae's neighborhood, Baptist Town, and past Avenue G, where Laura Mae lives. I gaze down her street as we pass it. It's filled with tiny clapboard houses sagging in the sun, some with paint peeling, porches rotting, and I try to picture Laura Mae there after work each day, stiffly lying on her bed, quiet as midnight, terrified the white students might knock on her door.

I look for white students, for Jo Ellen, for Vera. I look for colored men wearing straw hats and FREEDOM NOW T-shirts. I look for Gillette on his bike.

"It's hot as fluzions," says Mr. Bayard. Our windows are down and dust from the dirt road swirls all around us.

"Thanks for taking me along, Carol Ann," says Mr. Bayard. "I've been wanting to see this Freedom House for myself."

"I wouldn't come over here by myself," Polly's mother says, and then adds, "and now the *Commonwealth* can have its story, too."

"Not that it'll make the paper," says Mr. Bayard.

There's hardly a soul out and about, and I think all the coloreds must be finishing noon dinner, like we just did. The cicadas call from the trees and an old, yellow dog lolls in the cool dirt and dark shade under a rickety porch.

"Where are we?" I ask.

"This neighborhood is Gritney," says a chatty Mr. Bayard. "We left Baptist Town at the railroad tracks. Gritney is full of juke joints. I get calls in the middle of almost every Saturday night, some Negro who works for me wanting me to bail him out of jail after a fight at a juke joint. He got stabbed or he stole somebody's rent money."

"Do you bail him out?" Polly swats me, but I don't care.

"Jack," says Polly's mother. She's got an iron grip on the steering wheel and is leaning forward as she drives. It makes me think of when Parnell first learned to drive and I would ride with him and Daddy through the dirt roads on Uncle Vivian's plantation. "Aim high in steering!" Parnell would say as he put his hands at ten o'clock and two o'clock on the steering wheel and looked way out in front of him.

"I do," says Mr. Bayard. "I bail them out. I leave my warm bed to go down there in the wee hours and vouch for Adam or PeeToe or Moxie, or whoever got hisself in trouble." Mr. Bayard shakes his head like this is his cross to bear in life.

"What is bail?" I ask. Polly stares hard out her window like she's not listening to me, but I know she's hanging on every word.

"You post bail to get out of jail and go home," says Mr. Bayard. "It's a certain amount of money the court asks you to hand over to ensure you'll show up for a trial at a later date."

I know I'm pressing my luck, but I have to know. "Did someone post bail for the colored boy at the Leflore?"

"No need to," says Mr. Bayard, who seems happy to answer me, just like he's reporting the news. Polly's mother sits up straighter in the driver's seat but doesn't say anything.

Mr. Bayard continues. "The police didn't put him in jail. The city attorney was there when they brought him in and got him released. He's just a kid. Nobody wants a kid in jail."

"Mr. Carr?" I ask. "Mary Margaret's father?"

"The very one," says Mr. Bayard. "Now *there's* a body that gets calls in the middle of the night!"

"Jack, *please*," says Polly's mother, and that shuts up Mr. Bayard, who I think would make a fine gossip at Meemaw's bridge table.

So Raymond didn't go to jail. I'm surprised at how relieved I feel.

Mr. Bayard wipes his face with a handkerchief. "Where is this Freedom House, Carol Ann?"

"708 Avenue N," says Polly's mother. "Right up here, I think." She swings the station wagon right, onto Avenue N, and cruises slowly down the crumbling road.

Suddenly we come upon a gaggle of grown-ups, colored and white, about the age of Parnell or Jo Ellen, standing and talking — and laughing — on a freshly painted porch. Portulacas, Meemaw's least favorite flower, spill out of a pie pan on the wide porch rail and a tabby cat sleeps next to them. The patch of grass in front needs cutting. A radio plays from somewhere in the house.

"This must be the place," says Mr. Bayard. Polly's mother pulls to the side of the road and we stare for what feels like forever, as Mr. Bayard adds, "These aren't our coloreds." Another eon passes and Mr. Bayard says, "I think these coloreds are paid civil rights workers from somewhere else."

Polly's mother turns off the engine but keeps her hand on the keys.

The workers are sizing us up, too, but they don't seem to think we're a problem, and I'm certain we don't scream trouble. We are kids — two of us are, anyway — and all four of us look confused.

The agitators stand in twos and threes, with clipboards and papers. I see two colored men in straw hats, one in a button-down shirt and one in a FREEDOM NOW T-shirt. The girls are wearing shirtwaist dresses. None of them is Jo Ellen. They all look meltingly hot and are blinking into the sun, using their hands for sun visors. I can tell they like one another. A white girl laughs at something a Negro boy says, and then they hug each other. I blink at the sight.

"Lord have mercy," says Polly's mother. Finally she pulls the keys from the ignition and says, "Both of you. Come with us," as if it might be more dangerous to leave us in the car than take us inside the Freedom House. That suits me fine. She eyeballs Polly with a look I don't understand, but Polly does. She whispers to me, "Proverbs 22:6. 'Train up a child in the way he should go: and when he is old, he will not depart from it.'"

Smooth as silk, I answer her. "Romans 12:2. 'And be not conformed to this world: but be ye transformed by the renewing of your mind. . . .'"

We step out of the car and enter another world.

PART 3
ENGAGEMENT

Joshua fought the battle of Jericho
And the walls came tumblin' down.

— African American spiritual

CALLIN' OUT AROUND

ARE YOU READY FOR A

After a cross is burned in front of a freedom house, it becomes a freedom sign.

THE WORLD,

BRAND-NEW BEAT?

From "Dancing in the Street" by Ivy Jo Hunter, Marvin Gaye, William Stevenson, sung by Martha and the Vandellas, released by Barry Gordy/Motown, 1964

SUMMER'S HERE
AND THE TIME
IS RIGHT

FOR
DANCIN'
IN THE
STREET!

The SNICK "office" in Greenwood is like a front company headquarters during wartime.

From "SNCC: The Battle-Scarred Youngsters" by Howard Zinn in *The Nation,* October 5, 1963

Summer volunteers Lenora Thurman, Elinor Tideman, and Sue Miller.

ALL WE NEED IS MUSIC, SWEET MUSIC, THERE'LL BE MUSIC EVERYWHERE

Summer volunteers at COFO Freedom House in Meridian, Mississippi.

Summer volunteer Bruce Solomon of Brooklyn, New York, teaches a class at a Freedom School in Jackson, Mississippi.

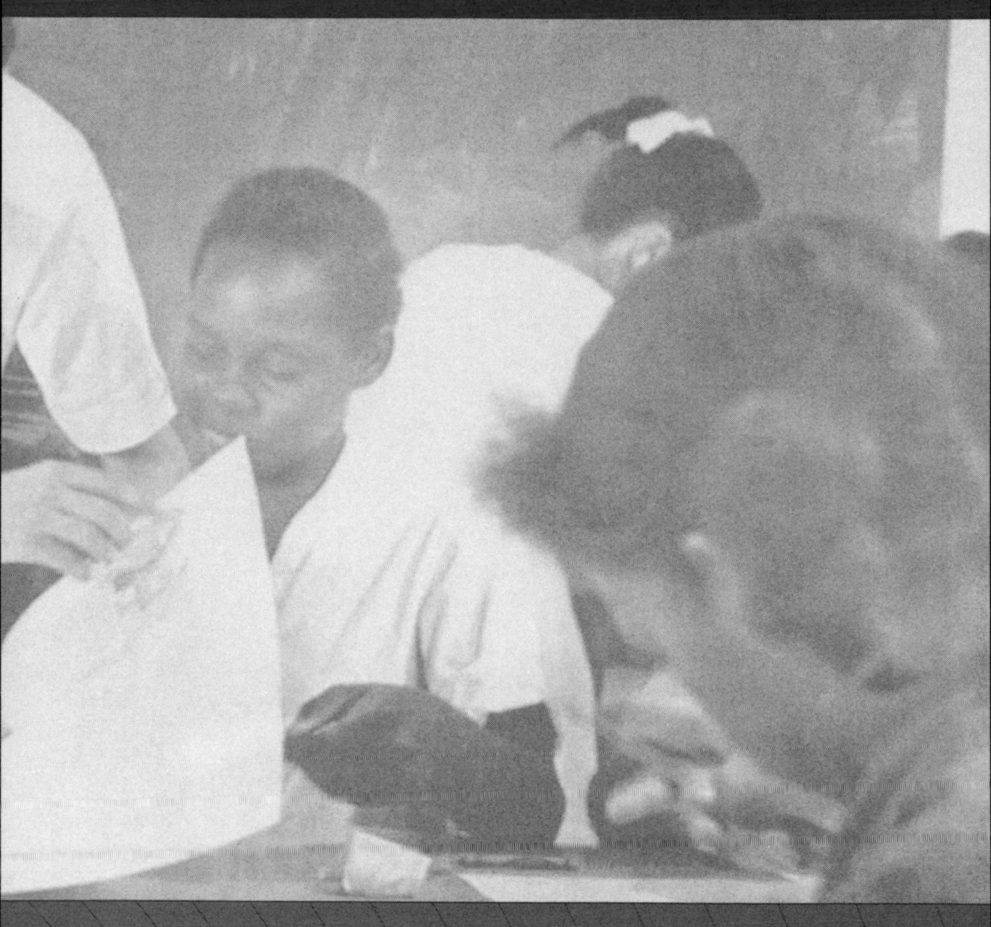

OH, IT DOESN'T MATTER WHAT YOU WEAR, JUST AS LONG AS YOU ARE THERE

Local teenagers dancing to the jukebox at Beddingfield's store near Mileston, Mississippi. Summer volunteers Abe Osheroff and Jim Boebel were building the Mileston Community Center.

SO COME ON
EVERY GUY,
GRAB A GIRL
EVERYWHERE,
AROUND THE
WORLD

Reverend Jim Nance, canvassing, registering voters outside of Hattiesburg, Mississippi, during Freedom Summer. In the summer of 1964, COFO workers started wearing straw hats to distinguish them from SNCC and other volunteers in Mississippi.

"They set up schools in Negro churches, and many of the local Negroes were wary of their being in their neighborhoods and refused to have anything to do with them. . . . We spent one day going around to some of the Freedom Schools and observing them and talking to them. Most of them looked as if they had not had a bath or washed their hair in a month. When we got back to the house for lunch the first thing we did was give our hands a good scrubbing. It was quite an experience."

From the journals of UPI reporter and Greenwood, Mississippi, resident Sara Criss

Summer volunteer Anthony "Arrow" Beaulieu (from San Francisco, California; a student at Dartmouth College) writes a letter while sitting on top of a U.S. mailbox in front of True Light Baptist Church in Hattiesburg, Mississippi.

THIS IS AN INVITATION, ACROSS THE NATION, A CHANCE FOR FOLKS TO MEET

LET'S FORM A BIG STRONG LINE, AND GET IN TIME,

WE'RE DANCIN' IN THE STREET

Reading in the Freedom House library, Hattiesburg, Mississippi, summer 1964.

The sign originally said *States Rights — Racial Integrity.*

SNCC Field Secretary Sandy Leigh (New York City), director of the Hattiesburg project, stands near the blackboard he uses to illustrate his Mississippi Freedom Democratic Party (MFDP) lecture to Freedom School students in the sanctuary of True Light Baptist Church.

WAY DOWN IN L.A., EVERY DAY THEY'RE DANCIN' IN THE STREET

ACROSS THE OCEAN BLUE, ME AND YOU

WE'RE DANCIN' IN THE STREET!

45

As soon as we're out of the car, all the talking stops. A tall Negro man who says his name is Sam Block introduces himself and says welcome, asks if he can help us, and Mr. Bayard says we're from the paper and would like just a few minutes to talk. Sam, who is a sharp dresser, like Parnell, tells us the volunteers have been there for a lunchtime meeting and are just leaving for their afternoon's work — they all say hey to us and introduce themselves. Sally, Linda, two Bobs, Lawrence, Eli, Mary, Bambi, Dick, Carol, Heather, Wally, Bruce.

"Come on in," says Sam as the volunteers drift off to wherever they're supposed to go and whatever they're supposed to do. Knock on Laura Mae's door, maybe.

Inside, two fans blow the hot air around the room. The tangy smells of potato salad and collards make me hungry — I never did eat my sandwiches.

Two colored boys play Ping-Pong at a table set up where a living room might have been once. An old couch sags next to the wall. A colored girl sits at a huge, heavy desk, typing on a huge, heavy typewriter. I have never seen a colored girl with a typing job.

The girl, who can't be much older than me and Polly and whose name is Ida Mae, greets us, surprise in her voice, and tells us we can talk with the community center coordinator upstairs, so we go upstairs to the library, where it's even hotter than downstairs and where there are more fans, and where we find colored kids sprawled on the scuffed wooden floor, coloring with a new box of crayons. There are books everywhere in piles, in boxes, and on shelves that look new against the freshly painted walls.

"Hello?" says Polly's mother when she sees no community center coordinator in the room.

"Oh! I'll get her!" says one of the coloring girls, who turns out to be Ree, the girl who was at church with Jo Ellen. She's wearing dirty white tennis shoes with white socks and a too-short dress that ties in the back with a sash. Her hair has at least six pigtails in it. She doesn't recognize me.

She runs into another room and comes out pulling Jo Ellen by the hand. *Jo Ellen!* She's wearing another shirtwaist dress and has a bandanna around her hair, tied at the back of her neck. Her locket practically screams my name. My every cell begins to vibrate. My heart does a pitty-pat and tries to leap out of my chest and hug her.

"Hello!" she says. She's not sure whether to walk toward us or not, which makes Ree suddenly shy. The other kids sit up and pay attention to us, too, but they don't say a word. One of them is William, from the church. His mouth forms a small O — he recognizes me.

Mr. Bayard again makes introductions and says we just want to talk with someone about the work the volunteers are doing this summer, and Jo Ellen says she is in charge of the library and part of her job is to unpack and shelve all the books sent from all the kind people and supporters up north, who also send money to pay the bills and pay some of the field secretaries, which is what the bosses are called, I think.

I stand there through all this and hope Jo Ellen will notice me. Which she does. She saves her most beatific smile for me. "Hello again, Sunny."

I stammer out a hello. It feels like it's been a hundred years since I last saw her and my whole life changed.

"You know each other?" Polly's mother asks. Polly looks from Jo Ellen to me and back again. I want to scream at them, *This is my real mother! This is how my mother would love me if she were here! This is what it's like to have a mother! Don't you recognize her?* and other crazy things, but I don't say a word. Still, my pulse beats in my ears and I feel like crying. I can't help it.

Jo Ellen says, "Sunny was kind enough to give us directions one day when a friend and I were lost downtown." I see the light of recognition in Ree's face now.

Polly's mother nods like she gets it perfectly, which she doesn't. But she doesn't push me out the door and take me directly home, like Uncle Vivian did. Instead, she takes out her shorthand notebook and gets her interview. Polly and I are invited to browse the books, which we do. Suddenly I need to take a book from here. I need to take it and keep it near me, always, so I hide a copy of *Captains Courageous* in my shorts. It will be hard to walk to the car without being found out, but I can do it.

While I'm busy turning this way and that, trying to push the book down the front of my shorts, I'm half on the lookout for being seen, and half listening to the interview — or, more accurately, listening to Jo Ellen's lilting voice. It sounds like a lullaby to me, like all the voices I've ever dreamed of loving me, like it was created, this voice, just for me.

"Yes, we are registering voters — black and white — for the Mississippi Freedom Democratic Party, which is an alternative to the all-white Mississippi Democratic Party, which will not allow Negroes a voice or the vote."

"Neither will the Republicans, for that matter," says Sam, who has come up the stairs to see how we're doing. "Negroes cannot vote, period, in Mississippi — or in Alabama, or in Georgia, or in most states in the American South." He sounds like a history teacher or a reporter. His face is wide-open and weary, but his eyes are fiery and serious.

Polly's mother asks him, "Are you giving up on registering Negroes at the courthouses in Mississippi, then?"

"Oh, no," says Sam. "We are hoping to force President Johnson, Congress, and the Justice Department to pay attention to us and help us. Negroes in Mississippi would very much like to register to vote peacefully, but there are impossible tests they must pass, passages of the Constitution they must read and interpret, poll taxes they must pay, and of course there is the ever-present fear of reprisal and arrest. . . ."

Polly is pretending to read a copy of *Aesop's Fables*, which would have been easier to stuff down my shorts.

"And just what is the Mississippi Freedom Democratic Party?" asks Mr. Bayard.

"We are offering the MFDP as an alternative to the Democratic Party this presidential election season," says Sam as I wriggle and stuff. "We will have presidential and vice presidential candidates, we will hold a convention in Jackson, and we will go to Atlantic City in August, to the Democratic National Convention, and ask to be seated in place of the racist Democratic Party."

I don't understand half of what Sam is saying, but I do know that if Meemaw were here, she would be having an apoplexy. We'd need the smelling salts. I can tell by the bold tone of voice Sam is using. *Strident*, Meemaw would call it

"Where are you from, boy?" Immediately Mr. Bayard's face colors up. "I mean . . . where are you from?" he repeats.

Sam keeps his eyes on Mr. Bayard's. "I'm from Cleveland, Mississippi, Mr. Bayard, right here in the Delta, born and raised."

"Huh," says Mr. Bayard. He sticks his hands in his pockets and rocks back on his heels a little.

Polly's mother asks Jo Ellen, "And where are you from?"

"I'm from Camp Springs, Maryland," says Jo Ellen. "Just outside Washington, D.C. I'm a student at the University of Maryland."

I think I have never heard of a more beautifully named town. Camp Springs. I could be from Camp Springs. I could live there forever and be happy.

I stand at the front picture window and look out on Avenue N while I try to finesse the book down farther between my underwear and shorts. All I manage to do is squirm like I have to go to the bathroom in the worst way.

"We have an outhouse in the backyard," calls Jo Ellen in a helpful, loving voice.

"I'm fine," I call back, turning my head just enough to let her know I heard her and am A-OK.

"Freedom Day is July sixteenth, all across Mississippi, wherever we have Freedom Houses," says Jo Ellen in response to another question from Polly's mother. "We expect the FBI will be here in Greenwood, and the press, and anyone who is interested in seeing justice done in Mississippi. We expect the local police will be ready for us as well. We've stopped using the telephones here, as you might know, and use a WATS line now, for communication with Washington and with other COFO and SNCC offices. We don't trust the police not to listen in to our conversations, I'm sorry to say."

Or Miss May. I hear Boo in my head: *There will be more arrests.*

"I find it interesting you trust the local press enough to tell us all this," says Mr. Bayard.

Sam says, "We aren't telling you anything your police department doesn't already know. We would love to see this in print, in your local papers. We know it's not likely. We know we're not welcome in white Greenwood. But we feel we've got an important job to do here in Mississippi."

"Isn't your presence in the Negro community problematic for the Negroes as well?" asks Mr. Bayard.

Sam Block laughs. "You're right about that, I'll admit. I had to sleep in my car the first four months I worked in Greenwood! No one knew what to do with me. But that was two years ago. I'd say SNCC has earned the trust of most folks in the Negro community now. And the student volunteers this summer are working hard to earn that trust as well."

Polly comes and stands next to me, on my right. We watch a car with a whip antenna crawl by the Freedom House. Two white men are inside. A rifle leans across one's chest and tips out the open passenger window. As the car passes the house, the driver revs the engine and stirs up a rooster tail of dust behind it. Polly puts her hand on my arm as if she's saying, *Did you see what I saw in that car?* I nod.

"Excuse me," says Sam Block. He hurries downstairs and the colored kids clatter after him, all but Ree, who stays near Jo Ellen.

When I turn toward Polly, my left hip looks like it's jutting out six extra inches, like I've jammed a slab of bacon in my pocket . . . or a book down my shorts. Polly stares. She's working up a Bible verse about stealing, I can see it in her eyes, but instead she sighs and turns away from me and walks back to the grown-ups.

I jiggle the book around some more, and a huge triangle of it dips below my shorts hem.

"Would you like to check out that book?" asks Jo Ellen, just as nice as peach pie. "Anybody can borrow books from the lending library."

I feel my neck on fire. My cheeks are burned completely off. I want to answer, *What book?*, but I think I am too caught for that. So I just pull the book out and face down the stares of

Polly's mother, Mr. Bayard, and Ree. "I had an itch," I say. And no one laughs. I try again. "I hurt my knee." That's worse.

I hand the book to Jo Ellen and she says, "I'm going to keep this on my desk for you. You come back and read it anytime. I'm glad to see you again."

I nod my head and follow my people down the stairs, out the door, and into the car to ride home.

"You're getting really weird, Sunny," whispers Polly.

"I know" is all I can whisper back. I know.

46

"Why you did that by yourself?" Twill ask me. "We supposed to gone with you!"

"I know." That's what I tell him. "Next time."

"Half the town thinks you a hero and half think you crazy," say Jimmy. He hits pop flies out to left field. I catch 'em. Took me two years to save for my glove. It come from Memphis last year. Still breakin' it in.

"I know!" I burn the ball to Twill at second base, like they's a runner on first. No pitcher, just Jimmy hitting poppers for catchin' practice.

"Where you been all day?" Twill ask me.

"Workin'." That's all I got to say about it. I told Mr. Booker Wright his windas so dirty, it was keepin' customers from eating at Booker's Place. He told me to clean 'em for fifty cents, since I such a hero now. Or crazy. So I did. Told me he'd give me another fifty cents if I mopped the floors and cleaned the outhouse, so I did that, too. Then I went to the Chinaman's store and paid Mr. Lee his two dollars.

"No need," he say. "I donate to Freedom. Please."

I left the dollars on the counter. My job done.

Simon take the bat from Jimmy. "You see that *Jet* magazine with Cassius Clay and Malcolm X on the cover? Clay change his name to Muhammad Ali, and he a Muslim now."

"He the greatest!" say Jimmy.

"I am the greatest!" Twill say it like he mean it, like Cassius Clay say it.

"Willie Mays the greatest," I say.

"Willie's old," say Twill. "You can do better than that."

"Let's go watch the ball game at the white folks' field," I tell him.

"They don't let us," say Twill.

"New law say we can just waltz in and sit on those seats, free as we please," say Jimmy.

"We the FreedomMakers! Let's go," I tell 'em.

Jimmy change his mind. "You the hero, not us."

"They skin you alive, next time," say Twill. "Don't think they won't."

"What happened to the greatest? What happened to the FreedomMakers?" I yell. "You boys cowards!"

"No we not!"

"Then go home and get your dollar and meet me at that movie house!"

They scuffle and mumble and I tell 'em, "I go by myself, then. Chickens!" and I walk away. They think about it and runs after me.

"Come on, Ray! Let's do it! Right now!"

"You don't mean it," I tell 'em.

"We gon'!" they shout. "You watch! We as brave as you! We do it!"

"Go on, then," I say. "Show me. I'm make up my mind. I'm gon' to the ball game."

They walk off all bold and talkin' crazy about all they gon' do at that movie house.

They not gon'. They talk about makin' freedom, but they afraid.

And they not mad as me.

I take the long way home.

47

Thursday, July 9

Polly screams like she's been set on fire. "Hit it, Troy Allen!"

I'm sitting right next to her and have to cover my ears.

Troy Allen is up to bat and Polly is going to make sure he gets a hit, even if she has to wreck her vocal cords to do it.

"Don't let this get back to Paul," I tell her. "He may be the jealous type."

"She has no shame," says Mary Margaret, sitting on the other side of me. . . . Mary Margaret, who shrieked like a banshee when Gillette got on second base just minutes ago. But then, everybody cheered for Gillette, just as they're screaming for Troy Allen now. The game is close, and we're sitting in the screamer section. For the first time I notice: Gillette has a huge cheering section. He is that good. And, maybe, he is that known, finally. I wonder at the difference a year makes. A year, and baseball.

Polly swats at me and screams once more. "You can do it, Troy Allen!"

Troy Allen swings a third time and misses. He has struck out. Our section of the bleachers moans like we've just seen the *Titanic* go down. The sweat trickles down my back. I smash a mosquito on my leg. It's hot.

The score is still tied, 4–4, and we're in the top of the ninth inning. It's been a great game. Gillette is on second base. Two outs. The home team is full of kids we know, too — there are probably twenty teams of boys here in Greenwood playing

Dixie Youth Baseball. Our team is sponsored by the Coca-Cola plant this year. Our opponent's sponsor is Barrett's Pharmacy, so we all know one another in the bleachers, more or less.

From the press box, Allan Harper intones the out and announces the change on the field. I spy Daddy coming back to his seat with an armful of hot dogs for himself and Annabelle and Boo and Audrey, who is jumping up and down with the excitement of being allowed to stay up late enough to attend Gillette's ball game. She seems to have made a full recovery from whatever ailed her, no thanks to me. I wave at Daddy and he nods back at me, acknowledging that he knows where I am, he approves, and all is well.

Up comes Nick Marshall to bat, Gillette's new best friend, who, it turns out, is suddenly on Gillette's ball team. How did that happen? I ask the question out loud, as the Barrett's pitcher calls a time out to talk with his catcher and Allan Harper lets us all know what's happening.

"Oh, I know all about it," says Mary Margaret. "Gillette said, since he didn't get to play last summer when he arrived here after . . . well, you know, after your dad and his mom got married. The season was already under way, and he wanted to make sure Nick got to play this summer. So he told his coach about it and told him what a good player Nick is, and his coach said okay!"

I just stare at Mary Margaret Fitzgerald Carr. "How would you know all that?"

Mary Margaret brushes at her skirt and says, "I might have been over at Nick's one day last week when Gillette was there, too. I might have had lunch with them."

I can't believe it. "Who are you after? Nick or Gillette?" I spit it out.

Polly comes to Mary Margaret's rescue. "Sunny, that's mean."

"Well, really," I say, "since when do you go over to a boy's house for lunch, just lah-dee-dah, because you feel like it?"

Mary Margaret licks her lips and stares at her lap. "My dad had some business to discuss with Nick's dad," she says, then adds, "Your pastor! It had to do with your dad hiring Vidella from the church after she was fired."

"She quit!" I say.

"Okay! After she quit!" says Mary Margaret. "She quit?"

"She quit," I say, and I surprise myself with my conviction.

The umpire yells "Play ball!" and we're back in the game. On second base, Gillette takes off his cap and smooths back his hair, then replaces his cap and gives it a purposeful tug, just like he did at the pool that night so long ago.

"Nick is cute," says Polly, as Nick swings outside the batter's box while the pitcher and catcher practice a few throws.

"Stop it," I snap. "How many boyfriends do you need?"

"That's mean, too," says Mary Margaret.

"I know!" I say, as I toss up my hands. "I know. I can't help it! I know."

Polly fights back tears.

"I'm sorry, Polly, really I am." I pat on my friend. Then, for good measure, I apologize to Mary Margaret as well.

"You're under a lot of pressure," states Mary Margaret, like it's a fact known to the entire town. "Do we need to talk about those ladies from New York City who came to your house yesterday? Because I know all about New York City."

"I don't want to talk about it," I say. But I do. "Annabelle served them tea, and Vidella sat with them! I was the maid! I brought in the little sandwiches, and I had to help Annabelle do the dishes after!"

"Wow," says Mary Margaret. "What was it like?"

"There was a white woman from New York, and Annabelle and Boo. Then there was a colored lady from New York, and

Vidella. And another colored lady named Geneva, from here. They sat in the living room with china plates on their laps and the New York ladies said, "We support you. What can we do? What do you need?" They were all dressed like they were going to church. They went to the Freedom House to visit the agitators after that."

"Annabelle and Boo went to the Freedom House!" Mary Margaret crosses herself.

"No!" I correct her. "Just the New York ladies."

Nick steps up to the plate and I shout, "Hit it, Nick!" as much to apologize to Polly as to stop talking about this.

"Did the agitators come to the house?" asks Polly.

I shake my head. The ladies had a car. They drove off together and the colored lady sat in the backseat — and after she'd sat in our living room, just like company."

"Stee-rike one!" Barrett's catcher runs out to the pitcher's mound, and the pitcher and catcher have a little chat about how to strike out Nick Marshall.

"I think my mom's worried about yours," says Polly. "I heard her tell Dad that it's one thing to bring over potato salad to feed them, but another to host them in your own home."

"It's all Annabelle's fault!" I stamp my foot. "She's a troublemaker, bringing strangers to our house like that."

"Play ball!" screams the crowd. The catcher trots back to home plate.

"Hit it, Nick Marshall!" screams Polly.

"I think I might have to move out," I say, "like Parnell did."

"Parnell moved out?" says Polly.

Now it's my turn to get teary. "I don't know where he is. He hasn't been home for two days."

"Steeee-rike two!" yells the umpire. Half the crowd gives off ominous groans, while the other half, the Barrett's half, sends up a hopeful cheer.

"You could go to the Leflore and ask him what he thinks he's doing," says Mary Margaret.

"I could," I say, "but I'm not allowed to go to the Leflore right now, because things are so uncertain there. Did you see there are people picketing outside?"

"Who's picketing?" asks Mary Margaret.

"It's not the coloreds," I say. "It's whites. They don't want the theater selling tickets to coloreds."

The Barrett's pitcher throws the ball to second, to keep Gillette on base. Gillette touches the bag, then leans over with his hands on his knees and spits into the dirt at his feet.

"You should go with Jodie Lynn Bayard," says Polly. "Her family invited me to go to the movies with them tomorrow night, but Mama is worried and says I can't go. Annabelle might let you."

"Annabelle doesn't get to say what I can and can't do," I snip. I decide to go with the Bayards, right then and there. Never mind that Jodie Lynn doesn't really like me. I don't really like her, either.

"Ball one!" Allan Harper announces.

"Mama hasn't dared write a story about it," says Polly. "I heard her say so to Dad."

"Well, she should!" I say.

"It would only bring the big newspapers and television here," Polly tells us. "Mr. Bayard says it will blow over. He said he isn't going to let some foolish white people stop him from enjoying a night out with his family."

"Ball two!"

"That's brave or crazy," says Mary Margaret. "My dad says it's dangerous at the Leflore right now. They're the only business in town that's integrating."

"My mom and dad drive by there every night," says Polly, "just to see what's happening."

Daddy and Annabelle do, too, on the way home from Fairchild's each night. Everyone wants to know what's happening at the Leflore. I can't imagine what Parnell must worry about, every single night at work as he collects a dollar from whoever wants to see the show and shoves back a ticket along with seven cents. I need to see Parnell. He didn't even tell me good-bye.

"Ball three!" warns Allan Harper, and a voice yells, "Don't walk him, Billy Joe! Throw strikes!"

"I'm to stay away from the courthouse, too," says Mary Margaret.

"We'll need a new George, then," I say.

"Just as well." Mary Margaret says. "Can we pick a place on the ground?"

"Hit it, Nick!" Polly screams again, just as Nick Marshall wallops the ball way out into center field and way, way over the head of the center fielder — it could have been Willie Mays out there and it would have been over his head, too. Home run.

We are all on our feet, cheering, as we watch the boys round the bases. The whole team comes out of the dugout and claps on Gillette and Nick, the two newest boys in town, who are suddenly like good old boys who have lived in the Delta forever. It's got to make Gillette feel good. From the press box Allan Harper bellows his approval of the home run, and then immediately starts in on the sure-fire abilities of the Barrett's team to get the next batter out.

I'm going to tell Gillette I'm sorry, that's how good I feel all of a sudden.

And I want Gillette to talk to me.

I know three things about Gillette: He loves that old dog. He loves baseball. And he likes for me to come to his games.

So I am here. I am here when the bright lights snap on because dusk has fallen, and I am here when the next batter,

Jimmy Miller, strikes out, retiring the side, and I am here when the Coca-Cola team takes the field and Gillette trots into center field.

I am here when the first batter for the Barrett's team gets a base hit, and I am here when the next batter gets a hit, and when the third batter hits a double and drives in a base runner, bringing the score to 6–5, with two runners on base and a chance for Barrett's to tie the game once again, or even win.

I am here, sitting in the bleachers, surrounded by screaming — hollering right along with everyone else — when the next batter for Barrett's hits a high fly ball that flirts between center and left field and sails back, back, back to the end of possibilities, back beyond where Gillette is running to reach it, and I am here when a colored boy in white high-top sneakers steps out of the shadows of dusk at the edge of the field and catches that ball with his gloved hand upturned and against his waist, a basket catch, just like Willie Mays.

I am here as that colored boy and Gillette almost collide, until Gillette veers sharp right and makes a circle. I am here as the entire ball field and bleachers stands as one person. We suck in our collective breath, as we watch Raymond toss the ball to Gillette and run off into the darkness, as Gillette catches the toss and burns it straight to second base as if nothing out of the ordinary has happened, where the second baseman catches it and tags the batter out. But the outfield umpire doesn't make the call. His mind is still back in center field, trying to make sense out of what has happened.

"*What* in tarnation was *that*?" yells Allan Harper over the loudspeaker, and now everyone is asking that question.

I don't tell a soul that I know the boy who appeared out of nowhere, and that he was the boy at the Leflore three nights ago. I keep this news to myself as everyone in the bleachers and on the field is asking *Who was that*? I know Gillette will keep it to himself, too. I am proud of how smoothly Gillette made the transition from surprise to business as usual. Just the facts, that's what he needs. And then he can decide.

Suddenly I can hear what Gillette was saying to me when we argued in the kitchen: *Think about how I must feel, Sunny. Think about it.* It occurs to me that I don't know how Gillette feels about most anything. Maybe he's right and I don't really know him, not really.

Both teams are on the field now, and Allan Harper announces that Coca-Cola is arguing that Gillette would have caught that ball and the game should be over, and Barrett's is saying Gillette never would have caught it, and their batter should be marked down for a home run, and men are on the edge of the ball field now, running into the woods, men are asking Gillette if he knows that boy — Gillette is shaking his head — parents are calling for order, and parents are calling for action. Polly and Mary Margaret are clambering down the bleachers to their parents, who are calling for them.

There's Daddy, waving me down as well, worry etched on his face. He was the one who comforted Annabelle this morning when the phone rang and someone told her she was vile for hosting paid Communist agitators from the North at her house. He's the one who said, "Don't worry about this, these people have nothing better to do, and this will pass."

He's the one who goes off to work each morning to face whoever walks through the front door at Fairchild's, hooligan or Hottentot, as Meemaw would say. I was listening by the telephone table when Daddy told Annabelle in the kitchen, "No matter what they believe, they still have to eat." But I know Daddy, and I could hear the quiver in his voice.

As I make my way down the bleachers, the thought dances on the hem of my attention: *Think about how your daddy must feel, Sunny. And what about Raymond? What does he feel?*

Now *there's* a brand-new mystery to figure out. I stare toward the darkness at the edge of the ball field and consider how Raymond caught that ball like he'd been standing there, in the shadows around the edge of the ball field at sunset, with nothing better to do than wait for that mysterious, magical moment when a baseball might curl toward the back of center field, drop into his life, and invite him to play.

48

On the way home from the ball game, we stop at Fairchild's, which is out of the way, so Daddy can check on the refrigerator that keeps threatening to stop working.

I wish someone would talk about what happened at the game tonight, but it's as if it never happened. The game was called a tie and everyone went home in a sort of daze after standing around and debating it for a while. And that's that.

Audrey has fallen asleep in Boo's lap. Boo is asleep, too, in the backseat between me and Gillette. She smells less like Vicks every day, thank goodness. Gillette hasn't spoken a word to me, and there's this whole big *thing* between us, just waiting to be talked about. He doesn't know the half of it.

Daddy pulls the car into the parking lot at the side of the building and tells me and Gillette to stay with Boo and Audrey. The windows are down and there's a little bit of a breeze. "We won't be long," he says.

"I'm coming in," I announce, and I get out of the car without asking permission. Daddy hardly notices. "I don't know what I'll do if the compressor's burned out," he tells Annabelle. "There's not another cooler big enough to hold all that's going to go bad overnight."

A note is taped to the front door. The writing is angry, scrawled in fat, black letters. Daddy can't keep me from it. By the light of the streetlamps, Daddy, Annabelle, and I read:

Send your "wife" back where she came from or make her behave, if you want to sell groceries in this town. You will hear from us!

Daddy pulls the note off the door, tears it into pieces, and throws it on the ground. "Ignore this," he says, but his voice has an edge to it I don't like. "These are not the decent people of this town. And there are plenty of them who will not let something like this happen."

"The decent people don't *do* anything!" says Annabelle. In the streetlamp's glow, she looks like a ghostly woman in distress in one of my monster movies. "Decent people are scared to speak up! Do you honestly think they're going to protect you, Jamie? Or me? I'm not even *from* the Delta. I'm already an interloper in their eyes. And I have children!"

"*We* have children," Daddy says firmly, looking from Annabelle to me, and seeing it's hopeless to keep me from it. "I'm not going to let a few misguided men on the Citizens' Council tell me what to do. That's why I said yes to hiring Vidella Brown when you pressed me about it."

"She needed a job," says Annabelle.

"Dozens of colored women need a job right now, Annabelle! Hiring a Negro who has lost her job because she tried to register to vote is an act of insurrection to some in this town."

"She quit."

"She had to. Her life would have been miserable there. Too many powerful people at church wanted her gone. And now the two of you — and your mother! — are conspiring to fix race relations in Greenwood all by yourselves!"

Daddy unlocks the door, walks inside, and turns on the lights. I like being in the light.

"Sunny," says Daddy, and I know he's going to tell me to wait outside. Then I see him decide that's not a good idea.

"Wait in my office," he orders. He picks up the pieces of the note and throws them in the trash inside the front door.

"Yessir." I make straight for his office like a good girl, but the office is in the front of the store, near the bakery. I'm disappointed I won't be able to hear the argument. But I needn't worry. Both Annabelle and Daddy are upset — I've never seen them like this — and I can hear them just fine from the front of the store without any of the usual store noises to muffle their conversation.

I turn on the office lights and begin to draw a tomato on some poster board. Maybe they're on special this week. One thing I discovered when I made signs for Daddy during my exile is that drawing is soothing.

"Many of those misguided men are your friends, Jamie," says Annabelle. "Lifelong friends! Business owners! Lawyers! Policemen! Nobody in this town wants integration — not even you! — and that's a fact. But it's coming."

"And that's the point," says Daddy. "It's coming. We can fight it, or we can ease into it. Inviting those women from the North to have tea at our house is not exactly easing into it!"

"I'm not doing it on my own," says Annabelle. "There is another group of us in Jackson and another in Hattiesburg. We're being careful. We need to know we're not alone down here, Jamie. We need help. I don't intend to be one of those people who cowers in her kitchen, afraid to speak out."

"The FBI is here to help," says Daddy. "I see them at the courthouse every day, watching."

"They don't *do* anything. We need people who will help us!"

I want to strangle Annabelle for creating all this trouble for Daddy.

Daddy tries to reason with her. I know, because he has used this tone of voice with me. "Use your discretion, Annabelle — that's all I'm saying. You could take lessons from Carol Ann."

"I used discretion for years," says Annabelle. "I was the very soul of discretion. I kept my mouth shut. It made things worse. In fact, it made me an accomplice."

"You're making up for lost time at my expense," Daddy says. "I have to work in this town! We have to live here! You're setting up the children to be ridiculed, and it has been hard enough for them."

"It may be hard. But how will they ever learn right from wrong if we don't teach them?" She lowers her voice to a loving level. "I know you know that."

There is a long pause. I step out of the office and tiptoe closer to the bakery to make sure I don't miss anything.

"I know that," says Daddy, his voice calmer now, too. "I just want you to be careful."

"Being careful would never have brought me you," says Annabelle. Then she adds in a softer voice, "Being careful, you would never have come for me that morning."

Daddy has nothing to say to that. Maybe they are hugging. I crane my neck to see down the canned goods aisle to the coolers. The giant cooler door sucks open.

Annabelle says, "It's okay to be scared."

There is another long pause. The cooler door bangs shut. "It's fine," Daddy says. "Let's go. I'll see if I can order a new compressor this week, just in case. We can't repair this one much longer."

I cut out my lights, Daddy cuts out his, and I give Annabelle my best look of disapproval as I step in front of her to walk out the door of Fairchild's. I hope she knows I heard every word.

They were meant for each other, Polly and Dorothy.

They were so different.

They were so alike.

Polly Speigel Cowan's German-Jewish family immigrated to the United States and peddled their way across the Midwest at the turn of the last century, and settled, finally, in Chicago, Illinois, among a thriving Jewish population, where they started a very successful mail-order furniture company called Speigel's and became wealthy.

Polly was born in 1913 after her family had left the city and moved to the Chicago suburb of Kenilworth. She was the only Jewish girl in her very white, very select, very upper-class neighborhood, and the only Jewish girl in her grade, every year, in school. She was not invited to parties or dances, and she didn't know why at first. But the other parents knew.

We don't mingle with those who
are not like us.

So Polly often felt like an outsider growing up, unwanted and excluded. But inside her family, her parents passed on to her the Reform Jewish faith:

Learn to do good, seek justice, rescue the oppressed, defend the orphan, plead for the widow.

Polly learned to think for herself, as she listened to family stories of European Jews losing their citizenship, countries, and lives in World War II. She understood that there were certain moments in history that compelled others to act. She learned to ask herself:

Is there something wrong with me, or is there something wrong with the world?

Because she knew herself, she knew the answer. She became a seeker and an adventurer. She married Lou Cowan — another adventurer — and made a life for her family in New York City, never forgetting that part of her job was to make the world a better place.

Enter Dorothy.

* * *

Dorothy Irene Height was born in 1912 in Richmond, Virginia. Her father was a building contractor and her mother was a nurse in the Negro hospital in Richmond. When she was four, Dorothy's family moved to Rankin, Pennsylvania, as part of the Negro Great Migration North. Hospitals in Pennsylvania wouldn't hire Negro nurses, so Dorothy's mother became a domestic worker. She joined the Pennsylvania Federation of Colored Women's Clubs and took Dorothy with her to every state and national meeting so Dorothy could see women working, organizing, and teaching themselves.

Dorothy grew up in a neighborhood with Italian, German, Croatian, and Jewish families, and mostly felt right at home.

> *"I have so many memories of being together with people who were so different from one another."*

Everyone felt different, but that was okay, in Dorothy's world. She attended public school with her different friends. Their teachers drilled them relentlessly in the English language until, no matter what language they spoke at home, they all knew perfect English as well. Dorothy was a good student.

When she arrived in New York City to attend Barnard College, the registrar told her that, yes, they had accepted her, but they hadn't known she was black, and they already had their quota of black students, thank you very much. Humiliated, different, Dorothy did not go home. She went directly to New York University and presented them with her acceptance letter from Barnard and her grades. They told her, "A girl with these kind of grades doesn't need an application to enroll at NYU."

Dorothy was on her way.

She knew how precious work was. She had seen her father hire so many men who came from the South, desperate for a job. She knew how important community was — she had seen it at home, and at her mother's meetings. And she knew how important dignity was.

Years later, when Dorothy was president of the National Council of Negro Women and everyone called her Dr. Height, she sat an arm's length from Martin Luther King, Jr., the only woman on the dais while Dr. King delivered his "I Have a Dream" speech at the March on Washington, August 28, 1963. Although she had helped organize the march, she had not been allowed to speak. But she knew who she really was, and by now she knew that women were powerful.

So how could women make change in the civil rights movement? Where was a woman's place? That was Dorothy's question, and Polly's as well.

They met at a meeting set up by Stephen Courier, who had started the Taconic Foundation in the early sixties, to encourage whites to donate to the civil rights movement. He invited wealthy white New Yorkers to a breakfast at the Carlysle Hotel, where they could meet civil rights leaders and hear their stories of the struggle in the South.

All the leaders at the meeting but Dorothy were men. When Stephen asked who might like to have volunteers from this audience to help with their work, the only person to raise her hand . . . was Dorothy.

And that's how these two very different women became colleagues. Polly became a volunteer for the National Council of Negro Women, and after the March on Washington, Polly and Dorothy began working on how women might best support women, in the fight for civil rights.

They put their heads together along with Doris Wilson, Susan Goodwillie, and others. The National Council of Negro Women, the Young Women's Christian Association, the National Council of Jewish Women, the National Council of Catholic Women, and the National Church Women came together to form the only civil rights program led by a national women's organization. It was about black liberation as part of human liberation, and justice for African Americans as part of justice for all people, all over the world. They called their project:

Wednesdays in Mississippi.

In the summer of 1964 — Freedom Summer — interracial teams of women flew from New York to Mississippi on a Tuesday. When they landed in Jackson, Mississippi, they got off the plane and acted like they didn't know one another. The white northern women were picked up by white southern women, and the black northern women by black southern women. It was too dangerous for them to ride, black and white, in cars, as friends, together, in 1964, in Mississippi.

They went to their hosts' homes, and on Wednesdays, they went out into Mississippi and met with a small group of women — the white northern women met with white southern women, and the black northern women met with black southern women — to let them know that they were not alone, that they had support, that here was money, here were supplies, here was good talk, and here were good stories — *Let's get to know one another,* they said. *Let's learn to trust one another. Tell us how it is for you, here in Mississippi, so we can take your stories back and share them.*

It was dangerous work! Southern white women were afraid for their husbands to find out — at first, the northern white women had to stay in hotels because the southern white women were so afraid of their neighbors discovering that they were housing agitators. But the northern black women always had homes to come to, as the southern black women were used to this fear, and knew how it felt.

They shared their lives, these women. Even though they were shaking, they held their heads high and dressed in their Sunday best — their pearls, their hats, their gloves, their most stylish dresses. They dared anyone to arrest them. And no one did.

Seven teams of northern women went to Mississippi in the summer of 1964. Forty-eight women. Thirty-two were white, sixteen were black; thirty-two were Protestants, six were Catholics, and eight were Jews. Forty-four had college degrees. Four were Ph.Ds. They were school teachers, businesswomen, board members, writers, sorority sisters, who could use their positions and social networks to create change. Polly called them "the Cadillac crowd." Their job was to build bridges of understanding.

These northern women and their southern counterparts became the shock-absorbers of change, working in a ministry of presence. They showed up, every week, all summer long, at different houses, for tea and talk. They coordinated with COFO and SNCC and toured the Freedom Schools and community centers. They brought supplies and food and resources, and they supported the student volunteers with their presence, like guardians, like mothers, like warrior women.

They noted the conditions in jails, they went to the courthouse when Freedom Workers were arrested, they observed the fear and the police behavior, and they heard story after story of courage from both blacks and whites. When suspicious southern whites asked them what they were doing, they replied: "We're just listening."

The northern women took home the stories of the southern women and they asked for funds, for money and supplies, to keep the movement going, and they got them.

And soon, women met together, black and white, southern and northern, in one place. When they sat down to eat together at a Mississippi restaurant, all the other diners got up and left. But because the Civil Rights Act had been passed, the restaurant was required to serve them. And did. The black kitchen help at first watched in disbelief, and then began to stand guard by the table, protectively, in a gesture of respect.

These women helped to change the South. The bravery it took for the southern women to open their homes was immense. But once a few did it, more would do it. The understanding that the South was changing — would have to change — melted more women's hearts — women who could now stand against their neighbors or husbands or families, and do the right thing.

When the summer was over, the *New York Times* ran a front-page story about Wednesdays in Mississippi that announced "Women Tear Down the Cotton Curtain." They were community organizers who went back to Mississippi in 1965 with "Workshops in Mississippi" and who continued, through the National Council of Negro Women, to develop a hunger program, a housing program, a health program, a careers program, and help for teenagers — all designed to put people into action on their own behalf, helping themselves, their families, and their communities. "It's in the neighborhoods and communities where the world begins," said Dorothy — Dr. Height. Voter registration was a main and natural component of this organizing. The Wednesday Women were part of the revolution.

As one of them said:

> *"We have learned here we can better understand each other when we talk together. We've learned we can work together and even sit together. We've learned we can eat together. Maybe we can learn to live together and die together."*

Freedom Summer and Wednesdays in Mississippi helped to reawaken the women's movement as women were united by their differences and their shared experiences.

Just like Polly and Dorothy. They became the best of friends, these two very different women. They never felt like outsiders with each other. They talked with each other every day, until the day Polly died too soon, in a house fire, in 1976. Dorothy, who'd had such severe asthma as a child that she wasn't expected to live beyond the age of sixteen, grew out of it as a teenager and went on to fool everyone — she lived to be ninety-eight years old. When she was ninety-five, she sat once again on the dais, this time to watch Barack Obama take the oath of office as president of the United States in 2008.

President Obama called Dr. Height "the godmother of the civil rights movement." How much of the election of the country's first African American president had to do with a group of courageous women who met every Wednesday in 1964 to ask questions and listen? How much was due to a young German-Jewish girl in Chicago who grew up to witness a moment in history and felt compelled to act? How much to an African American girl who grew up and remembered who she really was?

This is how it works. Everything is connected. Every choice matters. Every person is vital, and valuable, and worthy of respect.

49

We ride home together down Main Street while the night bugs harmonize in all their different voices, a mighty chorus from the trees and tall grasses. Boo and Audrey are awake now and sitting in the front seat between Daddy and Annabelle.

Boo tells Audrey about the time she played baseball with the boys when she was a little girl, every detail under the sun. I want to say "Time for the NoDoz" like Meemaw, but instead I close my eyes and concentrate on how sweet the night air feels against my face. I lift my chin to the breeze that cools the crease in my neck where the grit and the sweat gathers. I'm grateful for the extra space in the backseat.

I start to hum a tune to myself, to take my mind off nasty notes and the anger in Daddy's voice, the determination in Annabelle's. *Arguing! They were arguing*, I say to myself. Gillette laughs at Boo's descriptions of wearing pantaloons to play ball. Daddy turns left onto West Church Street. Instead of going all the way to Cotton and home to River Road, he turns right on Fulton Street, which means we're going to pass the Leflore.

"Can we stop and see Parnell?" I ask.

"We'll see," says Daddy.

Annabelle turns her head to smile at me, one of those stepmother smiles. "I know you miss him," she says as if she really does know me, which she doesn't. As if she wants to make up for me hearing her argue with Daddy.

"Do not," I sass. I close my eyes against anything she might say next. She can't tell me how I feel. She talks back to Daddy like she's in charge now. Well, she's not in charge of me.

Suddenly in a rushed and urgent voice Daddy says, "You kids get down on the floor."

"What?" I say.

"Do as you're told," Daddy says as serious as a heart attack, as he slows the car to a crawl. "Stay down."

Audrey wails as she is suddenly dumped at Annabelle's feet. Gillette and I are squashed on the floorboards behind the front seat, where the heat is stifling, and the air smells like dirty baseballs, me behind Daddy, Gillette behind Annabelle.

I can see Annabelle's face, worried, scared. She pulls her legs up onto the front seat to give Audrey more room. Boo soothes Audrey, who is whining.

I hear men talking, angry talk. I see the red blink of police car lights reflected off the ceiling of our car. Are we being stopped?

Gillette and I exchange a long look and I could almost cry over it because I know what it means. We're remembering — at the same time — that night we were almost arrested. And, even better, we know we can still talk to each other without even speaking. So we do.

Let's do it. Let's peek.

Suddenly we are compatriots again. I turn and face the door, then inch myself up enough to peer out the open window, and Gillette does the same on his side. We might only get one peek before we're caught, so I prepare to memorize all I see.

The headlights from half a dozen police cars flood the scene. A line of picketers walks in front of the Leflore, carrying handmade, painted signs:

KEEP GREENWOOD SEGREGATED!

DEFEND STATES' RIGHTS!

DO NOT CROSS PICKET LINE!

DO NOT PATRONIZE LEFLORE THEATER!

OWNERS ARE COMMUNISTS!

And the one that smacks me across the face:

COONS GO TO THIS THEATER

Daddy would never allow me to talk like that. Even Meemaw says only low-count people use that language.

Daddy is stopped at the traffic light on the corner of West Washington and Fulton Streets. The theater is on the opposite corner from my vision, so I inch up just another little bit, and turn my head to look. There's Parnell in the ticket booth, sitting as still as a statue, not one customer waiting to buy a ticket.

There are gaggles of men under the streetlights at the service stations on the other three corners. They are holding rifles in their hands, like they are daring anyone to enter the theater. Policemen stand beside their cars, arms crossed, watching but doing nothing.

"Rifles," murmurs Annabelle, like she would say *tarantulas.*

"That's Klan," says Daddy, plain and simple.

No one notices me and Gillette peering from our hiding place, not Daddy, not Annabelle. There is so much to look at. As one person, me and Gillette scoot up higher for a better view. My fingers curl around the metal where the open windows meet the body of the car.

A car with a whip antenna sits on the side of the street right in front of me. I blink when I realize Mr. Delay Beckwith is sitting in it. He looks directly at me, his eyes saying, *I see you and I know who you are*, and I sluice to the floor, shaking.

Just as the light turns green, the car behind us screeches into the opposite lane and guns it around us and then back into our lane ahead of us. Gillette and I both pop up onto the backseat in time to hear a terrific *craaaaash!* and see the splintering of glass and the scattering of pickets and the rushing of people to the ticket booth, where Parnell was sitting. The glass of the booth is completely shattered.

"Parnell!" I shout. I don't see him.

Daddy makes an immediate right turn into the alley instead of passing the theater and stomps on the brake so hard we lurch forward with the car. "Stay here!" he shouts as he throws the gearshift into PARK. We are left in the shadows of the alley as Daddy runs toward the lights.

Annabelle reaches her right arm to Audrey and her left arm back to us. "Wait here," she says as if she's sure we're about to jump from the car. Her voice shakes.

Gillette and I look out the back window. A police siren wails, then stops. Men with rifles, men with signs, are everywhere on the street, shouting. Someone throws a bottle and it shatters on the building, close to our car. Instinctively I shrink back and Audrey shrieks. Daddy appears at the open driver's door window. His voice is full of alarm. "I can't get in — they've got the doors locked from the inside. It's dangerous out here."

Immediately I know what to do. "I can get us in!" I shout, and I am out the door and clattering up the outside staircase on the side of the building in the dark before anyone can tell me not to. They are all right behind me, my entire family. I hear them, their hurrying feet clanging on the black metal stairs. I hear Gillette's stomping right behind me. I hear Annabelle helping Boo. I hear Gillette go back down to help them. I hear Daddy's two-at-a-time steps jostling the metal staircase, and Audrey's little-girl jouncing sounds — Daddy must be carrying her.

They're all right behind me, I think. *They're coming! Even though I can't see them, I know they're there.* The very thought breaks my heart with some sort of delirious, lunatic happiness or hopefulness, and here's what comes to me like a prayer: Hebrews 11:1. *Now faith is the substance of things hoped for, the evidence of things not seen.*

My heart slams in my chest so wildly I'm afraid it might burst. I pound on the projection room door for all I'm worth.

"Mr. Guston! Let me in! It's Sunny!"

50

"Now what?" says Daddy, to nobody in particular. We are safely inside the Leflore, in the projection room, crowding around the projector that is still showing *The Moon-Spinners*. We are almost to the part I was watching when the first bottle was thrown past my ear. Mr. Guston is eyeing us like we're creatures from the Black Lagoon invading his blinky darkness, and he doesn't know what to do with us.

"Thanks for letting us in," says Daddy. "Your doors are locked downstairs."

"I know," says Mr. Guston, squinting at us in the light that filters from the screen back to the projection room. "We're having a spot of trouble."

"They broke the glass in the ticket booth," says Daddy, "and I don't know if Parnell is all right."

"He's all right," says Mr. Guston. "He called me just a minute ago."

"You have a phone up here?"

"Oh, yes. They installed it just for me. They use it to wake me up if I don't get the reel changed in time." Mr. Guston is almost chatty. Audrey begins to whine and Gillette picks her up. Annabelle sits on the one seat in the room that Mr. Guston has offered her. Even in the shadows, I can see she's suddenly worn out. Maybe she's not supposed to run up metal staircases with her heart going ninety-to-nothing.

"Are there customers down there?" Daddy peers through one of the boxes cut into the wall for peering through on either side of the big projector hole.

"We still have customers," Mr. Guston says as he peers through the other box.

"They're not watching the movie," says Daddy. "Where are they?"

"I'd be hiding if I were them," says Mr. Guston. Then he adds, "Mr. Martini said to keep it rolling."

"Can I use the phone to call downstairs?" asks Daddy.

"Oh, yes. It's the same number. You just dial the number and hang up, it rings, and then you pick it up again and they'll pick it up downstairs, too. Here. I'll do it for you."

I hear the relief in Daddy's voice as he talks with Parnell. "He's all right," he says when he gets off the phone. Then he says, "I need to make one more call." He picks up the receiver again and dials.

When Mr. Carr comes on the line, we all get to hear what's happening as Daddy explains the situation to him. "There are three Negroes somewhere in the theater, all young men. Parnell sold them tickets. Everyone else has left, but there's a growing crowd out front, waiting to get the Negroes when they come out. It's a mean bunch. They've already broken the glass in the ticket booth, and some of them have rifles."

Gillette and I exchange a look in the shadows. *Is High-top here?*

Daddy listens to Mr. Carr for a long stretch. The projection room smells surround us: old cigarettes and fresh popcorn, alcohol to clean the projector lens, rubber cement to fix bits of broken film, and the white-hot smell of the bright projector light that animates every fragment of dust in its path to the screen.

"Our car is in the alley but close to the street," Daddy says to Mr. Carr. "It's not safe to go back out the way we came, and you'll be spotted if you show up there. You'll just draw a crowd."

Annabelle insists on giving up her seat to Boo, and Gillette puts Audrey on Boo's lap when Boo pats on her thighs, also insisting. Mr. Guston looks at me like he just can't believe I brought my entire family up the stairs and into this tiny projection room. Who would think to do such a thing? He gives my shoulder three confused pats. I give him a weak smile. "Sorry," I whisper, and he smiles at me in a resigned way.

Daddy cups his hand over the mouthpiece of the phone and asks Mr. Guston, "Is there a way down from here without using those outside stairs?"

"Yes," says Mr. Guston, "but it's steep and we never use it."

"Is it useable?"

"I expect it is."

"Do the exit doors at the back of the building work? Are they unlocked?"

"They have to work, and yes, they're unlocked during the show," says Mr. Guston. "That's the law."

I look through the boxed hole in the wall and watch the scene where Stratos pulls up the jewels from the cove and begins to fight with Mark and throws Mark overboard and then tries to run him over with the motorboat. No one throws a bottle and the movie plays on. Nikky steals a motorboat and convinces the sailors on a yacht to take her on board so she can talk to rich Madame Habib about the stolen jewels. The projector whirs away, oblivious to our plight.

Daddy says to Mr. Carr, "I'll meet you there in ten minutes. I'll let you in." Then he says to Mr. Guston, "Show me the stairs, please." And he tells us, "I'll go first to make sure the stairs are passable, you follow me. I don't want any of you outside by yourselves. We're going out the back door, where it's darkest and farthest from the crowds and we won't be seen. Stay together, stay with me. Everything will be fine. We'll find whoever's hiding and get them out safely. We'll all get out safely."

* * *

We creep, one by one, like the sections of a long caterpillar, down the steep wooden stairs. Mr. Guston refuses to come with us. "Got to stay with the picture," he says. Audrey cries softly in protest as Gillette tells her to keep her eyes closed and pretend it's a magic carpet ride. Audrey's not buying it for one cold minute. She clamps herself onto Gillette's back like she's riding horsey.

Daddy reaches the bottom of the stairs and shouts up to us. "Be *careful*! Come across the stage and wait for me to come get you. Gillette, you're in charge."

It's pitch-black in the stairwell, and we can hear through the walls the chanting and shouting boiling up outside. We sweep aside spiderwebs and feel our way down, keeping our palms on the cool concrete walls, as there is no banister to hold on to.

Annabelle is in front. Close to the bottom step, she slips and falls. Gillette is right behind her, scooping her up. Audrey screams as they stumble together to the landing, which is behind the screen and on the stage.

We each emerge into the light of *The Moon-Spinners* and rush to surround Annabelle. *Are you all right? Are you okay?* She assures us she is, holds on to Boo for a moment to catch her breath, and says, "Let's go," like this is a spy operation and she's second in command. Everyone follows her past the skyscraper-tall red velvet curtains and across the stage, behind the screen, to the opposite side. I swallow my pride and follow her, too. The movie is projected against all of us, so in a warped way, we are moving human screens.

I can see the patched hole in the screen, right in the middle, where that jughead Bobby Carpenter threw a gigantic dill pickle from the front row through the screen two years ago. Boy did he get it. They quit selling giant pickles at the concession after that.

Gillette has positioned himself at the top of the stage steps, as if he's guarding all of us while watching for Daddy. Boo is clearly worried about Annabelle and sticks close to her side. Audrey hugs me around the waist. I pick her up for a hug and she whispers in my ear. "You are *careful* today, Sunny!" and I whisper back, "You're right, Audrey. Let's watch the movie." I sit down and put her in my lap.

We watch *The Moon-Spinners* from the reverse side of the screen.

"You are an imposter!" says Madame Habib. "You are the girl from that English children's book who walked through the glass into a world of crazy people!"

"*Through the Looking Glass*," I say to Audrey. "Good book."

"Tell me," says Madame Habib, "do you often have adventures of this kind?"

"No. Never!" says Nikky. "This is the first one I've ever had in my life!"

Well, join the club, Nikky. Join the club. I'm having an adventure, too, a real adventure, right here in Greenwood, Mississippi. And I have decided that adventure may not be all it's cracked up to be.

"I have known many strange people in my life," Madame Habib tells Nikky, "but you are the most incredible."

The most incredible. A fifteen-year-old girl. How about that. She solves the mystery and saves the day.

"Let's go." Gillette waves us toward him and we scramble to meet him at the stage steps. I don't need to see the rest of *The Moon-Spinners*. Madame Habib is a good person. She won't buy the stolen emeralds. She'll give them back to Mark and he'll be able to clear his name. I know it's all going to work out now. Which is more than I can say for what's happening to us. Real life is so different from the movies.

Daddy is at the bottom of the steps, holding out a hand in the dark for each of us, in turn. As we come down the three steps and create a little pool of people near the front row, I see that we're not alone. The three Negro boys are with us — they've been found. None of them is Raymond and they all look scared to death. They stare at the floor, silent, so I'm silent, too. Gillette acknowledges them, though.

"Hey," he says.

"Hey," they each murmur, mostly with their bodies. They keep their gaze on the floor.

Mr. Martini, Mrs. Ferguson, and Mrs. Lefever are here, too. And, finally, Parnell comes down the aisle. "The money's in the safe," he tells Mr. Martini. "Mr. Guston's going to stop the movie when we leave and he'll wait for the crowd to disperse. Then he'll leave his usual way. He'll drive your car home, Jamie. We're all set."

I run into Parnell's arms like Audrey runs into mine. Parnell hugs me close. "It's all right," he says. "Everything's all right."

"No, it's not," I say. "I want to talk to you!"

"We're all going out the back door," says Daddy, pointing to the dimly lighted EXIT sign. "We'll be met by City Attorney Carr, City Commissioner Hammond, and the chief of police."

"Chief Lary?" I ask.

"Yes," says Daddy. He looks pointedly at the Negro boys and says, "Look at me, please." They do.

Daddy tells them, "This is the only time we'll be able to do this. They'll surround the back doors, too, next time, once they figure out how you got out. And we're not about to tell them *who* got you out."

"Yessir," they say together.

"We're going to take you home," Daddy says. The boys look at one another, and I know that look. Relief.

"Is everybody ready? Martini? Ladies?" Everyone nods. Nobody knows how it will turn out. Annabelle takes a step and woozes toward the floor. Daddy grabs her.

"She fell earlier," says Boo, so worried.

"What?" Daddy can command an escape operation, but something happening to Annabelle makes him look like he might crumble to dust.

"I'm *fine*," says Annabelle. She sounds like a soldier in this army, reporting for duty. "Really. I'm more exhausted than anything."

Daddy gathers himself together. "Call the doctor immediately when we get home," he directs Boo, and Boo nods that she will.

Daddy cautiously pushes open the back door of the theater, and there in the dark stand our rescuers. Chief Lary says, "All quiet back here so far, but let's hurry," and gives me a *you again* look. Mary Margaret's father shoots Daddy a short nod and I can read it. *Good work*. Daddy says to the Negroes, "You first," and they go — silently, quickly, and with surprise on their face — with Chief Lary to his police car. "We'll get them home," Chief Lary says. Gillette watches the boys watch him from inside the police car. He tugs on the brim of his baseball cap. Mr. Hammond takes Mrs. Lefever, Mrs. Ferguson, and Mr. Martini to his car. He says, "Good night, everyone. We were never here."

Mr. Carr opens the back door of his station wagon — the same car that went all the way to New York with all those Carr kids stuffed inside — and offers us a ride to freedom.

Daddy looks at us like we are the most precious jewels in the deepest sea.

"Let's go," he says.

We step out into the warm summer night.

51

That night, in our house, we surround ourselves with love and concern and regard for one another. We are gentle. We are kind. A small rain begins to fall, as if it's trying to cool down tempers all over the Delta, all over Mississippi. It works some magic on us, too. The earth is bathing, says Boo, and even the dirt, getting a bath, smells good and clean through the open windows.

Annabelle looks drawn down to a nub. Her eyes have dark circles under them. Sometimes I forget she's going to have a baby. The doctor tells Annabelle to get some rest. Lots of rest. The phone rings and Annabelle talks to Polly's mom for a little while, and I leave Polly a note in our bucket for tomorrow.

Parnell tells me he's living in an apartment building, sharing a bachelor pad with Randy Smithers, because his working at the Leflore might make us a target for crazies, at our house. I tell him Annabelle is doing a fine job of that all by herself now.

We turn on the air conditioner in the living room, and Boo serves everyone leftover sandwiches and glasses full of ice and Seven-Up. Daddy puts a long splash of gold liquid into his.

All the lamps all over the house are blazing and everyone takes turns telling the stories of the night, each with something different to add, until it sounds like *Bad Day at Black Rock* or *The Alamo*. There is even talk of how Sunny saved the day by thinking about the projection room staircase, but I don't feel like taking any credit for anything. Daddy's bravery is saluted, Audrey's bravery is applauded, everyone's bravery is noted. It makes us feel better or less scared, to hear all about it, over and over, again and again, like the Choctaw braves around a Delta campfire long ago, crowing after a successful escape from their enemies, but I decide I don't want to talk about it at all anymore.

Randy Smithers shows up at our house, out of uniform and rumpled from sleep, to pick up Parnell, and Parnell promises to come for noon dinner soon. Randy wants to know what kind of town is this that the police chief can rescue you but half the police force out front doesn't lift a finger.

Nobody does the dishes and nobody cares. Gillette half carries Ruth up the stairs because she's feeling too old to climb, and Audrey goes to bed with Annabelle and Daddy, who go upstairs holding hands. The nighttime smell of Vicks VapoRub comes thick from under Boo's bedroom door. The air conditioner is turned off downstairs, the lights are extinguished, and the fans hum like good company in each upstairs bedroom. The old house makes its creaking, going-to-sleep noises as the rain slips away and leaves the slow smell of the river on the air.

Gillette finds me in the upstairs alcove, where I'm sitting on the old dress-up box and watching the Yazoo drift under a quilt of freshly washed stars.

"His name is Raymond," I say.

Gillette sits on the window seat, where the breeze is best and the moonlight spills across his pajamas. "He could be as good as Willie Mays," he says. "I've watched him play."

"I know," I answer.

That's all. Just the facts. I am forgiven. I have forgiven him.

The summer frogs — even the old, fat bullfrogs — begin a mighty croaking all along the muddy riverbank and in all the wet trees. They are so happy for the rain. An owl hoots from a high tree nearby and a night bird comes to drink at the birdbath in the middle of the front yard. I imagine the moonflowers growing up and over the old George and blooming wide-open right now and smelling like magical summer.

"Did you ever want to go far away from here, on an adventure?" I ask.

"All the time," says Gillette.

"Really? Where would you go?"

"California."

I am surprised. "Why California?"

"Your grandmother's making me read *The Grapes of Wrath.* It makes me want to go on a trip to California."

"Is it an adventure story?" I ask.

"It's sad," Gillette says.

"Meemaw specializes in sad books," I say.

"But it's good," Gillette adds.

The breeze is cool and sweet. "I think I can sleep now," I say. "Can you?"

"I think so."

But we are reluctant to leave each other. There's so much to ask about and tell about the past three weeks. I don't know where or how to begin. I pick at the thin scab that has crusted over the cut on my knee.

"It must have been hard for you," I say. "Before."

When he doesn't answer me, I add, "Before you moved here."

Then, when he stays silent, I try again. "Maybe it still is."

Gillette scratches at a mosquito bite and says, "My mom is a good person. She cares about you."

I shrug in my I-don't-care way.

Gillette stands up. "She's the only mother I've got," he says. And then he looks at me with that familiar, brother-of-mine face and says, "The only one you've got, too."

I almost tell him about Jo Ellen then, but I decide not to. I'm going to keep Jo Ellen to myself. "I have a mother," I say in a voice that's more tired than defensive.

And that's that. We sit and watch the mysterious Yazoo for a long time, in the soft silence, together.

52

Wednesday, July 15, 1964

They start after supper and before dusk, the people arriving by foot, or in SNCC cars, and sometimes in buses from the plantations, from all over Baptist Town, Gritney, and Gee Pee, from the outlying farms in Browning and Shellmound, from tiny towns not big enough to hold their own mass meetings. They come, even if they aren't registered. They come for a sense of camaraderie and belonging, and to see what it's all about. They come to whatever colored church is hosting the meeting in Greenwood, and they come to give one another strength for the journey, the long, long journey to freedom. Now there is a mass meeting almost every night.

They lean on the "Everlasting Arms," that is their opening hymn tonight, and they sing it with the belief that they can find a way to be safe and secure from all alarms. The singing brings them together as one, and reminds them that they sang a hundred years ago for their freedom, and they are still not free.

Tonight, Cleveland Jordan, that dignified old warhorse of a mighty man, longtime member of the NAACP and courageous supporter of the Freedom Movement, leads them in a singsong chant full of feeling and power, with the people murmuring and shouting, "Yes, Lord!" and "Amen!" after each line.

Now, Father! Now, now, now, Lordie!
When we get through drinkin' tears for water
When we get through eatin' at unwelcome tables

When we get through shakin' unwelcome hands,
We children's all got to meet Death somewhere
Don't let us be afraid to die!
Rock me, rock me, Lordie!
Rock me until I won't have no fears
Land my spirit over in Beulah's Land,
Where I'll cease from worryin'!
Where I'll be at rest.
Father, I stretch my hand to thee!

Then he speaks:

"You all know me. I'm Cleveland Jordan, I am a citizen of Greenwood, I've lived here for fifty years. I have three sons and two daughters. I did some honest, long-life work here, setting rings in the street, and laying manholes and setting curbs, work that will be here for years and years, long after I am gone.

"We are going to the courthouse tomorrow, to register and vote, without any weapon at all. We're going humble. We're going meek. We're going with the spirit to treat both sides right.

"We are asking them kindly, 'Let us walk by your side!'"

Reverend Ebbie pipes up. "Behold how good and pleasant it is for brothers to dwell together in unity!" Reverend Tucker comes behind him: "Psalm 133!" And the people say, *Yes, Lord!* And it's hot. So hot the men's shirts stick to their backs and the women's hair is a wreck, and the fans roar and the microphone screeches and the bodies are packed close so everyone can be inside where it's safe.

Outside, Greenwood City police cars drive around and around the church, surrounding the block, over and over, taking down license plate numbers and waiting for people to come outside so they can take down names and put them in the next day's paper. But still they come.

The FBI is here, too. They are assigned to Greenwood as

observers. They have no authority to arrest or uphold the law. "This is a state matter," they say. Justice Attorney John Doar tells them, "We are here as witnesses. We are here not to interfere but just to observe and report any complaints back to the Justice Department. We are civil service employees."

"You! FBI!" yells Scarecrow Magee. "Do something! We being beat up out there!"

People begin to boo John Doar and his agents until Bob Moses takes the mic and says quietly, "We don't do that. John Doar is our friend. He's just being honest with you. We are working every channel we legally can, and so is he. Believe me, Washington, D.C., will notice us tomorrow. So will the world."

The energy shifts. Reverend Ebbie is proud to be speaking from his pulpit, from his church. "The entire state of Mississippi will participate in freedom tomorrow, July sixteenth! We will all march to the courthouse in Greenwood, and register to vote! Reverend Tucker got attacked by a police dog last year, tryin' to register, but he's still here! A hero! You can march with him tomorrow! There is strength in numbers!"

Paul and Silas, bound in jail
Had no money for to go their bail
Keep your eyes on the prize, hold on!

"No doubt about it, it's a dangerous business," says volunteer Bob Moses. "I've been in jail for weeks at a time, and so have many of you. Sam Block and Willie Peacock were shot at in front of the Freedom House one night as they were parked. White men drove close by the car, took a shotgun and blasted through the windows, and luckily no one in the car was injured. Whites do this because they're afraid of us! But we're not going anywhere."

Willie Peacock says, "There's not a night that the police don't trail us. They don't like us, but they're convinced now that Sam

Block is going to stay in Greenwood, and so am I, Willie Peacock, just like we had said, until we get a satisfactory number of Negroes registered to vote. You can't very well call me an outsider, 'cause I'm a Mississippian, and I was born in Tallahatchie County, just across the river!"

SNCC Dewey Greene says, "We want to hear your stories tonight! Who's brought us a story?"

They come to the podium, eager to share. And the song leaders lead them in choruses between each story.

"I know I'm not going to live long at the age of sixty, but I'm fighting for my grandchildren so they won't have to go through what I'm going through."

Paul and Silas began to shout
Doors popped open, and they walked out
Keep your eyes on the prize, hold on!

"We doesn't have enough money to buy clothes or food for our childrens to go to school, or to take care of school expenses for them. We don't get enough out of our jobs to cover our expenses at home, and some of us just only makes two dollars and a half a day. Light bills, gas bills, some of us the lights and gas cut off, and we've had some, near-like to froze this past winter. Fathers home all winter. . . ."

Well, the only chains that we can stand
Are the chains of hand in hand
Keep your eyes on the prize, hold on!

"Why do they hate us so bad? And we been workin' for them all our lives? They the ones ridin' in the fine cars, and our children goin' to school barefoot? But we not willing to stay down now! We're willing to fight! Amen!"

"Men who be on the police force ought to be the best men! They ought to be able to love humanity. Galatians 6: It read like this: 'Be not deceived whatever man sow, he gonna reap it.'"

Got my hand on the freedom plow
Wouldn't take nothing for my journey now
Keep your eyes on the prize, hold on!

"I want to vote and I want to be able to say who I want in office and what I feel about it, and if one in office that beats Negroes over the head, I want to put 'em out! We are willing to die for it. So our children and our children's children may live."

Samuel Block was locked in jail
Had not money for to pay his bail
Keep your eyes on the prize, hold on!

"Last winter, people were standing in line in front of the church, waiting for food, while their plantation owner was riding by in the streets, calling out their names and telling them to leave and go back to the plantations, and they were telling him that they were going to stand there and get their food because their children were hungry."

Wade in the water
Wade in the water, children
Wade in the water
God's gonna trouble the water!

"I've had threats to my life," says Reverend Aaron Johnson, "because I opened my church for a meeting. But I did it! People were afraid to come in at first, but when they did, we rocked that church. We rocked that church that night. I said, 'Well, if I die, I had a good time tonight. I had a *good* time tonight!'

Ain't scared of your jail because I want my
freedom! I want my freedom now!
Ain't scared of your dogs because I want my
freedom! I want my freedom now!
Gonna keep on fighting till I get my freedom!
'Cause I want my freedom now!

Fannie Lou Hamer has come from Ruleville. "I got throwed off the plantation the day I tried to register to vote, so I went that Friday night and spent the night with Miss Mary Tucker in Ruleville, and people who knew I was there, they shot into that house sixteen times and I had to leave and go to Tallahatchie County and I lived there until December, and I'm back in Ruleville, and I be's harassed, and I have quite a few things to go through. . . .

"Since I went down to register, it's been bloodhounds in front of my door. We're being harassed! And whether I work at home, or wash, the bills go higher and higher. Everything to put me out of Ruleville is being done, but I'll be right there, fighting for freedom, until God say 'enough done.'

"There's nothing that will keep me and get my spirit down, because now I'm in the fight for freedom!"

We shall not
We shall not be moved
Just like a tree that's planted by the waters
We shall not be moved!

"I'm telling you why you're poor — you don't have the vote! I'm telling you why you're uneducated — you don't have the vote! We want hundreds of you to line up in front of the courthouse in Greenwood tomorrow — which, I know, is the home of the Citizens' Council, in the heart of the Delta in Mississippi — but we want you to ask to be registered to vote, even if you can't read or write. This is nothing to be ashamed of. It's a shame on earth to live in poverty, and you don't have to, if you are willing to stand up for your rights as an American citizen and VOTE."

This little light of mine, I'm gonna let it shine!

"Shoot a Negro and watch him run, that's what he said. But this is a new Negro, and you tell old man Buff Hammond down there at the courthouse that we ain't running anymore! You can send us to the penitentiary, you can send us to the prison farm, but we don't care! We ain't scared of your jail now, because we want our freedom!"

Governor Johnson, don't you know
Mississippi is the next to go!
Keep your eyes on the prize, hold on!

SNCC Dewey again: "I'd like to ask for everybody in the audience that has been down and attempted to register to raise your hand! (No foolin' now!) See? There's a number of hands! Now. How do you feel, those who have gone down to register to vote? Do you feel like you are doing something you should, and that you are a part of this fight?"

YEAH! AMEN!

"So see? Now, I see there are more of us sittin' out in the audience that didn't raise their hand! So see . . . we still have a lot of work to do.

"We are ALL in this struggle! We are fighting for you, too, regardless of whether you are interested in yourself or not! You should take a part in this! Join hands with us! Walk down to the courthouse and let people know you want to be first-class citizens, that you are tired of being second-class citizens! My friends, as long as you stay second-class citizens, you will never get the things you should have!"

Then a SNCC volunteer introduces Rita Schwerner, wife of CORE Freedom Worker Mickey Schwerner, who has been missing since June 21, the summer solstice, and the first day of Freedom Summer. Mickey disappeared with Andy Goodman and James Chaney, somewhere near Philadelphia, Mississippi. The Philadelphia police were the last to see the three alive. They were working at the Freedom House in Meridian, Mississippi, but many of the summer volunteers in Greenwood knew them. Andy, only twenty years old, was in the same training group as Jo Ellen in Ohio.

"One hundred and fifty FBI agents have been assigned to Philadelphia, to look for our three companions," says the summer volunteer introducing Rita. "They found the burned-out shell of their car right away — it was half submerged in the Bogue Chitto Swamp — but they are still looking for Andy, James, and Mickey. And Rita has something to say."

There is no applause, just a hush, as a thin woman, not yet twenty-five years old, wearing a simple sheath dress, comes to the podium and begins to speak softly. She has the stage to herself.

"I know what fear is," she says, "and I know it makes you think, *I'm not going to do this*, or *I'm not going to do that*, because the risk is too great. But I know that you can risk much more by doing nothing. It's not unnatural to be afraid, but you're cheating your children if your being afraid stops them from having something."

The crowd so thoughtfully and politely listens to and watches this pale, young white woman from New York who has likely lost her husband to the cause, who is standing there, telling them to register. And then she quietly walks off the stage to many amens, and another volunteer begins to wind up the crowd one last time.

"There are men and women in Greenwood's jail, fighting for you! And me! And Mississippi! You see, I am from Mississippi, too! That's why I'm fighting for you! People have tried to leave Mississippi and go up north to live, but it's not better up north, not really, and that's not my home. *This* is my home. I plan to stay here and make Mississippi a better place to live! And as long as we continue to go up north and run away from the situation, we will never make it any better.

"You know what happened in Money nine years ago! Emmett Till was murdered! And you had voter registration workers walking the roads of Money this morning! Walking the streets of black Greenwood! Walking for freedom! Are you going to walk with them? Are you going to let them walk alone?"

NO! *Ain't gonna let no jailhouse turn me 'round!*

"You know what happened to Louis Allen and Herbert Lee and to countless black men who ended up at the end of a shotgun or a noose! And what about Medgar! Medgar Evers, who was gunned down, shot in the back, by a coward?"

He is not crazy enough to utter the name of that coward, Byron De La Beckwith from Greenwood, Mississippi, but the entire room knows who it is.

Ain't gonna let segregation turn me 'round!

"And so! We need you all. Undertakers, grocers, preachers, teachers, bricklayers, garbage collectors, cotton choppers, whatever you do — you iron, you clean, you wash, you cook, you drive, you sit, you sew. Tomorrow morning, we'd like for all of those who didn't raise their hands, to meet us, at our office, at eight thirty in the morning, so we all can go to the courthouse and become first-class citizens! If you live on the plantations, we'll send a bus for you. If you live too far to walk, we'll pick you up. But you have to come. Will you do it?"

A thunderous, roaring *yes!* rolls over the room like it might combine with the heat of the day and explode through the roof.

FREEDOM! FREEDOM! FREEDOM NOW!

And then the closing prayer.

"Our Father in Heaven and in Earth! Oh, the Lily of the Valley, the bright and morning star, the fairest of ten thousand to my soul! Oh, my Father, you said you would come to our rescue, if we would only call you in faith! We want more faith, our God! We want a closer walk with you! Our calm and heavenly friend! A light to shine on our road, to lead us on to thee. We want more faith, that we may be able to ask you for what we need here in this torn world. Oh Lordy, oh Lordy, don't leave us here in this distress which we're now going through because we know you have all power in Heaven and in Earth. And with your help, we shall overcome. Amen."

Deep in my heart, I do believe,
that we shall overcome some day.

Pap Bullis holds his daughter Glory's hand. Glory holds her mother Libby's hand. Libby holds her friend Vidella's hand. Vidella holds her husband Sheldon's hand, Sheldon holds summer volunteer Jo Ellen's hand, and on down the aisles, black and white together holding hands and singing "we shall overcome," overcoming they aren't sure what some days, and some days it's one another, but still they come. Most of the summer workers are from far away and are white, and young, and tired, and earnest, and scared, and oh-so-full of hope. They are not perfect. Neither are the folks whose hands they hold. But they are there. They are all there. And tomorrow they will all be counted.

53

Thursday, July 16, 1964
Freedom Day

"Jamie!"

Uncle Vivian's voice, booming from the kitchen. The sun has barely blossomed. Uncle Vivian must have come in through the unlocked kitchen door without even knocking.

I hear Daddy's feet hit the floor — it's so early he's not even up yet.

"They've walked off! They've walked off the plantation!" Uncle Vivian is at the bottom of our stairs now, roaring for Daddy. "Jamie!"

I leap out of bed and throw on my clothes. I haven't seen Uncle Vivian since that day at the courthouse when he marched me home. So much has happened.

Booths at the Thompson-Turner Drugstore have disappeared. Now Foster Hamilton can make you a malted, but you can't sit inside the drugstore and drink it. What good is that?

The pool is still closed. Until further notice. I can't stand to go anywhere near it. It's the saddest-looking thing on this earth. Mary Margaret says there are dandelions growing in the deep end where dirt has sifted in and has no way to get out.

They've taken the drinking fountain out of the courthouse and have locked all the bathrooms.

The Crystal Grill and almost all the other Greenwood restaurants are now private clubs. You have to pay three dollars for a special card to show through a little peephole if you want to come in and eat there. Daddy says we're just not going.

The library has reopened, but all the seats have been removed. There is nowhere to sit unless you are Miss Cantrell or the other librarians. What good is a library if you can't even sit down and read in it?

The Leflore is still open, but hardly anyone goes to the movies now, especially since Mr. Bayard and his family went anyway, to see *The Chalk Garden*, the day after all the commotion. There was a picket line and they walked right through it and bought their tickets and went in. Somebody shot a bullet through their front window after they got home. They left town immediately, supposedly on vacation, and might not come back. Polly's mother says Mr. Bayard has lost his job at the paper. I wish I'd liked Jodie Lynn Bayard a little better while she was here. Where will they go now?

But none of this is as important to Uncle Vivian as his cotton crop.

"Gone!" he shouts as he and Daddy make for the kitchen, me flying down the stairs and into the hallway right behind them.

"Every cotton truck I sent out this morning had a mole on it — a young black turk whose job it was to see my choppers got off the truck and came to the courthouse to register to vote! All of them! Today! Every one! We've finally had good rain and I need those choppers!"

Daddy fills the coffeepot with water and reaches for the can of Maxwell House. "Slow down," he says. "Did they come to the farm or not?"

"Oh, they came!" shouts Uncle Vivian. He opens the refrigerator and searches for orange juice, his favorite. He slams the door. "Then they left! I watched them do it! They pinned buttons to their shirts, they handed out papers, and they told my workers — my workers! — to come with them, and they did!"

"All of them?" Daddy spoons coffee into the top of the percolator.

"All the young ones," says Uncle Vivian. "They're my strongest and fastest choppers. They threw their hoes down and walked out, every one of them! Only five colored women were left standing there. What am I going to do with five old Negro women and dozens of acres of weeds?"

"It's three miles back to town," says Daddy.

"They picked them up in buses. I passed one on the way over here. Fulla Nigras singing. They've got buses! To take them to the courthouse!"

Daddy says, "I don't know what I can do about it, Vivian. What do you need?"

Annabelle walks past me and puts her hand on my shoulder to say good morning. I let her. She pours Uncle Vivian his orange juice.

"I need you to round them up!" shouts Uncle Vivian.

"What?" Daddy takes the sugar bowl down from the shelf and tests it with a finger to make sure it's sugar. The clock strikes three, which means it's six.

"I've got one of my cotton trucks out front. It's got some grain sacks in it, but it will still hold at least twenty men — more if they hang off the sides. They'll all be at the courthouse to register soon, and I want you to offer them a chance to come back and work for me — no questions asked, no recriminations, if they come back this morning. They'll all be arrested at the courthouse, anyway, and they know it."

"What they know is that you need them and will take them back, whether they register or not," Daddy says.

"They can't make their three fifty a day while they're in jail," growls Uncle Vivian.

Annabelle lights the flame under the percolator and takes the milk out of the refrigerator. "Sunny, this is a grown-up conversation," she says, which is a command for me to leave.

I bristle at her. I actually show her my teeth. If I were a porcupine, I'd shoot her a quill.

Daddy notices me for the first time. "Off you go, Sunny," he says. Then he turns back to the conversation. "You know I can't do that, Vivian. I've got to be at the store this morning."

"Ben Arnold can open the store — he's done it before. Come on. They're all over at that Freedom House now — I heard those snakes in the grass tell them where to go. You can go get them right now and be done before the store opens. You can make two, three runs in my truck and be done with it. I'd go, but they won't come for me, you know that. They'll be afraid of me."

Annabelle says, "Sunny . . ."

Daddy waves me off and I go, without so much as a howdee-do from Uncle Vivian, whose face is the color of purple heliotrope. But I stop at the phone table in the hallway. Gillette's coming from the opposite direction with Ruth. I put up a finger to shush him. He quietly lets Ruth out the front door.

Daddy says, "Annabelle, sit," and I hear a chair scrape out from under the kitchen table.

"I'm fine," she says. "Women have fallen on their cans for centuries and still had healthy babies."

"Their cans?" says Daddy.

This seems to soften Uncle Vivian a smidge. "How you doin', Miss Annabelle?" he asks.

"I do fine, Vivian," Annabelle repeats. "Let me make you an egg."

Gillette walks past me and into the kitchen, so I follow him.

"What's happening?" he asks.

Uncle Vivian skirts the subject and says, "I need an irrigation system, but I'm going to have to bring in a good enough crop this year to pay for one. I'm here to talk about it with your . . . your . . ."

"Dad," says Gillette.

Daddy gives Gillette a smile. "Let me get dressed," he says, "and shave, so I can think. Vivian, you eat. The courthouse doesn't open until nine o'clock. We've got time for breakfast."

"Jamie —" Uncle Vivian protests, but Daddy is gone.

Polly's mother sticks her head in the door. "I saw you were up," she says. "Hello, Vivian." Uncle Vivian waves a hand in a resigned way. He waves at me then, too, and I lift a hand to him in return, but we keep the kitchen table between us.

Polly's mother looks at me and Gillette as if she's deciding but then goes on. "It's already started. The national news trucks and reporters are all over the courthouse lawn. The FBI is there, too. You'll see cars parked in front of my house throughout the day, and news people coming and going. I've got the only Teletype machine in Greenwood that isn't at the newspaper office, and I've told them they can share it, as well as the darkroom, to file their stories. Just so you know what's happening next door. I'm covering the story for the *Appeal*. I'll be scarce."

"Thank you, Carol Ann," says Annabelle. Polly's mother disappears as swiftly as she came. Annabelle ties on her apron and I notice her tummy is good and poochy now. She surely is going to have a baby. I know that having-a-baby look. Mary Margaret's mother has it almost every year.

"What's happening?" Gillette asks again.

"There's a voter registration drive for the Negroes today," says Annabelle. She begins breaking eggs into a glass bowl on the counter. Uncle Vivian is almost bland, compared to how fired-up he was earlier. He slaps back the screen door, trundles down the porch steps, and walks off, toward George, where the night's slippery moonflower blossoms are closing and dropping to the ground, just as Boo enters the kitchen in her bathrobe. Her hair is sticking out six ways to Sunday.

"It's not going to go well," Annabelle says. She heads for the coffeepot, removes the grounds, and starts to pour everyone a cup of coffee. "That's why all the press is here. They'll all be arrested if they picket — coloreds, students, paid workers, all of them. It won't be pretty."

There will be more arrests.

Suddenly I'm in a rush to leave the kitchen. Jo Ellen will be at the courthouse! "I've got to go!" I announce. I'm halfway through the dining room when Annabelle comes after me and calls, "Wait!"

I stop, obedient, and turn to face her. She stands near the china cabinet, using her apron to wipe her hands. From the kitchen comes the clacking of bowls and spoons and Boo talking about her mother's old Singer sewing machine. It's just the two of us, me and Annabelle, and it's a standoff. We need holsters. I don't know which of us looks more determined.

"Sunny," Annabelle begins. There is resolve in her voice — or is it alarm? "You are absolutely *forbidden* to go near the courthouse today, do you understand? Anywhere you go today, you've got to tell me you're going."

If I could shoot flames from my eyes, this would be the time to do it. *How dare you?* That's what I want to say to her — *How dare you*? but that's not good enough. I swallow in order to give myself time to think.

Annabelle repeats herself. "Sunny, do you hear me? You *will not* go to the courthouse today."

And that's when I find the just-right words for my stepmother and say them, quietly and forcefully, in a voice only she can hear:

"Watch me."

54

Pap got hisself a case of worries this morning. Ma'am say, "Wilson Bullis, you gon' come get in that register line with me, ain't not two ways about it! Nobody gon' be here makin' you dinner or supper, not today, and not tomorrow, if you don't come get in that line!"

Pap just growl. "We can't even use the same bathrooms whites use or eat from the same dishes, just how you think we gonna get the vote and one day elect us a Negro sheriff?"

"We gon' figure it out, Wilson," say Ma'am. "That's what we gon' do."

She dressed in her best Sunday dress, and Pap wearing a bow tie.

Ree over to Miss Liberty Belle Fortuna's, where she looked after all day, along with sixteen other childrens. Miss Liberty Belle does folks' hair in her beauty parlor back of her house, but she won't have no customers today. She got herself registered last year. Everybody say it because a white man sweet on her, but nobody talk about that to her face.

My job to be ready. "Whatever we need," say SNCC Casey from Indiana. She got yellow hair like Jo Ellen. "There will be volunteers on the phone, and they'll tell you where to run. We'll have volunteer stations at the Colored Elks Hall and the Freedom House all day."

"I've never been arrested," say SNCC Eli. "I *want* to go to jail. I've never been."

"Me, neither," say SNCC Evelyn Ellis. "Won't that look grand: Ellis versus the State of Mississippi!"

Stokely say, "Now hold up! This is serious business! *I'm nervous.* I don't want to go to jail. There have been cars circling the office all morning. George and Bob are out there taking down license plate numbers. I don't want any funny business here. Anybody wants to get killed, they can just go out into the middle of the street, but leave the office. This is not going to be a fun day."

Everybody quiet and back to work, they get assignments.

Simon and Jimmy and Twill and me help make signs. Protest signs for the pickets. Jo Ellen gon' be a picket. Vera, too. Ma'am made 'em a big breakfast with the eggs from Scarecrow Magee's farm. Even Freddie and Chuff nailing signs to sticks.

Ida Mae grab her forms and march out the door. "Where you gon'?"

"I'm gon' to help!" she say. "When Martha Lamb turn 'em down, I be right there with a form for the MFDP. We get 'em registered for Atlantic City!"

"Gonna be a long day," say SNCC Bob. White Bob. "Can we count on you and your FreedomMakers here?"

"I reckon you can." That's what I tell him.

SNCCs and COFOs and COREs — Freedom workers everywhere, straw hats on the COFOs. So many of our people — hundreds — gon' to the courthouse to stand in line all day if they has to. All the COFOs gonna stand with 'em. The SNCCs gonna picket. SNCCs will be arrested.

"Plan for it," say Stokely. "Carry a toothbrush and some change for the phone. Stick 'em in your pants pockets."

"It's going to be like a war out there," say SNCC Dewey. "And we are a well-prepared army. Let's go."

"You can't go, Dorie," say SNCC Bob. Black Bob. "You're too far along. You stay here and take care of that baby."

"I signed up," say Dorie. She our neighbor. She gonna have a baby in September.

"It's too dangerous," say SNCC Bob. But Dorie get on the bus to the courthouse. Bob can't stop her.

Nobody stop this army today.

55

I am on my bike and flying down River Road before you can say "Crackerjack." I lean to the right and sail onto Cotton and see that the parking lot at the back of the courthouse is peppered with police cars. I pretend I'm on urgent business, cross the street between a row of parked cars, and skim across the grass until I'm under the sheltering tent of magnolias. I jump off my bike while it's still moving and my Beatles wig falls out of the basket. I grab it and tug it onto my head, over my unbrushed hair. You never know when you might need a disguise.

Even if Annabelle comes looking for me — which she won't, she's supposed to rest — she'll never find me here.

The morning is still misty with dew, and already so much is happening. Once I get high enough, I can see cars are parked all down Cotton Street, and on both sides of Market Street in front of the courthouse. The parked cars are full of people watching. There are the trucks that say NBC and CBS, and there are the big cameras on legs, on the edges of the grass near the courthouse steps and near the curbs.

A line of Negroes stretches from the courthouse door all the way down the front walk to the sidewalk, where the line bends toward Fulton Street and the Confederate memorial statue. They are all dressed up, these Negroes, like they're going to church. Flowered dresses and shiny shoes and Sunday hats and pressed trousers and neckties. More come and get in line as they are dropped off by the carload. I don't see any buses except for the black bus I saw two Negroes painting the day I rode off to visit the pool that morning eons ago. It's parked in the middle of Market Street, which is blocked off to traffic. The white letters painted on it spell out *Greenwood Police.*

Chief Lary stands on the grass with his bullhorn, shouting orders. "You cannot picket! You can try to register, but you cannot picket! Governor Johnson has just signed a bill prohibiting picketing in public places! If you picket, you will be arrested!"

There are no pickets, but there are reporters everywhere. Men with cameras, men with notebooks and pencils, and there's Polly's mother near the Confederate memorial, talking with them, with her camera around her neck, nervous, I can tell. She keeps scanning the crowd behind the sawhorses to see who's in it. She watches every car that drives by on Fulton Street.

There are wooden sawhorses all along the opposite side of Market Street, and behind them stand onlookers, like this is a show and they've got a ticket to watch it. There are an awful lot of them and I'll bet they've been deputized. I've seen them do that in the movies, when the sheriff needs help to go after the bad guys and has to call up a posse.

There are people in the courthouse already, hanging out of open windows upstairs, sitting on the ledges downstairs, and watching. It's like the circus has come to town and everyone has turned out to wait for it, only there are no elephants.

Then the circus arrives. The buses Uncle Vivian talked about. There are two of them, full of pickets, some colored, some white. They tumble off the bus with signs that say *FREEDOM NOW!* and *WE WANT TO VOTE!* and *ONE MAN ONE VOTE!* Jo Ellen and Vera are on the first bus. I sit up so suddenly I almost fall off my branch.

Chief Lary yells at the pickets through his megaphone and tells them they will be arrested, they cannot picket here. "We will let you in, three at a time, to register," he hollers, "but there will be no picketing!"

The pickets start carrying their signs, quietly walking single file down the sidewalk, going the opposite way of the Negroes on the sidewalk who are waiting to register, which means they are walking toward Cotton Street and toward my magnolias. Some leave the line and stand on the grass next to the Negroes who are standing on the front walk. Jo Ellen is one of those. Jo Ellen's sign reads *REGISTER TO VOTE!* Vera stays on the picket line. Her sign reads *END THE LITERACY TEST!*

The day is heating up and I'm already sweating. I should take off my wig, but I feel safer with it on. I keep having to switch positions in George so I can see what I want to see between the branches and so my can isn't too sore. *Can*. That was funny, I admit.

Here come the police who were in the back parking lot. They run right in front of the magnolias and I get a good, close look at them. They wear helmets and carry their billy clubs, some waving them in the air. There are so many of them.

They line up on either side of the sidewalk, where they are joined by the deputized sheriff's posse from behind the saw-horses. They form a wall along either side of the picket line. As each picket comes to the end of the block and tries to turn around, a policeman shouts, "You are under arrest!" and two men, one from each side of the sidewalk, haul the picket by the arms to the black bus. Another policeman tears up the picket's sign. Each time, the picket goes limp, and the policemen have to drag him to the bus.

The Negroes standing in line to register watch all this and shift nervously. Some of them look angry. Some wipe their faces with handkerchiefs. But none of them gets out of line.

"You are under arrest!" yells the next policeman as he and the one on the opposite side grab the next picket, and then the whole line of policemen shifts up one so the next two police-men can be ready for the next picket.

Some of the policemen are rough, hauling those picket bodies across the street and to the waiting bus, but the pickets go peacefully — you'd think they were trying to get arrested. I watch Vera, who is as old as Meemaw or Boo, being dragged across the street to the black bus. I think I might need to throw up, even though I had no breakfast. Last night's supper queases into my throat anyway.

I keep my eye on Jo Ellen, who is still standing next to the line of Negroes waiting for the courthouse doors to open, until I hear a girl's voice yell, "Keep your hands off my sister!" and I see two policemen dragging a Negro picket girl down the sidewalk and across the street to the bus. Reporters are running and photographers are taking pictures and the girl is screaming now, screaming bloody murder.

She must be a grown-up because it's clear she is going to have a baby and yet they are dragging her down the sidewalk. Her tummy is bigger than Annabelle's. It's almost the size of the pictures we see of Mary at Christmas just before she has Jesus. She might have that baby any minute, that's what I think, and she's still screaming, this girl, and they are still dragging her to the bus, and she frees one arm from one policeman, and she's lying on the ground, on her back, and the other policeman keeps pulling at her like he's going to rip her other arm out of its socket, and then I do throw up, I vomit something green and vile, right onto the magnolia leaves in front of me. My stomach does a flip-flop into my chest, and my throat is raw with the sour taste. I want some water to wash out my mouth, and I have none.

There is a ruckus now, as the summer workers and the pickets and the Negroes in line are all upset about the expecting Negro girl being dragged to the bus. But the pickets don't push back. They don't fight, but the ones already on the bus start to shout, "Freedom! Freedom! Freedom!" and the pickets still in the line start singing, "Not gonna let Chief Lary turn me 'round!" but they don't get out of line. They just keep getting arrested, one by one, and filling up the bus until the bus can't hold any more of them and it takes off for somewhere with "Freedom! Freedom! Freedom!" still ringing from inside of it, and another bus comes up behind it as it's let through the sawhorse barriers.

"Stay in line!" yells a straw-hat colored man as he is hauled off to the next bus, "Freedom!" And then I see the Negro man Sam get arrested, and then the police begin pulling on the pickets who aren't marching, who are just standing in the grass with their signs, and that includes Jo Ellen. Jo Ellen is arrested and I can't stand to watch her be dragged across the grass by bullies with their clubs and helmets and guns. They rip up her sign and tear her skirt and bruise her arms as she's hauled without protest, limp and obedient, onto the bus where everyone is screaming "Freedom! Freedom! Freedom!" so loud and beating on the windows so furiously and stomping so rhythmically they are rocking that bus and sending their chant up to heaven.

I burst into tears and scream my own war cry: "Stop it! Stop it! Stop it!"

But no one can hear me.

WOKE UP THIS MORNING WITH MY MIND STAYED ON FREEDOM — HALLELUJAH!

From "Woke Up This Morning with My Mind Stayed on Freedom," traditional

Willy James Earl, leading a meeting in song, Greenwood, Mississippi.

TALKING WITH MY MIND STAYED ON FREEDOM!

SNCC worker Monroe Sharp is dragged to a Greenwood police bus on Freedom Day, July 16, 1964.

Freedom Day in Greenwood, Mississippi.

THINKING AND MOVING WITH MY MIND STAYED ON FREEDOM!

SINGING AND PRAYING WITH MY MIND STAYED ON FREEDOM!

Freedom Day in Greenwood, Mississippi.

Waiting in line to register on Freedom Day in Greenwood, Mississippi, July 16, 1964.

In line, waiting to register to vote on Freedom Day in Greenwood, Mississippi.

NOW I WOKE UP THIS MORNING WITH MY MIND, IT WAS STAYED ON FREEDOM

HALLELUJAH!

56

As soon as Jo Ellen's bus is filled, it starts to move and I move with it. Down from the tree like lightning, I skid and scrape and finally tumble until I am at the bottom and out from under the magnolia's skirts, scrambling across the courthouse lawn. I don't care who sees me.

I run for my life across the grass. Negroes in line scatter out of my way when they see me coming. The police posse moves the sawhorses and the bus turns left at the corner of Market and Fulton — it's going across the bridge and will get away from me! I cut catty-corner across the grass to catch it — maybe if I scream it will stop — but it doesn't go all the way across the bridge, it turns left again, onto River Road!

I can get in front of it if I hurry!

I run close to the building, make my turn, and run the long side of the courthouse with a stitch in my side. As I reach the far corner, I have to bend over double to catch my breath, my hands on my knees. *Wait for me, wait!*

But I don't have to worry. The bus is not going anywhere. It's pulling into the parking lot behind the courthouse. I stumble toward that corner of the building, running in the deep morning shadows between the towering azaleas and the cool marble of the walls. I'm running behind the jail now. The bus made almost a complete circle and is in the parking lot at Cotton Street, disgorging its passengers, who are singing:

O Freedom! O Freedom! O Freedom over me!
And before I'll be a slave,

I'll be buried in my grave,
And go home to my Lord and be free!

Policemen are on either side of the pickets, pushing them into the back of the courthouse — the jail! — and I am so close I could talk to them from here. They get quiet as they leave the bus. One of the policemen says to a girl, "What happened to you, pretty?" and here comes Mama off the bus and I start to run to her, to call to her. *Wait for me!*

The only thing that stops me is Deputy Davis, who comes out of the jail waving his nightstick high in the air before he cracks it over the head of one of the pickets, a white boy who kept singing as he got off the bus. Now the boy yelps as he rolls into a ball and begins to bleed all over his shirt and the parking lot. There are no reporters back here, no photographers to take a picture.

I need to help Mama. I need to get Daddy. I need to go home. Instead, I sink to the ground in the corner near a crape myrtle and try to catch my breath. I don't know what to do. I'm half out of my head with fear. I can't catch my breath. I think I might faint. I know that's not Mama. I know it's Jo Ellen. I know that, but I don't care.

I lick my lips, hug my knees to my chest, and try to make myself small. Small. I start to rock myself ever so slightly, back and forth, then side to side, then back and forth again. How is the boy who is bleeding? How is the girl who's expecting? How is my Jo Ellen? What is happening to them? What is happening to them all? As long as I rock myself and make myself small, I am safe and no one can see me.

After some time has gone by, I hear singing again. Singing and clapping from inside the jail.

Oh, freedom! Oh, freedom! All over again.

Then there is quiet. Then shouting. "We want a lawyer! We

want to make a phone call! We are human beings! We want freedom!" and I realize, they are all in jail, every one of them, and their windows are open. The boys are on my side, the Cotton Street side. The girls' voices are coming from the Fulton Street side. I walk to that side of the jail and look up. They are three stories up and they can't see me. But if I climb the magnolias on this side of the courthouse, I might be able to see them.

Under and up I go, while listening to them sing and shout and pray and sing some more. They sound happy to be in jail. They sound excited. I am calmed by this and hope they are really okay.

Once I get high enough, I can see straight through the windows of the jail cell on the corner. It's big. There are thick metal bars on the windows, and the glass is propped open with a stick. The white girls are in this cell. One yells, "It's hot in here!" Another yells, "Water!"

Beds hang from the walls and are stacked like bunk beds. I don't know how to talk to these girls. I don't know if Jo Ellen is even with them, so I just watch, and it makes me feel better to see them. I edge as close as I can to an opening in the branches that gives me a clear view.

From my vantage point, I can also watch the traffic come across the bridge and into Greenwood. I can see the Confederate memorial, and I can see there are still reporters and photographers talking to folks and taking pictures, but the show is over. There aren't nearly as many policemen as there were. The sawhorses across Market Street are gone and cars cruise down Market now. All the pickets are in jail.

I watch for a long time as people start to drift away, but the Negroes stay in their long line, which doesn't look like it has moved at all. I see some straw hats with them, so I know they've got their Civil Righters with them. I wonder how long they'll stand there.

I wonder how long I can stay in this tree. I'm hungry, I'm thirsty, and I'm hot. A colored girl runs onto the grass below me and calls up to the girls. "Hey! Who's up there?"

"We are!" call the white girls as they rush the windows.

"They took seventy-six to the county jail!" the colored girl shouts. "All of them colored. The rest of you are here."

"How many arrested altogether?" shouts a girl in the jail cell.

"One hundred eleven," the girl shouts back. A policeman on a motorcycle putts around the corner and slows down to watch what's happening. The girl walks off as if she'd never been talking to them. The policeman follows her slowly as she walks, and then zooms on.

"Hey! There's a kid in the tree!" shouts how-many-altogether girl.

The girls crowd the windows. "Hey, girl!" they say. "Hey!" They are so excited to see me. "What are you doing up here? Did you come to see us?"

I blink at them, not knowing what to say, or where to even begin. Then Jo Ellen shows up at the windows and I know why I'm there. "Hey, Sunny," she says again, with that crooked smile. "You've got a mop on your head."

I reach up and pull off my wig. I'm instantly cooler. "I forgot about that," I say. I want them all to go away so I can talk with Jo Ellen all by myself. At the same time, I am fascinated by them. "Are you okay?" I ask.

"We're fine," says Jo Ellen. "We did our job."

"What was your job?"

"It was our job to pack the jails today, all over Mississippi," says Jo Ellen, "to get the press to notice us, to get on the news, to let the whole country see what's happening here, and to get help. To get Washington to send people to protect us down here, to protect the Negroes so they can register to vote without being beaten or harassed."

"We want to embarrass Washington!" shouts one of them. They like having an audience.

"We aren't going to eat," says another one. "Hunger strike until we're out."

"We'll be out tomorrow," says a third. "Our lawyers know we're here. And the story will be all over the news tonight. Go watch us!"

"We're a little crazy right now," says Jo Ellen. "Getting arrested will do that to you."

I can't think of anything else to say. "Are you sure you're all right?" I ask again.

"We're fine for now," says Jo Ellen. "Are you?"

"I'm okay," I tell her. "I just wanted to be sure."

"That's very sweet of you," says Jo Ellen, as the other girls drift away from the windows. "Is that a wig you've got there?"

"It's a Beatles wig," I say, half embarrassed that I am sitting in a tree holding a Beatles wig while people are being arrested and thrown in jail.

"My little sister loves the Beatles!" says Jo Ellen. "She has all their records."

"How old is she?" I ask.

"She's about your age, I'd guess," says Jo Ellen. "Thirteen."

"I'll be thirteen in September," I say. "My brother's already thirteen."

"It's good to see you again," says Jo Ellen, like it's the most natural thing in the world to find me in a tree outside her jail cell window, like this sort of thing happens to her — or between us — every day.

"Maybe I'll come tomorrow to make sure you're out," I say hesitantly.

"That would be nice," says Jo Ellen, "but you don't have to do that."

"Where is your locket?" I ask her.

"I didn't wear it today," she says, surprised at my question. "I thought it might get lost. But I wore shorts under my skirt, and I've got my toothbrush and comb in my pocket."

"It must be special," I say. "The locket, I mean."

"Oh, yes, it is," says Jo Ellen. "Very special. My mother gave it to me."

"Are there pictures in it?"

"Not yet," says Jo Ellen.

"We want to make a phone call!" shouts a girl inside. The boys start singing from the other side of the jail, and the girls begin singing with them. Jo Ellen smiles at me. "I've got to go," she says. "Will you be okay getting down?"

"I do this all the time," I assure her. "See you tomorrow."

"I'll count on it," says Jo Ellen. "We'll watch for you."

She's counting on me. She'll watch for me. And she's okay. That's all I need to know.

Walter Cronkite is all over the story that night, but no one gets out of jail the next day, or the next, or the next. The Negroes who line the courthouse sidewalks and wait the entire day to register to vote are allowed in by twos and threes to take the literacy test.

Martha Lamb, the county registrar, does not pass one of them.

57

I slap through the back screen door, ready for another face-off with Annabelle, but I don't care. When you've seen what I've seen, a face-off with Annabelle seems tame. When you've had the kind of talk I've just had with Jo Ellen, Annabelle is a sap. I can handle Annabelle, especially if she doesn't tell on me to Daddy.

I've left my bike on the back porch with my wig stuffed in the basket. I found thirteen cents in the basket, too. I left it there. It might come in handy.

Boo is leaving the kitchen with a glass of iced tea and a cookie. She's barefoot and she grins at me. "*Guiding Light*!" she says, and spritzes out to the living room.

I have never seen Meemaw's bare feet.

"Where's Vidella?" I ask.

"Don't know," says Boo.

"Where is everybody else?"

"I'm not sure. Audrey is napping, and Annabelle is with her."

"What about noon dinner?" I ask. "What about lunch?"

"Help yourself," says Boo as she turns on the air conditioner and the television set.

I go to Polly's house. Her mother was right. There are newspaper people there, all over the kitchen, taking turns filing stories for their newspapers at her Teletype machine. One man says he's from *Time* magazine. I stand next to him and read the blocky print on the yellow pages that curl up and out of the machine. I read and think, *I was there.*

Polly is making grilled cheese sandwiches. "Want one?" she asks me.

Right then and there I decide that if Jo Ellen won't eat until she's out of jail, neither will I, even though I'm half starved already and I really want that grilled cheese sandwich. But I just drink water. Three full glasses. "Not hungry," I say.

In the living room, Polly's family maid, Mary Wade, is ironing starched pillowcases and watching *Guiding Light*.

I sit at Polly's kitchen table and watch Mary Wade iron, watch Polly make grilled cheese sandwiches, and think, *My life isn't like this at all anymore. Not at all.* Polly's right, I'm getting really weird, but she doesn't know the first thing about my weirdness. And I can't tell her about it. She wouldn't believe me. *I* wouldn't believe me.

So instead of telling her what I want her to know, I ask my friend, "Any more Paul stories?" which thrills Polly to her toes. We go upstairs to her room and listen to the Beatles and the Dave Clark Five. I get to hear all the stories she's written about her and Paul since the last time I listened to all the stories she'd written about her and Paul. They're good stories.

"What about *your* adventures?" asks Polly when she's all storied out.

The upstairs air conditioner takes all the heat out of Polly's bedroom. I am more sleepy than hungry. "Can I lie on your bed for a while?" I ask. "It's so hot outside."

"Sure," says Polly. "Do you want to spend the night? Daddy's off to Memphis selling pickles and we'll have something fun for supper."

"Okay." I kick off my Keds and peel off my socks and crawl under the covers of Polly's double bed. I think, *When you grow up the only kid in a family with both a mother and a father, you get a big bed.* I stretch out into the cool of the crisp, white sheets that Mary Wade irons every week. Such a delicious feeling, so comforting and clean, right in the middle of the afternoon. I like being taken care of.

"Thanks," I say to my friend. And that's the last thing I remember before Polly wakes me up for supper.

58

Vidella has been arrested. That's why she's not at our house. She was one of the pickets. And, it turns out, she's more than that. She's the secretary of the Greenwood Chapter of the NAACP, which stands for the National Association for the Advancement of Colored People. The NAACP is a partner with CORE and SNCC and part of COFO, who is sponsoring Freedom Summer. Whatever all that means.

I know this because I sit up and read the Teletype at Polly's house for hours while Polly and her mother sleep. I slept all afternoon, then refused supper — I said I wasn't feeling well, which I'm not — watched *The Flintstones*, *The Donna Reed Show*, and *My Three Sons*, with Polly eating popcorn and me refusing it — not easy, believe me.

I like being at Polly's, but tonight it feels echoey and empty. There are too many people at my house, but at least I'm never alone in the middle of the night.

I can't stop reading the Teletype news. The metal box says UNITED PRESS INTERNATIONAL in large white letters, and the pages keep printing, even while everyone is asleep. "We never turn it off," says Polly. Stories come in from reporters all across the Delta, and I feast my eyes on them, partly to keep from feasting on the leftover macaroni and cheese in the refrigerator. A hunger strike is no simple thing. My mind turns to Jo Ellen in jail. Is she comfortable? Are there enough beds? Is she as hungry as I am?

Tick-tick-tick-tick-type-type-type from the Teletype. A Negro church is bombed in the night in Merigold. A cross is burned in somebody's yard in Clarksdale. A mass meeting is held at a Negro church in Greenwood. Greenwood! Also in Greenwood, six Negroes are arrested and held in jail for disturbing the peace at the Leflore Theater. Names are listed. One of them is:

RAYMOND BULLIS, NEGRO, AGE 14.

I want to go home.

I tear off a whole bunch of the Teletype coming out of the machine, including the story about Raymond Bullis. I rip it across, just the way I saw the newspaper men tear off their stories earlier. I need it, so I take it.

Then I tiptoe out the back door of Polly's house and walk across the night grass in my pajamas. The moonflowers scent the air I breathe and I am glad for their familiar smell. I turn the knob at the back door and let myself in, quiet as a tiny, brown field mouse. The clock strikes nine, which means its twelve o'clock. Midnight. The stove light was left on in the kitchen and I see the bowls set out on the counter for breakfast, the coffeepot ready to be assembled for the morning's coffee.

I step around all the creaks on the stairs and go to Gillette's room. I open his door slowly, without knocking.

"Hey." Gillette says it before I do. I step in and close the door behind me.

"You're awake," I say.

"I thought you were at Polly's."

"I wanted to come home."

"Yeah."

I pull out Gillette's desk chair, sit on it, and fold my legs crisscross under me. Gillette sits up in bed and props his pillows behind his back, against his headboard. His San Francisco Giants pennant is on the wall above his head. "What's happening?" he asks.

I sniff. "Oh, Gillette. Everything."

"Tell me," he says. The nicest invitation.

But I can't. I just can't.

"Your boy got arrested" — that's what I can tell him. "Hightop. Raymond. I read it on the Teletype at Polly's tonight." I hoist my Teletype papers at him, to show him I've got proof.

"Is he in jail?"

"I guess so. He was at the Leflore again, with some others."

"Is Parnell okay?"

I hadn't even thought about Parnell. What's wrong with me? Then Gillette says, "He called here tonight. He must be all right."

I nod, relieved. "What are we going to do?"

"There's nothing *to* do," says Gillette.

"Have you talked to him?" I ask.

"Parnell?"

"No, Raymond."

"No. I never have. Why?"

"I just wondered."

"Have you ever talked to him?" Gillette asks me.

"No. What would we say?"

"I'd say 'good catch.'"

I smile. "Good night, brother."

"Good night, Sunny."

Good catch.

59

Sunday, July 19, 1964

There's a weird thing about not eating I didn't know. After the first day, when you're so hungry you could eat a freezer full of ice-cream sandwiches, or even a boat of lima beans, you're not so hungry anymore. After the second day, your mind doesn't work so well anymore. After that, you have to go to bed, and that's that.

Jo Ellen isn't eating, either — none of them is eating. The colored girls are in a different cell, and the boys are separated, too. I've checked on Jo Ellen for two days, and she is worried. They are all worried. They can't make phone calls and they haven't seen their lawyers. They haven't seen a judge. No one knows how long they will be in jail. They are hungry. I am, too.

"We won't eat their food," says Jo Ellen.

We have great food at my house — it turns out Boo is a good cook — and I won't eat it. I am crazy and I am determined. But I won't be able to fool Daddy and Annabelle much longer. "I don't feel good" can only get me so far. And honest, I really don't feel good anymore. I don't think I can climb a tree until I eat again.

It about kills me not to eat Sunday dinner, which we have over at Polly's today, with Mary Margaret attending. "Are you sick?" Parnell asks me, and I just shake my head. "My mom's a nurse," says Randy Smithers, unhelpful as can be. Randy takes Parnell to work and says he's going to hang around in case of trouble. Parnell says he's got to find a new job.

We all migrate to our house for dessert on the porch, where Daddy talks with Mr. Carr when he comes to pick up Mary Margaret. They have figured out that Vidella is at the county work farm, where she got sentenced to thirty days. Thirty days!

"We can probably get her out sooner," says Mr. Carr.

"You are delusional, Sunny," chides Mary Margaret when I temporarily lose my mind during dessert — cherry cobbler with homemade vanilla ice cream — and start babbling to her and Polly about being in jail and climbing trees and police brutality — a phrase I got from the Teletype sheets I brought home. "You're having hallucinations."

I want to say, *So are you, if you think baton twirling is your next big talent*, when Mary Margaret breaks the porch light trying to show us her left-backhand-release-double-knuckle-pop . . . and she isn't even on the porch.

"Stick to singing," says Polly, which makes me laugh so hard I fall off the step. I drink another lemonade and Mary Margaret tells me that at least she has a talent. Huh.

All the dads sit on the porch with lemonades while Mr. Carr tells Daddy and Mr. Campbell that he and the judge at the courthouse are trying to figure out what to do with all the Civil Righters in jail. Their lawyers are stuck somewhere, but I don't understand that. What I do understand is that I need to lie down.

"I'm worried about that girl," I hear Polly's mother say to Annabelle as I excuse myself and go inside. "Has she seen a doctor? And what's all this talk about going to jail and climbing trees?"

"So, Gillette . . . ," says Mary Margaret with a little giggle in her voice, and I can't even stick around to see what will happen next.

Run, brother — that's all I can think, and that makes me laugh, too, all the way into the kitchen. By the time I reach the refrigerator I forget where I'm going. Oh, right, the bedroom. I'm going to bed.

It's a funny thing, hunger. It gnaws away at your mind, as well as your body. It makes you say things you don't realize you're saying. It makes you forget what you already said. It makes the world fuzzy, and it makes your stomach so very empty.

All the windows are open. I sit at the kitchen table by myself and stare at the salt and pepper shakers like they're the most amazing objects I've ever seen in my life, as I listen to the sounds of Mary Margaret leaving with her dad, and Daddy hitting Gillette pop flies in the front yard, and Audrey playing with the hose, filling her wading pool with Boo's help while Boo tells her a story about riding pecan tree branches when she was a little girl, shaking the nuts to the ground, and collecting sacks of pecans to crack for pies.

I'm concentrating so hard on the salt and pepper shakers I don't see them anymore, and I don't hear Annabelle until she pulls out a chair and sits next to me.

"She's very pretty," she says.

I blink at Annabelle. "Who?"

Annabelle reaches into her dress pocket and pulls out my picture of *Miranda, age 18*. In a voice she might use to soothe a skittish kitten, Annabelle says, "I found it when I was vacuuming yesterday. It was under your bed. I almost sucked it up. I'm so glad I didn't." She puts the picture on the kitchen table and says, "I was thinking maybe you'd like to put it in a frame on your dresser."

I stare at the picture so long my tears drip onto the table. Annabelle gently moves the picture out of teardrop range and I say, "It doesn't belong to me. I took it from Meemaw's house. Without her permission."

Annabelle ignores my admission of theft. "I wonder what she was thinking in this picture, and where she was going," she says. A lawn mower starts up somewhere in the neighborhood.

"I don't know very much," I say. Then I hiccup. "I think she handed me to Daddy and ran away." I wipe my eyes. "But nobody wants to tell me that."

Annabelle sighs. "That's a hard thing to tell. And a hard thing to believe, too." In the distance a train whistle blows and I picture the crossing at the compress, the crossing near the pool.

"Maybe she just wanted to have an adventure first," I say, "and then she didn't know how to come back." Annabelle draws me a glass of water from the sink and hands it to me along with a napkin for my nose.

"Do you want to know what I think?" she asks, and suddenly I do. I really do. I nod my head but keep my eyes on the picture in front of me. My head feels hollow and my eyes sting.

"I think love is a mystery," says Annabelle. "We never know where it may come from or how it may surprise us or when it may ask us to do the impossible. But we know one thing about love. It is steady. It is brave. And you are one of the bravest people I know."

I wipe my nose and look at my stepmother. "I am?"

"You are."

"But I'm afraid all the time," I say.

"It's okay to be afraid," Annabelle assures me. "I'm afraid, too."

"You are?"

"Yes. I am. But I know something about being afraid that helps me."

"What is it?"

"I know that you don't have to be afraid by yourself. You don't have to be alone with what scares you."

I consider this as the sounds of Audrey and Boo, shrieking and splashing, split my concentration.

"Okay," I say, and I get up to leave the table.

"I'm going to scramble some eggs, and I want you to eat them," says Annabelle.

"No," I say. I drink some water.

"And then," Annabelle continues, "we'll make some food for those kids at the courthouse."

I choke and Annabelle claps me on the back.

"What are you talking about?" I say, but I can't sound innocent. I am completely empty.

"Mr. Carr said the kids at the courthouse aren't eating. Let's take them some food. They must be hungry."

"You don't even know them."

"I know you," says Annabelle. "And something tells me they're important to you."

I sit down, surprised. "People in this town surely don't like them," I say. "I always thought people in Greenwood were good people, but I've seen some bad things. . . ."

Annabelle brushes a curl out of her face and says, "Being good is not a straight line, Sunny. Being good is not being ever-obedient and never making mistakes. Being good is more complicated than that."

I tuck my flyaway hair behind my ears. "What does that mean?"

Annabelle says, "It's good to be your own person and to be bold. But it's good to understand when to listen to someone else who is trying to keep you safe. It's good to understand when to think about the safety of others. It's good to think about how your actions affect others. That's why people in this town — good people, black and white — are so careful. They are afraid to take risks, but that's not necessarily a bad thing. Sometimes it's best to do what feels safe, and sometimes it's better to do what you know is right, even though the cost may be high. It's hard to tell the difference, especially when, if you do nothing, it gives a chance for those who would do harm, to do it."

"Like Mr. Delay and his friends."

"Yes."

"How can you tell when to take a risk and when to do nothing?" I ask.

"I don't know." Annabelle picks at a crumb on the table, leftover from breakfast, then says, "Practice, maybe. Every time you make a mistake, you get another chance to practice. And that's what's important. Keep practicing and you'll get better at knowing the difference."

I nod my head, but I'm not sure I understand.

Then Annabelle says, "I still practice."

I pick up the picture of *Miranda, age 18*, and I see Jo Ellen smiling her crooked smile at me, hungry, at the courthouse jail.

"Thank you," I whisper to Annabelle.

"You're welcome," she says.

He was in Rome, Italy, and eighteen years old, when he won the gold medal — the Olympic light heavyweight boxing crown — at the 1960 Olympic games. Legend has it, he refused to take that medal off, even to sleep.

Legend goes on to say that when he returned home to Louisville, Kentucky, Cassius Marcellus Clay stood on a bridge and hurled his Olympic gold medal into the river because he discovered that he still wasn't allowed to be served in a white-owned restaurant, that all the medals in the world wouldn't matter to white, segregated America in 1960. A Negro had to understand his place.

But not Cassius. He got busy carving himself a new place. He opened his mouth and shouted, "I am the Greatest! I am the King of the World!" He would go on to hold the world heavyweight title three times, he would convert to a faith that America was afraid of, and he would go to jail rather than violate his principles. But first he had to become Muhammad Ali.

Ali was born Cassius Marcellus Clay, Jr., in 1942, smack in the middle of World War II. In Louisville, the grocery store man was white. The bus drivers were white. The store owners were white. Cassius asked his father:

"Daddy, what do the colored people do?"

Cassius's father was nicknamed "Cash." He wanted to be a painter of fine paintings, an artist, but he had to settle for being the best sign painter in Louisville. So he told everyone he met, "I am the Greatest!" and he held forth at the supper table about the injustices suffered by Negroes. Cassius's mom, Odessa, raised Cassius and his younger brother, Rudy, and also worked in the wealthy white part of town as a family maid. When Cassius saw whites driving by in their fancy cars and clothes, he asked his father:

"Daddy, why can't I be rich?"

Cash pointed to his son's brown hands and said, "That's why you can't be rich."

While Cassius grew up, America struggled with itself over segregation.

In 1954, when Cassius was twelve, the U.S. Supreme Court decided that American schools could no longer be segregated, in a decision called *Brown v. the Board of Education.* The new law made no difference in Louisville, or in much of the American South, as whites largely ignored *Brown,* schools remained segregated, and Cassius attended an all-black high school where, even though he was not a good student, his teachers and principal worked with him to make sure he graduated. They already saw his potential.

Go, Cassius!

Brown put the South on notice. *You must integrate! Desegregate!* Whites were worried, scared. Blacks were cautious, and yet they pushed against the old rules.

That's when Rosa sat down and Martin stood up, in Montgomery, Alabama. It's also when Emmett Till was murdered in Money, Mississippi. Cassius and Emmett were the same age. Cash brought home the *Jet* magazine with pictures of Emmett's broken body. He made his boys look. *"This is what they do to us!"* he said.

Cash railed, and Cassius stared hard at the pictures of a beaten Emmett pulled out of the river, a boy his age who went out into the world and didn't come home. Emmett hadn't had any quarrel with those white men who killed him. This fact would stay with Cassius, and would inform his life and his decisions.

So would Vietnam, a tiny country in Asia that Cassius had never heard of when he was twelve. So would Allah, who Cassius would discover as a young man, and who he would follow through the Nation of Islam, the Sunni Muslims, and, eventually, the Sufis.

But boxing came first. It came first because — also when Cassius was twelve — *someone stole his bicycle.*

His *brand-new* Schwinn.
You never saw a kid so mad!

WATCH OUT!

Cassius grabbed hold of Joe Martin, a policeman who also trained young boxers, and yelled for help — *I'm gonna whup whoever stole it!* — and Joe told him, *Then you'd better learn to fight first!*

That's how it began. Many years later, Cassius — Ali — would say:

> *"When I was eight and ten years old, I'd walk out of my house at two in the morning and look up at the sky for an angel or a revelation from God telling me what to do. I never got the answer. Then my bike got stolen and I started boxing and it was like God telling me that boxing was my responsibility."*

He weighed eighty-eight pounds when he was twelve years old, but he didn't let being scrawny stop him. He rose at four in the morning to train and he worked harder than anyone else at Joe Martin's gym. He never missed a meal. He was disciplined, determined, and had something to hold on to. Finally, he had something to *do*. He said:

> *"Boxing kept me out of trouble."*

It also took him out into the world.

As he ran out of Louisville and into the world without his Olympic gold medal, as he pummeled and pounded and battered his opponents and racked up more than two dozen wins in a row, he became the heavyweight champion of the world, all while developing his signature doggerel poetry and chatter, partly to keep his fears at bay.

He was just twenty-two years old before his first heavyweight bout against the champ, Sonny Liston, in 1964, four months before one thousand souls came marching into Mississippi for Freedom Summer.

Liston learned to box in the Missouri State Penitentiary, where he served time for armed robbery. He was ferocious! Massively muscled! The most formidable fighter of his time. The mob loved him! No one wanted to get in the ring with Liston. He had knocked out Floyd Patterson twice — both times in the first round!

Cassius was nearly hysterical with fear, but you would never have known it from his chatter. He called Liston a "big, ugly bear" and said he would "donate him to the zoo" after he won. In the history of boxing, no one had ever seen an opponent talk like this, brag like this, bait his opponent like this.

But inside, Cassius was so afraid that he asked his friend, Malcolm X, to fly to the match to be by his side. Malcolm reminded Cassius, over and over again, about how David slew Goliath and how he, Cassius, could beat this Goliath. Which he did, in a stunning twenty-one round TKO — technical knockout — decision.

He was a marvel, something the sports world had never seen before. He moved his arms and his legs at the same time, and he threw his punches while he was in motion. It was hard to hit a moving target, and he never stopped moving —

"Float like a butterfly, sting like a bee!"

Many in white America had rooted for Liston, as a black man who might keep a sassy Negro in line. But it wasn't going to be that way. Clay changed his name to Ali, and went on boxing . . . and composing poems.

This is the legend of Cassius Clay
The most beautiful fighter in the world today.
He talks a great deal, and brags indeed-y,
of a muscular punch that's incredibly speed-y.

Americans either loved him or hated him, there was no in between. To those who wouldn't call him Ali, he said:

> *"Changing my name was one of the most important things that happened to me in my life. It freed me from the identity given to my family by slave masters. People change their names all the time, and no one complains . . . actors and actresses change their names. The Pope changes his name!"*

Ali was on fire. He fought Liston again and defeated him, two weeks before Martin Luther King, Jr., led six hundred fifty marchers through Selma, Alabama. He fought Floyd Patterson and won. He fought all comers!

But what Ali could not foresee was that a tiny country in Southeast Asia was about to trip him up. . . .

Ho Chi Minh's 1945 letters to Harry Truman asking for U.S. help to fight the French (who claimed ownership of Indochina) went unanswered, so Ho made friends with the Russians and Chinese — the Communists — who helped the Viet Minh army hoist the French out of Vietnam.

As a result, Vietnam was partitioned into two countries — North Vietnam and South Vietnam. This had happened in 1954 . . . coincidentally, when Cassius was twelve, and when no one in America had heard of Vietnam.

But now, in 1964, every American knew about Vietnam, because somehow America was involved in helping the South Vietnamese keep the North Vietnamese Communists out of their country and, if you believed what you were told, out of America, and out of the rest of the world.

American boys registered for the draft when they turned eighteen, and took selective service entrance exams. Cassius had dutifully registered, and he had failed his tests. Twice. He had never done well in school, and he didn't do any better now.

Suddenly America needed more and more soldiers for the fight against the Communists in Southeast Asia. Ali's test scores were suddenly declared high enough to draft him into the U.S. Army and send him to Vietnam, right in the middle of his heavyweight championship career.

And Ali would not go.

Did he remember the tales his father told at the kitchen table about how Negroes were not treated fairly in white America?

Did he remember his first trainer, Joe Martin, telling him he'd better learn to fight first?

Did he remember Emmett Till, who would never be able to fight again?

Ali stood before the U.S. Draft board in 1966 and said no. He said, "I ain't got no quarrel with them Vietcong." And, suddenly, a wave swept over America, of young men, white and black, who were being drafted and could articulate, thanks to Ali, the accidental patron saint of the antiwar movement, why they didn't want to go to Vietnam.

Ali said more:

> *"Why should they ask me to put on a uniform and go ten thousand miles from home and drop bombs and bullets on brown people in Vietnam while so-called Negro people in Louisville are treated like dogs and denied simple human rights?"*

He refused to go to Vietnam on religious grounds, saying the Holy Koran said believers were not to participate in war, not even to aid in passing a cup of water to the wounded. He kept on talking.

> *"America is my birth country. They make the rules, and if they want to put me in jail, they'll put me in jail. I'll go to jail. But I'm an American, and I'm not running away."*

They put him in jail. They stripped him of his heavyweight title, and for three years, he could not fight. He kept on talking.

> *"I don't have to be what you want me to be. I'm free to be what I want."*

In 1971, the U.S. Supreme Court overturned Ali's conviction and he reclaimed his heavyweight boxing title, fighting Joe Frazier, Floyd Patterson, Ken Norton, George Foreman, Larry Holmes . . .

The Rumble in the Jungle!
The Thrilla in Manila!
Rope a Dope!
The Greatest was back!

He was older and he was slower, but Ali was King, and America loved him.

In the 1980s he developed Parkinson's Syndrome, probably from all that fighting, all that battering to the head, and he retired from boxing.

He went home to Louisville, because he could go home. A museum was opened in his honor. He could eat wherever he wanted. America had changed. Ali had changed. Young men who had watched Ali's fight had changed.

In 1996, the Summer Olympics were held in Atlanta, Georgia. The opening ceremonies focused on the rebirth of the American South after the Civil War. Muhammad Ali wore all white and carefully jogged up the lighted trail in the Olympic stadium, where he lit the Olympic torch. Then he received a replacement gold medal for his boxing victory in the 1960 Summer Olympic games.

He held his head high while America cheered for the legend who had lived according to his conscience, who said, "I wasn't trying to be a leader. I just wanted to be free."

60

"But it's Sunday!" Daddy says, leaning the bat against the porch. "It's her only day off."

"That's the point," says Annabelle, patting Daddy's cheek like she's so happy to be putting on this party he has agreed to. "Your mother would never allow it during the week."

"True enough," says Daddy.

"Sunny, bring me some sugar!" she calls after us. "I'm going to make a pound cake!"

Daddy takes me and Gillette with him to Colored Town, where we knock on Laura Mae's door. "We're not the white students!" I yell. We ask her if she might consider it. She's still in her church clothes and doesn't want to come, I can tell, but she does, anyway. Daddy says we'll pay her half a day's wages and bring her right back.

We stop at Fairchild's to pick up a cooked ham, Annabelle's sugar, and some bread from the bakery case. The store is closed up tight, but its good smells are leftover from the week, and I'm glad Daddy and Annabelle aren't fighting by the cooler anymore. Gillette snaps open a paper sack and fills it with grapes, peaches, and a bunch of bananas. I throw in a handful of candy bars.

"Hey!" says Daddy.

"It's important! Everybody in jail needs candy!" I say it like I know from firsthand experience.

Gillette slips in some comic books from the rack in the back. I grab a copy of *Look* magazine and *True Romance*.

"*True Romance*?" says Gillette. I shrug.

"What else do we need, Laura Mae?" asks Daddy.

Laura Mae is hesitant at first, then she goes on a no-nonsense shopping spree. She loads a box with hot dogs and buns and pickle relish and aluminum foil to wrap the hot dogs in, waxed paper, a roll of paper towels, and two packages of baloney and sliced American cheese for the bread and some Ritz Crackers and Cheez Whiz.

Daddy says "How many people are in this jail?" and I answer, "One hundred eleven minus seventy-six!"

Laura Mae throws in three bags of Lay's Potato Chips and three bags of Fritos.

"Finished?" asks Daddy.

Laura Mae adds two cans of Reddi-wip and says, "That'll do it."

Daddy hands Gillette three cartons of Coca-Cola and says, "We can put them in a tub of ice and they can share." THINGS GO BETTER WITH COKE is the slogan on the cartons. The glass bottles clink together as Gillette tries to carry them all to the trunk at once while Daddy goes to the freezer for ice.

We drive home up Walthall Street, and Daddy turns on the radio. Gillette fiddles with the stations so he can find a ball game.

"The Giants don't play until three thirty," he says.

"The White Sox are at home in Chicago," says Daddy.

"I got a son in Chicago," says Laura Mae in a quiet voice only I hear because I'm sitting in the backseat next to her.

"I didn't know that, Laura Mae," I tell her. Laura Mae folds her hands in her lap and stares out the open window.

"What's his name?" I ask.

"David," says Laura Mae. "Like the king who slew Goliath."

"He had a mighty slingshot," I say.

Laura Mae nods. "It's all in the Bible. 'Now the Philistines gathered together their armies to battle.'"

"David wrote the Psalms," I say.

"'The Lord is my shepherd,'" says Laura Mae.

"'I shall not want,'" I answer. "Psalm twenty-three."

"Yes," says Laura Mae. She goes back to staring out the window.

Gillette gets the game on the radio. "The Yankees!" he says.

"Roger Maris," I spout. "Right field."

"Wow!" Daddy is impressed.

"That's right." Gillette smiles, pleased that I'm learning. I'm pleased that he's pleased.

"Lord, Lord," says Laura Mae as we pass the colored funeral home. She clasps her hands together like she's going to pray and says, softly, "Emmett, Emmett, Emmett. This gon' be bad as that poor chile Emmett before it all over."

"Who's Emmett?" I ask.

Laura Mae fixes me with her dark brown eyes and says, "Throwed in the river when he your age. Beaten and throwed away in the river. Right up the road yonder. A summertime, just like now. He didn't do nothing but be a black chile talkin' to a white lady. Now these white kids come down here and stir up trouble and colored children gon' die again. They already some disappear. And then they gon' go home, these white kids, and we gon' be left to Mister. Ain't no good gon' come out of this."

Her story gives me the creeps. Laura Mae takes a handkerchief out of her dress pocket and wipes her face. "Y'all don't need me now, I just a' soon go home."

"I need you, Laura Mae," I say, and I mean it. I reach over and take her hand. She lets me.

"Honeychile."

I think about the river and the boy named Emmett and the boy named Raymond, and how he's probably in the same jail as my Jo Ellen now. I wish he could have some of this feast.

"Laura Mae, do you know a colored boy named Raymond Bullis?"

"Everybody knows Ray," says Laura Mae. "He got a lot to prove, that boy."

I want to hit the back of the front seat and squeal at Gillette, *Forget the ball game! There's treasure right here in the backseat! Is there anything more amazing than this?*

"You know Raymond?" asks Laura Mae.

"I never met him," I say, which is true. "I saw his name in the paper."

"He in jail, for sure," says Laura Mae. "Can't leave well enough alone. He and that crowd of his. They all cousins, some from the farm at Browning. Troublemakers." I hear pride in her voice.

"We could feed them tonight, too," I suggest.

Laura Mae sits a little higher in the seat. "That's a thought," she says.

"That's a thought," I say.

Four hours later, it's suppertime and we have packed three large boxes with ham or baloney and cheese sandwiches made by me, fried chicken made by Laura Mae, biscuits made by Boo, and a warm pound cake made by Annabelle, plus everything else from Fairchild's. I have eaten some of everything. And I put a Milky Way in the freezer to eat later.

Gillette is our packer. Laura Mae is our designated food-taker — "because we can't do that," says Daddy, and Annabelle agrees. But Laura Mae refuses to do it.

"Somebody see me down at the courthouse like that, Miss Eloise fire me, sure enough," she says. "And I needs this job. But I know who will do it."

Daddy calls one of the colored cab companies to come get Laura Mae. We tote three boxes and one tin tub full of Cokes on ice to the cab. Daddy gives the cabdriver enough money to make all his runs.

"Levon's good," says Laura Mae about the cab driver. "Some gets paid to be spies for the white mens. You got to know who you can trust."

Daddy arranges with Levon to take the food and Laura Mae to Baptist Town, where she knows who she can trust to take her place at the Freedom House and take the food to the jailhouse door. Levon and the summer volunteers will make sure it gets delivered.

"See what's keeping Laura Mae," Daddy says when we've got everything ready.

I find Laura Mae packing a grocery sack. She's wrapping the last sandwich in waxed paper. "This is special for Ray and those troublemakers," she says. I nod.

"How we gon' make sure he gets it?" she asks me.

"Put his name on it," I tell her. I rummage through the junk drawer and produce a Magic Marker

"How that works?" asks Laura Mae.

I pull off the top and hear that hollow *pop!* sound. The smell of the black ink stings my nose. I hand the marker to Laura Mae.

"I don't have my glasses," she says.

"You don't wear glasses," I tell her.

"I do today," she says.

I don't know why she's being so difficult. I grab the bag and write in big letters:

FOR RAYMOND BULLIS

Laura Mae inspects my writing. "That looks right," she says.

"Thank you," I snip. "Anything else?"

"Yes," says Laura Mae. She tears a piece of brown paper off

an empty sack and puts it on the counter in front of me. "Write 'freedom' on this one," she says. "Write it pretty."

"Really?"

Laura Mae nods yes.

Freedom. I write it pretty. I make it look brave.

"Thank you." Laura Mae tucks the piece of paper between the ham sandwich and the waxed paper, double wraps the sandwich, and puts it in the bag. She rolls the bag down as far as it will go, takes off the apron Annabelle loaned her, and says, "That's good."

Our food gets delivered and eaten, every last crumb.

61

Simon, Chuff, Freddie, Twill, Jimmy, and me, the FreedomMakers, arrested at the movies. Aunt Geneva beside herself. She come to the courthouse with a lawyer and got her some mad, made so much noise. We watchin' while she swing her big purse and hit one police in the head, punch him in the eye, wrestle him right to the floor. He don't want nobody to know about it, and so the police let her boys go, but they don't let me go. "He's a repeat offender," they say.

Freddie and Chuff, they eighteen. They sent to the county work farm.

They put me in with the colored SNCC mens. Now I got my own dinner bag.

"Somebody thinks you're mighty special, boy," jailer say. "Who'd your mama pay to write your name that pretty?"

Extra chicken and cake — share it. And a present, wrapped up. *Freedom*. Put it in my pocket. Somebody tellin' me "Freedom."

Four days we in jail, SNCCs and me, and Ma'am worried sick.

Pap teary, when I get home. SNCCs say they got a job for me and the FreedomMakers, real job. "Quit that theater, boy. Do something useful. Slim Henderson, that policeman who hauled Dorie down the sidewalk — he owns a grocery store in Baptist Town."

"I know it," I say. "Henderson's."

"Folks don't need to shop at a white man's store when he hurts Negroes," say SNCC Stokely. "You go tell people.

Do something constructive, stop tryin' to get yourselves killed."

"I got to run it by 'em, See what they say."

They say yes.

At Freedom House, SNCC Bob say, "It's called a boycott."

I say, "Boycott 'em all."

We gon' get started after King come. Mama cleaning our house top to toes. Ironing her best dress. "King comin'!" She sing it. And King come, with four cars of FBI men and most of black Greenwood crowding him from all sides, wherever he walk, the Greenwood Colored Marching Band steppin' high in front of him.

Black Elks Hall only place big enough to hold the crowd. It rock to the heavens that night and noise bust out the roof.

People on top of people, cryin', singin', moanin', shoutin', *YES, LAWD!*

We want Freedom!

King shout from the mountaintop:

"There is power in unity, power in numbers! Keep this movement moving! Keep climbing! If you can't fly, run! If you can't run, walk! If you can't walk, crawl! But by all means, keep moving! Walk together, children, and don't you get weary!

"Register for Freedom Democratic Party now! Sign up! Be counted!"

Simon and Twill and Jimmy and even me — eyes shiny. King walkin' our street next day, crowds press in, every cranny, cars parade, horns blare, suddenly nobody care who drive by slow, lookin' to take down names! King say hello to Ma'am on her porch, say *register*. "I done it!" she say. Everybody scramble for forms and Ida Mae holdin' 'em.

Ma'am call out, "No Martha Lamb! No police! No jail! Register! *Yes, lawd.*"

Now a prop plane circle low overhead and drop a shower of papers over everybody. I grab me one.

"A gift from the Klan," say the man with King. He shout to the crowd, "Keep moving!"

King's crowd move along like a wave, but I turn over the paper and read it. I read it again. And again.

Then I tear those hateful words into tiny pieces while I set my jaw tight like a prizefighter, like Muhammad Ali going for the knockout.

Gonna get me some Slim Henderson.

I put my hand in my pocket and smooth that brown paper with my fingers.

Freedom.

TO THOSE OF YOU *NIGGERS* WHO GAVE OR GIVE AID AND COMFORT TO THIS CIVIL RIGHTS SCUM, WE ADVISE YOU THAT YOUR IDENTITIES ARE IN THE PROPER HANDS AND *YOU WILL BE REMEMBERED.* WE KNOW THAT THE NIGGER OWNER OF COLLINS SHOE SHOP ON JOHNSON STREET "ENTERTAINED" MARTIN LUTHER KING WHEN THE "BIG NIGGER" CAME TO GREENWOOD. WE KNOW OF OTHERS AND WE SAY TO YOU — AFTER THE SHOUTING AND THE PLATE-PASSING AND STUPID STREET DEMONSTRATIONS ARE OVER AND THE IMPORTED AGITATORS HAVE ALL GONE, ONE THING IS SURE AND CERTAIN — YOU ARE STILL GOING TO BE *NIGGERS* AND WE ARE STILL GOING TO BE WHITE MEN. YOU HAVE CHOSEN YOUR BEDS AND NOW YOU MUST LIE IN THEM.

— KKK leaflet dropped in colored sections of Greenwood after the visit of Martin Luther King, Jr.

62

Saturday, August 8, 1964

"You could work at the store!" shouts Daddy. I've never heard him sound like this. He looks like somebody told him his best friend just died. The morning sun beams through the tall windows in the dining room and plays across a wooden bowl of fruit on the table. It's so empty and quiet in the dining room, like it's a little world unto itself, while in the living room we've got World War III.

"I don't want to work at the store," shouts Parnell. "I never did!" Parnell never shouts, either. No one in this family is a shouter but me.

"Go back to Oxford!"

"I'm not college material," says Parnell. "I never wanted to go to Ole Miss. You wanted me to. That was a waste of a year. I feel like I'm wasting my whole life!"

Annabelle is still in bed this morning. Audrey has started sleeping with Boo. Gillette spent the night at Nick's. I am sitting in a corner of the couch with a warm Pop-Tart on a paper towel in my lap and a glass of cold milk on the end table.

Daddy paces in the living room. "I don't understand why you have to enlist. There are better jobs than the one at the Leflore."

"Where?" says Parnell. "I don't want to work at the plantation. I don't want to work at the Buckeye, or at any other place that'll have me, I don't want to move to Memphis or Jackson, I want to get out of here, see the world!"

An adventure! Parnell wants an adventure. I knew it.

"You'll see Vietnam, that's what you'll see!" cries Daddy. "Did Randy talk you into this just so he could make his quota?"

"There are lots of men signing up — even some coloreds — now that there's a call for troops," replies Parnell. "It's better than getting bricks thrown at me through the glass at the Leflore or fighting off the mobs that congregate every time one of those Bullis brothers shows up. I'm getting a bad name in this town just because I work there. Now I've quit."

"I've had a bad name in this town for years!" Daddy hollers. "You just hold up your head and live through it!"

"Not me!" Parnell hurls back at Daddy. "You're old, Jamie. I'm only nineteen."

"That's the point! You're still a kid."

Parnell takes a breath. "I haven't been a kid since Mama and Daddy died." He says it softly, and Daddy calms down. He stops pacing, rubs his face with his hands, sighs, and says, "I know." That's all.

Parnell sounds like he's the parent now and Daddy is his boy. "Randy will still be here, signing up folks. I hope you have him for dinner sometimes. He'd appreciate that."

Randy will never be a substitute for Parnell. I feel like crying and I don't even know what it means that Parnell has enlisted.

Daddy shakes his head and walks out of the room. Parnell looks at me with a half smile and says, "Got any pie for a soldier?"

"I'll make you one," I say, although without Laura Mae or Vidella, I just have to hope that Boo or Annabelle can help me. "Are you leaving, Parnell?"

"Yes," he tells me. He sits in the chair by the television. "I leave for basic training in two weeks. Then I go wherever they send me — but I'll be home before that."

I am not hungry anymore. "Will you go to Vietnam?" I ask because it's on the news all the time now, and all I know is it's far away and we have to fight the Communists.

"Probably," Parnell says

"I don't want you to go."

"You're going to be so busy in school and with your friends, you won't even miss me."

"That's not true. And you know it."

He comes to me and tugs at my chin. "Do we still have a date to go to Memphis and see *A Hard Day's Night*?" I nod. Parnell promised to take me, Polly, and Mary Margaret next weekend. No one dares to go see it at the Leflore. Mrs. Campbell might come with us and let us visit her newspaper's office. It was going to be the highlight of summer before school started again, but right this minute, I don't even care. Right this minute, I don't even remember one Beatles song I ever knew.

"I want it to be like it was," I say, "with the Leflore open and everybody happy, and you letting me in for free. . . ."

"I didn't let you in for free," says Parnell. "I always paid for your ticket."

"You did?"

"Nothing is what it seems, is it?" says Parnell. He tries to get a smile out of me, but I'm not going to cooperate.

Audrey shuffles into the room, sleepy, and tries to crawl on my lap. I hand her my Pop-Tart. "You are sharing today, Sunny," she whispers as she snuggles next to me and starts nibbling. Ruth pads in behind her, and Parnell gives her a pat and lets her out the front door.

"I have to go," says Parnell. "Somebody filled lightbulbs with red paint and threw them inside the lobby last night — paint bombs — and it's a mess. I'm going to help Mr. Martini clean up what we can. But I'll be here for Sunday dinner.

Annabelle says she's cooking and Meemaw and Uncle Vivian are coming."

"Come by yourself," I say, like it's an order, and Parnell says okay, he will. Red paint. In lightbulbs. Splattered all over the Leflore lobby. Poor Mr. Martini.

"Let's go, Sunny, we're late!" calls Daddy in a tragic voice from the kitchen. Time for work. Gillette will meet us. It's Saturday, and everybody and his brother will come, from town and from the country, for groceries, so we need all hands on deck to bag them, and Gillette will make deliveries, too. We can count on a busy day.

What we don't count on are all the Civil Righters on Johnson Street, where the Negroes shop on Saturday. They are standing on corners with papers, talking to every Negro that passes by. We stop at the light at Main and Johnson and watch them. I look for Jo Ellen, but I don't see her. There are police cars, too, and policemen, watching, along with men in suits, just standing there, also watching. It's already blistering hot. How can they stand to wear those suit jackets?

"What are they doing?" I ask Daddy. I've never seen the Civil Righters in town before, except at the courthouse.

"I don't know," says Daddy, sounding tired already, and it's not even nine o'clock.

Chief Lary is out with his bullhorn again. "You must be off the sidewalks! You are impeding foot traffic!" he yells. The light turns green and Daddy crosses over Johnson to the block that holds Fairchild's, only to find more Civil Righters near our store. He swings into the parking lot and slams the car door as he gets out. "Get away from my store!" he yells at the white students on the corner.

"We have a right to be wherever we want in public, sir," says a white boy in a checked shirt.

"What are you doing?" Daddy yells.

"We're registering voters for the Mississippi Freedom Democratic Party," says the white boy. "Anyone can register. It's a new party. You don't have to go to the courthouse. Are you registered to vote?"

Daddy slams through the front door of Fairchild's with me on his heels.

Mr. Arnold, who opened the store so Daddy could talk with Parnell, says, "Customers aren't going to want to get close to these agitators."

Daddy picks up the phone and says, "Get me the police, Miss May."

Five minutes later, Deputy Davis swaggers through the front door. I am bagging Mrs. Murchison's groceries and she is staring out the front picture window at the Civil Righters talking to the Negroes trying to shop at our store. She looks as nervous as a polecat facing a shotgun, and so do the Negroes. She forgets to give me a tip and she doesn't tell me I'm a doodle. Deputy Davis escorts her to her car like he's protecting the queen of England and comes back to talk to Daddy. They go into his office.

And that's when Raymond shows up. He's got a sign that reads, DON'T SHOP WHERE YOU CAN'T WORK. What? Mrs. Maple stops ringing up orders. I stop bagging. We all gawk at Raymond and his sign. I walk to the front window to get a better look.

Isaiah Nixon, who has been restocking the canned goods shelf, notices how quiet it is suddenly and comes to the front of the store and stands next to me. He takes one look at Raymond and says, "Boy got the wrong store," and walks out front in his long, white apron. Daddy and Deputy Davis are right behind him. "Raymond!" Isaiah shouts. "I work here! Coloreds shop *and* work here."

"I know that," says Raymond in a smug voice.

"This ain't right," says Isaiah. "Go pick on Henderson's but leave this place alone."

Deputy Davis grabs Raymond by the arm and says, "You again! You're under arrest, boy, for picketing."

A small crowd has gathered. Raymond almost smiles, as if he knew Deputy Davis was in Fairchild's and he knew he'd be arrested. He wrenches his arm away and says, "You tell that to the whites you let picket the Leflore every night!"

And that's when Deputy Davis clubs Raymond. Right over the head, he clubs him and beats him to the ground. I press my palms against the window and watch. I feel helpless. Sick to my stomach. I can't believe what I'm seeing and I can't look away. Raymond curls himself into a ball and covers his head with his arms and still, Deputy Davis hits him with his club.

"Hey!" yells Daddy. Civil Righters and Isaiah rush to help but Deputy Davis holds his club high, threatening them, and they stand back. Gillette, arriving on his bike, jumps off and runs the few feet to Raymond. He doesn't hesitate — he helps Raymond up with both hands. He's holding him, helping him up. Raymond's nose is bleeding. He's got a nasty cut over one eye. The blood trickles down the side of his face.

Deputy Davis grabs Raymond from Gillette and shoves him down the sidewalk to his police car. "*Show's over*," he snarls.

Gillette follows them to the police car. I run outside and grab Daddy's hand. He pulls me to him. A train approaches the crossing at Main and Johnson. Its sharp, insistent whistle slices the summer morning as Raymond is handcuffed and stuffed into the back of the police car. He stares at Gillette through the closed window, and Gillette stares right back, like a silent sentry, a witness to all of it. I take a step toward them but Daddy holds me back. "Enough," he says. His voice chokes in his throat.

The train rumbles through and Daddy repeats himself. "Enough."

63

Finally the end of the longest day at Fairchild's. Customers were unsure of us all day long, with the Civil Righters outside trying to register the coloreds to vote. The police were up and down Johnson Street all day with clubs and helmets and sirens and bullhorns. People were arrested, mostly agitators, and now I think some of the outside agitators are really inside agitators and live here, like Raymond.

Annabelle showed up to help count the money into the ledger and put it in the safe. Audrey stayed home with Boo. Vidella comes back to us tomorrow, and I hope I'm brave enough to ask her what it was like at the county work farm. I wonder if she'll look different.

Isaiah finishes mopping the floors and is the last worker to leave. Daddy thanks him for his help today, and I know he doesn't mean just stocking shelves.

"I'll see y'all on Monday," says Isaiah, firm and strong.

"Bye, Isaiah," I say, then, "Mr. Isaiah," and that is my thank-you.

Isaiah Nixon tips his hat. "Miss Sunny," he says.

Annabelle and I are easier with each other. Daddy has noticed it even though I can tell he doesn't know why, which means Annabelle is a keeper of one of my secrets now, and I don't know what to make of that. We're polite with each other, the way you are when you've shared too much with somebody and wish maybe you hadn't.

Annabelle put Meemaw's picture of *Miranda, age 18*, into a little frame and placed it on my nightstand. I liked it better when it was hidden, so I've put it back in the drawer. Annabelle said we can tell Meemaw about it privately, when she comes to Sunday dinner tomorrow, but I'm not going to do that.

I can let Annabelle live with us, and I can be nice to her, but I can't tell her what weighs heaviest on my heart. Maybe it's not explainable, but I feel it. It's there, this longing that I can't name, pressing down like a cold, hard stone.

"Ice cream tonight," Annabelle says as we step outside to a quiet seven o'clock, and lock the doors to Fairchild's. Gillette bikes off to catch the end of a ball game.

"Home after!" he yells. Ruth, who showed up after lunch and slept for hours in the cool of Daddy's office, trots after him.

"I'll pick you up in the truck!" Daddy calls. "If it rains, bike here and wait for me under the awning!"

We haven't had one minute to talk to each other all day, me and Gillette, but we've been extra good to each other. I can tell we've had our minds on the same thing, all day, without saying so. *Raymond.*

I wonder if Gillette is really going to the game. The sky is the color of a fresh, hot bruise, and thunder grumbles far off in the clouds.

It is so hot, we eat supper on TV trays in the air-conditioned living room while the thunder bellyaches and we watch the Smothers Brothers sing "Michael Row the Boat Ashore" on *Hootenanny.* "This is an old Negro spiritual!" says Dickie Smothers as he introduces the song.

I've sung that song in Bible School for years, and I know the Bible verse I memorized to go with it. *Daniel 12:1 — And at that time shall Michael stand up, the great prince which standeth for the children of thy people: and there shall be a time of trouble, such as never was since there was a nation even to that same time: and at that time thy people shall be delivered, every one that shall be found written in the book.*

I could have won that Bible verse contest. I should go write Polly and tell her so right now. Thunder rolls and crackles and the television blips with snowy lines. Boo jumps up and bangs on it so it rights itself.

The phone rings and Daddy answers it while Tommy Smothers interrupts the song, like he always does, and says, "I want to go back to the beginning and take it one more time from the top," and Dickie Smothers says, "We hum this verse, Tommy," and Tommy says, "I know, but I want everybody to join in this time," and Dick says okay and the audience starts to laugh because Tommy is Tommy so they know he's about to do something silly. Lightning makes the lamps dim and a fresh breeze tugs at the windows. Annabelle takes a sleeping Audrey upstairs and says, "I'll get the bedroom windows."

Daddy says, "That's good to know, Martin," so I know he's talking to Mary Margaret's father, who must be at the police station or city hall or the courthouse, where he seems to be all the time now. I want to know what's happened to Raymond, so I slip off the couch, but Daddy waves me away when he sees me coming and turns his back to me. "How is he?" he asks. "Is he out on bail?"

Tommy Smothers says in his dopey way, "Gang, in a world torn asunder by strife and by unhappiness, what sound in the world enters into our heart and brings love and brotherhood but the sound of people's voices joining together in singing? So let's lift the rafters, people, let's fill this room with the most joyous sound known to man: people. People singing . . ."

Everyone in the audience laughs and Tommy keeps talking in his silly way, and yet it makes sense, and the audience keeps laughing, and Daddy keeps talking to Mr. Carr on the phone. "Are they all out, then?" he asks. I creep closer to the hall and the phone table. Lightning. Thunder. "How did you manage it?"

"For in the ether of the air," Tommy continues, "with the great sky of . . . of . . . of the faraway land, fill this sky, the musical sky, with voices intertwining themselves in a giant choral arrangement, like colors in your mind, and lines going up and down, as the voices of people join together."

Boo laughs just as the downdraft sluices through our windows, blowing the curtains and riffling the pages of the *TV Guide* on the coffee table. Lightning slices the sky like a long, white scar, and thunder cracks it open. The rain comes as a deafening downpour. Three sides of our house are bordered by porches, so we don't have to close those windows. Boo stands in front of the television and turns up the sound.

Daddy says, "I see. Thanks for letting me know."

"So, friends," says Tommy Smothers, "let's fill this room with love. Let's fill this room with music and song, for people driving by, maybe outside, they'll be in their car, and we'll be in here singing, and they'll be driving by, and as they drive by they'll probably say . . . what the heck is going *on* in there?"

Boo hoots, turns off the television, and walks to the back of the house to close the dining room windows while singing, "Jordan's river is deep and wide, hallelujah. Got a home on the other side, hallelujah."

Boom! I go to the kitchen and close those windows as we get ourselves a roaring summer storm, and about time. If we're lucky, it will rain for hours and Uncle Vivian's parched cotton will get a nice, long drink. Boo starts to crumble corn bread into buttermilk for her dessert. I go see if there's any more to hear about Raymond.

Daddy hangs up the phone. He rests his forehead on the wall over the telephone table. His hands close over the top of the ladder-back chair, and his shoulders slump forward.

"Daddy?" I step close to him but don't know whether or not to touch him. "Daddy?"

He takes a deep breath and turns to me. Two fat tears. They make my heart lurch. "What is it?"

He smiles. "I'm just tired, Sunny," he says in a tender voice. "I'm glad it's over."

"What's over?"

Boo comes out of the kitchen with her tall glass of buttermilk corn bread in one hand, a teaspoon in the other.

"The kids go home tomorrow." Daddy gives Boo a smile of relief. "Mr. Carr says they didn't even want to fool with them at the courthouse, so they let 'em all go. They know they're leaving in the morning and they just want them out of town."

"Thank the Lord," says Boo. She puts her dessert on the phone table. "I'm going to go tell Annabelle."

"Tell her I'm heading out to get Gillette," he says in a weary voice. He rubs his hands over his face, back and forth, and breaths out a huge sigh.

"I'll do it!" Boo calls as she marches to the stairs and twinkles up.

But I need to know more. I am anxious for news.

"How's Raymond?" I ask.

Daddy peeks out from between his fingers. "Who is Raymond?"

Suddenly I'm caught. Thunder booms like Jesus bowling in heaven. Rain pours like God opened all the faucets. Daddy stares at me with his tired face. I'm tired, too. I'm tired of keeping secrets.

"I know that colored boy who picketed the store." I feel my face flush.

Daddy raises an eybrow. "You do?" That's all. He keeps his hands at his face.

I take a breath. "His name is Raymond Bullis. He was in the pool the night me and Gillette trespassed. We didn't know he was there, and he ran off. He's the same boy who caught the fly ball at Gillette's ball game. And he's the same boy who was at the Leflore the night I got caught there. I know him."

Daddy's fingers cover his eyes again. I feel the weight on my heart of that cold, hard stone, but still I ask.

"Is he all right?" I want to ask more. *Do you still love me?*

Daddy removes his hands from his face and stares at me like he's seeing me for the first time.

"He's all right," he tells me. "He got banged up — you saw that." His voice chokes. "But he's all right."

He's all right. "Thank you," I say in my quietest voice.

A tiny eternity passes between us as we stand together in the hallway of our house, by the phone table, wondering what to say to each other.

"I'm glad you know," Daddy says finally. "It helps to know, doesn't it?"

"Yes," I tell him. "It does."

"Here's something else for you to know, then," says Daddy. He pulls the chair out from under the phone table and sits at it, so that we're the same height and can look at each other, eye-to-eye. "You're my girl. You will always be my girl."

My throat fills with tears. "You've got Annabelle now. And Audrey. And another baby, too."

Daddy takes my hands in his. "You will *always* be my girl."

Then he hugs me to him and I hug him back. "Daddy."

Another crack of thunder brings Daddy to his feet.

"Now," he says. "Want to go with me to get your brother?"

We get drenched running from the house to the car.

We ride into the storm of our lives.

64

We gon' to Beulah's to celebrate.

Everybody out of jail, so quick, after picketing and registering folks in downtown Greenwood. Everybody sayin' good-bye to friends. So many of 'em goes home tomorrow, or to the Democrat Convention in Atlantic City, New Jersey. Long trip. I want to go, but "You're too young yet, Ray," say SNCC Bob. "Your time is coming, believe me, and it won't be long. Patience, my man. We need you. You've done well. So proud of you."

Some SNCCs will stay in Greenwood, in Mississippi, the ones that said they would. Most will go back to college and they lives somewheres else.

They showed us what we can do, how we can do it. They did it, too, right next to us.

We gon' keep on fightin'.

Keep on walkin', keep on talkin', marchin' up to Freedom Land.

Ain't gonna let nobody turn us 'round!

I beaten and bruised, but I here.

And I got a job to do. Keep on being arrested until they let anybody watch a movie at the Leflore. Keep on gettin' arrested until Chief Lary sick of me. Keep gettin' arrested until no more arrestin' to do.

But tonight we got us a party. We gon' all go to Beulah's and say good-bye together. The FreedomMakers comin', SNCCs comin', COREs and COFOs, everybody comin', all our friends. Even Dorie here, feelin' good, still carryin' that baby. Proud a herself. "I'm gon' tell him what his mama went through with him in her belly!"

Ma'am say, "You take it easy over at Beulah's, Raymond." Ree said, "I wanna go!" but I tell her no, she too young. Jo Ellen, she say she'll tell Ree bye in the morning. Jo Ellen say, "You coming, Ray?" and she smile at me, crooked smile. For the first time, I look her full in the face and smile back. "Yeah, I'm comin'."

But I tired, that's what I know when I sit in that car with all those people. At Beulah's, bodies pile out, but not me. It rain to beat the band and it feel good to be alone a minute.

"Come on, Raymond!" say Twill, Jimmy, Simon, Jo Ellen, two Bobs.

"You one of our heroes today!"

"I gon' wait a minute," I say, "till this rain let up."

Don't feel like running across no street.

Head hurt. Back hurt. Face hurt. Sore. Feel great.

So I scoot over to the wheel of the SNCC car. Put my hands at ten o'clock and two o'clock, like Simon taught me. I be drivin' soon. Already drive the truck over the pasture at the Browning Farm, which gonna be Simon's farm one day.

Look out the windshield, can't see a thing, just sheets and sheets of rain.

Thump-a-thump-a-thump-a on the roof, like drums.

Streets filling up with rain. Tires swimming in water.

Rest my head on the steering wheel to wait.

Don't want to think.

Tired.

So tired.

65

Gillette is standing under the awning in front of Fairchild's. He tosses his bike into the truck bed and jumps in the cab with us. We are all three wet and clammy and close, sitting across the long bench seat. I am in the middle.

"Ruth is missing!" Gillette shouts over the din of the rain pounding on the truck roof. "The storm scared her and she ran off!"

"Which way?" shouts Daddy.

"That way!" Gillette points down Main Street, and into Baptist Town. Daddy pulls the car away from the curb and slowly starts driving in that direction. Lightning spotlights the street ahead of us as well as a red pickup truck with a white stripe on the side, which passes us and sprays water like a hose across the windshield.

"Crack your window," says Daddy as he rolls his down and, slows to a crawl. "I can't see."

Gillette obliges. "She could be anywhere," he says, anxious. He hands me a towel from Daddy's tackle box. I wipe the windsheld as best I can.

"The streets are flooding," says Daddy. "I don't think there are gutters in this part of town, but at least we're on pavement. See anything?"

Gillette calls out the open window "Ruth!" but his voice is lost in the downpour. We're getting soaked with the windows down, but the rain begins to let up. "Ruth!"

"Won't she come home on her own, Gillette?" I mean it as a comfort. "She gets to the store by herself all the time."

But Gillette won't be comforted. "She's old! She could drown out here!"

I doubt it. "She'll find a porch to get on, Gillette."

"Hush, Sunny," Daddy is anxious, too. "We're going to give it a few minutes."

I sit on my hands so I'll keep my mouth shut. We cruise down Main as the rain lessens and I listen to the insistent thwacking of the wipers on the windshield, and the sucking and sloshing sound of the truck tires plowing through the river of rain on the street. At least we're not on one of the dirt roads. We'd get stuck in the mud for sure.

Daddy says, "I don't know, Gillette," and Gillette says, "She's probably gone to the colored ball fields."

Daddy, leaning over to peer through the rain, says, "Why would she go there?"

"Because I've been going there," Gillette tells him.

Daddy risks a quick look at Gillette and then puts his eyes back on the road. "I don't know where that is."

"Turn here," Gillette says.

We turn onto a street where the water is so high it's climbing the porch steps. "Definitely no storm drains over here," says Daddy. "We're going to have to turn around."

"You can get to it on Henry," Gillette tells him.

Daddy backs down Gibbs and out to Main Street. The red pickup truck passes us again. We all take note and I think Gillette searches the truck bed with his eyes to see if an old red dog is in it. Empty.

Daddy tries Henry, a street on higher ground and nearer the railroad tracks, but still a street full of water. The rain begins to taper off as the wipers *slap-slap-slap* and Daddy rolls his window down farther to get more air in the car. I wipe at the windshield again and keep my mouth shut. A long lightning bolt gives the houses along the street a ghostly glow.

"I don't think we're going to find her this way, Gillette," says Daddy. Gillette has no answer. We crawl past shotgun houses with tired porches and no lights on in the almost-dark, until, on our left, there is a house with lights lit everywhere, inside and out, like Christmas, with happy people on the porch, singing, white people, students — they are agitators, I can tell. I strain to pick them out, to see if one of them is Jo Ellen, and there she is, on the porch in a blue shirtwaist dress, laughing with a colored girl who's also wearing a shirtwaist dress.

The cold, hard stone on my heart begins to lift when I see her, and I want to run to her, to tell her I still love her, when a colored woman in an apron comes onto the porch and signals them in, and I see an unlighted sign that says, BEULAH'S CAFÉ, and I suppose this house is Beulah's house and she feeds the Civil Righters.

Everybody streams into Beulah's yelling, "Ray! Come in and eat!" and gesturing to a car parked across from Beulah's. But no one leaves the car. *Raymond!* I elbow Gillette who, I know, has noticed, but he's beside himself scanning for Ruth at the same time.

"Well," says Daddy, breaking to a stop and peering out the window. "Looks like we found something else entirely." Then all three of us notice the truck waiting at the other end of Henry Street. Its lights are trained on us, and another streak of lightning shows us it's the same red truck that passed us twice.

I keep my mouth shut but my stomach begins to churn.

Daddy grips the steering wheel so tightly his knuckles are white. He pulls to the right, to the edge of the street, and slows to a stop behind the car with Raymond in it, so the other truck can pass us down this narrow street. It's still raining, but the thunder sounds like it's closed up in a closet, farther and farther away. The red truck comes slowly down Henry Street, toward us.

And then I'm in a horror movie of my own. I breathe in slow motion as the window of the truck that approaches us slides down and a rifle appears, its barrel sticking out like a monster's ugly tongue, as it shoots once — *pop!* — into the car where Raymond is sitting. There is no shattering of glass, just that *pop!* as the truck speeds off in a grotesque blur, passing us like a fanged creature in the falling dark, racing away like a coward.

Daddy opens his door and yells, "Stay here!" and starts running for Beulah's. Gillette is already out of the truck and I am right behind him. Ruth runs from between two shotgun houses and into the road in front of us and Gillette swerves to grab her. I race for the car with Raymond in it.

The invaders spill out of the house behind Daddy. One of them reaches the car just as I do and jerks open the front driver's seat door. The window has one perfect hole in it and the glass around it cracks like a giant, radiant spiderweb. Raymond falls out of the car and into the street, into the river of rain running beneath him. He turns the water red.

66

"Give me your shirt!" yells SNCC Bob — white Bob — as he peels off his undershirt and begins to wrap it around Raymond's head. Another SNCC hands him his shirt and Bob uses that one, too. "Tie it tight!" The other SNCC yells. "Put pressure on it!"

"Get in the backseat!" yells SNCC Bob as Jo Ellen — Jo Ellen — opens the back door, and I don't even think about it, I just climb in, right after Jo Ellen. My heart hammers against my ribs, but I won't leave her, and — a new thought — I won't leave Raymond. In seconds, he is lifted into the backseat of the car by many hands, including hands from Jo Ellen's side of the car who have opened the other back door to receive Raymond. Jo Ellen helps, I help, and soon Raymond is lying across us, his head wrapped in a shirt bandage, already red and leaking. Raymond is bleeding all over us.

"I'll call the office!" yells one of the students.

"Don't use the phone!" yells Bob. "We'll call them from the radio in the car!"

"Call the police!" yells the other SNCC. "Call them now!"

"Call the hospital!" yells someone else. "Call the colored doctor!"

"We're right behind you!" yells another.

SNCC Bob leaps into the front seat with the other SNCC, who I now recognize as Sam Block at the Freedom House. He jumps into the passenger seat. Both of them are shirtless because their shirts are Raymond's bandages. Bob screams the car away toward the hospital. I don't know if Gillette caught

Ruth or came back to the car. I don't know if Daddy saw me get into the car. I don't know, I don't know. All I know is that Raymond is alive and his eyes are open. His head is in Jo Ellen's lap, and he is bleeding all over us. I can't take my eyes off him. "Are you holding it tight, keeping pressure on the wound?" yells Bob.

"Yes!" shouts Jo Ellen.

We don't say a thing, me and Jo Ellen. It's as if she expected me to be here, in this moment, and here I am. We take a corner too fast and Jo Ellen says, "Easy, Bob."

"Is he breathing?" asks Bob.

"Yes," says Jo Ellen.

"We're getting help, Ray!" Bob yells from the front seat. "Hold on, buddy!"

The windows are down and I'm grateful for the wind and rain pelting our faces.

Me and Jo Ellen stare at Raymond and he stares at us. I feel it bubble up in me before I can stop it, and I say, "You're hurt."

Raymond blinks.

"You're shot," says Jo Ellen.

Another blink.

"We're taking you to the hospital," she says. "It will be all right. Hold on. Hold my hand." Raymond doesn't move. Jo Ellen says as if she's just realized it, "I don't have a hand to give him."

So I give him mine, like it's the most natural thing in the world. I grab it and he grabs back. His grip says, *I'm scared. Don't let me go*, so I don't.

I look out the window to see where we are and find the old Greenwood cemetery on our right, so I know we're close to the hospital — we're almost there. *Hurry, hurry!* The two SNCCs in the front seat talk on their car radio while the car races wildly down the street, and Raymond bobbles on our laps, his bandages completely red, and my lap, Jo Ellen's lap — the whole seat — sticky with his blood. I should feel like vomiting, but I can't feel a thing.

"Call Justice on the WATS line so the Greenwood operators can't listen in," says Sam Block to somebody on the other end of the line. "Make sure you speak to Doar. We have his home number. We want the FBI out here. And call the networks. Now. We need cameras and reporters."

Raymond blinks again, squeezes my hand so hard, and stares at me so steadily, like he wants to ask a question, until I think I must answer him.

I lean my head close to his so it seems more private, and I whisper, "It was me, in the pool."

He blinks and keeps his eyes on my face like he's memorizing it.

"I didn't know you then," I say.

The nighttime lights of the Leflore County Hospital beam toward us, as if they're saying, *This way . . . this way . . . that's right, this way.*

We pull up to the emergency room entrance. Six policemen are there, in the glaring light under the overhang, standing with their arms crossed, daring us to go through the sliding doors. Bob and Sam are out of the car lickety-split and arguing with them. Chief Lary isn't with them and neither is Deputy Davis.

"This is the white entrance," says one of them. *They knew we were coming.*

"But he's shot!" sputters Bob. "He needs help!"

"Colored entrance is on the other side," says another policeman. He puts a hand on his billy club.

Without another word, Bob and Sam race back to the car and we drive with the tires shrieking around to the other side of the hospital. I hold on to Raymond as best I can, and Jo

Ellen keeps him from falling off the backseat. His grip starts to fade and I hold on to him harder.

There is one large light fixture here at the colored entrance, a dim yellow porch light, with moths dancing around it. The same six policemen walk out of the colored entrance and stand with their arms crossed. They must have walked across the lobby, from one side to the other, just like that.

Bob races for the door. "We need a stretcher!" he says in a desperate voice.

A policeman holds out his billy club and keeps Bob from going inside. "You can't go in without a shirt."

"My shirt's on his head!" shouts Bob. "He's been shot in the head!"

"Tell someone to bring out a stretcher," pleads Sam.

"Can't do that," says another officer, calm as you please.

Jo Ellen gives me an order. "Hold his head here! Keep pressure on it!" She is out of the car in a flash. She marches through the little crowd of policemen in her bloody blue dress, and into the hospital. I have to let go of Raymond's hand to hold on to his head. I don't know what to do but sit there with Raymond's head in my lap, my hands trying to hold his brains in. "We're here," I tell him. "Everything's going to be okay."

And that's when he closes his eyes and leaves us.

67

My mind not mine no more. It drifts. To that girl in the pool, holding my head. "It was me." To that boy with the old, red dog — he been biking over to our ball field, watchin' us play. Never say a word, just ride by so slow, and stop sometimes, at the far corner, his glove hanging off the handle bars, like he want to ask to play, then push off.

To Ma'am and Pap, eatin' they cold supper at home, one lightbulb over the table, swaying over the room, all the windows open, the bugs making such a racket, I can't hear what Ma'am and Pap say, but they happy. They smilin' at each other. They registered for the MFDP. They gon' elect the first black sheriff in Greenwood and the first black president of the United States one day, I know it.

I float on my back in that city pool, smiling wide in that cool, clear water, and I hear Ree jump in, and Twill, and Simon, and Jimmy, and then comes Jo Ellen and SNCC friends, black and white, and Deputy Davis family and Mr. Jamie Fairchild at the store, and Mr. Martini at the movies, and there's that girl again. She say, "You're hurt," and I reach up to touch my head but I touch her hand instead, and she hold it, hold it tight, she say, "It will be all right," and I believe it. I feel so good, floating.

I float to Crosley Field in Ohio, where the Giants play the Reds, and I see my man Willie Mays catch a pop to center field to put the batter out. "You gon' be in the Hall of Fame, Willie," I whispers to him. "You not too old." Willie look right at me and say, "Ray, we Southern boys got to stick together. I came up from nuthin', too. You keep playin' ball, you hear? It's not your time yet."

Freddie and Chuff, they next, they wearin' uniforms so crisp, so smart. "We signed up, Ray, we gon' to Vietnam. No future in this town, in Greenwood, so we gon' go see the world." Twill with them now, he say, "I'm right behind you boys, yes sirree," and I say, "Wait . . ." but they gone already, and that girl, she hold my hand and say, "Here. Here's someone you know. . . ."

Then she come to me, just like she real, Adele. She stretch out her long, black arm, her long fingers on her fine, long hand. "Here I am, Ray, my beautiful brother. Here I am."

Shimmery and soft and smiling, Adele. She say, "You know your name, Raymond, what it means? Wise protector. Like a king. That's you, Ray. You're a king."

"That's what they teach Ree at the Freedom School," I tell Adele. "She come home saying, 'We was all kings and queens in Africa!'"

Adele smile and start to hum so soft, in that voice so fine. "Leaning on the Everlasting Arms."

"I can go now," I tell her. "I can float to heaven with you, Adele. Let me come with you. 'Michael row the boat ashore, hallelujah,' I am come. Marchin' up to Freedom Land."

68

Two carloads of SNCCs are right behind us.

"We need someone to find a pay phone and stay on the phone with the office, let them hear everything that's happening so they can be on the WATS line relaying it," says Bob. "The rest of you go back to the office so you don't get arrested for parading without a permit or disturbing the peace or some other trumped-up charge."

"Where's the doctor?" asks one person.

"On the way," says another.

Dr. Norwood lives right next door. He would be here by now, if they called him, but he doesn't come. I almost mention his name, to help my new friends, but I don't know what to do or if that's the right thing. No one so far has even noticed me. They haven't registered I'm not one of them yet. They don't have time to think about it.

Jo Ellen pushes a stretcher outside and hands help put Raymond on it. He's breathing, but he's not conscious. His white high-top sneakers are wet and muddy. Jo Ellen disappears into the colored emergency room with Raymond. I strut through the colored entrance right behind her. Somebody else comes inside to use the phone and call again for the colored doctor to come to the hospital. "There's just one," says a SNCC named Sally, "but we've got a SNCC doctor out at Browning on call this week — somebody go out and get him."

None of the white doctors or nurses will tend to Raymond. A white doctor walks through the lobby in his white coat and silver stethoscope and acts like he doesn't see us. I can tell he sees the policemen, though. The folks behind the front counter stay busy with papers. A nurse comes to the counter to pick up a folder and doesn't say a word. They are all white. We must be invisible. Or maybe they're afraid of the police and the men who are gathering with them, just like they gathered at the Leflore.

Someone has brought shirts for Bob and Sam. They come inside and talk to each person in the room. "Can you help?" Their voices are desperate. "He'll die without help!"

I run to the doctor walking briskly away from the lobby and plead with him. "I am covered in his blood and nothing has happened to me!" The doctor won't listen to me.

"Whose girl are you?" asks one of the policemen.

"I'm my own girl," I say as I stalk right past them the way I saw Jo Ellen do. They don't stop me.

A SNCC named Linda is on the phone with the Freedom House. Raymond is still on the stretcher in the emergency room. "Here's the colored doctor," says Jo Ellen just as he arrives. Bob and Sam and others cluster around him.

"You'll need to get him out of Greenwood," the colored doctor says in a low voice. "They'll kill him, sure as I'm standing here. Somebody will come in here and finish the job. But let's get him stable first and see what's happening."

Bob and Sam help the doctor and a colored nurse wheel Raymond down a long hallway. Jo Ellen takes my hand and pulls me to some old wooden chairs against a wall. There is a lone lamp in the room for light, and it is full dark outside. The policemen go outside where they talk in twos and threes, waiting for whatever comes next. Other men arrive. Some carry rifles, but they stay outside. I am so numb I can't even be afraid anymore. I wonder if Mrs Campbell's Teletype machine is typing away right now with this story. But it probably isn't, because she's not here. Nobody is here to report this story.

"We're a mess," says Jo Ellen. Her voice is shaky. "Is there a bathroom we can use?"

I go looking. "Whites Only," I report back.

"I don't want to use that one," says Jo Ellen. "I can wait."

"I'll wait, too, then," I say.

"They're going to take him to Jackson," Linda tells us. "We've got money for an ambulance. His family is on the way. We've sent a SNCC car to pick them up. They're very upset. Of course." She goes back to the phones.

"Now what?" I say. My legs are shaking.

"Now we wait," says Jo Ellen.

"I should call my house," I say. "They don't know where I am."

"Where do you live?" asks Jo Ellen.

"I live right up the road," I tell her. "This is River Road — you can smell the Yazoo when you're outside. I live up toward town."

"How do you manage to show up so unexpectedly?" Jo Ellen smiles a tired smile.

"Luck, I guess," is all I can think to say. "I don't plan it that way."

"Does your mother know you're here?"

"I don't have a mother," I tell her. My face prickles up with feelings, and I don't want to cry so I say, "Do you? Of course you do, you said so."

"Oh, yes," says Jo Ellen. "I have a mother. I'd like to call her right now, as a matter of fact."

"Why don't you?" I ask.

"She would worry about me. I don't want her to worry. And my friends will take care of me." Jo Ellen is suddenly teary. "But they aren't my mother."

"You must be very close to her," I offer.

"We fight a lot," Jo Ellen says with a laugh. "She didn't want me to come here. My dad had to talk her into giving her permission, because I'm not twenty-one yet."

"How old are you?"

"I'm twenty."

"What's your sister's name? The one who likes the Beatles?"

"Her name is Frances, but we call her Franny. I miss her."

"Do you miss your mother?"

"Oh, yes," says Jo Ellen. "You know what they say, absence makes the heart grow fonder. I go home tomorrow, and I'm sure we'll fight again. But you know, I've been thinking about it a lot lately. It must be hard to be a mother. If I had a daughter who was so different from me, I might have a hard time understanding her as well. What's important is what you do. That's what I think. If you show up, if you try, if you love, even badly sometimes . . . well, that's what counts. And my mother loves me — I know she does."

Now I am teary, too. "My mother didn't love me." And as I say it, I realize it's the truth. What a truth to have to live with. It makes me shake.

Jo Ellen's face caves in. "I'm so sorry, Sunny," she whispers.

"I don't know why." I sniff and wish I had something to wipe my nose with. My hands are caked with blood.

"She didn't know you," Jo Ellen says simply and quietly. "That's all. She didn't know you."

"I'm a big mouth," I say.

"How lucky for the world," Jo Ellen replies. "We wouldn't be here in Mississippi if it weren't for the big mouths."

"I'm not sure that's such a good thing," I tell her. "You've ruined my life this summer."

"Are you sure about that?"

"Yes!" I say. "Maybe. I don't understand it. I'm not sure about anything right now except I know my mother didn't love me."

I'm trying to tell her she's the mother I never had, but I don't know how.

Jo Ellen pulls her chair around to face me. She touches my arm. "Anyone who knows you has to love you. You are a wonderful girl. There must be so many people in your life who love you."

"I have a stepmother," I say as tears choke my throat. "But she's not you."

It takes her a moment to understand what I'm trying to tell her. I'm not sure I can stand to be with her much longer.

Then she does something that breaks my heart. She takes off her locket, and in a move that's as graceful as any mother's could be, she laces it around my neck. "I want you to have this," she says. "To remember me by."

Then I do cry.

"Will you remember me?" I ask her.

"Oh, yes," she says. "You are the girl with so much love to give, who waited for her mother to appear, the summer she turned thirteen."

"Yes," I tell her. "Yes, I did."

And at that moment, the doors whisk open on the opposite side of the hospital, at the white emergency room entrance, and Annabelle presses in, looking for me. She knew I was here. She knew to come get me. She came.

"And here she is," says Jo Ellen. "Someone who loves you very much. I can tell."

Annabelle is soaked to the skin. Her face wears the torment of not knowing. She is suffocating in worry, drenched in dread, but there is a steady, unwavering look in her eyes. She will claim me. That is what her eyes say. She *will* claim me for her own, because she loves me.

I stand to meet her. She takes one look at me waiting for her, hanging by a thread in the colored emergency room wearing the blood of a boy from Baptist Town and carrying inside me the truth about *Miranda, age 18*. I look at her like she's finally come for me, my mother.

I have finally allowed her to come.

Annabelle flies across the waiting room to catch me up in her arms and lift that cold, heavy stone right off my heart.

WE SHALL NOT, WE SHALL NOT BE MOVED

From "We Shall Not Be Moved," traditional

Dr. Martin Luther King, Jr., encourages Greenwood citizens to register for the Mississippi Freedom Democratic Party.

New voters registering for the MFDP.

LIKE A TREE THAT'S PLANTED BY THE WATER, WE SHALL NOT BE MOVED!

I SUPPORT FREEDOM DEMOCRATS

Ella Baker, founder of SNCC, speaks to the Mississippi Freedom Party Delegation at the Democratic National Convention in Atlantic City, New Jersey, August 1964.

"If the Freedom party is not seated now, I question America. Is this America, the land of the free and the home of the brave, where we have to sleep with our telephones off the hooks because our lives be threatened daily, because we want to live as decent human beings, in America?"

MFDP spokesperson and delegate Fannie Lou Hamer at the Democratic National Convention in Atlantic City, August 1964

"The President will not allow that illiterate woman to speak from the floor of the convention."

Vice President Hubert Humphrey

The Mississippi Freedom Democratic Party was offered two at-large seats at the Democratic National Convention but was denied representation or a vote. The MFDP was not seated in Atlantic City but did succeed in showing America that, if given the opportunity to register, black Americans would turn out in droves to VOTE and become first-class citizens. Its challenge to the all-white Democratic Party helped pass the Voting Rights Act of 1965.

No voting qualification or prerequisite to voting, or standard, practice, or procedure shall be imposed or applied by any State or political subdivision to deny or abridge the right of any citizen of the United States to vote on account of race or color.

Section 2 of the Voting Rights Act of 1965

BLACK AND
WHITE TOGETHER,
WE SHALL NOT
BE MOVED!

WE'RE FIGHTING FOR OUR FREEDOM, WE SHALL NOT BE MOVED!

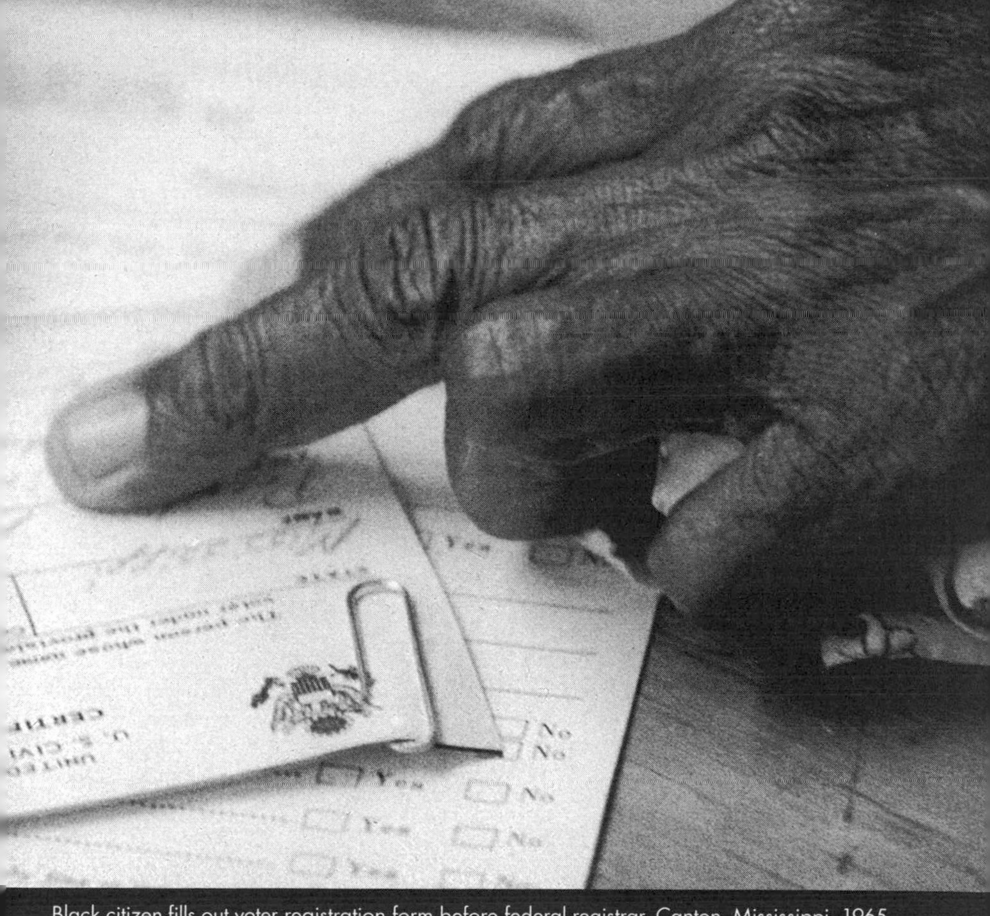

Black citizen fills out voter registration form before federal registrar, Canton, Mississippi, 1965.

The button says "I am registered, are you?" Sumter, South Carolina, 1965.

LIKE A TREE THAT'S PLANTED BY THE WATER, WE SHALL NOT BE MOVED!

69

Saturday, September 26, 1964

Gillette and I pedal to Colored Town as fast as our legs will take us.

"708 Avenue N," I tell him.

"I know where it is," he says. "This way."

We travel River Road behind the courthouse, past the jail, and past my magnolias. We need a new George, but now that school has started again, we're busy trying to figure out junior high and seventh grade. George has had to wait.

"Don't turn here," says Gillette as we cross over Fulton Street, then Howard Street, and then Main Street and all the way up to Lamar with the Yazoo on our left all the way. We are on the east side of town now, where I hardly ever go.

We swing right onto Lamar and fly past an old neighborhood of brick houses just waking up to this September Saturday, neighborhoods where newspapers wait on front stoops and cats stretch in the warming sun and tricycles have been left on the driveway to be accidentally run over.

The train whistle blows. "We're gonna get stopped at the tracks!" I shout.

"Sounds like a short one!" Gillette calls back. "Not a long freight. Do you want me to slow down?"

"Hey. I didn't get top awards on the President's Council for Physical Fitness for nothing! Let's go!"

"You did not!"

I laugh. "I know! I have no talent for sit-ups and I couldn't do a pull-up if my life depended on it."

"Bobby Carpenter can do ten pull-ups in a row," says Gillette.

"He's a Neanderthal," I reply.

We reach the Crystal Grill and the railroad tracks at Johnson Street. The train is still crossing. I catch my breath.

"I told them we'd be back before lunch," Gillette says. "We have to be back in time."

"I know," I tell him. "Thanks for coming with me."

The caboose passes us and we cross the tracks. The cotton compress sits like a gray metal giant up against the tracks, winking at us with a thousand shiny eyes in the early-morning sun. We're in high cotton now and the pickers are in the fields from sunup to sundown every day. Wagons full of cotton from the gin keep the compress going all day and into the night, until Old Joe Black, who calls the compress, sings, "Sun is almost down, sun is almost down, Captain." The iron teeth will clamp the bales and press them down with such force, the steam will whistle up through the tin roof — I've seen it.

When the mornings are frosty and the compress is singing, the air around it is thick with steam. Long ago, cotton went down the Yazoo to the Mississippi to the port of New Orleans. Now it goes on the freight trains.

We steam past the compress and past Lusco's, where we had my twelfth birthday dinner a year ago, and on into another part of Colored Town I don't know.

Summer is good and over. Trucks load up with colored men and women and children in the foggy mornings. Colored kids won't go to school until the first of October, when the last bolls are picked. Uncle Vivian has started coming to our house for Sunday dinner, and so has Meemaw. Uncle Vivian is asking me about "those Bee-atles" again, so I think we're all right now. I tried to tell him what *A Hard Day's Night* was all about, but it was too confusing and he just shook his head.

It's almost like nothing ever happened here, except the restaurants are all private clubs now, and the pool is still closed, and the Leflore is closed now, too, and you still can't sit down at the library or the soda fountain. It's different. Nobody knows what to say, and there's an election in November, and I read on Polly's mother's Teletype that the FBI will be here then, to make sure all the Negroes who want to vote can vote, and peacefully.

We brake in front of the Freedom House, running our feet on the street to stop our bikes completely. "Go on," says Gillette.

"I'm going," I tell him, but I don't. We straddle our bikes in front of the Freedom House and soon a SNCC comes to the door, his hands shielding his eyes from the morning sun. I recognize him. It's Sam Block.

"Hey! Are you Sunny?" he asks. I nod. "I thought I recognized you. You were at the hospital that night, weren't you? You were here before, too, at the office, yes?" I nod. "Jo Ellen thought you might come by. I've got something for you. Wait right here."

Gillette stares at me and I shrug. He knows all my secrets now. Everyone does. I gave my picture of *Miranda, age 18*, back to Meemaw, and she didn't make me feel bad for taking it. She put it on the stereo cabinet at her house, so now I see it whenever I go visit her and Laura Mae, and that's enough. I took *Kon-Tiki* back on the first day of school. I didn't tell on myself, I just slipped it back on the shelf, where it belongs. I can check it out any time I want. I still have three postcards from Mary Margaret's trip to New York City, but I'm ready to give two of those back, too.

Sam Block comes back outside and hands me a book. "For you," he says, "from all of us. Jo Ellen picked it out." I take it and know right away what it is. *Captains Courageous.* "Thanks for your help," says Sam.

I'm all choked up. "Thanks" is all I manage. Then Gillette tweaks me with his elbow and I remember. I reach into my bike basket and pull out my Beatles wig. "Could you send this to Jo Ellen for me? I think her sister, Franny, would like it."

Sam Block smiles. "Sure," he says. "I'd be happy to."

"And just a minute," I say, suddenly sure. I lift Jo Ellen's locket from around my neck and wrap it gently inside the Beatles wig. "Tell her I really needed this when she gave it to me, but now I want her to have it back. I know it was special to her."

"Sure," says Sam. He looks at us as if he's not sure what else to say. There is an awkward moment, and then Gillette adjusts his baseball cap and says, "How is Ray?"

Sam says, "He's coming along. You'll find him at the ball field, if you want him. They were organizing a pickup game this morning."

Gillette nods and makes like he's going to push off, so I do, too. I put my new book in my bike basket. "See you around," I say, because I don't know what else to say.

"We'll be here," says Sam. The place is so quiet, compared to all the noise and people and busy-ness of the summer. I don't see any cars circling, either. It's downright peaceful. The birds are making a racket, and the morning cicadas are already busy at work.

I follow Gillette to the colored ball field. "This is how you do it," he says. He stops his bike at the corner near an enormous, scraggly bunch of bushes full of berries, and I stop next to him. We can see the action without being seen. I don't consider that behind every shanty house window, somebody is probably looking out at us, wondering what we're doing, two white kids in Baptist Town.

A whole passel of boys is on the field, in no particular order, just standing around catching pop flies. Raymond is the batter. He's standing at home plate, in his dirty high-top sneakers, pointing to where he's going to hit the next ball, then he tosses it in the air above him and hits it to that exact place, one ball after another. *Craaaack!*

"Unbelievable," says Gillette.

"I know," I say. "I didn't think for a minute he was going to live." I wonder if his brains are still the same, and I wonder what his scars look like.

"No, his hitting," says Gillette. "He's not running, but I've watched him run the bases. He's so fast — or he was. And you've seen him catch. He's real good. He's like Mays. . . . It would be a lot of fun to play with him."

A car cruises past us, slow, with a white man in it, and that's our signal to go. "Come on," says Gillette. "It's getting late."

We turn our bikes around and start for home. Gillette takes the corner ahead of me, while I take one last look back. Raymond Bullis is standing still, outside the batter's box, holding his bat with two hands and looking right at me. My heart does a flutter in my chest as I turn my attention back to the road and where I'm going, but I know he saw me. *And I saw you, boy in the high-top sneakers. I saw you.*

At home, the picnic table is set for a party. Balloons are fixed to the front porch. The barbecue grill is hot and my friends will be over to see me soon and celebrate. Audrey skips down the front steps and hurls herself at me before I'm off my bike. "You are older today, Sunny! You are a teenager!" she says, and I laugh. I lean my bike against the porch and pick up Audrey and squeeze her. "Yes, I am! And *you* are in kindergarten!"

Boo calls from the upstairs window on the third floor. "Yoo-hoooo! Wait for me! Sunny, I just got off the phone with your meemaw. You've got a letter from Parnell that she picked up at the post office for you — she's bringing it over. Don't start without me!"

A very pregnant Annabelle comes out the front door with a birthday cake, and Daddy is right behind her, holding a platter of hot dogs and hamburgers for the grill.

Gillette says, "I didn't get you anything for your birthday."

"Oh, yes, you did," I tell him. The Westminster chimes start their noon chiming, grand and eloquent and deep, and I know what I want for my birthday. I want these people. For better or for worse. Forever and ever. Amen.

I'm connected to everything. That's what the Westminster chimes tell me in their ringing. Each of us is small, all by ourselves, but we are *big*, when we stick together. I am connected to everyone, even that boy in Baptist Town. And I do have talents. I am steady. I am brave. Annabelle told me so.

When Polly heard all my secrets, she said, "You didn't need to solve the mysteries, Sunny. You *are* the mystery!"

And I realize, she's right. I am my greatest mystery, my finest discovery. Is there anything more amazing than that?

I may not have a talking parrot or a flying fish or a balsa-wood raft in the Pacific, but I have had other adventures, right here, in this town, in this summer, and I think I'm done for a while with adventure.

Daddy always says, "My everyday life is adventure enough for me."

Maybe. I haven't given up on packing my suitcase some day and taking off to see the world.

But I won't run away. I'll tell them I'm going. I'll send them postcards. I'll invite them to visit. I'll grow up. Maybe I'll fall in love. *Yeah, yeah, yeah.*

But no matter where I wander, no matter how far I go, one thing I know to my bones:

I will always, always come home.

U.S. helicopters leave a battlefield in South Vietnam's Mekong Delta on July 11, 1964, after depositing Vietnamese troops in the swampy terrain for an assault on a village in the background.

THE EASTERN WORLD, IT IS EXPLODING, VIOLENCE FLARIN', BULLETS LOADIN'

From "The Eve of Destruction" by P. F. Sloan, sung by Barry McGuire, released by Dunhill, 1965

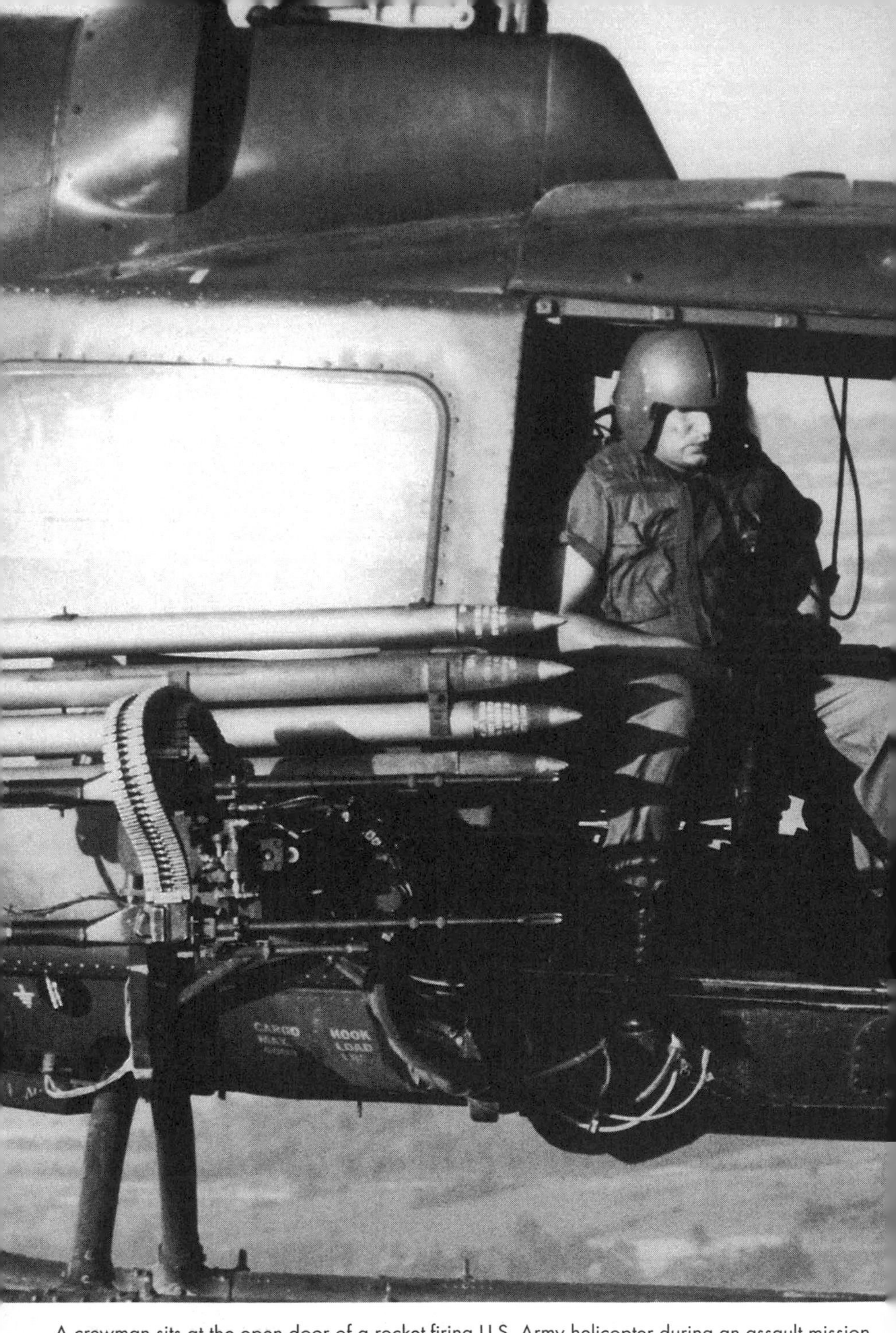

A crewman sits at the open door of a rocket-firing U.S. Army helicopter during an assault mission in the jungle area near Bien Hoa, north of Saigon, in South Vietnam on January 18, 1964.

President Lyndon Johnson authorizes phase two of Operation Rolling Thunder, the first show of saturation bombing use in the Vietnam War, designed to force North Vietnam to stop supporting Vietcong guerrillas in the South.

March 2, 1965

YOU'RE OLD ENOUGH TO KILL,

DUP

SSS Form 1 (Rev. 4-20-67)

SELECTIVE SERVICE SYSTEM

REGISTRATION CERTIFICATE

THIS IS TO CERTIFY THAT IN ACCORDANCE WITH THE SELECTIVE SERVICE LAW

(FIRST NAME)	(MIDDLE NAME)	(LAST NAME)
Dennis	Michael	Mannion

SELECTIVE SERVICE NO. 6 9 46 72

DATE OF BIRTH: Feb. 4, 1946 — PLACE OF BIRTH: Springfield, Mass.

COLOR EYES: Blue — COLOR HAIR: Brown — HEIGHT: 5 FT. 8½ IN. — WEIGHT: 174

Other obvious physical characteristics: none

WAS DULY REGISTERED ON THE 11 DAY OF Feb 19 64

(MEMBER OR EXECUTIVE SECRETARY, OR CLERK OF LOCAL BOARD)

(REGISTRANT'S SIGNATURE)

BUT NOT FOR VOTIN'

Major Giai, background, second from right, commander of South Vietnam's airborne brigade, is about to place a Vietnamese medal of honor on the casket of Captain Thomas W. McCarthy of Fayetteville, North Carolina, in a ceremony at Saigon Airport on March 5, 1964. Captain McCarthy, an American advisor to Vietnamese forces, was killed in an engagement with communist Vietcong guerrillas near the Cambodian frontier.

BUT YOU TELL ME
OVER AND OVER
AND OVER AGAIN,
MY FRIEND

ON MARCH 8, 1965, 3,500 U.S. MARINES

from the 9th Marine Expeditionary Brigade land at China Beach, near Da Nang in South Vietnam; they are the first U.S. combat troops to arrive in Vietnam. They join the 23,000 military advisors already in Vietnam. They were met by Vietnamese sightseers, children with leis, and four American soldiers carrying a large sign: ***Welcome Gallant Marines.***

A South Vietnamese armored personnel carrier provides its kind of life insurance as a farmer resumes work in a rice paddy. The newly harvested rice crop was destroyed and many rice paddies were scorched by fire during bitter fighting between government troops and the Communist Vietcong, March 7, 1964.

AH, YOU DON'T WE'RE ON THE DESTRUCTION

Flying low over the jungle, an A-1 Skyraider drops five-hundred-pound bombs on a Vietcong position below as smoke rises from a previous pass at the target, December 26, 1964.

"The other ascent into the unknown," June 10, 1965

"LAST SUMMER I WENT TO MISSISSIPPI

to join the struggle there for civil rights. This fall I am engaged in another phase of the same struggle, this time in Berkeley. . . . In Mississippi an autocratic and powerful minority rules, through organized violence, to suppress the vast, virtually powerless majority. In California, the privileged minority manipulates the university bureaucracy to suppress the students' political expression."

Berkeley Free Speech Movement leader
Mario Savio to protesting students

"DO YOU BELIEVE IN MAGIC?"

The Lovin' Spoonful, 1965

"THIS IS THE DAWNING OF THE AGE OF AQUARIUS."

From HAIR, 1967

war is not healthy for children and other living things

A NOTE ABOUT FREEDOM SUMMER

No one wanted to go to Mississippi in the early 1960s to fight for civil rights. The Magnolia State seemed genteel and cultured from the outside, but under its manicured surface, for anyone who wanted to change the rigid status quo, Mississippi was too scary, too violent, and too unknown.

The Rev. Dr. Martin Luther King, Jr., and his confidantes in the Southern Christian Leadership Conference (SCLC) considered the prospect of working for civil rights in Mississippi too risky. They concentrated their efforts in Alabama and Georgia — certainly dangerous as well. In 1960, Ella Baker recruited Bob Moses for her newly formed SNCC — the Student Nonviolent Coordinating Committee — to go to Mississippi to begin talking with the courageous few — mostly members of the Mississippi NAACP — about how SNCC might be of assistance in supporting black Mississippi's struggle for equal rights. Very quickly, Bob Moses realized that securing the vote for Mississippi's black citizens was paramount for real change.

SNCC had already begun to recruit financial support, and "Friends of SNCC" chapters opened in many cities outside the American South, including Chicago, San Francisco, Boston, and New York City. SNCC's newspaper, *The Student Voice*, kept these friends apprised of what was really happening with SNCC's work in southern cities. (The southern press often did not report these stories, or misreported them.) The "Friends" kept money flowing (sometimes trickling) into SNCC's coffers so it could have funds to pay rent for Freedom Schools, community centers, and offices; to buy transportation; to secure bail for arrested workers; to pay a few field secretaries a modest sum (ten dollars per week); and to buy supplies and food and other essentials. Field secretaries were workers who organized the operations at a Freedom House.

When northern students heard what their southern counterparts were doing, many said, in effect, *injustice anywhere is everyone's concern*, and they began to picket northern branches of chain stores such as Woolworth's and Kress & Co. that were segregated in the south. Thus was born the early SNCC tradition of blacks working with whites for a common goal.

Instead of swooping into a beleaguered city, leading the local people to victory, and then leaving, SNCC would quietly, one-on-one, visit, reach out, engender trust, and help find leaders and black institutions from within those communities; educate and support them; and encourage them to lead themselves and their communities for years to come. In Mississippi, SNCC partnered with CORE, the NAACP, and the SCLC to form COFO. SNCC and CORE took the lead, and SNCC moved its national headquarters from Atlanta to Greenwood, Mississippi, for Freedom Summer.

They had their work cut out for them.

The American South had existed on a cotton economy for more than a hundred years, an economy made possible by the back-breaking work of the large number of slaves who lived on the plantations. In 1865, after the Civil War and the emancipation of the slaves, Reconstruction was the federal efforts designed to reunite the nation and ensure the full rights of citizenship for all freed slaves. The South declared itself free of most federal authority, and "states' rights" became the way the South made sure that Negroes remained disenfranchised, without their civil rights.

The state laws that were passed during and after Reconstruction by these southern states were called Jim Crow laws, and southern states adamantly claimed their right to uphold them. None was as fierce as Mississippi, which is why white Mississippians saw themselves as "invaded" in the summer of 1964.

The idea of separate but equal facilities for whites and blacks was sanctioned by the U.S. Supreme Court in 1896, as part of overturning Reconstruction gains. The U.S. government, for the most part, did not interfere with states' rights until 1964, when the Civil Rights Act of 1964 overturned Jim Crow and gave equal status to African Americans. The Voting Rights Act of 1965 abolished the literacy test and ensured African Americans had the right to vote.

This overthrowing of Jim Crow by the federal government was a revolution. And it came with its battles. One of those battles was Freedom Summer. In the one hundred years between the Civil War and the Civil Rights Act, Jim Crow laws had set African Americans back to where they had been during the long years of slavery: without protection, without rights, without a voice, without access to jobs and services, without adequate education, and without the opportunity to fashion a life created from their dreams and hopes. This situation was particularly stark in the South, where black labor was still needed in the years following the Civil War, to pick cotton and tend to white families who had become used to their comforts being provided for them. Blacks whose mothers and fathers had been slaves often remained on the plantations as sharecroppers who now had to be paid for their labor. The sharecropping system was little better than slavery, however, and it kept blacks poor and with few options. Retribution was swift and violent against any blacks who complained or advocated for themselves. Loss of jobs, loss of a means to feed a family, loss of home and health, beatings, jail, and death were real possibilities.

It had become clear to whites that they were outnumbered by blacks in many cities and towns in the South, and this fact scared southern whites; if African Americans got "uppity" and insisted on the vote, or on equal employment opportunities, or on adequate education for their children, what would be next?

Even though *Brown v. the Board of Education* in 1954 declared that "separate educational facilities are inherently unequal," southern states ignored the decision. Influential whites declared that "race mixing" would ruin both races, and public schools remained segregated. Money set aside for education of black students was negligible. By the time the Civil Rights Act of 1964 was passed, Mississippi whites didn't expect it would have much effect on them. They were prepared to ignore it in favor of their states' rights to do as they pleased.

In 1964, 45 percent of Mississippi's population was black, but only 5 percent of blacks were registered to vote. A mock Freedom Vote in 1963, however, where blacks could vote for governor at mock polls set up by SNCC, had been so successful that SNCC believed blacks would turn out in great numbers to vote, if they had the chance, in the 1964 presidential election. So planning started for a Mississippi Summer Project.

The architects of Freedom Summer counted on almost a thousand white students and others coming from outside the South, coming mostly from Ivy League colleges, coming from families of means, to be noticed by the national press when they came to Mississippi in 1964.

Lawyers, doctors, and ministers also volunteered time and expertise. Friends of SNCC sent money, books, and supplies, as kids from all over the United States were recruited on college campuses, submitted applications, went to training in Ohio, joined SNCC and CORE, and worked as members of COFO in Mississippi in 1964, registering black voters, setting up community centers and Freedom Schools, and attending mass meetings, working one-on-one to encourage black Mississippians to fearlessly stand up for their rights.

Three volunteers were murdered by members of the Mississippi White Knights of the Ku Klux Klan, the Neshoba County Sheriff's Office, and the Philadelphia Police Department, outside Philadelphia, Mississippi, on the first day of Freedom Summer, June 21, 1964. Andrew Goodman, age twenty, was from New York City and had attended the first volunteer training session in Ohio. He came to Mississippi with Michael Schwerner, age twenty-four, also from New York City and who was already working for

CORE in Meridian, Mississippi; and James Chaney, age twenty-one, who lived in Meridian and was a local CORE volunteer.

Immediately, the national press was covering Mississippi like it had never noticed it before. Certainly one reason was that Andy and Mickey were white, and their deaths alongside James Chaney's attracted national attention. More than a dozen black Mississippians' bodies were discovered during the search for the three summer volunteers. It would be over forty days before their bodies were found buried in an earthen dam, and over forty years before the last of the killers — the last the prosecutors had adequate documentation to indict — was brought to justice.

During the course of the summer, scores of summer volunteers across Mississippi were beaten, some were injured critically, over one thousand were arrested (including local citizens), thirty-seven black churches were bombed or burned, and thirty black homes or businesses were destroyed.

But Mississippi came awake. Thirty Freedom Schools were established in the state, with the hope that one thousand students would enroll. Three thousand showed up. The Mississippi Freedom Democratic Party — one of the major accomplishments of Freedom Summer — registered over eighty thousand black voters; held a state convention in Jackson, Mississippi; and sent a delegation to the Democratic National Convention to ask to be seated in place of the all-white Democratic Party of Mississippi. Although they failed to be seated, they made noise and put America on notice, with delegate Fannie Lou Hamer asking a national audience, "I question America! Is this America?" and "I am sick and tired of being sick and tired!"

The actions of the MFDP bolstered support for the Voting Rights Act that was passed in 1965. The Voting Rights Act set up federal oversight for elections, but it still took over a decade for Mississippi to fully comply, even though by 1966, 60 percent of black Mississippians had become registered voters.

Mississippi continued to pass laws designed to keep blacks from having power in the voting process. The MFDP challenged every one of them until, by the 1990s, Mississippi had more black elected officials than any other state.

In 1986, Mike Espy was elected Mississippi's first black U.S. congressman since Reconstruction. In 1987, Toni Seawright, a black woman, was crowned Miss Mississippi. In 2014, 28 percent of Mississippi's elected state legislature is black, and there are scores of black mayors, police officers, and county officials.

U.S. Congressman John Lewis of Georgia, former chairman of SNCC and tireless civil rights activist, has said Freedom Summer "literally brought the country to Mississippi. People were able to see the horror and evil of blatant racial discrimination. If it hadn't been for the veterans of Freedom Summer, there would be no Barack Obama."

However, Mississippi remains one of the poorest states in the nation, and the Delta remains its poorest pocket of poverty.

"The Promised Land is still far off," says journalist Hodding Carter III, who grew up in the Delta. "Black folks are still on the outside, looking in, when it comes to jobs, equal education, housing, etc. But here, sadly enough, that does not much distinguish Mississippi from the rest of the country. What did distinguish us — racism red of fang and claw, in the saddle and riding hard — no longer prevails. What is in the heart of individuals is one thing; how they now find they must operate in public is another. We are talking about fundamental change, which has left the state still far from the mountaintop, but it has been climbing for some time. It may go sideways from time to time, but it isn't going back."

At heart, *Revolution* is a story about what it means to be a citizen of this country, to live in a democracy, to be a member of a family, to nurture your friendships, to look beyond what you understand, to ask questions, and to tend to your community, your own backyard. What are your responsibilities? What must you do to empower yourself and others?

Your vote is your voice. It is your most powerful weapon of choice.

It can change the world.

ACKNOWLEDGMENTS

I want to thank the writers who told this story before I did and whose excellent memoirs and works of nonfiction paved the way for this book, especially Bruce Watson's *Freedom Summer*, Sally Belfrage's *Freedom Summer;* Charles M. Payne's *I've Got the Light of Freedom: The Organizing Tradition and the Mississippi Freedom Struggle*, John Dittmer's *Local People: The Struggle for Civil Rights in Mississippi*, Endesha Ida Mae Holland's *From the Mississippi Delta*, and many others, some of which you'll find in the bibliography. Thanks to Sarah Campbell for book suggestions along the way.

Many thanks to everyone at the McCain Library's Civil Rights Archive at the University of Southern Mississippi, for making available to me their storehouse of civil rights papers, and particularly Freedom Summer materials, on my several visits, and for their help with permissions. Thanks especially to Diane Ross, Cindy Lawler, and Elizabeth La Beaud, and to Ellen Ruffin and Danielle Bishop for so graciously welcoming me back to my Mississippi roots.

Thanks to Alice Bernstein for helping me track down some errant photo credits. Thanks to summer volunteer Dick Atlee for his honest and compelling stories of working in southern Mississippi in the sixties, and to Sarah Corson for abiding encouragement and for connecting me with Dick. Thanks to good sport and former classmate, Jim Epps, for allowing me the use of his uncle Vivian's good name.

Sincere thanks to the civil rights photographers whose work graces (literally) this book, and for their courage and contribution to the world's understanding of Freedom Summer. I wanted to name them here, so I have captioned their photos. Special thanks to Bob Adelman, whose gracious correspondence with me gave me a window into a photographer's life shooting the sixties, and who gave me much-needed perspective, not to mention an offer to come visit him in Miami. Or Mexico. Which I will do. Thank you.

The Civil Rights Movement Veterans website, crmvets.org, was a great source of material for my research, and led me to some wonderful contacts, including webmaster Bruce Hartford, photographer Wally Roberts, and the marvelous Heather Booth, all of whom were summer volunteers in 1964. The crmvets website also led me to Linda Wetmore's story, which I tell in this book through Jo Ellen Chapman. Jo Ellen is in no way Linda Wetmore, but I was so moved by her courage and forthrightness, and her story of being with Silas McGee the night he was shot, I wanted to retell it. I knew I needed to put Sunny in that car, so Linda's story gave me a way for Sunny to be part of the Movement.

Thanks to summer project volunteers whose letters home allow the world a glimpse into their experiences in 1964, especially Zoya Zeman, Matt Zwerling, and Chude Pam Parker Allen. The correspondence between Zoya and her father, Nathan Zeman (a doctor who also volunteered in Mississippi in 1964), was my doorway into thinking about Freedom Summer as a viable project for the sixties trilogy.

Author, teacher, and historian Curtis Wilkie was a reporter for the *Delta Democrat-Times* in 1964. He turned on a dime and met me early on at Square Books in Oxford, Mississippi, to share his experiences during Freedom Summer, even though I forgot to bring my notebook with me because I was so awestruck. Instead, I used the paper sack that housed his book, *Dixie: A Personal Odyssey Through Events That Shaped the Modern South*. Thank you.

Context was what I needed for such a complex story, and I found lots of it in Greenwood itself. I visited several times, in all seasons, and I want to thank Jamie and Kelly Kornegay of Turnrow Books, as well as Ben Arnold and Tad Russell, and everyone who breathes life into this extraordinary independent bookstore in the Mississippi Delta, for all they did to take good care of me, make me welcome, and introduce me to local Greenwood. Jamie first put

Sally Belfrage's memoir into my hands and said, "It's about Greenwood." That was the spark.

Jamie and Kelly introduced me to Mary Carol Miller, whose mother, Sara Criss, was the Greenwood bureau chief for the *Memphis Commercial Appeal* during Freedom Summer — a rare opportunity for a woman in the sixties. Mary Carol grew up with a UPI Teletype machine in the kitchen and a darkroom under the stairs for developing photos. Mary Carol and her sister, Cathy, sometimes accompanied Sara on assignment. Sara kept copies of all her newspaper stories during the civil rights years in Mississippi as well as a detailed diary that Mary Carol generously allowed me to use for my research. This was treasure, pure and simple.

Jamie and Kelly also introduced me to Mary and Sylvester Hoover, and some of their friends, in Baptist Town. Mary spent an afternoon traipsing all over "black" Greenwood with me, and took me to the Wade Plantation, where she grew up; to Money, Mississippi, to see Bryant's store for my Emmett Till research; and also to Robert Johnson's grave, just because.

I first met Marianne Richardson when I did an author visit at Heritage School in Newnan, Georgia, in 2002. When I told Marianne I was writing a story centered in Greenwood, Mississippi, Marianne told me she had grown up in Greenwood, which led to us taking a road trip from Atlanta to Greenwood one long weekend in January 2011.

In addition to allowing me to appropriate bits of their lives into *Revolution*, Marianne and Mary Carol drove all over kingdom come with me and showed me the markers I needed to internalize in order to tell this story, including the location of Byron De La Beckwith's family home and the location of the Freedom House in Baptist Town. Marianne introduced me to her former classmates, including Allan Hammons, who lives with a treasure trove of Greenwood memorabilia, both literally and in his head, and who is largely responsible for the Mississippi Blues Trail markers; and Carolyn McAdams, the current mayor of Greenwood, who offered me the keys to the city's history. Thank you.

Thanks also to Van Richardson and Larry Killebrew for helpful and essential details about the operation of Liberty Cash Grocery and about Dixie Youth Baseball in Greenwood in the sixties.

Thanks to the folks at Greenwood Utilities for opening their storehouse, which was once the shower house for the Greenwood City Pool, and for allowing me to walk the private parking lot that was once the pool itself. It was thrilling and sobering to find the blue-tiled edges of the pool peeking up from the worn asphalt, almost fifty years after its burial.

Mary Carol Miller's uncle, Gray Evans, was the city attorney for Greenwood in 1964 and was largely responsible, along with some other forward-thinking people, for mitigating the level of violence in Greenwood during Freedom Summer. I interviewed Judge Evans and his wife, Tricia, in 2011, and want to thank them for their time and stories. Such incredible, vital people. Martin Carr is based loosely on a portrait of Judge Evans and the stories he told me, but in no way is meant to be him. I could not create a character sweeping enough to match Judge Evans's integrity and courage.

Through Sara Criss's diary I was led to the Reverend Eade Anderson, who was the pastor of First Presbyterian Church in Greenwood in 1964. I interviewed him in the summer of 2012 in Montreat, North Carolina, and want to thank him for his generosity and heart. Pastor Marshall is loosely based on Reverend Anderson, but is in no way the same person. Vidella Brown is based on the heroic Lou Emma Allen, a secretary for the NAACP in 1964, who was an aide in First Presbyterian's kindergarten. She quit her job after her attempts to register to vote caused a tremendous stir in the church. Reverend Anderson's family hired her to work for them.

Also in Greenwood, Kelvin Scott took good care of me at the Alluvian Hotel each time I visited. Hannah Wiles went on a research trip with me to Medgar Evers's home in Jackson, and up into the Delta, so I could get a sense of the geography and expanse of the Delta. Jim Allen drove me through the Delta in 2005 and took me deep into cotton fields so I could get a sense of what it might be like to stand in the middle of them in the heat of the day, even though I didn't have to pick cotton. Jim Pearce drove me through the green swamps, black bayous, and dusty dirt back roads of the Delta, in search of the Tallahatchie Bridge.

Grateful thanks to Liza Cowan and Holly Cowan Shulman for the materials they shared with me and for spending long hours on e-mail and phone to talk about their astonishing mother, Polly Cowan, and her friendship with the exceptional Dorothy Height, for the Wednesdays in Mississippi biography. Particular thanks to Holly for impressing upon me the fact that one could not understand the many different mind-sets surrounding Freedom Summer without understanding Jim Crow, which led me back to research.

I want to thank my Mississippi cousin, Carol Booth, who provided such essential encouragement and support, as did all my Mississippi family. Thanks to the High Test Girls for listening to me talk about this story every year on retreat in New England, and for listening to me read chunks of it out loud. There is nothing like a good listener.

Trusted and essential readers were Zachary Wiles, Nancy Werlin, Joanne Stanbridge, Dian Curtis Regan, Jane Kurtz, and Marianne Richardson. Lucky me. Thank you. Love to Deborah Hopkinson, who kept telling me, in all my flagging moments (and there were many), that I could do it. Thanks and love to Robin Hoffman for checking in on me and telling me I wasn't forgotten.

Grateful yeah-yeah-yeahs to my friend and Beatles expert Tommy Archibald for his insight and intelligence, and to all my cherished friends in Atlanta for their steadfast support and encouragement along the way. Thanks to Steven "Stokely" Malk for his solid steadiness and resolute confidence in me. Thanks to my family for sustenance and understanding. A shoop-shoop kiss for my husband, Jim, who is clown, wise man, great love, and expert listener. Thanks for doing all those dishes and shepherding the cats.

I continue to count my blessings at my good fortune in finding my Scholastic family, who take such breathtaking risks with me. Thank you to Els Rijper and Erin Black for valiant and unflagging permissions work, to Phil Falco for his fantastic design genius, to Rachael Hicks for her infinite patience and production wizardry, to Susan Jeffers for her exacting and smart copyediting skills, and to Jody Revenson for her proofreading. Thank you to my friends in marketing and publicity who make sure my books find an audience and who always extend such a warm welcome to me. I love working with you.

Finally, heartfelt and ardent thanks to my editor, King David Levithan, who wields a mighty slingshot and slays Goliaths every day in the service of story. I am honored to be a scribbler in your army.

A BEGINNING BIBLIOGRAPHY

There are so many excellent sources that document, from differing perspectives, Freedom Summer and the American Civil Rights Movement of the sixties. Here are some the sources I turned to most often while researching and writing *Revolution*. (Other sources can be found on my website, www.deborahwiles.com.) I used many books, but you will also find pertinent websites and DVDs that will add to your knowledge of Freedom Summer and United States history in 1964, including, specifically, the presidency of Lyndon Baines Johnson, the escalation of the war in Vietnam, the boxing career of Cassius Clay/Muhammad Ali, the history of Mississippi and Greenwood in particular, and the architecture of Wednesdays in Mississippi, along with the ephemera and social and cultural markers of the mid-sixties. I hope they help you learn more about this time in our nation's history and think critically about your important place in the amazing continuum.

WORKS CITED

Adelman, Bob, and Charles Johnson. *Mine Eyes Have Seen: Bearing Witness to the Struggle for Civil Rights*. New York: Time Home Entertainment, 2007.

Belfrage, Sally, *Freedom Summer*. New York: Viking Press, 1965.

Bingham, Howard L., and Max Wallace, *Muhammad Ali's Greatest Fight: Cassius Clay vs. the United States of America*. New York: M. Evans & Company, 2000.

Bloom, Alexander, and Wini Breines, *"Takin' It to the Streets": A Sixties Reader*. New York: Oxford University Press, 1995.

Branch, Taylor, *Pillar of Fire: America in the King Years 1963–65*. New York: Simon & Schuster, 1998.

Burner, Eric, *And Gently He Shall Lead Them: Robert Parris Moses and Civil Rights in Mississippi*. New York: New York University Press, 1994.

Cagin, Seth, and Philip Dray, *We Are Not Afraid: The Story of Goodman, Schwerner, and Chaney, and the Civil Rights Campaign for Mississippi*. New York: Macmillan, 1988.

Caro, Robert A., *The Years of Lyndon Johnson*. New York: Alfred A. Knopf, 1982–2012.

Carson, Clayborne, *In Struggle: SNCC and the Black Awakening of the 1960s*. Cambridge, MA: Harvard University Press, 1981.

Carson, Clayborne, et. al., *The Eyes on the Prize: Civil Rights Reader: Documents, Speeches, and Firsthand Accounts from the Black Freedom Struggle*. New York: Penguin Books, 1991.

Cobb, James C., *The Most Southern Place on Earth: The Mississippi Delta and the Roots of Regional Identity*. New York: Oxford University Press, 1992.

Collier-Thomas, Bettye, and V. P. Franklin, *My Soul Is a Witness: A Chronology of the Civil Rights Era, 1954–1965*. New York: Henry Holt, 2000.

Curry, Constance, et. al., *Deep in Our Hearts: Nine White Women in the Freedom Movement*. Athens: University of Georgia Press, 2000.

Davies, David R., ed., *The Press and Race: Mississippi Journalists Confront the Movement*. Jackson: University Press of Mississippi, 2001.

Dittmer, John, *Local People: The Struggle for Civil Rights in Mississippi*. Champaign: University of Illinois Press, 1994.

Du Bois, W. E. B., *The Souls of Black Folk*. New York: Dodd, Mead, 1961.

Fleming, Karl, *Son of the Rough South: An Uncivil Memoir*. New York: PublicAffairs, 2005.

Grubin, David, James Callanan, and Michael Bacon, *The American Experience: RFK*. Hollywood, CA: PBS Home Video, 2004. DVD.

Height, Dorothy, *Open Wide the Freedom Gates: A Memoir*. New York: PublicAffairs, 2003.

Heyerdahl, Thor, *Kon-Tiki*. Chicago: Rand McNally, 1950.

Holland, Endesha Ida Mae, *From the Mississippi Delta: A Memoir*. New York: Simon & Schuster, 1997.

Holt, Len, *The Summer That Didn't End: The Story of the Mississippi Civil Rights Project of 1964*. New York: Morrow, 1965.

Kelen, Leslie G., ed., *This Light of Ours: Activist Photographers of the Civil Rights Movement*. Jackson: University Press of Mississippi, 2011.

Martinez, Elizabeth Sutherland, ed., *Letters from Mississippi*. New York: McGraw-Hill, 1965.

McAdam, Doug, *Freedom Summer*. New York: Oxford University Press, 1988.

McCullough, David G, and David Grubin, *The American Experience: LBJ*. Alexandria, VA: PBS Home Video, 2006. DVD.

Moody, Anne. *Coming of Age in Mississippi*. New York: Dial Press, 1968.

Mills, Hayley, Eli Wallach, Peter McEnery, Joan Greenwood, Michael Dyne (screenplay), Mary Stewart (book), *The Moon-Spinners*. Directed by James Neilson. Burbank, CA: Walt Disney Productions, recorded 1965, accessed 2003. DVD.

Morris, Willie, *The Ghosts of Medgar Evers: A Tale of Race, Murder, Mississippi, and Hollywood.* New York: Random House, 1998.

Moses, Robert P., and Charles E. Cobb, *Radical Equations: Math Literacy and Civil Rights.* Boston: Beacon Press, 2001.

Murray, Albert, *South to a Very Old Place.* New York: McGraw-Hill, 1971.

Neill, William L., *Coming Apart: An Informal History of America in the 1960's.* Chicago: Quadrangle Books, 1971.

Payne, Charles M., *I've Got the Light of Freedom: The Organizing Tradition and the Mississippi Freedom Struggle.* Berkeley: University of California Press, 1995.

Perlstein, Rick, *Nixonland: The Rise of a President and the Fracturing of America.* New York: Scribner, 2008.

Randall, Herbert, and Dr. Bobs M. Tusa, *Faces of Freedom Summer.* Tuscaloosa: University of Alabama Press, 2001.

Remnick, David, *King of the World: Muhammad Ali and the Rise of an American Hero.* New York: Random House, 1998.

Roberts, Gene, and Hank Klibanoff, *The Race Beat: The Press, the Civil Rights Struggle, and the Awakening of a Nation.* New York: Knopf, 2006.

Shakoor, Jordana Y., *Civil Rights Childhood.* Jackson: University Press of Mississippi, 1999.

Silver, James W., *Mississippi: The Closed Society*. New York: Harcourt, Brace & World, 1964.

Sokol, Jason, *There Goes My Everything: White Southerners in the Age of Civil Rights, 1945–1975*. New York: Alfred A. Knopf, 2006.

Stewart, Mary, *The Moon-Spinners*. New York: William Morrow and Company, 1963.

Sugarman, Tracy, *We Had Sneakers, They Had Guns: The Kids Who Fought for Civil Rights in Mississippi*. Syracuse, NY: Syracuse University Press, 2009.

"The Story of Greenwood, Mississippi," Produced by Guy Carawan, web download, Folkways Records FD 5593, recorded 1965, Smithsonian Center for Folklife and Cultural Heritage, 2013. http://www.folkways.si.edu/the-story-of-greenwood-mississippi/african-american-spoken-american-history/music/album/smithsonian.

Vollers, Maryanne, *Ghosts of Mississippi: The Murder of Medgar Evers, the Trials of Byron De La Beckwith, and the Haunting of the New South*. Boston: Little, Brown, 1995.

Watson, Bruce, *Freedom Summer: The Savage Season That Made Mississippi Burn and Made America a Democracy*. New York: Viking, 2010.

Whitehead, Donny, and Mary Carol Miller, *Greenwood*. Charleston, SC: Arcadia Publishing, 2009.

Wilkie, Curtis, *Dixie: A Personal Odyssey Through Events That Shaped the Modern South*. New York: Scribner, 2001.

Woods, Randall B., *LBJ: Architect of American Ambition*. New York: Free Press, 2006.

Woodward, C. Vann, *The Strange Career of Jim Crow*. New York: Oxford University Press, 1974.

Zellner, Bob, and Constance Curry, *The Wrong Side of Murder Creek: A White Southerner in the Freedom Movement*. Montgomery, AL: NewSouth Books, 2008.

WEBSITES

"Civil Rights in Mississippi Digital Archive," The University of Southern Mississippi Digital Collections, accessed 2013, http://digilib.usm.edu/crmda.php.

Civil Rights Movement Veterans (CORE, NAACP, SCLC, SNCC), Hosted by Tougaloo College, Tougaloo, MS, accessed 2013, http://www.crmvet.org.

"Greenwood, Mississippi," About Greenwood, Mississippi, Donny Whitehead, accessed 2013, aboutgreenwoodms.com/.

Wednesdays in Mississippi: Civil Rights as Women's Work, Hosted by University of Houston Center for Public History, accessed 2013, http://www.history.uh.edu/cph/WIMS/.

Wednesdays in Mississippi, WIMS Film Project, accessed 2013, http://wimsfilmproject.com/.

PHOTOS

Photos copyrighted ©

DUST JACKET

Back jacket, clockwise from top left: *COFO brochure*, McCain Library and Archives, The University of Southern Mississippi; *Freedom Day in Greenwood, Mississippi*, Ted Polumbaum/Newseum; *burned cross*, Tamio Wakayama/Take Stock/The Image Works; *volunteer workers*, Steve Schapiro/Corbis; *science class*, Matt Herron/Take Stock/The Image Works;

AIN'T GONNA LET NOBODY TURN ME AROUND

Page 6: *March on Washington*, Warren K Leffler/USN&WR COLL/Library of Congress; 9: *World's Fair*, CLPjr/cc-by-sa-2.0; 10: *Boston Core demonstration*, Bettmann/Corbis; 13: *Mississippi map*, McCain Library and Archives, The University of Southern Mississippi; 14–15: *demonstrators at pool*, Danny Lyon/Magnum; 16: *demonstration in Brooklyn, NY*, © Bob Adelman; 18–19: *SNCC field workers*, Herbert Randall/McCain Library and Archives, The University of Southern Mississippi; 20: *poster*, Matt Herron/Take Stock/The Image Works; 24–25: *Staughton Lynd*, Herbert Randall/McCain Library and Archives, The University of Southern Mississippi; 26: *non-violent training session*, Mark Levy Collection, Department of Special Collections and Archives, Queens College, CUNY; 28–29: *The Beatles*, Bettmann/Corbis; 30–31: *Vietnam river patrol*, Horst Faas/AP Photo; 33: *Willie Mays*, Ralph Morse/Time Life Pictures/Getty Images; 34: *Rev. Joe Carter*, © Bob Adelman; 37: *COFO brochure*, McCain Library and Archives, The University of Southern Mississippi; 38–39: *volunteer workers*, Steve Schapiro/Corbis; 53: *Dick Landerman*, Herbert Randall/ McCain Library and Archives, The University of Southern Mississippi; 64: *Bob Moses*, George Ballis/Take Stock/The Image Works;

TWIST! AND SHOUT!

96–97: *Vietnam soldier*, Horst Faas/AP Photo; 98–99: *troops wading*, Larry Burrows/Time Life Pictures/Getty Images; 101: *Chubby Checker*, Ralph Crane/Time Life Pictures/Getty Images; 103: *George C. Wallace*, AP Photo; 104: *KKK*, Popperfoto/Getty Images; 114: *Freedom School students*, Photo by Ken Thompson, Courtesy of the General Board of Global Ministries of the United Methodist Church. Used by permission; 114: *sign*, George Ballis/Take Stock/The Image Works;

DOWN BY THE RIVERSIDE

130–131: *Sunday Best*, Matt Herron/Take Stock/The Image Works; 132, 133: *Summer volunteers*, Donna Garde/Mark Levy Collection, Department of Special Collections and Archives, Queens College, CUNY; 134–135: *science class*, Matt Herron/Take Stock/The Image Works; 138: *Missing poster*, Bettmann/Corbis; 140: *Vietnamese family crosses field*, Horst Faas/ AP Photo; 142: *sign*, © Bob Adelman; 184: *Willie James Shaw*, Matt Heron/Take Stock/The Image Works; 193: *Lyndon Baines Johnson*, LBJ Presidential Library;

WHEN THE SAINTS GO MARCHING IN

289: *NAACP pamphlet*, Library of Congress; 290–291: *men reading*, Herbert Randall/McCain Library and Archives, The University of Southern Mississippi; 292–293: *burnt-out car*, State of Mississippi, Attorney General's Office/AP Photo; 294: *Freedom Press Office*, Bettmann/Corbis;

DANCING IN THE STREET

314–315: *Burned cross*, Tamio Wakayama/Take Stock/The Image Works; 317: *Summer volunteers*, JAB/AP Photo; 318–319: *Summer volunteers teaching*, BH/AP Photo; 318: *COFO Freedom House interior*, Mark Levy Collection, Department of Special Collections and Archives, Queens College, CUNY; 320: *local teens dancing*, Matt Herron/Take Stock/The Image Works; 322: *Rev. Jim Nance*, 324: *Summer volunteer writing*, 325: *Freedom House library*, Herbert Randall/McCain Library and Archives, The University of Southern Mississippi; 326: *sign*, Matt Herron/Take Stock/The Image Works; 327: *Sandy Leigh*, Herbert Randall/McCain Library and Archives, The University of Southern Mississippi; 329: *SNCC members*, Danny Lyon/Magnum; 353: *Wednesdays in Mississippi*, National Park Service; Mary McLeod Bethune Council House National Historic Site; DC-WaMMB; National Archives for Black Women's History. Photographer unknown

WOKE UP THIS MORNING WITH MY MIND STAYED ON FREEDOM

403: *Willy James Earl*, Photo by Ken Thompson, Courtesy of the General Board of Global Ministries of the United Methodist Church. Used by permission; 404–405: *Monroe Sharp*, 406: *Freedom Day in Greenwood, Mississippi*, 409: *dragged by police*, 410–411: *court steps*, 412–413: *waiting in line*, Ted Polumbaum/Newseum; 432: *Cassius Clay*, Harry Harris/AP Photo;

WE SHALL NOT BE MOVED

480–481: *Rev. Dr. Martin Luther King, Jr.*, Jim Bourdier/AP Photo; 482–483: *voters registering*, Herbert Randall/McCain Library and Archives, The University of Southern Mississippi; 484: *Ella Baker*, George Ballis/Take Stock/The Image Works; 486–487: *voter registration form*, Matt Herron/Take Stock/The Image Works; 488: *voter button*, © Bob Adelman;

THE EVE OF DESTRUCTION

496–497: *US helicopters*, AP Photo; 498–499: *US Army helicopter*, Horst Faas/AP Photo; 500: *registration card*, Mike Ross, Record-Journal/AP Photo; 501: *US soldier casket*, AP Photo; 503: *Vietnam rice paddies*, Bettmann/Corbis; 504–505: *A-1 Skyraider bomb attack*, Horst Faas/AP Photo; 506: *political cartoon*, A 1965 Herblock Cartoon, © The Herb Block Foundation; 509: *poster*, Sunflower design and words by Lorraine Art Schneider, image and text © 1968, 2003 by Another Mother for Peace, Inc. (AMP) (www.anothermother.org).

WORDS/LYRICS

Page 1: *"I, Too"* from THE COLLECTED POEMS OF LANGSTON HUGHES by Langston Hughes, edited by Arnold Rampersad with David Roessel, Associate Editor, copyright © 1994 by the Estate of Langston Hughes. Used by permission of Alfred A. Knopf, an imprint of the Knopf Doubleday Publishing Group, a division of Random House LLC. All rights reserved. Any third party use of this material, outside of this publication, is prohibited. Interested parties must apply directly to Random House LLC for permission. Reprinted by permission of Harold Ober Associates Incorporated.

Page 3: Excerpt from speech delivered by Rev. Dr. Martin Luther King, Jr., at the March on Washington. Reprinted by arrangement with The Heirs to the Estate of Martin Luther King Jr., c/o Writers House as agent for the

ABOUT THE AUTHOR

DEBORAH WILES was born in Alabama and spent her summers in a small Mississippi town. (Both of her parents were from Mississippi, and much of her extended family still lives there.) Her books include the picture book *Freedom Summer*, which takes place at the same time as *Revolution*, and the novels *Love, Ruby Lavender*; *The Aurora County All-Stars*; and *Each Little Bird That Sings*, a National Book Award finalist. The first book in The Sixties Trilogy, *Countdown*, received five starred reviews upon its publication and has appeared on many state award lists.

Deborah lives in Atlanta, Georgia. You can visit her on the web at www.deborahwiles.com.

This book was edited by David Levithan and designed by Phil Falco. Its documentary features were coordinated by Erin Black and Els Rijper. The text was set in Futura, a typeface designed by Paul Renner between 1924 and 1926. The display type was set in FF Identification 04S, designed by Rian Hughes in 1993. The book was typeset at Jouve North America and printed and bound at R. R. Donnelley in Crawfordsville, Indiana. The production was supervised by Rachael Hicks. The manufacturing was supervised by Angelique Browne.